Terry Pratchett is the acclaimed creator of the Discworld series,
started in 1983 with *The Colour of Magic*, and which has now reached
38 novels. Worldwide sales of his books are now 60 million, and they have
been translated into 37 languages. Terry Pratchett was knighted
for services to literature in 2009.

INTRODUCING DISCWORLD

The Discworld series is a continuous history of a world not totally unlike
our own, except that it is a flat disc carried on the backs of four elephants
astride a giant turtle floating through space, and that it is peopled by, among
others, wizards, dwarves, policemen, thieves, beggars, vampires and witches.
Within the history of Discworld there are many individual stories, which
can be read in any order, but reading them in sequence can increase your
enjoyment through the accumulation of all the fine detail that contributes
to the teeming imaginative complexity of this brilliantly conceived world.

The Discworld® series

Have you read them all?

———————— **Other books about Discworld** ————————

THE ART OF DISCWORLD
(with Paul Kidby)

THE WIT AND WISDOM OF DISCWORLD
(compiled by Stephen Briggs)

THE FOLKLORE OF DISCWORLD
(with Jacqueline Simpson)

———————— Discworld maps ————————

THE STREETS OF ANKH-MORPORK
(with Stephen Briggs, painted by Stephen Player)

THE DISCWORLD MAPP
(with Stephen Briggs, painted by Stephen Player)

A TOURIST GUIDE TO LANCRE – A DISCWORLD MAPP
(with Stephen Briggs, illustrated by Paul Kidby)

DEATH'S DOMAIN
(with Paul Kidby)

A complete list of Terry Pratchett ebooks and audio books as well as other books
based on the Discworld series – illustrated screenplays, graphic novels,
comics and plays – can be found on
www.terrypratchett.co.uk

———————— Non-Discworld books ————————

THE DARK SIDE OF THE SUN

STRATA

THE UNADULTERATED CAT (illustrated by Gray Jolliffe)

GOOD OMENS (with Neil Gaiman)

———— Non-Discworld novels for younger readers ————

THE CARPET PEOPLE

TRUCKERS

DIGGERS

WINGS

ONLY YOU CAN SAVE MANKIND*

JOHNNY AND THE DEAD

JOHNNY AND THE BOMB

NATION

*www.ifnotyouthenwho.com

FEET OF CLAY

A Discworld® Novel

Terry Pratchett

CORGI BOOKS

FEET OF CLAY
A CORGI BOOK : 9780552153256

Originally published in Great Britain by
Victor Gollancz Ltd

PRINTING HISTORY
Gollancz edition published 1996
Corgi edition published 1997

17 19 20 18

Set in Minion by Kestrel Data, Exeter, Devon.

Corgi Books are published by Transworld Publishers,
61–63 Uxbridge Road, London W5 5SA,
a division of The Random House Group Ltd.

Addresses for Random House Group Ltd companies outside the UK
can be found at: www.randomhouse.co.uk
The Random House Group Ltd Reg. No. 954009.

Printed and bound in Great Britain by
Cox & Wyman Ltd, Reading, Berkshire.

The Random House Group Limited supports The Forest Stewardship
Council (FSC), the leading international forest certification organisation.
All our titles that are printed on Greenpeace approved FSC certified paper
carry the FSC logo. Our paper procurement policy can be found at:
www.rbooks.co.uk/environment.

Edward St John de Nobbes, Earl of Ankh

Mr Gerhardt Sock, Butcher

The Vetinari Family

The Guild of Assassins

Mr Rudolph Potts, Baker

The Guild of Thieves

Mr Arthur Carry, Candlemaker

The Vimes Family (now withdrawn)

Reproduced by Kind Permission of the Royal College of Heralds, Mollymog Street, Ankh-Morpork

FEET OF CLAY

It was a warm spring night when a fist knocked at the door so hard that the hinges bent.

A man opened it and peered out into the street. There was mist coming off the river and it was a cloudy night. He might as well have tried to see through white velvet.

But he thought afterwards that there had been shapes out there, just beyond the light spilling out into the road. A lot of shapes, watching him carefully. He thought maybe there'd been very faint points of light . . .

There was no mistaking the shape right in front of him, though. It was big and dark red and looked like a child's clay model of a man. Its eyes were two embers.

'Well? What do you want at this time of night?'

The golem handed him a slate, on which was written:

WE HEAR YOU WANT A GOLEM.

Of course, golems couldn't speak, could they?

'Hah. *Want*, yes. *Afford*, no. I've been asking around but it's wicked the prices you're going for these days . . .'

The golem rubbed the words off the slate and wrote:

TO YOU, ONE HUNDRED DOLLARS.

'You're for sale?'

NO.

The golem lurched aside. Another one stepped into the light.

It was also a golem, the man could see that. But it wasn't like the usual lumpen clay things that you occasionally saw. This one gleamed like a newly polished statue, perfect down to the detailing of the clothes. It reminded him of one of the old pictures of the city's kings, all haughty stance and imperious haircut. In fact, it even had a small coronet moulded on to its head.

'A hundred dollars?' the man said suspiciously. 'What's wrong with it? Who's selling it?'

NOTHING IS WRONG. PERFECT IN ALL DETAIL. NINETY DOLLARS.

'Sounds like someone wants to get rid of it in a hurry . . .'

GOLEM MUST WORK. GOLEM MUST HAVE A MASTER.

'Yeah, right, but you hear stories . . . Going mad and making too many things, and that.'

NOT MAD. EIGHTY DOLLARS.

'It looks . . . new,' said the man, tapping the gleaming chest. 'But no one's making golems any more, that's what's keeping the price up beyond the purse of the small business—' He stopped. '*Is* someone making them again?'

EIGHTY DOLLARS.

'I heard the priests banned making 'em years ago. A man could get in a *lot* of trouble.'

SEVENTY DOLLARS.

'Who's doing it?'

SIXTY DOLLARS.

'Is he selling them to Albertson? Or Spadger and Williams? It's hard enough competing as it is, and they've got the money to invest in new plant—'

FIFTY DOLLARS.

The man walked around the golem. 'A man can't sit by and watch his company collapse under him because of unfair price cutting, I mean to say . . .'

FORTY DOLLARS.

'Religion is all very well, but what do prophets know about profits, eh? Hmm . . .' He looked up at the shapeless golem in the shadows. 'Was that "thirty dollars" I just saw you write?'

YES.

'I've always liked dealing wholesale. Wait one moment.' He went back inside and returned with a handful of coins. 'Will you be selling any to them other bastards?'

NO.

'Good. Tell your boss it's a pleasure to do business with him. Get along inside, Sunny Jim.'

The white golem walked into the factory. The man, glancing from side to side, trotted in after it and shut the door.

Deeper shadows moved in the dark. There was a faint hissing. Then, rocking slightly, the big heavy shapes moved away.

Shortly afterwards, and around the corner, a beggar holding out a hopeful hand for alms was amazed to find himself suddenly richer by a whole thirty dollars.*

The Discworld turned against the glittering backdrop of space, spinning very gently on the backs of the four giant elephants that perched on the shell of Great A'Tuin the star turtle. Continents drifted slowly past, topped by weather systems that themselves turned gently against the flow, like waltzers spinning counter to the whirl of the dance. A billion tons of geography rolled slowly through the sky.

People look down on stuff like geography and meteorology, and not only because they're standing on one and being soaked by the other. They don't look quite like real science.† But geography is only physics slowed down and with a few trees stuck on it, and meteorology is full of excitingly fashionable chaos and complexity. And summer isn't a time. It's a place as well. Summer is a moving creature and likes to go south for the winter.

Even on the Discworld, with its tiny orbiting sun tilting over the turning world, the seasons moved. In Ankh-Morpork, greatest of its cities, spring was nudged aside by summer, and summer was prodded in the back by autumn.

Geographically speaking, there was not a lot of

---

*He subsequently got dead-drunk and was shanghaied aboard a merchantman bound for strange and foreign parts, where he met lots of young ladies who didn't wear many clothes. He eventually died from stepping on a tiger. A good deed goes around the world.
†That is to say, the sort you can use to give something three extra legs and then blow it up.

difference within the city itself, although in late spring the scum on the river was often a nice emerald green. The mist of spring became the fog of autumn, which mixed with fumes and smoke from the magical quarter and the workshops of the alchemists until it seemed to have a thick, choking life of its own.

And time moved on.

Autumn fog pressed itself against the midnight window-panes.

Blood ran in a trickle across the pages of a rare volume of religious essays, which had been torn in half.

There had been no need for that, thought Father Tubelcek.

A further thought suggested that there had been no need to hit him either. But Father Tubelcek had never been very concerned about that sort of thing. People healed, books didn't. He reached out shakily and tried to gather up the pages, but slumped back again.

The room was spinning.

The door swung open. Heavy footsteps creaked across the floor – one footstep at least, and one dragging noise.

Step. Drag. Step. Drag.

Father Tubelcek tried to focus. '*You?*' he croaked.

Nod.

'Pick . . . up the . . . books.'

The old priest watched as the books were retrieved and piled carefully with fingers not well suited to the task.

The newcomer took a quill pen from the debris, carefully wrote something on a scrap of paper, then rolled it up and placed it delicately between Father Tubelcek's lips.

The dying priest tried to smile.

'We don't work like that,' he mumbled, the little cylinder wobbling like a last cigarette. 'We . . . make . . . our . . . own . . . w . . .'

The kneeling figure watched him for a while and then, taking great care, leaned forward slowly and closed his eyes.

Commander Sir Samuel Vimes, Ankh-Morpork City Guard, frowned at himself in the mirror and began to shave.

The razor was a sword of freedom. Shaving was an act of rebellion.

These days, someone ran his bath (every day! – you wouldn't think the human skin could stand it). And someone laid out his clothes (such clothes!). And someone cooked his meals (what meals! – he was putting on weight, he knew). And someone even polished his boots (and such boots! – no cardboard-soled wrecks but big, well-fitting boots of genuine shiny leather). There was someone to do nearly everything for him, but there were some things a man ought to do for himself, and one of them was shaving.

He knew that Lady Sybil mildly disapproved. Her father had never shaved himself in his life. He had a man for it. Vimes had protested that he'd spent too many years trudging the night-time streets to

be happy about anyone else wielding a blade anywhere near his neck, but the *real* reason, the
unspoken reason, was that he hated the very idea of
the world being divided into the shaved and the
shavers. Or those who wore the shiny boots and
those who cleaned the mud off them. Every time he
saw Willikins the butler fold his, Vimes's, clothes,
he suppressed a terrible urge to kick the butler's
shiny backside as an affront to the dignity of man.

The razor moved calmly over the stubble of the
night.

Yesterday there had been some official dinner.
He couldn't recall now what it had been for. He
seemed to spend his whole life at the things. Arch,
giggling women and braying young men who'd been
at the back of the line when the chins were handed
out. And, as usual, he'd come back through the
fog-bound city in a filthy temper with himself.

He'd noticed a light under the kitchen door and
heard conversation and laughter, and had gone in.
Willikins was there, with the old man who stoked the
boiler, and the head gardener, and the boy who
cleaned the spoons and lit the fires. They were playing cards. There were bottles of beer on the table.

He'd pulled up a chair, and cracked a few jokes
and asked to be dealt in. They'd been . . . welcoming.
In a way. But as the game progressed Vimes had
been aware of the universe crystallizing around him.
It was like becoming a cogwheel in a glass clock.
There was no laughter. They'd called him 'sir' and
kept clearing their throats. Everything was very . . .
careful.

17

Finally he'd mumbled an excuse and stumbled out. Halfway along the passage he'd thought he'd heard a comment followed by . . . well, maybe it was only a chuckle. But it *might* have been a snigger.

The razor carefully circumnavigated the nose.

Hah. A couple of years ago a man like Willikins would have allowed him into the kitchen only on sufferance. And would have made him take his boots off.

So that's your life now, Commander Sir Samuel Vimes. A jumped-up copper to the nobs and a nob to the rest, eh?

He frowned at the reflection in the mirror.

He'd started out in the gutter, true enough. And now he was on three meat meals a day, good boots, a warm bed at night and, come to that, a wife too. Good old Sybil – although she did tend to talk about curtains these days, but Sergeant Colon had said this happened to wives and was a biological thing and perfectly normal.

He'd actually been rather attached to his old cheap boots. He could read the street in them, the soles were so thin. It'd got so that he could tell where he was on a pitch-dark night just by the feel of the cobbles. Ah, well . . .

There was something mildly strange about Sam Vimes's shaving mirror. It was slightly convex, so that it reflected more of the room than a flat mirror would do, and it gave a very good view of the out-buildings and gardens beyond the window.

Hmm. Going thin on top. Definitely a receding

scalp there. Less hair to comb but, on the other hand, more face to wash . . .

There was a flicker in the glass.

He moved sideways and ducked.

The mirror smashed.

There was the sound of feet somewhere beyond the broken window, and then a crash and a scream.

Vimes straightened up. He fished the largest piece of mirror out of the shaving bowl and propped it up on the black crossbow bolt that had buried itself in the wall.

He finished shaving.

Then he rang the bell for the butler. Willikins materialized. 'Sir?'

Vimes rinsed the razor. 'Get the boy to nip along to the glazier, will you?'

The butler's eyes flickered to the window and then to the shattered mirror. 'Yes, sir. And the bill to go to the Assassins' Guild again, sir?'

'With my compliments. And while he's out he's to call in at that shop in Five And Seven Yard and get me another shaving mirror. The dwarf there knows the kind I like.'

'Yes, sir. And I shall fetch a dustpan and brush directly, sir. Shall I inform her ladyship of this eventuality, sir?'

'No. She always says it's my fault for encouraging them.'

'Very good, sir,' said Willikins.

He dematerialized.

Sam Vimes dried himself off and went downstairs to the morning-room, where he opened the cabinet and took out the new crossbow Sybil had given to him as a wedding present. Sam Vimes was used to the old guard crossbows, which had a nasty habit of firing backwards in a tight corner, but this was a Burleigh and Stronginthearm made-to-measure job with the oiled walnut stock. There was none finer, it was said.

Then he selected a thin cigar and strolled out into the garden.

There was a commotion coming from the dragon house. Vimes entered, and shut the door behind him. He rested the crossbow against the door.

The yammering and squeaking increased. Little gouts of flame puffed above the thick walls of the hatching pens.

Vimes leaned over the nearest one. He picked up a newly hatched dragonette and tickled it under the chin. As it flamed excitedly he lit his cigar and savoured the smoke.

He blew a smoke ring at the figure hanging from the ceiling. 'Good morning,' he said.

The figure twisted frantically. By an amazing feat of muscle control it had managed to catch a foot around a beam as it fell, but it couldn't quite pull itself up. Dropping was not to be thought of. A dozen baby dragons were underneath it, jumping up and down excitedly and flaming.

'Er . . . good morning,' said the hanging figure.

'Turned out nice again,' said Vimes, picking up a bucket of coal. 'Although the fog will be back later, I expect.'

He took a small nugget and tossed it to the dragons. They squabbled for it.

Vimes gripped another lump. The young dragon that had caught the coal already had a distinctly longer and hotter flame.

'I suppose,' said the young man, 'that I could not prevail upon you to let me down?'

Another dragon caught some coal and belched a fireball. The young man swung desperately to avoid it.

'Guess,' said Vimes.

'I suspect, on reflection, that it was foolish of me to choose the roof,' said the assassin.

'Probably,' said Vimes. He'd spent several hours a few weeks ago sawing through joists and carefully balancing the roof tiles.

'I should have dropped off the wall and used the shrubbery.'

'Possibly,' said Vimes. He'd set a bear-trap in the shrubbery.

He took some more coal. 'I suppose you wouldn't tell me who hired you?'

'I'm afraid not, sir. You know the rules.'

Vimes nodded gravely. 'We had Lady Selachii's son up before the Patrician last week,' said Vimes. 'Now, *there*'s a lad who needs to learn that "no" doesn't mean "yes, please".'

'Could be, sir.'

'And then there was that business with Lord Rust's boy. You can't shoot servants for putting your shoes the wrong way round, you know. It's too messy. He'll have to learn right from left like the rest of us. And right from wrong, too.'

'I hear what you say, sir.'

'We seem to have reached an impasse,' said Vimes.

'It seems so, sir.'

Vimes aimed a lump at a small bronze and green dragon, which caught it expertly. The heat was getting intense.

'What I don't understand,' he said, 'is why you fellows mainly try it here or at the office. I mean, I walk around a lot, don't I? You could shoot me down in the street, couldn't you?'

'What? Like some common murderer, sir?'

Vimes nodded. It was black and twisted, but the Assassins' Guild had honour of a sort. 'How much was I worth?'

'Twenty thousand, sir.'

'It should be higher,' said Vimes.

'I agree.' If the assassin got back to the guild it would be, Vimes thought. Assassins valued their own lives quite highly.

'Let me see now,' said Vimes, examining the end of his cigar. 'Guild takes fifty per cent. That leaves ten thousand dollars.'

The assassin seemed to consider this, and then reached up to his belt and tossed a bag rather clumsily towards Vimes, who caught it.

Vimes picked up his crossbow. 'It seems to me,' he said, 'that if a man were to be let go he might well make it to the door with no more than superficial burns. If he were fast. How fast are you?'

There was no answer.

'Of course, he'd have to be desperate,' said Vimes, wedging the crossbow on the feed table and taking a piece of cord out of his pocket. He lashed the cord to a nail and fastened the other end to the crossbow's string. Then, standing carefully to one side, he eased the trigger.

The string moved very slightly.

The assassin, watching him upside down, seemed to have stopped breathing.

Vimes puffed at his cigar until the end was an inferno. Then he took it out of his mouth and leaned it against the restraining cord so that it would have just a fraction of an inch to burn before the string began to smoulder.

'I'll leave the door unlocked,' he said. 'I've never been an unreasonable man. I shall watch your career with interest.'

He tossed the rest of the coals to the dragons, and stepped outside.

It looked like being another eventful day in Ankh-Morpork, and it had only just begun.

As Vimes reached the house he heard a whoosh, a click, and the sound of someone running very fast towards the ornamental lake. He smiled.

Willikins was waiting with his coat. 'Remember you have an appointment with his lordship at eleven, Sir Samuel.'

'Yes, yes,' said Vimes.

'And you are to go and see the Heralds at ten. Her ladyship was very explicit, sir. Her exact words were, "Tell him he's not to try to wriggle out of it again," sir.'

'Oh, very well.'

'And her ladyship said please to try not to upset anyone.'

'Tell her I'll try.'

'And your sedan chair is outside, sir.'

Vimes sighed. 'Thank you. There's a man in the ornamental lake. Fish him out and give him a cup of tea, will you? Promising lad, I thought.'

'Certainly, sir.'

The chair. Oh, yes, the chair. It had been a wedding present from the Patrician. Lord Vetinari knew that Vimes loved walking the streets of the city, and so it was very typical of the man that he presented him with something that did not allow him to do so.

It was waiting outside. The two bearers straightened up expectantly.

Sir Samuel Vimes, Commander of the City Watch, rebelled again. Perhaps he *did* have to use the damn thing, but . . .

He looked at the front man and motioned with a thumb to the chair's door. 'Get in,' he commanded.

'But sir—'

'It's a nice morning,' said Vimes, taking off his coat again. 'I'll drive myself.'

'Dearest Mumm & Dad . . .'

Captain Carrot of the Ankh-Morpork City Watch was on his day off. He had a routine. First he had breakfast in some handy café. Then he wrote his letter home. Letters home always gave him some trouble. Letters *from* his parents were always interesting, being full of mining statistics and exciting news about new shafts and promising seams. All *he* had to write about were murders and such things as that.

He chewed the end of his pencil for a moment.

Well, it has been an intresting week again [he wrote]. I am running around like a flye with a blue bottom and No Mistake! We are opening another Watch House at Chittling Street which is handy for the Shades, so now we have no Less than 4 including Dolly Sisters and Long Wall, and I am the only Captain so I am around at all hours. Persnally I sometimes mifs the cameraderry of the old days when it was just me and Nobby and Sergeant Colon but this is the Century of the Fruitbat. Sergeant Colon is going to retire at the end of the month, he says Mrs Colon wants him to buy a farm, he says he is looking forward to the peace of the country and being Close to Nature, I'm sure you would wish him well. My friend Nobby is still Nobby only more than he was.

Carrot absent-mindedly took a half-eaten mutton chop from his breakfast plate and held it out below the table. There was an *unk*.

Anyway, back to the jobb, also I am sure I have told you about the Cable Street Particulars, although they are still based in Pseudopolis Yard, people do not like it when Watchmen do not wear uniforms but Commander Vimes says criminals dont wear uniforms either so be d*mned to the lot of them.

Carrot paused. It said a lot about Captain Carrot that, even after almost two years in Ankh-Morpork, he was still uneasy about 'd*mned'.

Commander Vimes says you have to have secret policemen because there are secret crimes . . .

Carrot paused again. He loved his uniform. He didn't have any other clothes. The idea of Watchmen in disguise *was* . . . well, it was unthinkable. It was like those pirates who sailed under false colours. It was like spies. However, he went on dutifully:

. . . and Commander Vimes knows what he is talking about I am sure. He says it's not like old fashioned police work which was catching the poor devils too stupid to run away!! Anyhow it all means a lot more work and new faces in the Watch.

While he waited for a new sentence to form, Carrot took a sausage from his plate and lowered it.

There was another *unk*.

The waiter bustled up.

'Another helping, Mr Carrot? On the house.' Every restaurant and eatery in Ankh-Morpork offered free food to Carrot, in the certain and happy knowledge that he would always insist on paying.

'No, indeed, that was very good. Here we are . . . twenty pence and keep the change,' said Carrot.

'How's your young lady? Haven't seen her today.'

'Angua? Oh, she's . . . around and about, you know. I shall definitely tell her you asked after her, though.'

The dwarf nodded happily, and bustled off.

Carrot wrote another few dutiful lines and then said, very softly, 'Is that horse and cart still outside Ironcrust's bakery?'

There was a whine from under the table.

'Really? That's odd. All the deliveries were over hours ago and the flour and grit doesn't usually arrive until the afternoon. Driver still sitting there?'

Something barked, quietly.

'And that looks quite a good horse for a delivery cart. And, you know, normally you'd expect the driver to put a nosebag on. And it's the last Thursday in the month. Which is payday at Ironcrust's.' Carrot laid down his pencil and waved a hand politely to catch the waiter's eye.

'Cup of acorn coffee, Mr Gimlet? To take away?'

In the Dwarf Bread Museum, in Whirligig Alley, Mr Hopkinson the curator was somewhat excited. Apart from other considerations, he'd just been murdered. But at the moment he was choosing to consider this as an annoying background detail.

He'd been beaten to death with a loaf of bread. This is unlikely even in the worst of human bakeries, but dwarf bread has amazing properties as a weapon of offence. Dwarfs regard baking as part of the art of warfare. When they make rock cakes, no simile is intended.

'Look at this dent here,' said Hopkinson. 'It's quite *ruined* the crust!'

AND YOUR SKULL TOO, said Death.

'Oh, yes,' said Hopkinson, in the voice of one who regards skulls as ten a penny but is well aware of the rarity value of a good bread exhibit. 'But what was wrong with a simple cosh? Or even a hammer? I could have provided one if asked.'

Death, who was by nature an obsessive personality himself, realized that he was in the presence of a master. The late Mr Hopkinson had a squeaky voice and wore his spectacles on a length of black tape – his ghost now wore their spiritual counterpart – and these were always the signs of a mind that polished the undersides of furniture and stored paperclips by size.

'It really is too bad,' said Mr Hopkinson. 'And ungrateful, too, after the help I gave them with the oven. I really feel I shall have to complain.'

MR HOPKINSON, ARE YOU FULLY AWARE THAT YOU ARE DEAD?

'Dead?' trilled the curator. 'Oh, no. I can't possibly be dead. Not at the moment. It's simply not convenient. I haven't even catalogued the combat muffins.'

NEVERTHELESS.

'No, no. I'm sorry, but it just won't do. You will have to wait. I really cannot be bothered with that sort of nonsense.'

Death was nonplussed. Most people were, after the initial confusion, somewhat relieved when they died. A subconscious weight had been removed. The other cosmic shoe had dropped. The worst had happened and they could, metaphorically, get on with their lives. Few people treated it as a simple annoyance that might go away if you complained enough.

Mr Hopkinson's hand went through a tabletop. 'Oh.'

YOU SEE?

'This is most uncalled-for. Couldn't you have arranged a less awkward time?'

ONLY BY CONSULTATION WITH YOUR MURDERER.

'It all seems very badly organized. I wish to make a complaint. I pay my taxes, after all.'

I AM DEATH, NOT TAXES. *I* TURN UP ONLY ONCE.

The shade of Mr Hopkinson began to fade. 'It's simply that I've always tried to plan ahead in a sensible way . . .'

I FIND THE BEST APPROACH IS TO TAKE LIFE AS IT COMES.

'That seems very irresponsible . . .'

IT'S ALWAYS WORKED FOR ME.

The sedan chair came to a halt outside Pseudopolis Yard. Vimes left the runners to park it and strode in, putting his coat back on.

There had been a time, and it seemed like only yesterday, when the Watch House had been almost empty. There'd be old Sergeant Colon dozing in his chair, and Corporal Nobbs's washing drying in front of the stove. And then suddenly it had all changed . . .

Sergeant Colon was waiting for him with a clipboard. 'Got the reports from the other Watch Houses, sir,' he said, trotting along beside Vimes.

'Anything special?'

'Bin a bit of an odd murder, sir. Down in one of them old houses on Misbegot Bridge. Some old priest. Dunno much about it. The patrol just said it ought to be looked at.'

'Who found him?'

'Constable Visit, sir.'

'Oh, gods.'

'Yessir.'

'I'll try to get along there this morning. Anything else?'

'Corporal Nobbs is sick, sir.'

'Oh, I know *that*.'

'I mean *off* sick, sir.'

'Not his granny's funeral this time?'

'Nossir.'

'How many's he had this year, by the way?'

'Seven, sir.'

'Very odd family, the Nobbses.'

'Yessir.'

'Fred, you don't have to keep calling me "sir".'

'Got comp'ny, sir,' said the sergeant, glancing meaningfully towards a bench in the main office. 'Come for that alchemy job.'

A dwarf smiled nervously at Vimes.

'All right,' said Vimes. 'I'll see him in my office.' He reached into his coat and took out the assassin's money pouch. 'Put it in the Widows and Orphans Fund, will you, Fred?'

'Right. Oh, well done, sir. Any more windfalls like this and we'll soon be able to afford some more widows.'

Sergeant Colon went back to his desk, surreptitiously opened his drawer and pulled out the book he was reading. It was called *Animal Husbandry*. He'd been a bit worried about the title – you heard stories about strange folk in the country – but it turned out to be nothing more than a book about how cattle and pigs and sheep should breed.

Now he was wondering where to get a book that taught them how to read.

Upstairs, Vimes pushed open his office door carefully. The Assassins' Guild played to rules. You could say that about the bastards. It was terribly bad form to kill a bystander. Apart from anything else, you wouldn't get paid. So traps in his office were out of the question, because too many people were in and out of it every day. Even so, it paid to be careful. Vimes *was* good at making the kind of rich enemies who could afford to employ assassins. The assassins had to be lucky only once, but Vimes had to be lucky all the time.

He slipped into the room and glanced out of the window. He liked to work with it open, even in cold weather. He liked to hear the sounds of the city. But anyone trying to climb up or down to it would run into everything in the way of loose tiles, shifting handholds and treacherous drainpipes that Vimes's ingenuity could contrive. And Vimes had installed spiked railings down below. They were nice and ornamental but they were, above all, spiky.

So far, Vimes was winning.

There was a tentative knock at the door.

It had issued from the knuckles of the dwarf applicant. Vimes ushered him into the office, shut the door, and sat down at his desk.

'So,' he said. 'You're an alchemist. Acid stains on your hands and no eyebrows.'

'That's right, sir.'

'Not usual to find a dwarf in that line of work. You people always seem to toil in your uncle's foundry or something.'

You people, the dwarf noted. 'Can't get the hang of metal,' he said.

'A dwarf who can't get the hang of metal? That must be unique.'

'Pretty rare, sir. But I was quite good at alchemy.'

'Guild member?'

'Not any more, sir.'

'Oh? How did you leave the guild?'

'Through the roof, sir. But I'm pretty certain I know what I did wrong.'

Vimes leaned back. 'The alchemists are always blowing things up. I never heard of them getting sacked for it.'

'That's because no one's ever blown up the Guild Council, sir.'

'What, *all* of it?'

'Most of it, sir. All the easily detachable bits, at least.'

Vimes found he was automatically opening the bottom drawer of his desk. He pushed it shut again and, instead, shuffled the papers in front of him. 'What's your name, lad?'

The dwarf swallowed. This was clearly the bit he'd been dreading. 'Littlebottom, sir.'

Vimes didn't even look up.

'Ah, yes. It says here. That means you're from the Uberwald mountain area, yes?'

'Why . . . yes, sir,' said Littlebottom, mildly surprised. Humans generally couldn't distinguish between dwarf clans.

'Our Constable Angua comes from there,' said Vimes. 'Now . . . it says here your first name is . . . can't read Fred's handwriting . . . er . . .'

There was nothing for it. 'Cheery, sir,' said Cheery Littlebottom.

'Cheery, eh? Good to see the old naming traditions kept up. Cheery Littlebottom. Fine.'

Littlebottom watched carefully. Not the faintest glimmer of amusement had crossed Vimes's face.

'Yes, sir. Cheery Littlebottom,' he said. And there still wasn't as much as an extra wrinkle there. 'My father was Jolly. Jolly Littlebottom,' he added, as one might prod at a bad tooth to see when the pain will come.

'Really?'

'And . . . *his* father was Beaky Littlebottom.'

Not a trace, not a smidgeon of a grin twitched anywhere. Vimes merely pushed the paper aside.

'Well, we work for a living here, Littlebottom.'

'Yes, sir.'

'We don't blow things up, Littlebottom.'

'No, sir. I don't blow *everything* up, sir. Some just melts.'

Vimes drummed his fingers on the desk. 'Know anything about dead bodies?'

'They were only mildly concussed, sir.'

Vimes sighed. 'Listen. I know about how to be a copper. It's mainly walking and talking. But there's lots of things I don't know. You find the scene of a crime and there's some grey powder on the floor. What is it? *I* don't know. But you fellows know how to mix things up in bowls and can find out. And maybe the dead person doesn't seem to have a mark on them. Were they poisoned? It seems we need someone who knows what colour a liver is supposed to be. I want someone who can look at the ashtray and tell me what kind of cigars I smoke.'

'Pantweed's Slim Panatellas,' said Littlebottom automatically.

'Good gods!'

'You've left the packet on the table, sir.'

Vimes looked down. 'All right,' he said. 'So sometimes it's an easy answer. But sometimes it isn't. Sometimes we don't even know if it was the right question.'

He stood up. 'I can't say I like dwarfs much, Littlebottom. But I don't like trolls or humans either, so I suppose that's okay. Well, you're the only applicant. Thirty dollars a month, five dollars living-out allowance, I expect you to work to the job not the clock, there's some mythical creature called "overtime", only no one's even seen its footprints, if troll officers call you a gritsucker they're out, and if you call them rocks *you're* out, we're just one big family and, when you've been to a few domestic disputes, Littlebottom, I can assure you that you'll see the resemblance, we work as a team and we're pretty much making it up as we go along, and half the time we're not even certain what the law is, so it can get interesting, technically you'll rank as a corporal, only don't go giving orders to real policemen, you're on a month's trial, we'll give you some training just as soon as there's time, now, find an iconograph and meet me on Misbegot Bridge in . . . damn . . . better make it an hour. I've got to see about this blasted coat of arms. Still, dead bodies seldom get deader. Sergeant Detritus!'

There was a series of creaks as something heavy moved along the corridor outside and a troll opened the door.

'Yessir?'

'This is Corporal Littlebottom. Corporal Cheery Littlebottom, whose father was Jolly Littlebottom. Give him his badge, swear him in, show him where everything is. Very good, Corporal?'

'I shall try to be a credit to the uniform, sir,' said Littlebottom.

'Good,' said Vimes briskly. He looked at Detritus. 'Incidentally, Sergeant, I've got a report here that a troll in uniform nailed one of Chrysoprase's henchmen to a wall by his ears last night. Know anything about that?'

The troll wrinkled its enormous forehead. 'Does it say anything 'bout him selling bags of Slab to troll kids?'

'No. It says he was going to read spiritual literature to his dear old mother,' said Vimes.

'Did Hardcore say he saw dis troll's badge?'

'No, but he says the troll threatened to ram it where the sun doesn't shine,' said Vimes.

Detritus nodded gravely. 'Dat's a long way to go just to ruin a good badge,' he said.

'By the way,' said Vimes, 'that was a lucky guess of yours, guessing that it was Hardcore.'

'It come to me in a flash, sir,' said Detritus. 'I fort: what bastard who sells Slab to kids deserves bein' nailed up by his ears, sir, and . . . bingo. Dis idea just formed in my head.'

'That's what I thought.'

Cheery Littlebottom looked from one impassive face to the other. The Watchmen's eyes never left each other's face, but the words seemed to come from a little distance, as though both of them were reading an invisible script.

Then Detritus shook his head slowly. 'Musta been a impostor, sir. 'S easy to get helmets like ours. None of my trolls'd do anything like dat. Dat would be police brutality, sir.'

'Glad to hear it. Just for the look of the thing, though, I want you to check the trolls' lockers. The Silicon Anti-Defamation League are on to this one.'

'Yes, sir. An' if I find out it was one of my trolls I will be down on dat troll like a ton of rectang'lar buildin' things, sir.'

'Fine. Well, off you go, Littlebottom. Detritus will look after you.'

Littlebottom hesitated. This was uncanny. The man hadn't mentioned axes, or gold. He hadn't even said anything like 'You can make it big in the Watch'. Littlebottom felt really unbalanced.

'Er . . . I *did* tell you my name, didn't I, sir?'

'Yes. Got it down here,' said Vimes. 'Cheery Little-bottom. Yes?'

'Er . . . yes. That's right. Well, thank you, sir.'

Vimes listened to them go down the passage. Then he carefully shut the door and put his coat over his head so that no one would hear him laughing.

'Cheery Littlebottom!'

Cheery ran after the troll called Detritus. The Watch House was beginning to fill up. And it was clear that the Watch dealt with all *sorts* of things, and that many of them involved shouting.

Two uniformed trolls were standing in front of Sergeant Colon's high desk, with a slightly smaller troll between them. This troll was wearing a down-cast expression. It was also wearing a tutu and had a small pair of gauze wings glued to its back.

'—happen to know that trolls don't have *any* tradition of a Tooth Fairy,' Colon was saying. 'Especially not one called' – he looked down – 'Clinkerbell. So how about if we just call it breaking and entering without a Thieves' Guild licence?'

'Is racial prejudice, not letting trolls have a Tooth Fairy,' Clinkerbell muttered.

One of the troll guards upended a sack on the desk. Various items of silverware cascaded over the paperwork.

'And this is what you found under their pillows, was it?' said Colon.

'Bless dere little hearts,' said Clinkerbell.

At the next desk a tired dwarf was arguing with a vampire. 'Look,' he said, 'it's *not* murder. You're dead already, right?'

'He stuck them right in me!'

'Well, I've been down to interview the manager and he said it was an accident. He said he's got nothing against vampires at all. He says he was merely carrying three boxes of HB Eraser Tips and tripped over the edge of your cloak.'

'I don't see why I can't work where I like!'

'Yes, but . . . in a pencil factory?'

Detritus looked down at Littlebottom and grinned. 'Welcome to life in der big city, Littlebottom,' he said. 'Dat's an int'restin' name.'

'Is it?'

'Most dwarfs have names like Rockheaver or Stronginthearm.'

'Do they?'

Detritus was not one for the fine detail of relationships, but the edge in Littlebottom's voice got through to him. ''S a good name, though,' he said.

'What's Slab?' said Cheery.

'It are chloric ammonium an' radium mixed up. It give your head a tingle but melts troll brains. Big problem in der mountains and some buggers are makin' it here in der city and we tryin' to find how it get up dere. Mr Vimes is lettin' me run a' – Detritus concentrated – 'pub-lic a-ware-ness campaign tellin' people what happens to buggers who sells it to kids . . .' He waved a hand at a large and rather crudely done poster on the wall. It said:

Slab: Jus' say 'Aarrghaarrghpleeassennono-noUGH'.

He pushed open a door.

'Dis is der ole privy wot we don't use no more, you can use it for mixin' up stuff, it the only place we got now, you have to clean it up first 'cos it smells like a toilet in here.'

He opened another door. 'And this der locker room,' he said. 'You got your own peg and dat, and dere's dese panels for getting changed behind 'cos we knows you dwarfs is modest. It a good life if you don't weaken. Mr Vimes is okay but he a bit weird about some stuff, he keepin' on sayin' stuff like dis city is a meltin' pot an' all der scum floats to der top, and stuff like dat. I'll give you your helmet an' badge in a minute but first' – he opened a rather larger locker on the other side of the room, which had 'DTRiTUS' painted on it – 'I got to go and hide dis hammer.'

Two figures hurried out of Ironcrust's Dwarf Bakery ('T'Bread Wi' T'Edge'), threw themselves on to the cart and shouted at the driver to leave urgently.

He turned a pale face towards them and pointed to the road ahead.

There was a wolf there.

Not a usual kind of wolf. It had a blond coat, which around its ears was almost long enough to be a mane. And wolves did not normally sit calmly on their haunches in the middle of a street.

This one was growling. A long, low growl. It was the audible equivalent of a shortening fuse.

The horse was transfixed, too frightened to stay where it was but far too terrified to move.

One of the men carefully reached for a crossbow. The growl rose slightly. He even more carefully took his hand away. The growl subsided again.

'What is it?'

'It's a wolf!'

'In a city? What does it find to eat?'

'Oh, *why* did you have to ask that?'

'*Good* morning, gentlemen!' said Carrot, as he stopped leaning against the wall. 'Looks like the fog's rising again. Thieves' Guild licences, please?'

They turned. Carrot gave them a happy smile and nodded encouragingly.

One of the men patted his coat in a theatrical display of absentmindedness.

'Ah. Well. Er. Left the house in a bit of a hurry this morning, must've forgotten—'

'Section Two, Rule One of the Thieves' Guild Charter says that members must carry their cards on all professional occasions,' said Carrot.

'He's not even drawn his sword!' hissed the most stupid of the three-strong gang.

'He doesn't need to, he's got a loaded wolf.'

Someone was writing in the gloom, the scritching of their pen the only sound.

Until a door creaked open.

The writer turned as quick as a bird. 'You? I told you never to come back here!'

'I know, I know, but it's that damn *thing*! The

40

production line stopped and it got out and it's killed that priest!'

'Did anyone see it?'

'In the fog we had last night? I shouldn't think so. But—'

'Then it is not, ah-ha, a matter of significance.'

'No? They're not supposed to *kill* people. Well . . . that is,' the speaker conceded, 'not by smashing them on the head, anyway.'

'They will if so instructed.'

'I never told it to! Anyway, what if it turns on me?'

'On its master? It can't disobey the words in its head, man.'

The visitor sat down, shaking his head. 'Yeah, but which words? I don't know, I don't know, this is getting too much, that damn thing around all the time—'

'Making you a fat profit—'

'All right, all right, but this other stuff, the poison, I never—'

'Shut up! I'll see you again tonight. You can tell the others that I certainly do have a candidate. And if you dare come here again . . .'

The Ankh-Morpork Royal College of Heralds turned out to be a green gate in a wall in Mollymog Street. Vimes tugged on the bell-pull. Something clanged on the other side of the wall and immediately the place erupted in a cacophony of hoots, growls, whistles and trumpetings.

A voice shouted, 'Down, boy! Couchant! I said

couchant! No! *Not* rampant! And thee shall have a sugar lump like a good boy. William! Stop that at once! Put him down! Mildred, let go of Graham!'

The animal noises subsided a bit and footsteps approached. A wicket gate in the main door opened a fraction.

Vimes saw an inch-wide segment of a very short man.

'Yes? Are you the meat man?'

'Commander Vimes,' said Vimes. 'I have an appointment.'

The animal noises started up again.

'Eh?'

'*Commander Vimes!*' Vimes shouted.

'Oh. I suppose thee'd better come in.'

The door swung open. Vimes stepped through.

Silence fell. Several dozen pairs of eyes regarded Vimes with acute suspicion. Some of the eyes were small and red. Several were big and poked just above the surface of the scummy pond that occupied a lot of space in the yard. Some were on perches.

The yard was *full* of animals, but even they were crowded out by the *smell* of a yard full of animals. And most of them were clearly very old, which didn't do anything for the smell.

A toothless lion yawned at Vimes. A lion running, or at least lounging around loose, was amazing in itself, but not so amazing as the fact that it was being used as a cushion by an elderly gryphon, which was asleep with all four claws in the air.

There were hedgehogs, and a greying leopard, and moulting pelicans. Green water surged in the pond and a couple of hippos surfaced and yawned. Nothing was in a cage, and nothing was trying to eat anything else.

'Ah, it takes people like that, first time,' said the old man. He had a wooden leg. 'We're quite a happy little family.'

Vimes turned and found himself looking at a small owl. 'My gods,' he said. 'That's a morpork, isn't it?'

The old man's face broke into a happy smile. 'Ah, I can see thee knows thy heraldry,' he cackled. 'Daphne's ancestors came all the way from some islands on the other side of the Hub, so they did.'

Vimes took out his City Watch badge and stared at the coat of arms embossed thereon.

The old man looked over his shoulder. 'That's not her, o'course,' he said, indicating the owl perched on the Ankh. 'That was her great-grandma, Olive. A morpork on an ankh, see? That is a pune or play on words. Laugh? I nearly started. That's about as funny as you gets round here. We could do with a mate for her, tell you the truth. And a female hippo. I mean, his lordship says we've got two hippos, which is right enough, I'm just saying it's not natural for Roderick and Keith, I ain't passing judgement, it's just not right, that's all I'm saying. What was thy name again?'

'Vimes. Sir Samuel Vimes. My wife made the appointment.'

The old man cackled again. 'Ah, 'tis usually so.'

Moving quite fast despite his wooden leg, the old man led the way through the steaming mounds of multi-species dung to the building on the other side of the yard.

'I expect this is good for the garden, anyway,' said Vimes, trying to make conversation.

'I tried it on my rhubarb,' said the old man, pushing open the door. 'But it grew to twenty feet tall, sir, and then spontaneously caught fire. Mind where the wyvern's been, sir, he's been ill – oh, what a shame. Never mind, it'll scrape off beautiful when it dries. In thee goes, sir.'

The hall inside was as quiet and dark as the yard had been full of light and noise. There was the dry, tombstone smell of old books and church towers. Above him, when his eyes got used to the darkness, Vimes could make out hanging flags and banners. There were a few windows, but cobwebs and dead flies meant that the light they allowed in was merely grey.

The old man had shut the door and left him alone. Vimes watched through the window as he limped back to continue what he had been doing before Vimes's appearance.

What he had been doing was setting up a living coat of arms.

There was a large shield. Cabbages, actual cabbages, had been nailed to it. The old man said something that Vimes couldn't hear. The little owl fluttered from its perch and landed on a large ankh that had been glued to the top of the shield. The two hippos flopped out of their pool and took up station on either side.

The old man unfolded an easel in front of the

scene, placed a canvas on it, picked up a palette and brush, and shouted, 'Hup-la!'

The hippos reared, rather arthritically. The owl spread its wings.

'Good gods,' murmured Vimes. 'I always thought they just made it up!'

'Made it up, sir? Made it up?' said a voice behind him. 'We'd soon be in trouble if we made things up, oh dear me, yes.'

Vimes turned. Another little old man had appeared behind him, blinking happily through thick glasses. He had several scrolls under one arm.

'I'm sorry I couldn't meet you at the gate but we're very busy at the moment,' he said, holding out his spare hand. 'Croissant Rouge Pursuivant.'

'Er . . . you're a small red breakfast roll?' said Vimes, nonplussed.

'No, no. No. It means Red Crescent. It's my title, you see. Very ancient title. I'm a Herald. You'd be Sir Samuel Vimes, yes?'

'Yes.'

Red Crescent consulted a scroll. 'Good. Good. How do you feel about weasels?' he said.

'Weasels?'

'We have got some weasels, you see. I know they're not *strictly* a heraldic animal, but we seem to have some on the strength and frankly I think I'm going to have to let them go unless we can persuade someone to adopt them, and that'd upset Pardessus Chatain Pursuivant. He always locks himself in his shed when he's upset . . .'

'Pardessus . . . you mean the old man out there?'

said Vimes. 'I mean . . . why's he . . . I thought you
. . . I mean, a coat of arms is just a design. You don't
have to paint it from life!'

Red Crescent looked shocked. 'Well, I suppose if
you want to make a complete mockery of the whole
thing, yes, you could just *make it up*. You could do
that,' he said. 'Anyway . . . not weasels, then?'

'Personally I'd just as soon not bother,' said
Vimes. 'And certainly not with a weasel. My wife
said that dragons would—'

'Happily, the occasion will not arise,' said a voice
in the shadows.

It wasn't the right sort of voice to hear in any
kind of light. It was dust-dry. It sounded as if it came
from a mouth that had never known the pleasures of
spittle. It sounded dead. It was.

The bakery thieves considered their options.

'I've got my hand on my crossbow,' said the most
enterprising of the three.

The most realistic said, 'Have you? Well, I've got
my heart in my mouth.'

'Ooo,' said the third. 'I've got a weak heart, me . . .'

'Yeah, but what I mean is . . . he's not even
wearing a sword. If I take the wolf, the two of you
should be able to deal with him with *no* trouble,
right?'

The one clear thinker looked at Captain Carrot.
His armour shone. So did the muscles on his bare
arms. Even his *knees* gleamed.

'It seems to me that we have a bit of an impasse,
or stand-off,' said Captain Carrot.

'How about if we throw down the money?' said the clear thinker.

'That would certainly help matters.'

'And you'd let us go?'

'No. But it would definitely count in your favour and I would certainly speak up on your behalf.'

The bold one with the crossbow licked his lips and glanced from Carrot to the wolf. 'If you set it on us, I warn you, someone's going to get killed!' he warned.

'Yes, it could happen,' said Carrot, sadly. 'I'd prefer to avoid that, if at all possible.'

He raised his hands. There was something flat and round and about six inches across in each one. 'This,' he said, 'is dwarf bread. Some of Mr Iron-crust's best. It's not classic battle bread, of course, but it's probably good enough for slicing . . .'

Carrot's arm blurred. There was a brief flurry of sawdust, and the flat loaf spun to a stop halfway through the thick timbers of the cart and about half an inch away from the man with the weak heart and, as it turned out, a fragile bladder, too.

The man with the crossbow tore his attention away from the bread only when he felt a slight, damp pressure on his wrist.

There was no way that an animal could have moved that fast, but there it was, and the wolf's expression contrived to indicate very calmly that if the animal so desired the pressure could be increased more or less indefinitely.

'Call it off!' he said, flinging the bow away with his free hand. 'Tell it to let go!'

'Oh, I never tell her anything,' said Carrot. 'She makes up her own mind.'

There was a clatter of iron-shod boots and half a dozen axe-bearing dwarfs raced out of the bakery gates, kicking up sparks as they skidded to a halt beside Carrot.

'Get them!' shouted Mr Ironcrust. Carrot dropped a hand on top of the dwarf's helmet and turned him around.

'It's me, Mr Ironcrust,' he said. 'I believe these are the men?'

'Right you are, Captain Carrot!' said the dwarf baker. 'C'mon, lads! Let's hang 'em up by the *bura'zak-ka!**'

'Ooo,' murmured the weak of heart, damply.

'Now, now, Mr Ironcrust,' said Carrot patiently. 'We don't practise that punishment in Ankh-Morpork.†'

'They bashed Bjorn Tightbritches senseless! *And* they kicked Olaf Stronginthearm in the *bad'dhakz!*‡ We'll cut their—'

'Mr Ironcrust!'

The dwarf baker hesitated and then, to the amazement and relief of the thieves, took a step backwards. 'Yeah . . . all right, Captain Carrot. If you say so.'

'I have business elsewhere, but I would be grateful if you would take them and turn them over to the Thieves' Guild,' said Carrot.

---

*Town hall.
†Because Ankh-Morpork doesn't have a town hall.
‡Yeast bowl.

The quick thinker went pale. 'Oh, no! They get really *intense* about unlicensed thieving! *Anything* but the Thieves' Guild!'

Carrot turned. The light caught his face in a certain way. 'Anything?' he said.

The unlicensed thieves looked at one another, and then all spoke at once.

'The Thieves' Guild. Fine. No problem.'

'We *like* the Thieves' Guild.'

'Can't wait. Thieves' Guild, here I come.'

'Fine body of men.'

'Firm but fair.'

'Good,' said Carrot. 'Then everyone's happy. Oh, yes.' He dug into his money pouch. 'Here's five pence for the loaf, Mr Ironcrust. I've handled the other one, but you should be able to sand it off with no trouble.'

The dwarf blinked at the coins. '*You* want to pay *me* for saving *my* money?' he said.

'As a tax payer you are entitled to the protection of the Watch,' said Carrot.

There was a delicate pause. Mr Ironcrust stared at his feet. One or two of the other dwarfs started to snigger.

'I'll tell you what,' said Carrot, in a kindly voice, 'I'll come round when I get a moment and help you fill in the forms, how about that?'

A thief broke the embarrassed silence.

'Er . . . could your . . . little dog . . . let go of my arm, please?'

The wolf released its grip, jumped down and padded over to Carrot, who raised his hand to his helmet respectfully.

'Good day to you all,' he said, and strode away.

Thieves and victims watched him go.

'Is he *real*?' said the quick thinker.

There was a growl from the baker, then 'You bastards!' he shouted. 'You *bastards*!'

'Wha . . . what? You've got the money back, haven't you?'

Two of his employees had to hold Mr Ironcrust back.

'Three years!' he said. 'Three years and no one bothered! Three bloody years and not so much as a knock at the door! And he'll ask me! Oh, yes! He'll be *nice* about it! He'll probably even go and get the extra forms so I won't be put to the trouble! Why couldn't you buggers have just run away?'

Vimes peered around the shadowy, musty room. The voice might as well have come from a tomb.

A panicky look crossed the face of the little Herald. 'Perhaps Sir Samuel would be kind enough to step this way?' said the voice. It was chilly, clipping every syllable with precision. It was the kind of voice that didn't blink.

'That is, in fact, er . . . Dragon,' said Red Crescent.

Vimes reached for his sword.

'Dragon King of Arms,' said the man.

'*King* of Arms?' said Vimes.

'Merely a title,' said the voice. 'Pray enter.'

For some reason the words re-spelled themselves in Vimes's hindbrain as 'prey, enter'.

'King of Arms,' said the voice of Dragon, as

Vimes passed into the shadows of the inner sanctum. 'You will not need your sword, Commander. I have been Dragon King of Arms for more than five hundred years but I do not breathe fire, I assure you. Ah-ha. Ah-ha.'

'Ah-ha,' said Vimes. He couldn't see the figure clearly. The light came from a few high and grubby windows, and several dozen candles that burned with black-edged flames. There was a suggestion of hunched shoulders in the shape before him.

'Pray be seated,' said Dragon King of Arms. 'And I would be most indebted if you would look to your left and raise your chin.'

'And expose my neck, you mean?' said Vimes.

'Ah-ha. Ah-ha.'

The figure picked up a candelabrum and moved closer. A hand so skinny as to be skeletal gripped Vimes's chin and moved it gently this way and that.

'Ah, yes. You have the Vimes profile, certainly. But not the Vimes ears. Of course, your maternal grandmother was a Clamp. Ah-ha . . .'

The Vimes hand gripped the Vimes sword again. There was only one type of person that had that much strength in a body so apparently frail.

'I *thought* so! You *are* a vampire!' he said. 'You're a bloody *vampire.*'

'Ah-ha.' It might have been a laugh. It might have been a cough. 'Yes. Vampire, indeed. Yes, I've heard about your views on vampires. "Not really alive but not dead enough," I believe you have said. I think that is rather clever. Ah-ha. Vampire, yes. *Bloody,* no. Black puddings, yes. The acme of the butcher's art,

51

yes. And if all else fails there are plenty of kosher butchers down in Long Hogmeat. Ah-ha, yes. We all live in the best way we can. Ah-ha. Virgins are safe from me. Ah-ha. For several hundred years, more's the pity. Ah-ha.'

The shape, and the pool of candlelight, moved away.

'I'm afraid your time has been needlessly wasted, Commander Vimes.'

Vimes's eyes were growing accustomed to the flickering light. The room was full of books, in piles. None of them were on shelves. Each one sprouted bookmarks like squashed fingers.

'I don't understand,' he said. Either Dragon King of Arms had very hunched shoulders or there were wings under his shapeless robe. Some of them could fly like a bat, Vimes recalled. He wondered how old this one was. They could 'live' almost for ever . . .

'I believe you're here because it is considered, ah-ha, appropriate that you have a coat of arms. I am afraid that this is not possible. Ah-ha. A Vimes coat of arms *has* existed, but it cannot be resurrected. It would be against the rules.'

'What rules?'

There was a thump as a book was taken down and opened.

'I'm sure you know your ancestry, Commander. Your father was Thomas Vimes, his father was Gwilliam Vimes—'

'It's Old Stoneface, isn't it,' said Vimes flatly. 'It's something to do with Old Stoneface.'

'Indeed. Ah-ha. Suffer-Not-Injustice Vimes. Your ancestor. Old Stoneface, indeed, as he was called. Commander of the City Watch in 1688. And a regicide. He murdered the last king of Ankh-Morpork, as every schoolboy knows.'

'Executed!'

The shoulders shrugged. 'Nevertheless, the family crest was, as we say in heraldry, *Excretus Est Ex Altitudine*. That is to say, *Depositatum De Latrina*. Destroyed. Banned. Made incapable of resurrection. Lands confiscated, house pulled down, page torn out of history. Ah-ha. You know, Commander, it is interesting that so many of, ah-ha, "Old Stoneface's" descendants' – the inverted commas dropped neatly around the nickname like an old lady carefully picking up something nasty in a pair of tongs – 'have been officers of the Watch. I believe, Commander, that you too have acquired the nickname. Ah-ha. Ah-ha. I have wondered whether there is some inherited urge to expunge the infamy. Ah-ha.'

Vimes gritted his teeth. 'Are you telling me I *can't* have a coat of arms?'

'This is so. Ah-ha.'

'Because my ancestor killed a—' He paused. 'No, it wasn't even execution,' he said. 'You execute a human being. You *slaughter* an animal.'

'He was the king,' said Dragon mildly.

'Oh, yes. And it turned out that down in the dungeons he had machines for—'

'Commander,' said the vampire, holding up his hands, 'I feel you do not understand me. *Whatever else he was*, he was the king. You see, a crown is not like a Watchman's helmet, ah-ha. Even when you take it off, it's still on the head.'

'Stoneface took it off all right!'

'But the king did not even get a trial.'

'No willing judge could be found,' said Vimes.

'Except you . . . that is, your ancestor . . .'

'Well? Someone had to do it. Some monsters should not walk under the living sky.'

Dragon found the page he had been looking for and turned the book around. 'This was his escutcheon,' he said.

Vimes looked down at the familiar sign of the morpork owl perched on an ankh. It was atop a shield divided into four quarters, with a symbol in each quarter.

'What's this crown with a dagger through it?'

'Oh, a traditional symbol, ah-ha. Indicates his role as defender of the crown.'

'Really? And the bunch of rods with an axe in it?' He pointed.

'A fasces. Symbolizes that he is . . . *was* an officer of the law. And the axe was an interesting harbinger of things to come, yes? But axes, I'm afraid, solve nothing.'

Vimes stared at the third quarter. It contained a painting of what seemed to be a marble bust.

'Symbolizing his nickname, "Old Stoneface",' said Dragon helpfully. 'He asked that some reference be made. Sometimes heraldry is nothing more than the art of punning.'

'And this last one? A bunch of grapes? Bit of a boozer, was he?' said Vimes sourly.

'No. Ah-ha. Word play. Vimes = Vines.'

'Ah. The art of *bad* punning,' said Vimes. 'I bet that had you people rolling on the floor.'

Dragon shut the book and sighed. 'There is seldom a reward for those who do what must be done. Alas, such is precedent, and I am powerless.' The old voice brightened up. 'But, still . . . I was extremely pleased, Commander, to hear of your marriage to Lady Sybil. An *ex*cellent lineage. One of the most noble families in the city, ah-ha. The Ramkins, the Selachiis, the Venturis, the Nobbses, of course . . .'

'That's it, is it?' said Vimes. 'I just go now?'

'I seldom get visitors,' said Dragon. 'Generally people are seen by the Heralds, but I thought you should get a proper explanation. Ah-ha. We're so busy now. Once we dealt with *real* heraldry. But this, they tell me, is the Century of the Fruitbat. Now it seems that, as soon as a man opens his second meat-pie shop, he feels impelled to consider himself a gentleman.' He waved a thin white hand at three coats of arms pinned in a row on a board. 'The butcher, the baker and the candlestick-maker,' he sneered, but genteelly. 'Well, the candlemaker, in point of fact. Nothing will do but that we burrow through the records and prove them acceptably armigerous . . .'

Vimes glanced at the three shields. 'Haven't I seen that one before?' he said.

'Ah. Mr Arthur Carry the candlemaker,' said Dragon. 'Suddenly business is booming and he feels he must be a gentleman. A shield bisected by a bend sinister d'une mèche en metal gris – that is to say, a steel grey shield indicating his personal determination and zeal (how zealous, ah-ha, these businessmen are!) bisected by a wick. Upper half, a chandelle in a fenêtre avec rideaux houlant (a candle lighting a window with a warm glow, ah-ha), lower half two chandeliers illuminé (indicating the wretched man sells candles to rich and poor alike). Fortunately his father was a harbourmaster, which fact allowed us to *stretch* ourselves a little with a crest of a lampe au poisson (fish-shaped lamp), indicating both this and his son's current profession. The motto I left in the common modern tongue and is "Art Brought Forth the Candle". I'm sorry, ah-ha, it was naughty but I couldn't resist it.'

'My sides ache,' said Vimes. Something kicked his brain, trying to get attention.

'*This* one is for Mr Gerhardt Sock, president of the Butchers' Guild,' said Dragon. 'His wife's told him a coat of arms is the thing to have, and who are we to argue with the daughter of a tripe merchant, so we've made him a shield of red, for blood, and blue and white stripes, for a butcher's apron, bisected by a string of sausages, centralis a cleaver held in a gloved hand, a boxing glove, which is, ah-ha, the best we could do for "sock". Motto is *Futurus Meus est in Visceris,* which translates as "My Future is in (the) Entrails", both relating to his profession and, ah-ha, alluding to the old practice of telling—'

'—the future from entrails,' said Vimes. 'Amazing.' Whatever was trying to get into his attention was really jumping up and down now.

'While this one, ah-ha, is for Rudolph Potts of

the Bakers' Guild,' said Dragon, pointing to the third shield with a twig-thin finger. 'Can you read it, Commander?'

Vimes gave it a gloomy stare. 'Well, it's divided into three, and there's a rose, a flame and a pot,' he said. 'Er . . . bakers use fire and the pot's for water, I suppose . . .'

'And a pun on the name,' said Dragon.

'But, unless he's called Rosie, I . . .' Then Vimes blinked. 'A rose is a flower. Oh, good grief. Flower, flour. Flour, fire and water? The pot looks like a guzunder to me, though. A chamber pot?'

'The old word for baker was *pistor*,' said Dragon. 'Why, Commander, we shall make a Herald of you yet! And the motto?'

'*Quod Subigo Farinam*,' said Vimes, and wrinkled his forehead. '"Because" . . . "farinaceous" means to do with corn, or flour, doesn't it? . . . oh, no . . . "Because I Knead the Dough"?'

Dragon clapped his hands. 'Well done, sir!'

'This place must simply rock on those long winter evenings,' said Vimes. 'And that's heraldry, is it? Crossword clues and plays on words?'

'Of course there is a great deal more,' said the Dragon. 'These are simple. We more or less have to make them up. Whereas the escutcheon of an old family, such as the Nobbses . . .'

'*Nobbs*!' said Vimes, as the penny dropped. 'That's it! You said "Nobbs"! Before – when you were talking about old families!'

'Ah-ha. What? Oh, indeed. Yes. Oh, yes. A fine old family. Although now, sadly, in decay.'

'You don't mean Nobbs as in . . . Corporal Nobbs?' said Vimes, horror edging his words.

A book thumped open. In the orange light Vimes had a vague upside-down glimpse of shields, and a rambling, unpruned family tree.

'My word. Would that be a C. W. St J. Nobbs?'

'Er . . . yes. Yes!'

'Son of Sconner Nobbs and a lady referred to here as Maisie of Elm Street?'

'Probably.'

'Grandson of Slope Nobbs?'

'That sounds about right.'

'Who was the illegitimate son of Edward St John de Nobbes, Earl of Ankh, and a, ah-ha, a parlour-maid of unknown lineage?'

'Good gods!'

'The earl died without issue, except that which, ah-ha, resulted in Slope. We had not been able to trace the scion – hitherto, at any rate.'

'Good gods!'

'You know the gentleman?'

Vimes regarded with amazement a serious and positive sentence about Corporal Nobbs that included the word 'gentleman'. 'Er . . . yes,' he said.

'Is he a man of property?'

'Only other people's.'

'Well, ah-ha, do tell him. There is no land or money now, of course, but the title is still extant.'

'Sorry . . . let me make sure I understand this. Corporal Nobbs . . . *my* Corporal Nobbs . . . is *the Earl of Ankh*?'

'He would have to satisfy us as to proof of his lineage but, yes, it would appear so.'

Vimes stared into the gloom. Thus far in his life, Corporal Nobbs would have been unlikely to satisfy the examiners as to his species.

'Good gods!' Vimes said yet again. 'And I suppose *he* gets a coat of arms?'

'A particularly fine one.'

'Oh.'

Vimes hadn't even *wanted* a coat of arms. An hour ago he'd have cheerfully avoided this appointment as he had done so many times before. But . . .

'Nobby?' he said 'Good gods!'

'Well, well! This has been a *very* happy meeting,' said Dragon. 'I do so like to keep the records up to date. Ah-ha. Incidentally, how is young Captain Carrot getting along? I'm told his young lady is a werewolf. Ah-ha.'

'Really,' said Vimes.

'Ah-ha.' In the dark, Dragon made a movement that might have been a conspiratorial tap on the side of the nose. 'We know these things!'

'Captain Carrot is doing well,' said Vimes, as icily as he could manage. 'Captain Carrot always does well.'

He slammed the door when he went out. The candle flames wavered.

Constable Angua walked out of an alleyway, doing up her belt.

'That went very well, I thought,' said Carrot, 'and will go some way to earning us the respect of the community.'

'Pff! That man's sleeve! I doubt if he even knows the meaning of the word "laundry",' said Angua, wiping her mouth.

Automatically, they fell into step – the energy-saving policeman's walk, where the pendulum weight of the leg is used to propel the walker along with the minimum of effort. Walking was important, Vimes had always said, and because Vimes had said it Carrot believed it. Walking and talking. Walk far enough and talk to enough people and sooner or later you had an answer.

The respect of the community, thought Angua. That was a Carrot phrase. Well, in fact it was a Vimes phrase, although Sir Samuel usually spat after he said it. But Carrot *believed* it. It was Carrot who'd suggested to the Patrician that hardened criminals should be given the chance to 'serve the community' by redecorating the homes of the elderly, lending a new terror to old age and, given Ankh-Morpork's crime rate, leading to at least one old lady having her front room wallpapered so many times in six months that now she could only get into it sideways.*

'I've found something very interesting that you will be very interested to see,' said Carrot, after a while.

'That's interesting,' said Angua.

'But I'm not going to tell you what it is because I want it to be a surprise,' said Carrot.

---

*Commander Vimes, on the other hand, was all for giving criminals a short, sharp shock. It really depended on how tightly they could be tied to the lightning rod.

'Oh. Good.'

Angua walked in thought for a while and then said: 'I wonder if it will be as surprising as the collection of rock samples you showed me last week?'

'That *was* good, wasn't it?' said Carrot enthusiastically. 'I've been along that street dozens of times and never suspected there was a mineral museum there! All those silicates!'

'Amazing! You'd imagine people would be flocking to it, wouldn't you?'

'Yes, I can't think why they don't!'

Angua reminded herself that Carrot appeared to have in his soul not even a trace element of irony. She told herself that it wasn't his fault he'd been brought up by dwarfs in some mine, and really did think that bits of rock were interesting. The week before they'd visited an iron foundry. That had been interesting, too.

And yet . . . and yet . . . you couldn't help *liking* Carrot. Even people he was arresting liked Carrot. Even old ladies living in a permanent smell of fresh paint liked Carrot. *She* liked Carrot. A lot. Which was going to make leaving him all the harder.

She was a werewolf. That's all there was to it. You either spent your time trying to make sure people didn't find out or you let them find out and spent your time watching them keep their distance and whisper behind your back, although of course you'd have to turn round to watch that.

Carrot didn't mind. But he minded that other people minded. He minded that even quite friendly colleagues tended to carry a bit of silver somewhere on their person. She could see it upsetting him. She could see the tensions building up, and he didn't know how to deal with them.

It was just as her father had said. Get involved with humans other than at mealtimes and you might as well jump down a silver mine.

'Apparently there's going to be a huge firework display after the celebrations next year,' said Carrot. 'I like fireworks.'

'It beats me why Ankh-Morpork wants to celebrate the fact it had a civil war three hundred years ago,' said Angua, coming back to the here-and-now.

'Why not? We won,' said Carrot.

'Yes, but you lost, too.'

'Always look on the positive side, that's what I say. Ah, here we are.'

Angua looked up at the sign. She'd learned to read dwarf runes now.

'"Dwarf Bread Museum",' she said. 'Gosh. I can't wait.'

Carrot nodded happily and pushed open the door. There was a smell of ancient crusts.

'Coo-ee, Mr Hopkinson?' he called. There was no reply. 'He does go out sometimes,' he said.

'Probably when the excitement gets too much for him,' said Angua. 'Hopkinson? That's not a dwarf name, is it?'

'Oh, he's a human,' said Carrot, stepping inside. 'But an amazing authority. Bread's his life. He wrote the definitive work on offensive baking. Well . . . since he's not here I'll just take two tickets and leave tuppence on the desk.'

It didn't look as though Mr Hopkinson got many visitors. There was dust on the floor, and dust on the display cases, and a lot of dust on the exhibits. Most of them were the classic cowpat-like shape, an echo of their taste, but there were also buns, close-combat crumpets, deadly throwing toast and a huge dusty array of other shapes devised by a race that went in for food-fighting in a big and above all terminal way.

'What are we looking for?' Angua said. She sniffed. There was a nastily familiar tang in the air.

'It's . . . are you ready for this? . . . it's . . . the Battle Bread of B'hrian Bloodaxe!' said Carrot, rummaging in a desk by the entrance.

'A loaf of bread? You brought me here to see a loaf of bread?'

She sniffed again. Yes. Blood. *Fresh* blood.

'That's right,' said Carrot. 'It's only going to be here a couple of weeks on loan. It's the actual bread he personally wielded at the Battle of Koom Valley, killing fifty-seven trolls although' – and here Carrot's tone changed down from enthusiasm to civic respectability – 'that was a long time ago and we shouldn't let ancient history blind us to the realities of a multi-ethnic society in the Century of the Fruit-bat.'

There was a creak of a door.

Then: 'This battle bread,' said Angua, indistinctly. 'Black, isn't it? Quite a lot bigger than normal bread?'

'Yes, that's right,' said Carrot.

'And Mr Hopkinson . . . A short man? Little white pointy beard?'

'That's him.'

'And his head all smashed in?'

'What?'

'I think you'd better come and look,' said Angua, backing away.

Dragon King of Arms sat alone among his candles.

So that was Commander Sir Samuel Vimes, he mused. *Stupid man. Clearly can't see beyond the chip on his shoulder. And people like that rise to high office these days. Still, such people have their uses, which presumably is why Vetinari has elevated him. Stupid men are often capable of things the clever would not dare to contemplate . . .*

He sighed, and pulled another tome towards him. It was not much bigger than many others which lined his study, a fact which might have surprised anyone who knew its contents.

He was rather proud of it. It was quite an unusual piece of work, but he had been surprised – or would have been surprised, had Dragon been really surprised at anything at all for the last hundred years or so – at how easy some of it had been. He didn't even need to read it now. He knew it by heart. The family trees were properly planted, the words were down there on the page, and all he had to do was sing along.

The first page was headed: 'The Descent of King Carrot I, by the Grace of the Gods King of Ankh-Morpork'. A long and complex family tree occupied the next dozen pages until it reached: Married . . . The words there were merely pencilled in.

'Delphine Angua von Uberwald,' read the Dragon aloud. 'Father – and, ah-ha, *sire* – Baron Guye von Uberwald, also known as Silvertail; mother, Mme Serafine Soxe-Bloonberg, also known as Yellowfang, of Genua . . .'

It had been quite an achievement, that part. He had expected his agents to have had some difficulty with the more lupine areas of Angua's ancestry, but it turned out that mountain wolves took quite a lot of interest in that sort of thing as well. Angua's ancestors had definitely been among the leaders of the pack.

Dragon King of Arms grinned. As far as he was concerned, species was a secondary consideration. What really mattered in an individual was a good pedigree.

Ah, well. That was the future as it *might* have been.

He pushed the book aside. One of the advantages of a life much longer than average was that you saw how fragile the future was. Men said things like 'peace in our time' or 'an empire that will last a thousand years', and less than half a lifetime later no one even remembered who they were, let alone what they had said or where the mob had buried their ashes. What changed history were smaller things. Often a few strokes of the pen would do the trick.

He pulled another tome towards him. The frontispiece bore the words: 'The Descent of King . . .' Now, what would the man call himself? That at least was not calculable. Oh, well . . .

Dragon picked up his pencil and wrote: 'Nobbs'.

He smiled in the candlelit room.

People kept on talking about the true king of Ankh-Morpork, but history taught a cruel lesson. It said – often in words of blood – that the true king was the one who got crowned.

Books filled this room, too. That was the first impression – one of dank, oppressive bookishness.

The late Father Tubelcek was sprawled across a drift of fallen books. He was certainly dead. No one could have bled that much and still been alive. Or survived for long with a head like a deflated football. Someone must have hit him with a lump hammer.

'This old lady came running out screaming,' said Constable Visit, saluting. 'So I went in and it was just like this, sir.'

'*Just* like this, Constable Visit?'

'Yes, sir. And the name's Visit-The-Infidel-With-Explanatory-Pamphlets, sir.'

'Who was the old lady?'

'She says she's Mrs Kanacki, sir. She says she always brings him his meals. She says she does for him.'

'*Does* for him?'

'You know, sir. Cleaning and sweeping.'

There was, indeed, a tray on the floor, along with a broken bowl and some spilled porridge. The lady who did for the old man had been shocked to find that someone else had done for him first.

'Did she touch him?' he said.

'She says not, sir.'

Which meant the old priest had somehow achieved the *neatest* death Vimes had ever seen. His hands were crossed on his chest. His eyes had been closed.

And something had been put in his mouth. It looked like a rolled-up piece of paper. It gave the corpse a disconcertingly jaunty look, as though he'd decided to have a last cigarette after dying.

Vimes gingerly picked out the little scroll and unrolled it. It was covered with meticulously written but unfamiliar symbols. What made them particularly noteworthy was the fact that their author had apparently made use of the only liquid lying around in huge quantities.

'Yuk,' said Vimes. 'Written in *blood*. Does this mean anything to anyone?'

'Yes, sir!'

Vimes rolled his eyes. 'Yes, Constable Visit?'

'Visit-The-Infidel-With-Explanatory-Pamphlets, sir,' said Constable Visit, looking hurt.

'"The-Infidel-With-Explanatory-Pamphlets*". I was just about to say it, Constable,' said Vimes. 'Well?'

'It's an ancient Klatchian script,' said Constable Visit. 'One of the desert tribes called the Cenotines, sir. They had a sophisticated but fundamentally flawed . . .'

---

*Constable Visit was an Omnian, whose country's traditional approach to evangelism was to put unbelievers to torture and the sword. Things had become a lot more civilized these days but Omnians still had a strenuous and indefatigable approach to spreading the Word, and had merely changed the nature of the weapons. Constable Visit spent his days off in company with his co-religionist Smite-The-Unbeliever-With-Cunning-Arguments, ringing doorbells and causing people to hide behind the furniture everywhere in the city.

'Yes, yes, yes,' said Vimes, who could recognize the verbal foot getting ready to stick itself in the aural door. 'But do you know what it means?'

'I could find out, sir.'

'Good.'

'Incidentally, were you able by any chance to find time to have a look at those leaflets I gave you the other day, sir?'

'Been very busy!' said Vimes automatically.

'Not to worry, sir,' said Visit, and smiled the wan smile of those doing good against great odds. 'When you've got a moment will be fine.'

The old books that had been knocked from the shelves had spilled their pages everywhere. There were splashes of blood on many of them.

'Some of these look religious,' Vimes said. 'You might find something.' He turned. 'Detritus, have a look round, will you?'

Detritus paused in the act of laboriously drawing a chalk outline around the body. 'Yessir. What for, sir?'

'Anything you find.'

'Right, sir.'

With a grunt, Vimes hunkered down and prodded at a grey smear on the floor. 'Dirt,' he said.

'You get dat on floors, sir,' said Detritus, helpfully.

'Except this is off-white. We're on black loam,' said Vimes.

'Ah,' said Sergeant Detritus. 'A Clue.'

'Could be just dirt, of course.'

There was something else. Someone had made an

attempt to tidy up the books. They'd stacked several dozen of them in one neat towering pile, one book wide, largest books on the bottom, all the edges squared up with geometrical precision.

'Now that I *don't* understand,' said Vimes. 'There's a fight. The old man is viciously attacked. Then someone – maybe it was him, dying, maybe it was the murderer – writes something down using the poor man's own blood. And rolls it up neatly and pops it into his mouth like a sweetie. Then he does die and someone shuts his eyes and makes him tidy and piles these books up neatly and . . . does what? Walks out into the seething hurly-burly that is Ankh-Morpork?'

Sergeant Detritus's honest brow furrowed with the effort of thought. 'Could be a . . . could be dere's a footprint outside der window,' he said. 'Dat's always a Clue wort' lookin' for.'

Vimes sighed. Detritus, despite a room-temperature IQ, made a good copper and a damn good sergeant. He had that special type of stupidity that was hard to fool. But the only thing more difficult than getting him to grasp an idea was getting him to let go of it.*

---

*Detritus was particularly good when it came to asking questions. He had three basic ones. They were the direct ('Did you do it?'), the persistent ('Are you sure it wasn't you what done it?') and the subtle ('It was you what done it, wasn't it?'). Although they were not the most cunning questions ever devised, Detritus's talent was to go on patiently asking them for hours on end, until he got the right answer, which was generally something like: 'Yes! Yes! I did it! I did it! Now please tell me what it was I did!'

'Detritus,' he said, as kindly as possible. 'There's a thirty-foot drop into the river outside the window. There won't be—' He paused. This was the river Ankh, after all. 'Any footprints'd be bound to have oozed back by now,' he corrected himself. 'Almost certainly.'

He looked outside, though, just in case. The river gurgled and sucked below him. There were no footprints, even on its famously crusted surface. But there was another smear of dirt on the window-sill.

Vimes scratched some up, and sniffed at it.

'Looks like some more white clay,' he said.

He couldn't think of any white clay around the city. Once you got outside the walls it was thick black loam all the way to the Ramtops. A man walking across it would be two inches taller by the time he got to the other side of a field.

'White clay,' he said. 'Where the hell is white-clay country round here?'

'It a mystery,' said Detritus.

Vimes grinned mirthlessly. It *was* a mystery. And he didn't like mysteries. Mysteries had a way of getting bigger if you didn't solve them quickly. Mysteries pupped.

Mere *murders* happened all the time. And usually even Detritus could solve them. When a distraught woman was standing over a fallen husband holding a right-angled poker and crying 'He never should've said that about our Neville!' there was only a limited amount you could do to spin out the case beyond the next coffee break. And when various men or parts thereof were hanging from or nailed to various fixtures in the Mended Drum on a Saturday night, and the other clientele were all looking innocent, you didn't need even a Detritic intelligence to work out what had been happening.

He looked down at the late Father Tubelcek. It was amazing he'd bled so much, with his pipe-cleaner arms and toast-rack chest. He certainly wouldn't have been able to put up much of a fight.

Vimes leaned down and gently raised one of the corpse's eyelids. A milky blue eye with a black centre looked back at him from wherever the old priest was now.

A religious old man who lived in a couple of little poky rooms and obviously didn't go out much, from the smell. What kind of threat could he . . . ?

Constable Visit poked his head around the door. 'There's a dwarf down here with no eyebrows and a frizzled beard says you told him to come, sir,' he said. 'And some citizens say Father Tubelcek is their priest and they want to bury him decently.'

'Ah, that'll be Littlebottom. Send him up,' said Vimes, straightening. 'Tell the others they'll have to wait.'

Littlebottom climbed the stairs, took in the scene, and managed to reach the window in time to be sick.

'Better now?' said Vimes eventually.

'Er . . . yes. I hope so.'

'I'll leave you to it, then.'

'Er . . . what exactly did you want me to do?' said Littlebottom, but Vimes was already halfway down the stairs.

*   *   *

Angua growled. It was the signal to Carrot that he could open his eyes again.

Women, as Colon had remarked to Carrot once when he thought the lad needed advice, could be funny about little things. Maybe they didn't like to be seen without their make-up on, or insisted on buying smaller suitcases than men even though they always took more clothes. In Angua's case she didn't like to be seen *en route* from human to werewolf shape, or vice versa. It was just something she had a thing about, she said. Carrot could see her in either shape but not in the various ones she occupied on the way through, in case he never wanted to see her again.

Through werewolf eyes the world was *different*.

For one thing, it was in black-and-white. At least, that small part of it which as a human she'd thought of as 'vision' was monochrome – but who cared that vision had to take a back seat when smell drove instead, laughing and sticking its arm out of the window and making rude gestures at all the other senses? Afterwards, she always remembered the odours as colours and sounds. Blood was rich brown and deep bass, stale bread was a surprisingly tinkly bright blue, and every human being was a four-dimensional kaleidoscopic symphony. For nasal vision meant seeing through time as well as space: a man could stand still for a minute and, an hour later, there he'd still be, to the nose, his odours barely faded.

She prowled the aisles of the Dwarf Bread

Museum, muzzle to the ground. Then she went out into the alley for a while and tried there too.

After five minutes she padded back to Carrot and gave him the signal again.

When he re-opened his eyes she was pulling her shirt on over her head. That was one thing where humans had the edge. You couldn't beat a pair of hands.

'I thought you'd be down the street and following someone,' he said.

'Follow who?' said Angua.

'Pardon?'

'I can smell him, and you, and the bread, and that's it.'

'Nothing else?'

'Dirt. Dust. The usual stuff. Oh, there are some old traces, days old. I know you were in here last week, for example. There are lots of smells. Grease, meat, pine resin for some reason, old food . . . but I'll swear no living thing's been in here in the last day or so but him and us.'

'But you told me *everyone* leaves a trail.'

'They do.'

Carrot looked down at the late curator. However you phrased it, however broadly you applied your definitions, he definitely couldn't have committed suicide. Not with a loaf of bread.

'Vampires?' said Carrot. 'They can fly . . .'

Angua sighed. 'Carrot, I could tell if a vampire had been in here in the last *month*.'

'There's almost half a dollar in pennies in the drawer,' said Carrot. 'Anyway, a thief would be here for the Battle Bread, wouldn't they? It is a very valuable cultural artefact.'

'Has the poor man got any relatives?' said Angua.

'He's got an elderly sister, I believe. I come in once a month just to have a chat. He lets me handle the exhibits, you know.'

'That must be fun,' said Angua, before she could stop herself.

'It's very . . . satisfying, yes,' said Carrot solemnly. 'It reminds me of home.'

Angua sighed and stepped into the room behind the little museum. It was like the back rooms of museums everywhere, full of junk and things there is no room for on the shelves and also items of doubtful provenance, such as coins dated '52 BC'. There were some benches with shards of dwarf bread on them, a tidy tool rack with various sizes of kneading hammer, and papers all over the place. Against one wall, and occupying a large part of the room, was an oven.

'He researches old recipes,' said Carrot, who seemed to feel he had to promote the old man's expertise even in death.

Angua opened the oven door. Warmth spilled out into the room. 'Hell of a bake oven,' she said. 'What're these things?'

'Ah . . . I see he's been making drop scones,' said Carrot. 'Quite deadly at short range.'

She shut the door. 'Let's get back to the Yard and they can send someone out to—'

Angua stopped.

These were always the dangerous moments,

just after a shape-change this close to full moon. It wasn't so bad when she was a wolf. She was still as intelligent, or at least she *felt* as intelligent, although life was a lot simpler and so she was probably just extremely intelligent for a wolf. It was when she became a human again that things were difficult. For a few minutes, until the morphic field fully reasserted itself, all her senses were still keen; smells were still incredibly strong, and her ears could hear sounds way outside the stunted human range. And she could *think* more about the things she experienced. A wolf could sniff a lamp-post and know that old Bonzo had been past yesterday, and was feeling a bit under the weather, and was still being fed tripe by his owner, but a human mind could actually think about the whys and wherefores.

'There *is* something else,' she said, and breathed in gently. 'Faint. Not a living thing. But . . . can't you smell it? Something like dirt, but not quite. It's kind of . . . yellow-orange . . .'

'Um . . .' said Carrot, tactfully. 'Some of us don't have your nose.'

'I've smelled it before, somewhere in this town. Can't remember where . . . It's strong. Stronger than the other smells. It's a muddy smell.'

'Hah, well, on *these* streets . . .'

'No, it's not . . . *exactly* mud. Sharper. More treble.'

'You know, sometimes I envy you. It must be nice to be a wolf. Just for a while.'

'It has its drawbacks.' *Like fleas,* she thought, as they locked up the museum. *And the food. And the* constant nagging feeling that you should be wearing three bras at once.

She kept telling herself she had it under control and she did, in a way. She prowled the city on moonlit nights and, okay, there was the occasional chicken, but she always remembered where she'd been and went round next day to shove some money under the door.

It was hard to be a vegetarian who had to pick bits of meat out of her teeth in the morning. She was definitely on top of it, though.

Definitely, she reassured herself.

It was Angua's mind that prowled the night, not a werewolf mind. She was almost entirely sure of that. A werewolf wouldn't stop at chickens, not by a long way.

She shuddered.

Who was she kidding? It was easy to be a vegetarian by day. It was preventing yourself from becoming a humanitarian at night that took the real effort.

The first clocks were striking eleven as Vimes's sedan chair wobbled to a halt outside the Patrician's palace. Commander Vimes's legs were beginning to give out, but he ran up five flights of stairs as fast as possible and collapsed on a chair in the waiting salon.

Minutes went past.

You didn't knock on the Patrician's door. He summoned you in the certain knowledge that you would be there.

Vimes sat back, enjoying a moment's peace.

Something inside his coat went: 'Bing bing bingley bing!'

He sighed, pulled out a leather-bound package about the size of a small book, and opened it.

A friendly yet slightly worried face peered up at him from its cage.

'Yes?' said Vimes.

'Eleven a.m. Appointment with the Patrician.'

'Yes? Well? It's five past now.'

'Er. So you've had it, have you?' said the imp.

'No.'

'Shall I go on remembering it or what?'

'No. Anyway, you didn't remind me about the College of Arms at ten.'

The imp looked panic-stricken.

'That's Tuesday, isn't it? Could've sworn it was Tuesday.'

'It was an hour ago.'

'Oh.' The imp was downcast. 'Er. All right. Sorry. Um. Hey, I could tell you what time it is in Klatch, if you like. Or Genua. Or Hunghung. Any of those places. You name it.'

'I don't need to know the time in Klatch.'

'You might,' said the imp desperately. 'Think how people will be impressed if, during a dull moment of the conversation, you could say "Incidentally, in Klatch it's an hour ago". Or Bes Pelargic. Or Ephebe. Ask me. Go on. I don't mind. Any of those places.'

Vimes sighed inwardly. He had a notebook. He took notes in it. It was always useful. And then Sybil, gods bless her, had bought him this fifteen-function imp which did so many other things, although as far as he could see at least ten of its functions consisted of apologizing for its inefficiency in the other five.

'You could take a memo,' Vimes said.

'Wow! Really? Gosh! Okay. Right. *No* problem.'

Vimes cleared his throat. 'See Corporal Nobbs re time-keeping; also re Earldom.'

'Er . . . sorry, is this the memo?'

'Yes.'

'Sorry, you should have said "memo" first. I'm pretty certain it's in the manual.'

'All right, it *was* a memo.'

'Sorry, you have to say it again.'

'Memo: See Corporal Nobbs re time-keeping; also re Earldom.'

'Got it,' said the imp. 'Would you like to be reminded of this at any particular time?'

'The time here?' said Vimes, nastily. 'Or the time in, say, Klatch?'

'As a matter of fact, I can tell you what time it—'

'I think I'll write it in my notebook, if you don't mind,' said Vimes.

'Oh, well, if you prefer, I can recognize hand-writing,' said the imp proudly. 'I'm quite advanced.'

Vimes pulled out his notebook and held it up. 'Like this?' he said.

The imp squinted for a moment. 'Yep,' it said. 'That's handwriting, sure enough. Curly bits, spiky bits, all joined together. Yep. Handwriting. I'd recognize it anywhere.'

'Aren't you supposed to tell me what it says?'

The imp looked wary. 'Says?' it said. 'It's supposed to make noises?'

Vimes put the battered book away and shut the lid of the organizer. Then he sat back and carried on waiting.

Someone very clever – certainly someone much cleverer than whoever had trained that imp – must have made the clock for the Patrician's waiting room. It went tick-tock like any other clock. But somehow, and against all usual horological practice, the tick and the tock were irregular. Tick tock tick . . . and then the merest fraction of a second longer before . . . tock tick tock . . . and then a tick a fraction of a second earlier than the mind's ear was now prepared for. The effect was enough, after ten minutes, to reduce the thinking processes of even the best-prepared to a sort of porridge. The Patrician must have paid the clockmaker quite highly.

The clock said quarter past eleven.

Vimes walked over to the door and, despite precedent, knocked gently.

There was no sound from within, no murmur of distant voices.

He tried the handle. The door was unlocked.

Lord Vetinari had always said that punctuality was the politeness of princes.

Vimes went in.

Cheery dutifully scraped up the crumbly white dirt and then examined the corpse of the late Father Tubelcek.

Anatomy was an important study at the Alchemists' Guild, owing to the ancient theory that the human body represented a microcosm of the universe, although when you saw one opened up it was hard to imagine which part of the universe was small and purple and went *blomp-blomp* when you prodded it. But in any case you tended to pick up practical anatomy as you went along, and sometimes scraped it off the walls as well. When new students tried an experiment that was particularly successful in terms of explosive force, the result was often a cross between a major laboratory refit and a game of Hunt-the-other-Kidney.

The man had been killed by being repeatedly hit around the head. That was about all you could say. Some kind of very heavy blunt instrument.*

What else did Vimes expect Cheery to do?

He looked carefully at the rest of the body. There were no other obvious signs of violence, although . . . there were a few specks of blood on the man's fingers. But, then, there was blood everywhere.

A couple of fingernails were torn. Tubelcek had put up a fight, or at least had tried to shield himself with his hands.

Cheery looked more closely at the fingers. There was something piled under the nails. It had a waxy sheen, like thick grease. He couldn't imagine why it should be there, but maybe his job was to find out.

---

*It is a pervasive and beguiling myth that the people who design instruments of death end up being killed by them. There is *almost* no foundation in fact. Colonel Shrapnel wasn't blown up, M. Guillotin died with his head on, Colonel Gatling wasn't shot. If it hadn't been for the murder of cosh and blackjack maker Sir William Blunt-Instrument in an alleyway, the rumour would never have got started.

He conscientiously took an envelope out of his pocket and scraped the stuff into it, sealed it up and numbered it.

Then he took his iconograph out of its box and prepared to take a picture of the corpse.

As he did so, something caught his eye.

Father Tubelcek lay there, one eye still open as Vimes had left it, winking at eternity.

Cheery looked closer. He'd thought he'd imagined it. But . . .

Even now he wasn't sure. The mind could play tricks.

He opened the little door of the iconograph and spoke to the imp inside.

'Can you paint a picture of his eye, Sydney?' he said.

The imp squinted out through the lens. 'Just the eye?' it squeaked.

'Yes. As big as you can.'

'You're sick, mister.'

'And shut up,' said Cheery.

He propped the box on the table and sat back. From inside the box there came the swish-swish of brush strokes. At last there was the sound of a handle being turned, and a slightly damp picture rustled out of a slot.

Cheery peered at it. Then he knocked on the box. The hatch opened.

'Yes?'

'Bigger. So big it fills the whole paper. In fact' – Cheery squinted at the picture in his hands – 'just paint the pupil. The bit in the middle.'

'So it fills the whole paper? You're weird.'

Cheery propped the box nearer. There was a clicking of gears as the imp wound the lenses out, and then a few more seconds of busy brush work.

Another damp picture unwound. It showed a big black disc.

Well . . . mainly black.

Cheery looked closer. There was a hint, just a hint . . .

He rapped on the box again.

'Yes, Mr Dwarf Weird Person?' said the imp.

'The bit in the middle. Big as you can, thank you.'

The lenses wound out yet further.

Cheery waited anxiously. In the next room, he could hear Detritus patiently moving around.

The paper wound out for the third time, and the hatch opened. 'That's it,' said the imp. 'I've run out of black.'

And the paper *was* black . . . except for the tiny little area that wasn't.

The door to the stairs burst open and Constable Visit came in, borne along by the pressure of a small crowd. Cheery guiltily thrust the paper into his pocket.

'This is intolerable!' said a small man with a long black beard. 'We *demand* you let us in! Who're you, young man?'

'I'm Ch – I'm Corporal Littlebottom,' said Cheery. 'Look, I've got a badge . . .'

'Well, *Corporal*,' said the man, 'I am Wengel Raddley and I am a man of some standing in this community and I demand that you let us have poor Father Tubelcek this minute!'

'We're, er, we're trying to find out who killed him,' Cheery began.

There was a movement behind Cheery, and the faces in front of him suddenly looked very worried indeed. He turned to see Detritus in the doorway to the next room.

'Everyt'ing okay?' said the troll.

The changed fortunes of the Watch had allowed Detritus to have a proper breastplate rather than a piece of elephant battle armour. As was normal practice for the uniform of a sergeant, the armourer had attempted to do a stylized representation of muscles on it. As far as Detritus was concerned, he hadn't been able to get them all in.

'Is dere any trouble?' he said.

The crowd backed away.

'None at all, officer,' said Mr Raddley. 'You, er, just loomed suddenly, that's all . . .'

'Dis is correct,' said Detritus. 'I am a loomer. It often happen suddenly. So dere's no trouble, den?'

'No trouble whatsoever, officer.'

'Amazing t'ing, trouble,' rumbled Detritus thoughtfully. 'Always I go lookin' for trouble, an' when I find it people said it ain't dere.'

Mr Raddley drew himself up.

'But we want to take Father Tubelcek away to bury him,' he said.

Detritus turned to Cheery Littlebottom. 'You done everyt'ing you need?'

'I suppose so . . .'

'He dead?'

'Oh, yes.'

'He gonna get any better?'

'Better than dead? I doubt it.'

'Okay, den you people can take him away.'

The two Watchmen stood aside as the body was carried down the stairs.

'Why you takin' pictures of the dead man?' said Detritus.

'Well, er, it might be helpful to see how he was lying.'

Detritus nodded sagely. 'Ah, he was lyin', was he? An' him a holy man, too.'

Littlebottom pulled out the picture and looked at it again. It was *almost* black. But . . .

A constable arrived at the bottom of the stairs. 'Is there someone up there called' – there was a muffled snigger – 'Cheery Littlebottom?'

'Yes,' said Littlebottom gloomily.

'Well, Commander Vimes says you've to come to the Patrician's palace right now, all right?'

'Dat's *Corporal* Littlebottom you're talkin' to,' said Detritus.

'It's all right,' said Littlebottom. 'Nothing could make it any worse.'

Rumour is information distilled so finely that it can filter through anything. It does not need doors and windows – sometimes it doesn't even need people. It can exist free and wild, running from ear to ear without ever touching lips.

It had escaped already. From the high window of the Patrician's bedroom, Sam Vimes could see people drifting towards the palace. There wasn't a mob – there wasn't even what you might call a crowd – but the Brownian motion of the streets was bouncing more and more people in his direction.

He relaxed slightly when he saw one or two guards come through the gates.

On the bed, Lord Vetinari opened his eyes.

'Ah . . . Commander Vimes,' he murmured.

'What's been happening, sir?' said Vimes.

'I appear to be lying down, Vimes.'

'You were in your office, sir. Unconscious.'

'Dear me. I must have been . . . overdoing it. Well, thank you. If you would be kind enough to . . . help me up . . .'

Lord Vetinari tried to pull himself upright, swayed, and fell back again. His face was pale. Sweat beaded his forehead.

There was a knock at the door. Vimes opened it a fraction.

'It's me, sir. Fred Colon. I got a message. What's up?'

'Ah, Fred. Who've you got down there so far?'

'There's me and Constable Flint and Constable Slapper, sir.'

'Right. Someone's to go up to my place and get Willikins to bring me my street uniform. And my sword and crossbow. And an overnight bag. And some cigars. And tell Lady Sybil . . . tell Lady Sybil . . . well, they'll just have to tell Lady Sybil I've got to deal with things down here, that's all.'

'What's *happening,* sir? Someone downstairs said Lord Vetinari's dead!'

'Dead?' murmured the Patrician from his bed. 'Nonsense!' He jerked himself upright, swung his legs off the bed, and folded up. It was a slow, terrible collapse. Lord Vetinari was a tall man, so there was a long way to fall. And he did it by folding up a joint at a time. His ankles gave way and he fell on his knees. His knees hit the ground with a bang and he bent at the waist. Finally his forehead bounced on the carpet.

'Oh,' he said.

'His lordship's just a bit . . .' Vimes began – then he grabbed Colon and dragged him out of the room. 'I reckon he's been poisoned, Fred, and that's the truth of it.'

Colon looked horrified. 'Ye gods! Do you want me to get a doctor?'

'Are you mad? We want him to live!'

Vimes bit his lip. He'd said the words that were on his mind, and now, without a doubt, the faint smoke of rumour would drift out across the city. 'But someone ought to look at him . . .' he said aloud.

'Damn right!' said Colon. 'You want I should get a wizard?'

'How do we know it wasn't one of them?'

'Ye gods!'

Vimes tried to think. All the doctors in the city were employed by the guilds, and all the guilds hated Vetinari, so . . .

'When you've got enough people to spare a

runner, send him up to the stables on Kings Down to fetch Doughnut Jimmy,' he said.

Colon looked even more stricken. 'Doughnut? He doesn't know *anything* about doctoring! He dopes racehorses!'

'Just get him, Fred.'

'What if he won't come?'

'Then say that Commander Vimes knows why Laughing Boy didn't win the Quirm 100 Dollars last week, and say that I know Chrysoprase the troll lost ten thousand on that race.'

Colon was impressed. 'You've got a nasty twist of mind there, sir.'

'There's going to be a lot of people turning up pretty soon. I want a couple of Watchmen outside this room – trolls or dwarfs for preference – and no one is to come in without my permission, right?'

Colon's face contorted as various emotions fought for space. Finally he managed to say, 'But . . . *poisoned*? He's got food-tasters and everything!'

'Then maybe it was one of them, Fred.'

'My gods, sir! You don't trust *anyone*, do you?'

'No, Fred. Incidentally, was it you? Just kidding,' Vimes added quickly as Colon's face threatened to burst into tears. 'Off you go. We don't have much time.'

Vimes shut the door and leaned on it. Then he turned the key in the lock and moved a chair under the handle.

Finally he hauled the Patrician off the floor and rolled him on to the bed. There was a grunt from the man, and his eyelids flickered.

Poison, thought Vimes. *That's the worst of all. It doesn't make a noise, the poisoner can be miles away, you can't see it, often you can't really smell it or taste it, it could be anywhere – and there it is, doing its work . . .*

The Patrician opened his eyes.

'I would like a glass of water,' he said.

There was a jug and a glass by the bed. Vimes picked up the jug, and hesitated. 'I'll send someone to get some,' he said.

Lord Vetinari blinked, very slowly.

'Ah, Sir Samuel,' he said, 'but whom can you trust?'

There was a crowd in the big audience chamber when Vimes finally went downstairs. They were milling about, worried and unsure, and, like important men everywhere, when they were worried and unsure they got angry.

The first to bustle up to Vimes was Mr Boggis of the Guild of Thieves. 'What's going on, Vimes?' he demanded.

He met Vimes's stare. 'Sir Samuel, I mean,' he said, losing a certain amount of bustle.

'I believe Lord Vetinari has been poisoned,' said Vimes.

The background muttering stopped. Boggis realized that, since he had been the one to ask the question, he was now the man on the spot. 'Er . . . fatally?' he said.

In the silence, a pin would have clanged.

'Not yet,' said Vimes.

Around the hall there was a turning of heads. The

focus of the universal attention was Dr Downey, head of the Guild of Assassins.

Downey nodded. 'I'm not aware of any *arrangement* with regard to Lord Vetinari,' he said. 'Besides, as I am sure is common knowledge, we have set the price for the Patrician at one million dollars.'

'And who has that sort of money, indeed?' said Vimes.

'Well . . . you for one, Sir Samuel,' said Downey. There was some nervous laughter.

'We wish to see Lord Vetinari, in any case,' said Boggis.

'No.'

'No? And why not, pray?'

'Doctor's orders.'

'Really? Which doctor?'

Behind Vimes, Sergeant Colon shut his eyes.

'Dr James Folsom,' said Vimes.

It took a few seconds before someone worked this out. 'What? You can't mean . . . Doughnut Jimmy? He's a *horse* doctor!'

'So I understand,' said Vimes.

'But why?'

'Because many of his patients survive,' said Vimes. He raised his hands as the protests grew. 'And now, gentlemen, I must leave you. Somewhere there's a poisoner. I'd like to find him before he becomes a murderer.'

He went back up the stairs, trying to ignore the shouts behind him.

'You sure about old Doughnut, sir?' said Colon, catching him up.

'Well, do you trust him?' said Vimes.

'Doughnut? Of course not!'

'Right. He's untrustworthy, and so we don't trust him. So that's all right. But I've seen him revive a horse when everyone else said it was fit only for the knackers. Horse doctors *have* to get results, Fred.'

And that was true enough. When a human doctor, after much bleeding and cupping, finds that a patient has died out of sheer desperation, he can always say, 'Dear me, will of the gods, that will be thirty dollars please,' and walk away a free man. This is because human beings are not, technically, worth anything. A good racehorse, on the other hand, may be worth twenty thousand dollars. A doctor who lets one hurry off too soon to that great big paddock in the sky may well expect to hear, out of some dark alley, a voice saying something on the lines of 'Mr Chrysoprase is *very upset*', and find the brief remainder of his life full of incident.

'No one seems to know where Captain Carrot and Angua are,' said Colon. 'It's their day off. And Nobby's nowhere to be found.'

'Well, that's something to be thankful for . . .'

'Bingeley bingeley bong beep,' said a voice from Vimes's pocket.

He lifted out the little organizer and raised the flap.

'Yes?'

'Er . . . twelve noon,' said the imp. 'Lunch with Lady Sybil.'

It stared at their faces.

'Er . . . that's all right, isn't it?' it said.

*   *   *

Cheery Littlebottom wiped his brow.

'Commander Vimes is right. It *could* be arsenic,' he said. 'It looks like arsenic poisoning to me. Look at his colour.'

'Nasty stuff,' said Doughnut Jimmy. 'Has he been eating his bedding?'

'All the sheets seem to be here, so I suppose the answer is no.'

'How's he pissing?'

'Er. The usual way, I assume.'

Doughnut sucked at his teeth. He had amazing teeth. It was the second thing everyone noticed about him. They were the colour of the inside of an un-washed teapot.

'Walk him round a bit on the loose rein,' he said.

The Patrician opened his eyes. 'You *are* a doctor, aren't you?' he said.

Doughnut Jimmy gave him an uncertain look. He was not used to patients who could talk. 'Well, yeah . . . I have a lot of patients,' he said.

'Indeed? I have very little,' said the Patrician. He tried to lift himself off the bed, and slumped back.

'I'll mix up a draught,' said Doughnut Jimmy, backing away. 'You're to hold his nose and pour it down his throat twice a day, right? And no oats.'

He hurried out, leaving Cheery alone with the Patrician.

Corporal Littlebottom looked around the room. Vimes hadn't given him much instruction. He'd said: 'I'm sure it won't be the food-tasters. For all they know they might be asked to eat the whole plateful.

Still, we'll get Detritus to talk to them. You find out the *how*, right? And then leave the *who* to me.'

If you didn't eat or drink a poison, what else was left? Probably you could put it on a pad and make someone breathe it, or dribble some in their ear while they slept. Or they could touch it. Maybe a small dart . . . Or an insect bite . . .

The Patrician stirred, and looked at Cheery through watery red eyes. 'Tell me, young man, are you a policeman?'

'Er . . . just started, sir.'

'You appear to be of the dwarf persuasion.'

Cheery didn't bother to answer. There was no use denying it. Somehow, people could tell if you were a dwarf just by looking at you.

'Arsenic is a very popular poison,' said the Patrician. 'Hundreds of uses around the home. Crushed diamonds used to be in vogue for hundreds of years, despite the fact they never worked. Giant spiders, too, for some reason. Mercury is for those with patience, aquafortis for those without. Cantharides has its followers. Much can be done with the secretions of various animals. The bodily fluids of the caterpillar of the Quantum Weather Butterfly will render a man quite, quite helpless. But we return to arsenic like an old, old friend.'

There was a drowsiness in the Patrician's voice. 'Is that not so, young Vetinari? Yes indeed, sir. Correct. But where then shall we put it, seeing that all will look for it? In the last place they will look, sir. Wrong. Foolish. We put it where no one will look *at all* . . .'

The voice faded to a murmur.

The bed linen, Cheery thought. Even clothes. Into the skin, slowly . . .

Cheery hammered on the door. A guard opened it.

'Get another bed.'

'What?'

'Another bed. From anywhere. And fresh bed linen.'

He looked down. There wasn't much of a carpet on the floor. Even so, in a bedroom, where people might walk with bare feet . . .

'And take away this rug and bring another one.'

What else?

Detritus came in, nodded at Cheery, and looked carefully around the room. Finally he picked up a battered chair.

'Dis'll have to do,' he said. 'If he want, I can break der back off'f it.'

'What?' said Cheery.

'Ole Doughnut said for to get a stool sample,' said Detritus, going out again.

Cheery opened his mouth to stop the troll, and then shrugged. Anyway, the less furniture in here the better . . .

And that seemed about it, short of stripping the wallpaper off the wall.

Sam Vimes stared out of the window.

Vetinari hadn't bothered much in the way of bodyguards. He had used – that is, he still did use – food-tasters, but that was common enough. Mind you, Vetinari had added his own special twist. The tasters were well paid and treated, and they were all sons of the chief cook. But his main protection was that he was just that bit more useful alive than dead, from everyone's point of view. The big powerful guilds didn't like him, but they liked him in power a lot more than they liked the idea of someone from a rival guild in the Oblong Office. Besides, Lord Vetinari represented stability. It was a cold and clinical kind of stability, but part of his genius was the discovery that stability was what people wanted more than anything else.

He'd said to Vimes once, in this very room, standing at this very window: 'They think they want good government and justice for all, Vimes, yet what is it they really crave, deep in their hearts? Only that things go on as normal and tomorrow is pretty much like today.'

Now, Vimes turned around. 'What's my next move, Fred?'

'Dunno, sir.'

Vimes sat down in the Patrician's chair. 'Can you remember the last Patrician?'

'Old Lord Snapcase? And the one before him, Lord Winder. Oh, yeah. Nasty pieces of work, they were. At least this one didn't giggle or wear a dress.'

The past tense, thought Vimes. *It creeps in already. Not long past, but already very tense.*

'It's gone very quiet downstairs, Fred,' he said.

'Plotting don't make a lot of noise, sir, generally.'

'Vetinari's not dead, Fred.'

'Yessir. But he's not exactly in charge, is he?'

Vimes shrugged. 'No one's in charge, I suppose.'

'Could be, sir. There again, you never know your luck.'

Colon was standing stiffly to attention, with his eyes firmly fixed on the middle distance and his voice pitched carefully to avoid any hint of emotion in the words.

Vimes recognized the stance. He used it himself, when he had to. 'What do you mean, Fred?' he said.

'Not a thing, sir. Figure of speech, sir.'

Vimes sat back.

This morning, he thought, *I knew what the day held. I was going to see about that damn coat of arms. Then there was my usual meeting with Vetinari. I was going to read some reports after lunch, maybe go and see how they're getting on with the new Watch House in Chittling Street, and have an early night. Now Fred's suggesting . . . what?*

'Listen, Fred, if there *is* to be a new ruler, it won't be me.'

'Who'll it be, sir?' Colon's voice still held that slow, deliberate tone.

'How should I know? It could be . . .'

The gap opened ahead of him and he could feel his thoughts being sucked into it. 'You're talking about Captain Carrot, aren't you, Fred?'

'Could be, sir. I mean none of the guilds'd let some other guild bloke be ruler now, and everyone likes Captain Carrot, and, well . . . rumour's got about that he's the hair to the throne, sir.'

'There's no proof of that, Sergeant.'

'Not for me to say, sir. Dunno about that. Dunno

what *is* proof,' said Colon, with just a hint of defiance. 'But he's got that sword of his, and the birthmark shaped like a crown, and . . . well, everyone *knows* he's king. It's his krisma.'

Charisma, thought Vimes. *Oh, yes. Carrot has charisma. He makes something happen in people's heads. He can talk a charging leopard into giving up and handing over its teeth and doing good work in the community, and that would* really *upset the old ladies.*

Vimes distrusted charisma. 'No more kings, Fred.'

'Right you are, sir. By the way, Nobby's turned up.'

'The day gets worse and worse, Fred.'

'You said you'd talk to him about all these funerals, sir . . .'

'The job goes on, I suppose. All right, go and tell him to come up here.'

Vimes was left to himself.

No more kings. Vimes had difficulty in articulating why this should be so, why the concept revolted in his very bones. After all, a good many of the patricians had been as bad as any king. But they were . . . sort of . . . bad *on equal terms*. What set Vimes's teeth on edge was the idea that kings were a different kind of human being. A higher lifeform. Somehow magical. But, huh, there was *some* magic, at that. Ankh-Morpork still seemed to be littered with Royal this and Royal that, little old men who got paid a few pence a week to do a few meaningless chores, like the Master of the King's Keys or the Keeper of the

Crown Jewels, even though there were no keys and certainly no jewels.

Royalty was like dandelions. No matter how many heads you chopped off, the roots were still there underground, waiting to spring up again.

It seemed to be a chronic disease. It was as if even the most intelligent person had this little blank spot in their heads where someone had written: 'Kings. What a good idea.' Whoever had created humanity had left in a major design flaw. It was its tendency to bend at the knees.

There was a knock at the door. It should not be possible for a knock to sound surreptitious, yet this knock achieved it. It had harmonics. They told the hindbrain: the person knocking will, if no one eventually answers, open the door anyway and sidle in, whereupon he will certainly nick any smokes that are lying around, read any correspondence that catches his eye, open a few drawers, take a nip out of such bottles of alcohol as are discovered, but stop short of major crime because he is not criminal in the sense of making a moral decision but in the sense that a weasel is evil – it is built into his very shape. It was a knock with a lot to say for itself.

'Come in, Nobby,' said Vimes, wearily.

Corporal Nobbs sidled in. It was another special trait of his that he could sidle forwards as well as sideways.

He saluted awkwardly.

There was something absolutely changeless about Corporal Nobbs, Vimes told himself. Even Fred Colon had adapted to the changing nature of the

City Watch, but nothing altered Corporal Nobbs in any way. It wouldn't matter what you did to him, there was always something fundamentally *Nobby* about Corporal Nobbs.

'Nobby . . .'

'Yessir?'

'Er . . . take a seat, Nobby.'

Corporal Nobbs looked suspicious. This was not how a dressing-down was supposed to begin.

'Er, Fred said you wanted to see me, Mr Vimes, on account of time-keeping . . .'

'Did I? Did I? Oh, yes. Nobby, how many grand-mothers' funerals have you *really* been to?'

'Er . . . three . . .' said Nobby, uncomfortably.

'Three?'

'It turned out Nanny Nobbs weren't quite dead the first time.'

'So why have you taken all this time off?'

'Don't like to say, sir . . .'

'Why not?'

'You're gonna go spare, sir.'

'Spare?'

'You know, sir . . . throw a wobbler.'

'I *might*, Nobby.' Vimes sighed. 'But it'll be nothing to what'll get heaved if you *don't* tell me . . .'

'Thing is, it's the tricentre – tricera – this three-hundred-year celebration thing next year, Mr Vimes . . .'

'Yes?'

Nobby licked his lips. 'I dint like to ask for time off special. Fred said you were a bit sensitive about it all. But . . . you know I'm in the Peeled Nuts, sir . . .'

Vimes nodded. 'Those clowns who dress up and pretend to fight old battles with blunt swords,' he said.

'The Ankh-Morpork Historical Re-creation Society, sir,' said Nobby, a shade reproachfully.

'That's what I said.'

'Well . . . we're going to recreate the Battle of Ankh-Morpork for the celebrations, see. That means extra practice.'

'It all begins to make sense,' said Vimes, nodding wearily. 'You've been marching up and down with your tin pike, eh? In my time?'

'Er . . . not exactly, Mr Vimes . . . er . . . I've been riding up and down on my white horse, to tell the truth . . .'

'Oh? Playing at being a general, eh?'

'Er . . . a bit more'n a general, sir . . .'

'Go on.'

Nobby's adam's apple bobbed nervously. 'Er . . . I'm going to be King Lorenzo, sir. Er . . . you know . . . the last king, the one your . . . er . . .'

The air froze.

'*You* . . . are going to be . . .' Vimes began, unpeeling each word like a sullen grape of wrath.

'I said you'd go spare,' said Nobby. 'Fred Colon said you'd go spare, too.'

'*Why* are you—?'

'We drew lots, sir.'

'And you lost?'

Nobby squirmed. 'Er . . . not exactly *lost*, sir. Not *precisely* lost. More sort of *won*, sir. Everyone wanted to play him. I mean, you get a horse and a good costume and everything, sir. And he *was* a king, when all's said and done, sir.'

'The man was a vicious monster!'

'Well, it was all a long time ago, sir,' said Nobby anxiously.

Vimes calmed down a little. 'And who drew the straw to play Stoneface Vimes?'

'Er . . . er . . .'

'*Nobby!*'

Nobby hung his head. 'No one, sir. No one wanted to play him, sir.' The little corporal swallowed, and then plunged onwards with the air of a man determined to get it all over with. 'So we're making a man out of straw, sir, so he'll burn nicely when we throw him on the bonfire in the evening. There's going to be *fireworks*, sir,' he added, with dreadful certainty.

Vimes's face shut down. Nobby preferred it when people shouted. He had been shouted at for most of his life. He could handle shouting.

'No one wanted to be Stoneface Vimes,' Vimes said coldly.

'On account of him being on the losing side, sir.'

'Losing? Vimes's Ironheads *won*. He ruled the city for six months.'

Nobby squirmed again. 'Yeah, but . . . everyone in the Society says he didn't ought to of, sir. They said it was just a fluke, sir. After all, he was out-numbered ten to one, and he had warts, sir. And he was a bit of a bastard, sir, when all's said and done. He did chop off a king's head, sir. You got to be a bit of a nasty type to do that, sir. Saving your presence, Mr Vimes.'

Vimes shook his head. What did it matter, anyway? (But it *did* matter, somewhere.) It had all been a long time ago. It didn't matter what a bunch of deranged romantics thought. Facts were facts.

'All right, I understand,' he said. 'It's almost funny, really. Because there's something else I've got to tell you, Nobby.'

'Yessir?' said Nobby, looking relieved.

'Do you remember your father?'

Nobby looked about to panic again. 'What kind of question is that to suddenly ask anybody, sir?'

'Purely a social enquiry.'

'Old Sconner, sir? Not much, sir. Never used to see him much except when the milit'ry police used to come for to drag him outa the attic.'

'Do you know much about your, er, antecedents?'

'That is a lie, sir. I haven't got no antecedents, sir, no matter what you might have been tole.'

'Oh. Good. Er . . . you don't actually know what "antecedents" means, do you, Nobby?'

Nobby shifted uneasily. He didn't like being questioned by policemen, especially since he was one. 'Not in so many words, sir.'

'You never got told anything about your forebears?' Another worried expression crossed Nobby's face, so Vimes quickly added: 'Your ancestors?'

'Only old Sconner, sir. Sir . . . if all this is working up to asking about them sacks of vegetables which went missing from the shop in Treacle Mine Road, I was not anywhere near the—'

Vimes waved a hand vaguely. 'He didn't . . . leave you anything? Or anything?'

'Coupla scars, sir. And this trick elbow of mine. It aches sometimes, when the weather changes. I always remembers ole Sconner when the wind blows from the Hub.'

'Ah, right—'

'And this, o' course . . .' Nobby fished around behind his rusting breastplate. And that was a marvel, too. Even Sergeant Colon's armour could shine, if not actually gleam. But *any* metal anywhere near Nobby's skin corroded very quickly. The corporal pulled out a leather thong that hung around his neck. There was a gold ring on it. Despite the fact that gold cannot corrode, it had nevertheless developed a patina.

'He left it to me when he was on his deathbed,' said Nobby. 'Well, when I say "left it" . . .'

'Did he say anything?'

'Well, yeah, he did say "Give it back, you little bugger!", sir. See, 'e 'ad it on a string round his neck, sir, just like me. But it's not like a proper ring, sir. I'd have flogged it but it's all I got to remember him by. Except when the wind blows from the Hub.'

Vimes took the ring and rubbed it with a finger. It was a seal ring, with a coat of arms on it. Age and wear and the immediate presence of the body of Corporal Nobbs had made it quite unreadable.

'You are armigerous, Nobby.'

Nobby nodded. 'But I got a special shampoo for it, sir.'

Vimes sighed. He was an honest man. He'd always felt that was one of the bigger defects in his personality.

'When you've got a moment, nip along to the College of Heralds in Mollymog Street, will you? Take this ring with you and say I sent you.'

'Er . . .'

'It's all right. Nobby,' said Vimes. 'You won't get into trouble. Not as such.'

'If you say so, sir.'

'And you don't have to bother with the "sir", Nobby.'

'Yessir.'

When Nobby had gone Vimes reached behind the desk and picked up a faded copy of *Twurp's Peerage* or, as he personally thought of it, the guide to the criminal classes. You wouldn't find slum dwellers in these pages, but you would find their landlords. And, while it was regarded as pretty good evidence of criminality to be living in a slum, for some reason owning a whole street of them merely got you invited to the very best social occasions.

These days they seemed to be bringing out a new edition every week. Dragon had been right about one thing, at least. Everyone in Ankh-Morpork seemed to be hankering after more arms than they were born with.

He looked up *de Nobbes*.

There even *was* a damn coat of arms. One supporter of the shield was a hippo, presumably one of the royal hippos of Ankh-Morpork and therefore the ancestor of Roderick and Keith. The other was a bull of some sort, with a very Nobby-like expression; it was holding a golden ankh which, this being the de Nobbes coat of arms, it had probably stolen from somewhere. The shield was red and green; there was a white chevron with five apples on it. Quite what they had to do with warfare was unclear. Perhaps they were some kind of jolly visual pune or play on words that had had them slapping their thighs down at the Royal College of Arms, although probably if Dragon slapped his thigh too hard his leg would fall off.

It was easy enough to imagine an ennobled Nobbs. Because where Nobby went wrong was in thinking small. He sidled into places and pinched things that weren't worth much. If only he'd sidled into continents and stolen entire cities, slaughtering many of the inhabitants in the process, he'd have been a pillar of the community.

There was nothing in the book under 'Vimes'.

Suffer-Not-Injustice Vimes wasn't a pillar of the community. He killed a king with his own hands. It needed doing, but the community, whatever that was, didn't always like the people who did what needed to be done or said what had to be said. He put some other people to death as well, that was true, but the city had been lousy, there'd been a lot of stupid wars, we were practically part of the Klatchian empire. Sometimes you needed a bastard. History had wanted surgery. Sometimes Dr Chopper is the only surgeon to hand. There's something final about an axe. But kill one wretched king and everyone calls you a regicide. It wasn't as if it was a habit or anything . . .

Vimes had found old Stoneface's journal in the Unseen University library. The man had been hard, no doubt about that. But they were hard times. He'd written: 'In the Fyres of Struggle let us bake New Men, who Will Notte heed the old Lies.' But the old lies had won in the end.

He said to people: you're free. And they said hooray, and then he showed them what freedom costs and they called him a tyrant and, as soon as he'd been betrayed, they milled around a bit like barn-bred chickens who've seen the big world outside for the first time, and then they went back into the warm and shut the door—

'Bing bong bingely beep.'

Vimes sighed and pulled out his organizer.

'Yes?'

'Memo: Appointment with bootmaker, two p.m.,' said the imp.

'It's not two o'clock yet and that was Tuesday in any case,' said Vimes.

'So I'll cross it off the list of Things To Do, then?'

Vimes put the disorganized organizer back in his pocket and went and looked out of the window again.

Who had a motive for poisoning Lord Vetinari?

No, that wasn't the way to crack it. Probably, if you went to some outlying area of the city and confined your investigations to little old ladies who didn't get out much, what with all the wallpaper over the door and everything, you might be able to find someone *without* a motive. But the man stayed alive by always arranging matters so that a future without him represented a riskier business than a future with him still upright.

The only people, therefore, who'd risk killing him were madmen – and the gods knew Ankh-Morpork had enough of them – or someone who was absolutely confident that if the city collapsed he'd be standing on top of the pile.

If Fred were right – and the sergeant was generally a good indicator of how the man in the street thought because he *was* the man in the street – then that person was Captain Carrot. But Carrot was one of the few people in the city who seemed to like Vetinari.

Of course, there was one other person who stood to gain.

Damn, thought Vimes. *It's me, isn't it . . .*

There was another knock at the door. He didn't recognize this one.

He opened the door cautiously.

'It's me, sir. Littlebottom.'

'Come in, then.' It was nice to know there was at least one person in the world with more problems than him. 'How is his lordship?'

'Stable,' said Littlebottom.

'*Dead is* stable,' said Vimes.

'I mean he's alive, sir, and sitting up reading. Mr Doughnut made up some sticky stuff that tasted of seaweed, sir, and I mixed up some Gloobool's Salts. Sir, you know the old man in the house on the bridge?'

'What old . . . oh. Yes.' It seemed a long time ago. 'What about him?'

'Well . . . you asked me to look around and . . . I took some pictures. This is one, sir.' He handed Vimes a rectangle that was nearly all black.

'Odd. Where'd you get it?'

'Er . . . have you ever heard the story about dead men's eyes, sir?'

'Assume I haven't had a literary education, Little-bottom.'

'Well . . . they say . . .'

'*Who* say?'

'*They*, sir. You know, *they*.'

'The same people who're the "everyone" in "everyone knows"? The people who live in "the community"?'

'Yes, sir. I suppose so, sir.'

Vimes waved a hand. 'Oh, *them*. Well, go on.'

'They say that the last thing a dying man sees stays imprinted in his eyes, sir.'

'Oh, *that*. That's just an old story.'

'Yes. Amazing, really. I mean, if it weren't true, you'd have thought it wouldn't have survived, wouldn't you? I thought I saw this little red spark, so I got the imp to paint a really big picture before it faded completely. And, right in the centre . . .'

'Couldn't the imp have made it up?' said Vimes, staring at the picture again.

'They haven't got the imagination to lie, sir. What they see is what you get.'

'Glowing eyes.'

'Two red dots,' said Littlebottom, conscientiously,

'which might indeed be a pair of glowing eyes, sir.'

'Good point, Littlebottom.' Vimes rubbed his chin. 'Blast! I just hope it's not a god of some sort. That's all I need at a time like this. Can you make copies so I can send them to all the Watch Houses?'

'Yes, sir. The imp's got a good memory.'

'Hop to it, then.'

But before Littlebottom could go the door opened again. Vimes looked up. Carrot and Angua were there.

'Carrot? I thought you were on your day off?'

'We found a murder, sir! At the Dwarf Bread Museum. But when we got back to the Watch House they told us Lord Vetinari's dead!'

Did they? thought Vimes. *That's rumour for you. If we could modulate it with the truth, how useful it could be . . .*

'He's breathing well for a corpse,' he said. 'I think he'll be okay. Someone got past his guard, that's all. I've got a doctor to see him. Don't worry.'

Someone got past his guard, he thought. *Yes. And I'm his guard.*

'I hope the man's a leader in the field, that's all I can say,' said Carrot severely.

'He's even better than that – he's the doctor *to* the leaders of the field,' said Vimes. *I'm his guard and I didn't see it coming.*

'It'd be terrible for the city if anything happened to him!' said Carrot.

Vimes saw nothing but innocent concern behind

108

Carrot's forthright stare. 'It would, wouldn't it?' he said. 'Anyway, it's under control. You said there's been *another* murder?'

'At the Dwarf Bread Museum. Someone killed Mr Hopkinson with his own bread!'

'Made him eat it?'

'Hit him with it, sir,' said Carrot reproachfully. 'Battle Bread, sir.'

'Is he the old man with the white beard?'

'Yes, sir. You remember, I introduced you to him when I took you to see the Boomerang Biscuit exhibition.'

Angua thought she saw a faint wince of recollection speed guiltily across Vimes's face. 'Who's going around killing old men?' he said to the world at large.

'Don't know, sir. Constable Angua went *plain clothes*' – Carrot waggled his eyebrows conspiratorially – 'and couldn't find a sniff of anyone. And nothing was taken. This is what it was done with.'

The Battle Bread was much larger than an ordinary loaf. Vimes turned it over gingerly. 'Dwarfs throw it like a discus, right?'

'Yes, sir. At the Seven Mountains games last year Snori Shieldbiter took the tops off a line of six hard-boiled eggs at fifty yards, sir. And that was with just a standard hunting loaf. But *this* is, well, it's a cultural artefact. We haven't got the baking technology for bread like this any more. It's unique.'

'Valuable?'

'Very, sir.'

'Worth stealing?'

'You'd never be able to get rid of it! Every honest dwarf would recognize it!'

'Hmm. Did you hear about that priest being murdered on Misbegot Bridge?'

Carrot looked shocked. 'Not old Father Tubelcek? Really?'

Vimes stopped himself from asking: 'You know him, then?' Because Carrot knew *everyone*. If Carrot were to be dropped into some dense tropical jungle it'd be 'Hello, Mr Runs Swiftly Through The Trees! Good morning, Mr Talks To The Forest, what a splendid blowpipe! And what a novel place for a feather!'

'Did he have more than one enemy?' said Vimes.

'Sorry, sir? Why more than one?'

'I should say the fact that he had *one* is obvious, wouldn't you?'

'He is . . . he *was* a nice old chap,' said Carrot. 'Hardly stirred out. Spends . . . *spent* all his time with his books. Very religious. I mean, all kinds of religion. Studied them. Bit odd, but no harm in him. Why should anyone want to kill him? Or Mr Hopkinson? A pair of harmless old men?'

Vimes handed him the Battle Bread. 'We shall find out. Constable Angua, I want you to have a look at this one. Take . . . yes, take Corporal Littlebottom,' he said. 'He's been doing some work on it. Angua's from Uberwald too, Littlebottom. Maybe you've got friends in common, that sort of thing.'

Carrot nodded cheerfully. Angua's expression went wooden.

'Ah, h'druk g'har dWatch, Sh'rt'azs!' said Carrot.

'H'h Angua tConstable . . . Angua g'har, b'hk bargr'a Sh'rt'azs Kad'k . . .'*

Angua appeared to concentrate. 'Grr'dukk d'buz-h'drak . . .' she managed.

Carrot laughed. 'You just said "small delightful mining tool of a feminine nature"!'

Cheery stared at Angua, who returned the stare blankly while mumbling, 'Well, dwarfish is difficult if you haven't eaten gravel all your life . . .'

Cheery was still staring. 'Er . . . thank you,' he managed. 'Er . . . I'd better go and tidy up.'

'What about Lord Vetinari?' said Carrot.

'I'm putting my best man on that,' said Vimes. 'Trustworthy, reliable, knows the ins and outs of this place like the back of his hand. *I'm* handling it, in other words.'

Carrot's hopeful expression faded to hurt puzzlement. 'Don't you want me to?' he said. 'I could—'

'No. Indulge an old man. I want you to go back to the Watch House and take care of things.'

'What things?'

'Everything! Rise to the occasion. Move paper around. There's that new shift rota to draw up. Shout at people! Read reports!'

Carrot saluted. 'Yes, Commander Vimes.'

'Good. Off you go, then.'

And if anything happens to Vetinari, Vimes added to himself as the dejected Carrot went out, *no one will be able to say you were anywhere near him.*

---

*'Welcome, Corporal Smallbottom! This is Constable Angua . . . Angua, show Smallbottom how well you're learning dwarfish . . .'

*   *   *

The little grille in the gate of the Royal College of Arms snapped open, to the distant accompaniment of brayings and grunts. 'Yes?' said a voice, 'what dost *thee* want?'

'I'm Corporal Nobbs,' said Nobby.

An eye applied itself to the grille. It took in the full, dreadful extent of the godly handiwork that was Corporal Nobbs.

'Are you the baboon? We've had one on order for . . .'

'No. I've come about some coat with arms,' said Nobby.

'You?' said the voice. The owner of the voice made it very clear that he was aware there were degrees of nobility from something above kingship stretching all the way down to commoner, and that as far as Corporal Nobbs was concerned an entirely new category – commonest, perhaps – would have to be coined.

'I've been told,' said Nobby, miserably. 'It's about this ring I got.'

'Go round the back door,' said the voice.

Cheery was tidying away the makeshift equipment he'd set up in the privy when a sound made him look around. Angua was leaning against the doorway.

'What do you want?' he demanded.

'Nothing. I just thought I'd say: don't worry, I won't tell anyone if you don't want me to.'

'I don't know what you're talking about!'

'I think you're lying.'

Cheery dropped a test tube, and sagged on to a seat. 'How could you tell?' he said. 'Even other *dwarfs* can't tell! I've been so careful!'

'Shall we just say . . . I have special talents?' said Angua.

Cheery started to clean a beaker distractedly.

'I don't know why you're so upset,' said Angua. 'I thought dwarfs hardly recognized the difference between male and female, anyway. Half the dwarfs we bring in here on a No. 23 are female, I know that, and they're the ones that are hardest to subdue . . .'

'What's a No. 23?'

'"Running Screaming at People While Drunk and Trying to Cut Their Knees off",' said Angua. 'It's easier to give them numbers than write it down every time. Look, there's plenty of women in this town that'd love to do things the dwarf way. I mean, what're the choices they've got? Barmaid, seamstress or someone's wife. While *you* can do anything the men do . . .'

'Provided we do only what the men do,' said Cheery.

Angua paused. 'Oh,' she said. 'I *see*. Hah. Yes. I know *that* tune.'

'I can't hold an axe!' said Cheery. 'I'm scared of fights! I think songs about gold are stupid! I hate beer! I can't even drink dwarfishly! When I try to quaff I drown the dwarf behind me!'

'I can see that could be tricky,' said Angua.

'I saw a girl walk down the street here and some men *whistled* after her! And you can wear *dresses*! With *colours*!'

'Oh, dear.' Angua tried not to smile. 'How long have lady dwarfs felt like this? I thought they were happy with the way things are . . .'

'Oh, it's easy to be happy when you don't know any different,' said Cheery bitterly. 'Chain-mail trousers are fine if you've never heard of lingerry!'

'Li— oh, yes,' said Angua. 'Lingerie. Yes.' She tried to feel sympathetic and found that she was, really, but she did have to stop herself from saying that at least *you* don't have to find styles that can easily be undone by paws.

'I thought I could come here and get a different kind of job,' Cheery moaned. 'I'm good at needlework and I went to see the Guild of Seamstresses and—' She stopped, and blushed behind her beard.

'Yes,' said Angua. 'Lots of people make that mistake.' She stood up straight and brushed herself off. 'You've impressed Commander Vimes, anyway. I think you'll like it here. Everyone's got troubles in the Watch. Normal people don't become policemen. You'll get on fine.'

'Commander Vimes is a bit . . .' Cheery began.

'He's okay when he's in a good mood. He needs to drink but he doesn't dare to these days. You know: one drink is too many, two is not enough . . . And that makes him edgy. When he's in a bad mood he'll tread on your toes and then shout at you for not standing up straight.'

'*You're* normal,' said Cheery, shyly. 'I like *you*.'

Angua patted her on the head. 'You say that now,' she said, 'but when you've been around here for a while you'll find out that sometimes I can be a bitch . . . What's that?'

'What?'

'That . . . painting. With the eyes . . .'

'Or two points of red light,' said Cheery.

'Oh, yeah?'

'It's the last thing Father Tubelcek saw, I think,' said the dwarf.

Angua stared at the black rectangle. She sniffed. 'There it is again!'

Cheery took a step backwards. 'What? What?'

'Where's that smell coming from?' Angua demanded.

'Not me!' said Cheery hurriedly.

Angua grabbed a small dish from the bench and sniffed at it. 'This is it! I smelled this at the museum! What is it?'

'It's just clay. It was on the floor in the room where the old priest was killed,' said Cheery. 'Probably it came off someone's boot.'

Angua crumbled some of it between her fingers.

'I think it's just potters' clay,' said Cheery. 'We used to use it at the guild. For making pots,' she added, just in case Angua hadn't grasped things. 'You know? Crucibles and things. This looks like someone tried baking it but didn't get the heat right. See how it crumbles?'

'Pottery,' said Angua. 'I know a potter . . .'

She glanced down at the dwarf's iconograph again.

Please, no, she thought. Not one of *them*?

*   *   *

115

The front gate of the College of Arms – *both* front gates – were swung open. The two Heralds bobbed excitedly around Corporal Nobbs as he tottered out.

'Has your lordship got everything he requires?'

'Nfff,' said Nobby.

'If we can be of any help whatsoever—'

'Nnnf.'

'Any help at all—?'

'Nnnf.'

'Sorry about your boots, m'lord, but the wyvern's been ill. It'll brush off no trouble when it dries.'

Nobby tottered off along the lane.

'He even walks nobly, wouldn't you say?'

'More . . . nobbly than nobly, I think.'

'It's disgusting that he's a mere corporal, a man of his breeding.'

Igneous the troll backed away until he was up against his potter's wheel.

'I never done it,' he said.

'Done what?' said Angua.

Igneous hesitated.

Igneous was huge and . . . well, rocky. He moved around the streets of Ankh-Morpork like a small iceberg and, like an iceberg, there was more to him than immediately met the eye. He was known as a supplier of things. More or less any kind of things. And he was also a wall, which was the same as a fence only a lot harder and tougher to beat. Igneous never asked unnecessary questions, because he couldn't think of any.

'Nuffin,' he said, finally. Igneous had always

found the general denial was more reliable than the specific refutation.

'Glad to hear it,' said Angua. 'Now . . . where do you get your clay from?'

Igneous's face crinkled as he tried to work out where this line of questioning could possibly go. 'I got re-seats,' he said. 'Every bit prop'ly paid for.'

Angua nodded. It was probably true. Igneous, despite giving the appearance of not being able to count beyond ten without ripping off someone else's arm, and having an intimate involvement in the city's complex hierarchy of crime, was known to pay his bills. If you were going to be successful in the criminal world, you needed a reputation for honesty.

'Have you seen any like this before?' she said, holding out the sample.

'It *clay*,' said Igneous, relaxing a little. 'I see clay all der time. It don't have no serial number. Clay's clay. Got lumps of it out der back. You make bricks an pots and stuff outa it. Dere's loads of potters in dis town and we all got der stuff. Why you wanna know about clay?'

'Can't you tell where it came from?'

Igneous took the tiny piece, sniffed it, and rolled it between his fingers.

'Dis is crank,' he said, looking a lot happier now that the conversation was veering away from more personal concerns. 'Dat's like . . . crappy clay, jus' good enough for dem lady potters wi' dangly earrings wot make coffee mugs wot you can't lift wid both hands.' He rolled it again. 'Also, it got a lotta grog in it. Dat's bitsa old pots, all smashed up real small. Makes it stronger. Any potter got loadsa stuff like dis.' He rubbed it again. 'Dis has been sorta heated up but it ain't prop'ly baked.'

'But you can't say *where* it came from?'

'Outa der ground is der best I can do, lady,' said Igneous. He relaxed a little now it appeared that enquiries were not to do with such matters as a recent batch of hollow statues and subjects of a similar nature. As sometimes happened in these circumstances, he tried to be helpful. 'Come an' have a look at dis.'

He loped away. The Watchmen followed him through the warehouse, observed by a couple of dozen cautious trolls. No one liked to see policemen up close, especially if the reason you were working at Igneous's place was that it was nice and quiet and you wanted somewhere to lie low for a few weeks. Besides, while it was true that a lot of people came to Ankh-Morpork because it was a city of opportunity, sometimes it was the opportunity not to be hung, skewered or dismantled for whatever crimes you'd left behind in the mountains.

'Just don't look,' said Angua.

'Why?' said Cheery.

'Because there's just us and there's at least two dozen of them,' said Angua. 'And all our clothes were made for people with full sets of arms and legs.'

Igneous went through a doorway and out into the yard behind the factory. Pots were stacked high on pallets. Bricks were curing in long rows. And under a crude roof were several large mounds of clay.

'Dere,' said Igneous generously. 'Clay.'

'Is there a special name for it when it's piled up like that?' said Cheery timorously. She prodded the stuff.

'Yeah,' said Igneous. 'Dat's technic'ly wot we calls a *heap*.'

Angua shook her head sadly. So much for Clues. Clay was clay. She'd hoped there were all different sorts, and it turned out to be as common as dirt.

And then Igneous Helped the Police with Their Enquiries. 'D'you mind if youse goes out the back way?' he mumbled. 'Youse makes the help nervous an' I get pots I can't sell.'

He indicated a pair of wide doors in the rear wall, big enough for a cart to get through. Then he fumbled in his apron and produced a large key-ring.

The padlock on the gate was big and shiny and new.

'*You* are afraid of *theft*?' said Angua.

'Now, lady, dat's unfair,' said Igneous. 'Someone broke der ole lock when dey pinched some stuff tree, four munfs ago.'

'Disgusting, isn't it?' said Angua. 'Makes you wonder why you pay your taxes, I expect.'

In some ways Igneous was a *lot* brighter than, say, Mr Ironcrust. He ignored the remark. 'It was just stuff,' he said, ushering them towards the open gate as speedily as he dared.

'Was it clay they stole?' said Cheery.

'It don't cost much but it's the principle of the t'ing,' he said. 'It beat me why dey bothered. It come to somet'ng when half a ton of clay can jus' walk out the door.'

Angua looked at the lock again. 'Yes, indeed,' she said distantly.

The gate rattled shut behind them. They were outside, in an alley.

'Fancy anyone stealing a load of clay,' said Cheery. 'Did he tell the Watch?'

'I shouldn't think so,' said Angua. 'Wasps don't complain too loudly when they're stung. Anyway, Detritus thinks Igneous is mixed up with smuggling Slab to the mountains, and so he's itching for an excuse to have a poke around in there . . . Look, this is still technically my day off.' She stepped back and peered up at the high spiked wall around the yard. 'Could you bake clay in a baker's oven?' she said.

'Oh, no.'

'Doesn't get hot enough?'

'No, it's the wrong shape. Some of your pots'd be baked hard while others'd still be green. Why do you ask?'

Why *did* I ask? Angua thought. Oh, what the hell . . . 'Fancy a drink?'

'Not ale,' said Cheery quickly. 'And nowhere where you have to sing while you drink. Or slap your knees.'

Angua nodded understandingly. 'Somewhere, in fact, without dwarfs?'

'Er . . . yes . . .'

'Where *we're* going,' said Angua, 'that won't be a problem.'

*   *   *

The fog was rising fast. All morning it had hung around in alleys and cellars. Now it was moving back in for the night. It came out of the ground and up from the river and down from the sky, a clinging yellowish stinging blanket, the river Ankh in droplet form. It found its way through cracks and, against all common sense, managed to survive in lighted rooms, filling the air with an eye-watering haze and making the candles crackle. Outdoors, every figure loomed, every shape was a menace . . .

In a drab alley off a drab street Angua stopped, squared her shoulders, and pushed open a door.

The atmosphere in the long, low, *dark* room altered as she stepped inside. A moment of time rang like a glass bowl, and then there was a sense of relaxation. People turned back in their seats.

Well, they were seated. It was quite likely they were people.

Cheery moved closer to Angua. 'What's this place called?' she whispered.

'It hasn't really got a name,' said Angua, 'but sometimes we call it Biers.'

'It didn't *look* like an inn outside. How did you find it?'

'You don't. You . . . gravitate to it.'

Cheery looked around nervously. She wasn't sure where they were, apart from somewhere in the cattle-market district, somewhere up a maze of alleys.

Angua walked to the bar.

A deeper shadow appeared out of the gloom. 'Hello, Angua,' it said, in a deep, rolling voice. 'Fruit juice, is it?'

'Yes. Chilled.'

'And what about the dwarf?'

'She'll have him raw,' said a voice somewhere in the gloom. There was a ripple of laughter in the dark. Some of it sounded altogether too strange to Cheery. She couldn't imagine it issuing from normal lips. 'I'll have a fruit juice, too,' she quavered.

Angua glanced at the dwarf. She felt oddly grateful that the remark from the darkness seemed to have gone entirely over the small bullet head. She unhooked her badge and with care and deliberation laid it down on the counter. It went *perlink*. Then Angua leaned forward and showed the iconograph to the barman.

If it *was* a man. Cheery wasn't sure yet. A sign over the bar said 'Don't you ever change'.

'You know everything that's going on, Igor,' Angua said. 'Two old men got killed yesterday. And a load of clay got stolen from Igneous the troll recently. Did you ever hear about that?'

'What's that to you?'

'Killing old men is against the law,' said Angua. 'Of course, a lot of things are against the law, so we're very busy in the Watch. We like to be busy about *important* things. Otherwise we have to be busy about unimportant things. Are you hearing me?'

The shadow considered this. 'Go and take a seat,' it said. 'I'll bring your drinks.'

Angua led the way to a table in an alcove. The clientele lost interest in them. A buzz of conversation resumed.

'What *is* this place?' Cheery whispered.

'It's . . . a place where people can be themselves,' said Angua slowly. 'People who . . . have to be a little careful at other times. You know?'

'No . . .'

Angua sighed. 'Vampires, zombies, bogeymen, ghouls, oh my. The und—' She corrected herself. 'The differently alive,' she said. 'People who have to spend most of their time being very careful, not frightening people, *fitting in.* That's how it works here. Fit in, get a job, don't worry people, and you probably won't find a crowd outside with pitchforks and flaming torches. But sometimes it's good to go where everybody knows your shape.'

Now that Cheery's eyes had grown accustomed to the low light she could make out the variety of shapes on the benches. Some of them were a lot bigger than human. Some had pointy ears and long muzzles.

'Who's that girl?' she said. 'She looks . . . normal.'

'That's Violet. She's a tooth fairy. And next to her is Schleppel the bogeyman.'

In the far corner something sat huddled in a huge overcoat under a high, broad-brimmed pointed hat.

'And him?'

'That's old Man Trouble,' said Angua. 'If you know what's good for you, you *don't* mind him.'

'Er . . . any werewolves here?'

'One or two,' said Angua.

'*I hate* werewolves.'

'Oh?'

The oddest customer was sitting by herself, at a

small round table. She appeared to be a very old lady, in a shawl and a straw hat with flowers in it. She was staring in front of her with an expression of good-natured aimlessness, and in context looked more frightening than any of the shadowy figures.

'What is she?' Cheery hissed.

'Her? Oh, that's Mrs Gammage.'

'And what does she do?'

'Do? Well, she comes in here most days for a drink and some company. Sometimes we . . . *they* have a singsong. Old songs, that she remembers. She's practically blind. If you mean, is she an undead . . . no, she isn't. Not a vampire, a werewolf, a zombie or a bogeyman. Just an old lady.'

A huge shambling hairy thing paused at Mrs Gammage's table and put a glass in front of her.

'Port and lemon. There you goes, Mrs Gammage,' it rumbled.

'Cheers, Charlie!' the old lady cackled. 'How's the plumbing business?'

'Doing fine, love,' said the bogeyman, and vanished into the gloom.

'*That* was *a plumber*?' said Cheery.

'Of course not. I don't know who Charlie was. He probably died years ago. But she thinks the bogeyman is him, and who's going to tell her different?'

'You mean she doesn't *know* this place is—'

'Look, she's been coming here ever since the old days when it was the Crown and Axe,' said Angua. 'No one wants to spoil things. Everyone likes Mrs Gammage. They . . . watch out for her. Help her out in little ways.'

'How?'

'Well, I heard that last month someone broke into her hovel and stole some of her stuff . . .'

'*That* doesn't sound helpful.'

'. . . and it was all returned next day and a couple of thieves were found in the Shades with not a drop of blood left in their bodies.' Angua smiled, and her voice took on a mocking edge. 'You know, you get told a lot of bad things about the undead, but you never hear about the marvellous work they do in the community.'

Igor the barman appeared. He looked more or less human, apart from the hair on the back of his hands and the single unbifurcated eyebrow across his forehead. He tossed a couple of mats on the table and put their drinks down.

'You're probably wishing this *was* a dwarf bar,' said Angua. She lifted her beermat carefully and glanced at the underside.

Cheery looked around again. By now, if it *had* been a dwarf bar, the floor would be sticky with beer, the air would be full of flying quaff, and people would be singing. They'd probably be singing the latest dwarf tune, 'Gold, Gold, Gold', or one of the old favourites, like 'Gold, Gold, Gold', or the all-time biggie, 'Gold, Gold, Gold'. In a few minutes, the first axe would have been thrown.

'No,' she said, 'it could never be that bad.'

'Drink up,' said Angua. 'We've got to go and see . . . something.'

A large hairy hand grabbed Angua's wrist. She looked up into a terrifying face, all eyes and mouth and hair.

'Hello, Shlitzen,' she said calmly.

'Hah, I'm hearing where there's a baron who's really *unhappy* about you,' said Shlitzen, alcohol crystallizing on his breath.

'That's my business, Shlitzen,' said Angua. 'Why don't you just go back behind your door like the good bogeyman that you are?'

'Hah, he's sayin' where you're disgracin' the Old Country—'

'Let go, please,' said Angua. Her skin was white where Shlitzen was gripping her.

Cheery looked from the wrist to the bogeyman's shoulder. Rangy though the creature was, muscles were strung along the arm like beads on a wire.

'Hah, you wearin' a *badge*,' it sneered. 'What's a good we—?'

Angua moved so fast she was a blur. Her free hand pulled something from her belt and flipped it up and on to Shlitzen's head. He stopped, and stood swaying back and forth gently, making faint moaning sounds. On his head, flopping down around his ears like the knotted hanky of a style-impaired seaside sunbather, was a small square of heavy material.

Angua pushed back her chair and grabbed the beermat. The shadowy figures around the walls were muttering.

'Let's get out of here,' she said. 'Igor, give us half a minute and then you can take the blanket off him. Come on.'

They hurried out. The fog had already turned the sun into a mere suggestion, but it was vivid daylight compared to the gloom in Biers.

'What *happened* to him?' said Cheery, running to keep up with Angua's stride.

'Existential uncertainty,' Angua said. 'He doesn't know whether he exists or not. It's cruel, I know, but it's the only thing we've found that works against bogeymen. *Blue* fluffy blanket, for preference.' She noted Cheery's blank expression. 'Look, bogeymen go away if you put your head under the blankets. Everyone knows that, don't they? So if you put *their* head under a blanket . . .'

'Oh, I see. Ooo, that's *nasty*.'

'He'll feel all right in ten minutes.' Angua skimmed the beermat across the alley.

'What was he saying about a baron?'

'I wasn't really listening,' said Angua carefully.

Cheery shivered in the fog, but not just from the cold. 'He sounded like he came from Uberwald, like us. There was a baron who lived near us and he *hated* people to leave.'

'Yes . . .'

'The whole family were werewolves. One of them ate my second cousin.'

Angua's memory spun in a hurry. Old meals came back to haunt her from the time before she'd said, no, this is not the way to live. A dwarf, a dwarf . . . No, she was pretty sure she'd never . . . The family had always made fun of her eating habits . . .

'That's why I can't stand them,' said Cheery. 'Oh, people *say* they can be tamed but *I* say, once a wolf, always a wolf. You can't trust them. They're basically evil, aren't they? They could go back to the wild at any moment, I say.'

'Yes. You may be right.'

'And the worst thing is, most of the time they walk around looking just like real people.'

Angua blinked, glad of the twin disguises of the fog and Cheery's unquestioning confidence. 'Come on. We're nearly there.'

'Where?'

'We're going to see someone who's either our murderer or who knows who the murderer is.'

Cheery stopped. 'But you've got only a sword and I haven't even got that!'

'Don't worry, we won't need weapons.'

'Oh, good.'

'They wouldn't be any use.'

'Oh.'

Vimes opened his door to see what all the shouting was about down in the office. The corporal manning – or in this case dwarfing – the desk was having trouble.

'Again? How many times have you been killed this week?'

'I was minding my own business!' said the unseen complainer.

'Stacking garlic? You're a *vampire,* aren't you? I mean, let's see what jobs you have been doing . . . Post sharpener for a fencing firm, sunglasses tester for Argus opticians . . . Is it me, or is there some underlying trend here?'

'Excuse me, Commander Vimes?'

Vimes looked round into a smiling face that sought only to do good in the world, even if the world had other things it wanted done.

'Ah . . . Constable Visit, yes,' he said hurriedly. 'At the moment I'm afraid I'm rather busy, and I'm not even sure that I have got an immortal soul, ha-ha, and perhaps you could call again when . . .'

'It's about those words you asked me to check,' said Visit reproachfully.

'What words?'

'The ones Father Tubelcek wrote in his own blood? You said to try and find out what they meant?'

'Oh. Yes. Come on into my office.' Vimes relaxed. This wasn't going to be another one of those painful conversations about the state of his soul and the necessity of giving it a wash and brush-up before eternal damnation set in. This was going to be about something *important*.

'It's ancient Cenotine, sir. It's out of one of their holy books, although of course when I say "holy" it is a fact that they were basically misguided in a . . .'

'Yes, yes, I'm sure,' said Vimes, sitting down. 'Does it by any chance say "Mr X did it, aargh, aargh, aargh"?'

'No, sir. That phrase does not appear anywhere in any known holy book, sir.'

'Ah,' said Vimes.

'Besides, I looked at other documents in the room and the paper does not appear to be in the deceased's handwriting, sir.'

Vimes brightened up. 'Ah-ha! Someone else's? Does it say something like "Take that, you bastard, we've been waiting ages to get you for what you did all those years ago"?'

'No, sir. That phrase also does not appear in any holy book anywhere,' said Constable Visit, and hesitated. 'Except in the *Apocrypha* to *The Vengeful Testament of Offler*,' he added conscientiously. '*These* words are from the Cenotine *Book of Truth*,' he sniffed, 'as they called it. It's what their false god . . .'

'Could I just perhaps have the words and leave out the comparative religion?' said Vimes.

'Very well, sir.' Visit looked hurt, but unfolded a piece of paper and sniffed disparagingly. 'These are some of the rules that their god allegedly gave to the first people after he'd baked them out of clay, sir. Rules like "Thou shalt labour fruitfully all the days of your life", sir, and "Thou shalt not kill", and "Thou shalt be humble". That sort of thing.'

'Is that all?' said Vimes.

'Yes, sir,' said Visit.

'They're just religious quotations?'

'Yes, sir.'

'Any idea why it was in his mouth? Poor devil looked like he was having a last cigarette.'

'No, sir.'

'I could understand if it was one of the "smite your enemies" ones,' said Vimes. 'But that's just saying "get on with your work and don't make trouble".'

'Ceno was a rather liberal god, sir. Not big on commandments.'

'Sounds almost decent, as gods go.'

Visit looked disapproving. 'The Cenotines died through five hundred years of waging some of the bloodiest wars on the continent, sir.'

'Spare the thunderbolts and spoil the congregation, eh?' said Vimes.

'Pardon, sir?'

'Oh, nothing. Well thank you, Constable. I'll, er, see that Captain Carrot is informed and, thank you once again, don't let me keep you from—'

Vimes's desperately accelerating voice was too late to prevent Visit pulling a roll of paper out of his breastplate.

'I've brought you the latest *Unadorned Facts* magazine, sir, and also this month's *Battle Call,* which contains many articles that I'm sure will be of interest to you, including Pastor Nasal Pedlers' exhortation to the congregation to rise up and speak to people sincerely through their letterboxes, sir.'

'Er, thank you.'

'I can't help noticing that the pamphlets and magazines I gave you last week are still on your desk where I left them, sir.'

'Oh, yes, well, sorry, you know how it is, the amount of work these days, makes it so hard to find the time to—'

'It's never too soon to contemplate eternal damnation, sir.'

'I think about it all the time, Constable. Thank you.'

Unfair, thought Vimes, when Visit had gone. A note is left at the scene of a crime in my town and does it have the decency to be a death-threat? No. The last dying scrawl of a man determined to name his murderer? No. It's a bit of religious doggerel.

What's the good of Clues that are more mysterious than the mystery?

He scribbled a note on Visit's translation and chucked it into his In Tray.

Too late, Angua remembered why she avoided the slaughterhouse district at this time of the month.

She could change at will at any time. That's what people forgot about werewolves. But they remembered the important thing. Full moonlight was the *irresistible* trigger: the lunar rays reached down into the centre of her morphic memory and flipped all the switches, whether she wanted them switched or not. Full moon was only a couple of days away. And the delicious smell of the penned animals and the blood from the slaughterhouses was chiming against her strict vegetarianism. The clash was bringing on her PLT.

She glared at the shadowy building in front of her. 'I think we'll go round the back,' she said. 'And you can knock.'

'Me? They won't take any notice of me!' said Cheery.

'You show them your badge and tell them you're the Watch.'

'They'll ignore me! They'll laugh at me!'

'You're going to have to do it sooner or later. Go on.'

The door was opened by a stout man in a bloody apron. He was shocked to have his belt grabbed by one dwarf hand, while another dwarf hand was thrust in front of his face, holding a badge, and a dwarf voice in the region of his navel said, 'We're the Watch, right? Oh, yes! And if you don't let us in we'll have your guts for starters!'

'Good try,' murmured Angua. She lifted Cheery out of the way and smiled brightly at the butcher.

'Mr Sock? We'd like to speak to an employee of yours. Mr Dorfl.'

The man hadn't quite got over Cheery, but he managed to rally. '*Mr* Dorfl? What's he done now?'

'We'd just like to talk to him. May we come in?'

Mr Sock looked at Cheery, who was trembling with nerves and excitement. 'I have a choice?' he said.

'Let's say – you have a *kind* of choice,' said Angua.

She tried to close her nostrils against the beguiling miasma of blood. There was even a sausage factory on the premises. It used all the bits of animals no one would ever otherwise eat, or even recognize. The odours of the abattoir turned her human stomach but, deep inside, part of her sat up and drooled and begged at the mingling smells of pork and beef and lamb and mutton and . . .

'Rat?' she said, sniffing. 'I didn't know you supplied the dwarf market, Mr Sock.'

Mr Sock was suddenly a man who wished to be seen to be cooperative.

'Dorfl! Come here right now!'

There was the sound of footsteps and a figure emerged from behind a rack of beef carcases.

Some people had a thing about the undead. Angua knew Commander Vimes was uneasy in their presence, although he was getting better these days. People always needed someone to feel superior to. The living hated the undead, and the undead loathed – she felt her fists clench – the unalive.

The golem called Dorfl lurched a little because one leg was slightly shorter than the other. It didn't wear any clothes because there was nothing whatsoever to conceal, and so she could see the mottling on it where fresh clay had been added over the years. There was so much patching that she wondered how old it could be. Originally, some attempt had been made to depict human musculature, but the repairs had nearly obscured these. The thing looked like the kind of pots Igneous despised, the ones made by people who thought that because it was hand-made it was supposed to *look* as if it was hand-made, and that thumbprints baked in the clay were a sign of integrity.

That was it. The thing *looked* hand-made. Of course, over the years it had mostly made itself, one repair at a time. Its triangular eyes glowed faintly. There were no pupils, just the dark red glow of a banked fire.

It was holding a long, heavy cleaver. Cheery's stare gravitated to this and remained fixed on it in terrified fascination. The other hand grasped a piece of string, on the end of which was a large, hairy and very smelly goat.

'What are you doing, Dorfl?'

The golem nodded towards the goat.

'Feeding the yudasgoat?'

Dorfl nodded again.

'Have you got something to do, Mr Sock?' said Angua.

'No, I've . . .'

'You *have* got something to do, Mr Sock,' said Angua emphatically.

'Ah. Er? Yes. Er? Yes. Okay. I'll just go and see to the offal boilers . . .'

As the butcher walked away he stopped to wave a finger under the place where Dorfl's nose would be if the golem had had a nose.

'If you've been causing trouble . . .' he began.

'I expect those boilers could really do with attention,' said Angua sharply.

He hurried off.

There was silence in the yard, although the sounds of the city drifted in over the walls. From the other side of the slaughterhouse there was the occasional bleat of a worried sheep. Dorfl stood stock-still, holding his cleaver and looking down at the ground.

'Is it a troll made to look like a human?' whispered Cheery. 'Look at those *eyes*!'

'It's not a troll,' said Angua. 'It's a golem. A man of clay. It's a machine.'

'It *looks* like a human!'

'That's because it's a machine made for looking like a human.'

She walked around behind the thing. 'I'm going to read your chem, Dorfl,' she said.

The golem let go of the goat and raised the cleaver and brought it down sharply on to a chopping block beside Cheery, making the dwarf leap sideways.

Then it pulled around a slate that was slung over its shoulder on a piece of string, unhooked the pencil, and wrote:

YES.

When Angua put her hand up, Cheery realized that there was a thin line across the golem's forehead. To her horror, the entire top of the head flipped up. Angua, quite unperturbed, reached inside. Her hand came out holding a yellowing scroll.

The golem froze. The eyes faded.

Angua unrolled the paper. 'Some kind of holy writing,' she said. 'It always is. Some old dead religion.'

'You've killed it?'

'No. You can't take away what isn't there.' She put the scroll back and closed the head with a click.

The golem came alive again, the glow returning to its eyes.

Cheery had been holding her breath. It came out in a rush. 'What did you *do*?' she managed.

'Tell her, Dorfl,' said Angua.

The golem's thick fingers were a blur as the pencil scratched across the slate.

I AM A GOLEM. I WAS MADE OF CLAY. MY LIFE IS THE WORDS. BY MEANS OF WORDS OF PURPOSE IN MY HEAD I ACQUIRE LIFE. MY LIFE IS TO WORK. I OBEY ALL COMMANDS. I TAKE NO REST.

'What words of purpose?'

RELEVANT TEXTS THAT ARE THE FOCUS OF BELIEF. GOLEM MUST WORK. GOLEM MUST HAVE A MASTER.

The goat lay down beside the golem and started to chew cud.

'There have been two murders,' said Angua. 'I'm

136

pretty certain a golem did one and probably both. Can you tell us anything, Dorfl?'

'Sorry, look,' said Cheery. 'Are you telling me this . . . thing is powered by words? I mean . . . is *it* telling me it's powered by words?'

'Why not? Words *do* have power. Everyone knows that,' said Angua. 'There are more golems around than you might think. They're out of fashion now, but they last. They can work underwater, or in total darkness, or knee-deep in poison. For years. They don't need rest or feeding. They . . .'

'But that's slavery!' said Cheery.

'Of course it isn't. You might as well enslave a doorknob. Have you got anything to tell me, Dorfl?'

Cheery kept looking at the cleaver in the block. Words like *length* and *heavy* and *sharp* were filling her head more snugly than any words could have filled the clay skull of the golem.

Dorfl said nothing.

'How long have you been working here, Dorfl?'

NOW THREE HUNDRED DAYS ALREADY.

'And you have time off?'

TO MAKE A HOLLOW LAUGHING. WHAT WOULD I DO WITH TIME OFF?

'I mean, you're not always in the slaughterhouse?'

SOMETIMES I MAKE DELIVERIES.

'And meet other golems? Now *listen*, Dorfl, I *know* you things keep in touch somehow. And, if a golem is killing *real* people, I wouldn't give a busted teacup for your chances. Folk will be along here straight away with flaming torches. And sledge-hammers. You get my drift?'

The golem shrugged.

THEY CANNOT TAKE AWAY WHAT DOES NOT EXIST, it wrote.

Angua threw up her hands. 'I'm trying to be civilized,' she said. 'I could confiscate you right now. The charge would be Being Obstructive When It's Been a Long Day and I've Had Enough. Do you know Father Tubelcek?'

THE OLD PRIEST WHO LIVES ON THE BRIDGE.

'How come you know him?'

I HAVE MADE DELIVERIES THERE.

'He's been murdered. Where were you when he was killed?'

IN THE SLAUGHTERHOUSE.

'*How do you know?*'

Dorfl hesitated a moment. Then the next words were written very slowly, as if they had come from a long way away after a great deal of thought.

BECAUSE IT IS SOMETHING THAT MUST HAVE HAPPENED NOT LONG AGO, BECAUSE YOU ARE EXCITED. FOR THE LAST THREE DAYS I HAVE BEEN WORKING HERE.

'All the time?'

YES.

'Twenty-four hours a day?'

YES. MEN AND TROLLS HERE ON EVERY SHIFT, THEY WILL TELL YOU. DURING THE DAY I MUST SLAUGHTER, DRESS, QUARTER, JOINT AND BONE, AND AT NIGHT WITHOUT REST I MUST MAKE SAUSAGES AND BOIL UP THE LIVERS, HEARTS, TRIPES, KIDNEYS AND CHITTERLINGS.

'That's *awful*,' said Cheery.

The pencil blurred briefly.

CLOSE.

Dorfl turned his head slowly to look at Angua and wrote:

DO YOU NEED ME FURTHER?

'If we do, we know where to find you.'

I AM SORRY ABOUT THE OLD MAN.

'Good. Come on, Cheery.'

They felt the golem's eyes on them as they left the yard.

'It was lying,' said Cheery.

'Why do you say that?'

'It *looked* as if it was lying.'

'You're probably right,' said Angua. 'But you can see the size of the place. I bet we wouldn't be able to prove it'd stepped out for half an hour. I think I'll suggest that we put it under what Commander Vimes calls special surveillance.'

'What, like . . . plain clothes?'

'Something like that,' said Angua carefully.

'Funny to see a pet goat in a slaughterhouse, I thought,' said Cheery, as they walked on through the fog.

'What? Oh, you mean the yudasgoat,' said Angua. 'Most slaughterhouses have one. It's not a pet. I suppose you could call it an employee.'

'Employee? What kind of job could it possibly do?'

'Hah. Walk into the slaughterhouse every day. *That's* its job. Look, you've got a pen full of frightened animals, right? And they're milling around and leaderless . . . and there's this ramp into this building, looks very scary . . . and, hey, there's this goat, *it's* not scared, and so the flock follows it and' – Angua made a throat-slitting noise – 'only the goat walks out.'

'That's horrible!'

'I suppose it makes sense from the goat's point of view. At least it *does* walk out,' said Angua.

'How did you know about this?'

'Oh, you pick up all sorts of odds and ends of stuff in the Watch.'

'I've got a lot to learn, I can see,' said Cheery. 'I never thought you had to carry bits of blanket, for a start!'

'It's special equipment if you're dealing with the undead.'

'Well, I knew about garlic and vampires. Anything holy works on vampires. What else works on werewolves?'

'Sorry?' said Angua, who was still thinking about the golem.

'I've got a silver mail vest which I promised my family I'd wear, but is anything else good for werewolves?'

'A gin and tonic's always welcome,' said Angua distantly.

'Angua?'

'Hmm? Yes? What?'

'Someone told me there was a werewolf in the *Watch*! I can't believe that!'

Angua stopped and stared down at her.

'I mean, sooner or later the wolf comes through,' said Cheery. 'I'm surprised Commander Vimes allows it.'

'There is a werewolf in the Watch, yes,' said Angua.

'*I knew* there was something odd about Constable Visit.'

Angua's jaw dropped.

'He always looks hungry,' said Cheery. 'And he's got that odd smile all the time. I know a werewolf when I see one.'

'He *does* look a bit hungry, that's true,' said Angua. She couldn't think of anything else to say.

'Well, I'm going to be keeping my distance!'

'Fine,' said Angua.

'Angua . . .'

'Yes?'

'Why do you wear your badge on a collar round your neck?'

'What? Oh. Well . . . so it's always handy. You know. In any circumstances.'

'Do I need to do that?'

'I shouldn't think so.'

Mr Sock jumped. 'Dorfl, you damn stupid lump! *Never* sneak up behind a man on the bacon slicer! I've told you that before! Try to make some noise when you move, damn you!'

The golem held up its slate, which said:

TONIGHT I CANNOT WORK.

'What's this? The bacon slicer never asks for time off!'

IT IS A HOLY DAY.

Sock looked at the red eyes. Old Fishbine had said something about this, hadn't he, when he'd sold Dorfl? Something like: 'Sometimes it'll go off for a few hours because it's a holy day. It's the words in its head. If it doesn't go and trot off to its temple or whatever it is, the words'll stop working, don't ask me why. There's no point in stopping it.'

Five hundred and thirty dollars the thing had cost. He'd thought it was a bargain – and it *was* a bargain, no doubt about that. The damned thing only ever stopped working when it had run out of things to do. Sometimes not even then, according to the stories. You heard about golems flooding out houses because no one told them to stop carrying water from the well, or washing the dishes until the plates were thin as paper. Stupid things. But useful if you kept your eye on them.

And yet . . . and yet . . . he could see why no one seemed to keep them for long. It was the way the damned two-handed engine just stood there, taking it all in and putting it . . . where? And never complained. Or spoke at all.

A man could get worried about a bargain like that, and feel mightily relieved when he was writing out a receipt for the new owner.

'Seems to me there's been a *lot* of holy days lately,' Sock said.

SOME TIMES ARE MORE HOLY THAN OTHERS.

But they *couldn't* skive off, could they? Work was what a golem *did*.

'I don't know how we're going to manage . . .' Sock began.

IT IS A HOLY DAY.

'Oh, all *right*. You can have time off tomorrow.'

TONIGHT. HOLY DAY STARTS AT SUNSET.

'Be back quickly, then,' said Sock, weakly. 'Or I'll— You be back quickly, d'you hear?'

That was another thing. You couldn't threaten the creatures. You certainly couldn't withhold their pay, because they didn't get any. You couldn't frighten them. Fishbine had said that a weaver over Nap Hill way had ordered his golem to smash itself to bits with a hammer – and it had.

YES. I HEAR.

In a way, it didn't matter who they were. In fact, their anonymity was part of the whole business. *They* thought themselves part of the march of history, the tide of progress and the wave of the future. They were men who felt that The Time Had Come. Regimes can survive barbarian hordes, crazed terrorists and hooded secret societies, but they're in real trouble when prosperous and anonymous men sit around a big table and think thoughts like that.

One said, 'At least it's clean this way. No blood.'

'And it would be for the good of the city, of course.'

They nodded gravely. No one needed to say that what was good for them was good for Ankh-Morpork.

'And he won't die?'

'Apparently he can be kept merely . . . unwell. The dosage can be varied, I'm told.'

'Good. I'd rather have him unwell than dead. I wouldn't trust Vetinari to stay in a grave.'

'I've heard that he once said he'd prefer to be cremated, as a matter of fact.'

'Then I just hope they scatter the ashes really *widely*, that's all.'

'What about the Watch?'

'What about it?'

'Ah.'

Lord Vetinari opened his eyes. Against all rationality, his hair ached.

He concentrated, and a blur by the bed focused into the shape of Samuel Vimes.

'Ah, Vimes,' he said weakly.

'How are you feeling, sir?'

'Truly dreadful. Who was that little man with the incredibly bandy legs?'

'That was Doughnut Jimmy, sir. He used to be a jockey on a very fat horse.'

'A racehorse?'

'Apparently, sir.'

'A fat racehorse? Surely that could never win a race?'

'I don't believe it ever did, sir. But Jimmy made a lot of money by not winning races.'

'Ah. He gave me milk and some sort of sticky potion.' Vetinari concentrated. 'I was heartily sick.'

'So I understand, sir.'

'Funny phrase, that. *Heartily* sick. I wonder why it's a cliché? Sounds . . . jolly. Rather cheerful, really.'

'Yes, sir.'

'Feel like I've got a bad dose of 'flu, Vimes. Head not working properly.'

'Really, sir?'

The Patrician thought for a while. There was obviously something else on his mind. 'Why did he still smell of horses, Vimes?' he said at last.

'He's a horse doctor, sir. A damn good one. I

heard last month he treated Dire Fortune and it didn't fall over until the last furlong.'

'Doesn't sound helpful, Vimes.'

'Oh, I don't know, sir. The horse *had* dropped dead coming up to the starting line.'

'Ah. I *see*. Well, well, well. What a nasty suspicious mind you have, Vimes.'

'Thank you, sir.'

The Patrician raised himself on his elbows. 'Should toenails throb, Vimes?'

'Couldn't say, sir.'

'Now, I think I should like to read for a while. Life goes on, eh?'

Vimes went to the window. There was a nightmarish figure crouched on the edge of the balcony outside, staring into the thickening fog.

'Everything all right, Constable Downspout?'

'Eff, fir,' said the apparition.

'I'll shut the window now. The fog is coming in.'

'Fight oo are, fir.'

Vimes closed the window, trapping a few tendrils which gradually faded away.

'What was that?' said Lord Vetinari.

'Constable Downspout's a gargoyle, sir. He's no good on parade and bloody useless on the street, but when it comes to staying in one place, sir, you can't beat him. He's world champion at not moving. If you want the winner of the 100 Metres Standing Still, that's him. He spent three days on a roof in the rain when we caught the Park Lane Knobbler. Nothing'll get past him. And there's Corporal Gimletsson patrolling the corridor and Constable Glodsnephew on the floor below and Constables Flint and Moraine in the rooms on either side of you, and Sergeant Detritus will be around constantly so that if anyone nods off he'll kick arse, sir, and you'll know when he does that 'cos the poor bugger'll come right through the wall.'

'Well done, Vimes. Am I right in thinking that all my guards are non-human? They all seem to be dwarfs and trolls.'

'Safest way, sir.'

'You've thought of everything, Vimes.'

'Hope so, sir.'

'Thank you, Vimes.' Vetinari sat up and took a mass of papers off the bedside table. 'And now, don't let me detain you.'

Vimes's mouth dropped open.

Vetinari looked up. 'Was there anything else, Commander?'

'Well . . . I suppose not, sir. I suppose I'd just better run along, eh?'

'If you wouldn't mind. And I'm sure a lot of paperwork has accumulated in my office, so if you'd send someone to fetch it, I would be obliged.'

Vimes shut the door behind him, a little harder than necessary. Gods, it made him livid, the way Vetinari turned him on and off like a switch – and had as much natural gratitude as an alligator. The Patrician relied on Vimes doing his job, *knew* he'd do his job, and that was the extent of his thought on the matter. Well, one day, Vimes would . . . would . . .

. . . would bloody well do his job, of course,

because he didn't know how to do anything else. But realizing that made it all the worse.

Outside the palace the fog was thick and yellow. Vimes nodded to the guards on the door, and looked out at the clinging, swirling clouds.

It was almost a straight line to the Watch House in Pseudopolis Yard. And the fog had brought early night to the city. Not many people were on the streets; they stayed indoors, barring the windows against the damp shreds that seemed to leak in everywhere.

Yes . . . empty streets, a chilly night, dampness in the air . . .

Only one thing was needed to make it perfect. He sent the sedan men on home and walked back to one of the guards. 'You're Constable Lucker, aren't you?'

'Yessir, Sir Samuel.'

'What size boots do you take?'

Lucker looked panicky. 'What, sir?'

'It's a simple question, man!'

'Seven and a halfs, sir.'

'From old Plugger in New Cobblers? The cheap ones?'

'Yessir!'

'Can't have a man guarding the palace in cardboard boots!' said Vimes, with mock cheerfulness. 'Off with them, Constable. You can have mine. They've still got wyvern – well, whatever it is wyverns do – on them, but they'll fit you. Don't stand there with your mouth open. Give me your boots, man. You can keep mine.' Vimes added: 'I've got lots.'

The constable watched in frightened astonishment

as Vimes pulled on the cheap pair and stood upright, stamping a few times with his eyes shut. 'Ah,' he said. 'I'm in front of the palace, right?'

'Er . . . yes, sir. You've just come out of it, sir. It's this big building here.'

'Ah,' said Vimes brightly, 'but I'd know I was here, even if I hadn't!'

'Er . . .'

'It's the flagstones,' said Vimes. 'They're an unusual size and slightly dished in the middle. Hadn't you noticed? Your feet, lad! That's what you'll have to learn to think with!'

The bemused constable watched him disappear into the fog, stamping happily.

Corporal the Right Honourable the Earl of Ankh Nobby Nobbs pushed open the Watch-House door and staggered inside.

Sergeant Colon looked up from the desk, and gasped. 'You okay, Nobby?' he said, hurrying around to support the swaying figure.

'It's terrible, Fred. Terrible!'

'Here, take a seat. You're all pale.'

'I've been elevated, Fred!' moaned Nobby.

'Nasty! Did you see who did it?'

Nobby wordlessly handed him the scroll Dragon King of Arms had pressed into his hand, and flopped back. He took a tiny length of home-made cigarette from behind his ear and lit it with a shaking hand. 'I dunno, I'm sure,' he said. 'You do your best, you keep your head down, you don't make any trouble, and then something like this happens to you.'

Colon read the scroll slowly, his lips moving when he came to difficult words like 'and' and 'the'. 'Nobby, you've read this? It says you're a *lord*!'

'The old man said they'd have to do a lot of checking up but he thought it was pretty clear what with the ring and all. Fred, what am I gonna *do*?'

'Sit back and eat off ermine plates, I should think!'

'That's just it, Fred. There's no money. No big house. No land. Not a brass farthing!'

'What, nothing?'

'Not a dried pea, Fred.'

'I thought all the upper crust had pots of money.'

'Well, I'm the crust on its uppers, Fred. I don't know anything about lording! I don't want to have to wear posh clothes and go to hunt balls and all that stuff.'

Sergeant Colon sat down beside him. 'You never suspected you'd got any posh connections?'

'Well . . . my cousin Vincent once got done for indecently assaulting the Duchess of Quirm's house-maid . . .'

'Chambermaid or scullery maid?'

'Scullery maid, I think.'

'Probably doesn't count, then. Does anyone else know about this?'

'Well, *she* did, and she went and told . . .'

'I mean about your lordshipping.'

'Only Mr Vimes.'

'Well, there you are,' said Sergeant Colon, handing him back the scroll. 'You don't have to tell anyone. Then you don't *have* to go around wearing golden trousers, and you needn't hunt balls unless you've lost 'em. You just sit there, and I'll fetch you a cup of tea, how about that? We'll see it through, don't you worry.'

'You're a toff, Fred.'

'That makes two of us, m'lord!' Colon waggled his eyebrows. 'Get it? Get it?'

'Don't, Fred,' said Nobby wearily.

The Watch-House door opened.

Fog poured in like smoke. In the midst of it were two red eyes. The parting shreds revealed the massive figure of a golem.

'Umpk,' said Sergeant Colon.

The golem held up its slate:

I HAVE COME TO YOU.

'Yeah. Yeah. Yeah. I've, er, yeah, I can see that,' said Colon.

Dorfl turned the slate around. The other side read:

I GIVE MYSELF UP FOR MURDER. IT WAS I WHO KILLED THE OLD PRIEST. THE CRIME IS SOLVED.

Colon, once his lips had stopped moving, scurried behind the suddenly very flimsy defences of his desk and scrabbled through the papers there.

'You keep it covered, Nobby,' he said. 'Make sure it don't run off.'

'Why's *it* going to run off?' said Nobby.

Sergeant Colon found a relatively clean piece of paper.

'Well, well, well, I, well, I guess I'd better . . . What's your name?'

The golem wrote:
DORFL.

By the time he was on the Brass Bridge (medium-sized cobbles of the rounded sort they called 'cat heads', quite a few missing) Vimes was already beginning to wonder if he'd done the right thing.

Autumn fogs were always thick, but he'd never known it this bad. The pall muffled the sounds of the city and turned the brightest lights into dim glows, even though in theory the sun hadn't set yet.

He walked along by the parapet. A squat, glistening shape loomed in the fog. It was one of the wooden hippos, some distant ancestor of Roderick or Keith. There were four on either side, all looking out towards the sea.

Vimes had walked past them thousands of times. They were old friends. He'd often stood in the lee of one on chilly nights, when he was looking for somewhere out of trouble.

That's what it used to be like, wasn't it? It hardly seemed that long ago. Just a handful of them in the Watch, staying out of trouble. And then Carrot had arrived, and suddenly the narrow circuit of their lives had opened up, and there were nearly thirty men (oh, including trolls and dwarfs and miscellaneous) in the Watch now, and they didn't skulk around keeping out of trouble, they went *looking* for trouble, and they found it everywhere they looked. Funny, that. As Vetinari had pointed out in that way of his, the more policemen you had, the more crimes seemed to be committed. But the Watch was back and out there on the streets, and if they weren't actually as good as Detritus at kicking arse they were definitely prodding buttock.

He lit a match on a hippo's toenail and cupped his hand around it to shield his cigar from the damp.

These murders, now. No one would care if the Watch didn't care. Two old men, murdered on the same day. Nothing stolen . . . He corrected himself: nothing *apparently* stolen. Of course, the thing about things that were stolen was that the bloody things weren't there. They almost certainly hadn't been fooling around with other people's wives. They probably couldn't remember what fooling around was. One spent his time among old religious books; the other, for gods' sakes, was an authority on the aggressive uses of baking.

People would probably say they had lived blameless lives.

But Vimes was a policeman. *No one* lived a completely blameless life. It might be just possible, by lying very still in a cellar somewhere, to get through a day without committing a crime. But only just. And, even then, you were probably guilty of loitering.

Anyway, Angua seemed to have taken this case personally. She always had a soft spot for the underdog.

So did Vimes. You had to. Not because they were pure or noble, because they weren't. You had to be on the side of underdogs because they weren't overdogs.

Everyone in this city looked after themselves. That's what the guilds were for. People banded together against other people. The guild looked after you from the cradle to the grave or, in the case of the Assassins, to other people's graves. They even maintained the law, or at least they had done, after a fashion. Thieving without a licence was punishable by death for the first offence.* The Thieves' Guild saw to that. The arrangement sounded unreal, but it worked.

It worked like a machine. That was fine except for the occasional people who got crushed in the wheels.

The damp cobbles felt reassuringly real under his soles.

Gods, he'd missed this. He'd patrolled alone in the old days. When there was just him, and the stones glistened around 3 a.m., it all seemed to make sense somehow—

He stopped.

Around him, the world became a crystal of horror, the special horror that has nothing to do with fangs or ichor or ghosts but has everything to do with the familiar becoming unfamiliar.

Something fundamental was wrong.

It took a few dreadful seconds for his mind to supply the details of what his subconscious had noticed. There had been five statues along the parapet on this side.

But there should have been four.

---

*The Ankh-Morpork view of crime and punishment was that the penalty for the first offence should prevent the possibility of a second offence.

He turned very slowly and walked back to the last one. It was a hippo, all right.

So was the next one. There was graffiti on it. Nothing supernatural had 'Zaz Ys A Wonker' scrawled on it.

It seemed to him that it didn't take quite so long to get to the next one, and when he *looked* at it . . .

Two red points of light flared in the fog above him.

Something big and dark leapt down, knocked him to the ground and disappeared into the gloom.

Vimes struggled to his feet, shook his head and set off after it. No thought was involved. It is the ancient instinct of terriers and policemen to chase anything that runs away.

As he ran he felt automatically for his bell, which would summon other Watchmen, but the Commander of the Watch didn't carry a bell. Commanders of the Watch were on their own.

In Vimes's squalid office Captain Carrot stared at a piece of paper:

Repairs to Guttering, Watch House, Pseudopolis Yard. New downpipe, 35° Micklewhite bend, four right-angled trusses, labour and making good. $16.35p.

There were more like them, including Constable Downspout's pigeon bill. He knew Sergeant Colon objected to the idea of a policeman being paid in pigeons, but Constable Downspout was a gargoyle and gargoyles had no concept of money. But they knew a pigeon when they ate it.

Still, things were improving. When Carrot had arrived the entire Watch's petty cash had been kept on a shelf in a tin marked 'Stronginthearm's Armour Polish for Gleaming Cohorts' and, if money was needed for anything, all you had had to do was go and find Nobby and force him to give it back.

Then there was the letter from a resident in Park Lane, one of the most select addresses in the city:

Commander Vimes,
  The Night Watch patrol in this street appears to be made up entirely of dwarfs. I have nothing against dwarfs amongst their own kind, at least they are not trolls, but one hears stories and I have daughters in the house. I demand that this situation is remedied instantly otherwise I shall have no option but to take up the matter with Lord Vetinari, who is a personal friend.
  I am, sir, your obt. servant,
    Joshua H. Catterail

This was police work, was it? He wondered if Mr Vimes were trying to tell him something. There were other letters. The Community Co-ordinator of Equal Heights for Dwarfs was demanding that dwarfs in the Watch be allowed to carry an axe rather than the traditional sword, and should be sent to investigate only those crimes committed by tall people. The Thieves' Guild was complaining that Commander

Vimes had said publicly that most thefts were committed by thieves.

You'd need the wisdom of King Isiahdanu to tackle them, and these were only *today's* letters.

He picked up the next one and read: 'Translation of text found in Fr Tubelcek's mouth. Why? SV.'

Carrot dutifully read the translation.

'In his mouth? Someone tried to put *words* in his mouth?' said Carrot, to the silent room.

He shivered, but not because of the cold that came from fear. Vimes's office was always cold. Vimes was an outdoors person. Fog was dancing in the open window, little fingers of it drifting in the light.

The next paper down the heap was a copy of Cheery's iconograph. Carrot stared at the two blurred red eyes.

'Captain Carrot?'

He half-turned his head, but kept looking at the picture.

'Yes, Fred?'

'We've got the murderer! We've got 'im!'

'Is he a golem?'

'How did you know that?'

The tincture of night began to suffuse the soup of the afternoon.

Lord Vetinari considered the sentence, and found it good. He liked 'tincture' particularly. Tincture. *Tinc*ture. It was a distinguished word, and pleasantly countered by the flatness of 'soup'. The soup of the afternoon. Yes. In which may well be found the croutons of teatime.

He was aware that he was a little light-headed. He'd never have thought a sentence like that in a normal frame of mind.

In the fog outside the window, just visible by the candlelight, he saw the crouching shape of Constable Downspout.

A gargoyle, eh? He'd wondered why the Watch was indented for five pigeons a week on its wages bill. A gargoyle in the Watch, whose job it was to watch. That would be Captain Carrot's idea.

Lord Vetinari got up carefully from the bed and closed the shutters. He walked slowly to his writing table, pulled his journal out of its drawer, then tugged out a wad of manuscript and unstoppered the ink bottle.

Now then, where had he got to?

Chapter Eight, he read unsteadily, *The Rites of Man.*

Ah, yes . . .

'Concerning Truth,' he wrote, 'that which May be Spoken as Events Dictate, but should be Heard on Every Ocasfion . . .'

He wondered how he could work 'soup of the afternoon' into the treatise, or at least 'tincture of night'.

The pen scratched across the paper.

Unheeded on the floor lay the tray that had contained a bowl of nourishing gruel, concerning which he had resolved to have strong words with the cook when he felt better. It had been tasted by three tasters, including Sergeant Detritus, who was unlikely to be poisoned by anything that worked on humans or even by most things that worked on trolls . . . but probably by most things that worked on trolls.

The door was locked. Occasionally he could hear the reassuring creak of Detritus on his rounds. Outside the window, the fog condensed on Constable Downspout.

Vetinari dipped the pen in the ink and started a new page. Every so often he consulted the leather-bound journal, licking his fingers delicately to turn the thin pages.

Tendrils of fog slipped in around the shutters and brushed against the wall until they were frightened away by the candlelight.

Vimes pounded through the fog after the fleeing figure. It wasn't quite so fast as him, despite the twinges in his legs and one or two warning stabs from his left knee, but whenever he came close to it some muffled pedestrian got in the way, or a cart pulled out of a cross-street.*

His soles told him that they'd gone right down Broad Way and had turned left into Nonesuch Street (small square paving stones). The fog was even thicker here, trapped between the trees of the park.

*This always happens in *any* police chase *anywhere*. A heavily laden lorry will *always* pull out of a side alley in front of the pursuit.

If vehicles aren't involved, then it'll be a man with a rack of garments. Or two men with a large sheet of glass.

There's probably some kind of secret society behind all this.

But Vimes was triumphant. You've missed your turning if you're heading for the Shades, my lad! There's only the Ankh Bridge now and there'll be a guard on that—

His feet told him something else. They said: 'Wet leaves, that's Nonesuch Street in the autumn. Small square paving stones with occasional treacherous drifts of wet leaves.'

They said it too late.

Vimes landed on his chin in the gutter, staggered upright, fell over again as the rest of the universe spun past, got up, tottered a few steps in the wrong direction, fell over again and decided to accept the majority vote for a while.

Dorfl was standing quietly in the station office, heavy arms folded across its chest. In front of the golem was the crossbow belonging to Sergeant Detritus, which had been converted from an ancient siege weapon. It fired a six-foot-long iron arrow. Nobby sat behind it, his finger on the trigger.

'Put it away, Nobby! You can't fire that in here!' said Carrot. 'You *know* we never find where the arrows stop!'

'We wrestled a confession out of it,' said Sergeant Colon, hopping up and down. 'It kept on admitting it but we got it to confess in the end! And we've got these other crimes we'd like taken into consideration.'

Dorfl held up its slate.

I AM GUILTY.

Something fell out of its hand.

It was short, and white. A piece of matchstick, by the look of it. Carrot picked it up and stared at it. Then he looked at the list Colon had drawn up. It was quite long, and consisted of every unsolved crime in the city for the past couple of months.

'It's confessed to all these?'

'Not yet,' said Nobby.

'We haven't read 'em all out yet,' said Colon.

Dorfl wrote:

I DID EVERYTHING.

'Hey!' said Colon. 'Mr Vimes is going to be really pleased with us!'

Carrot walked up to the golem. There was a faint orange glow in its eyes.

'Did you kill Father Tubelcek?' he said.

YES.

'See?' said Sergeant Colon. 'You can't argue with that.'

'Why did you do it?' said Carrot.

No reply.

'And Mr Hopkinson at the Bread Museum?'

YES.

'You beat him to death with an iron bar?' said Carrot.

YES.

'Hang on,' said Colon, 'I thought you said he was . . . ?'

'Leave it, Fred,' said Carrot. '*Why* did you kill the old man, Dorfl?'

No reply.

'Does there have to be a reason? You can't trust

160

golems, my dad always used to say,' said Colon. 'Turn on you soon as look at you, he said.'

'Have they ever killed anyone?' said Carrot.

'Not for want of thinking about it,' said Colon darkly. 'My dad said he had to work with one once and it used to look at him all the time. He'd turn around and there it would be . . . looking at him.'

Dorfl sat staring straight in front.

'Shine a candle in its eyes!' said Nobby.

Carrot pulled a chair across the floor and straddled it, facing Dorfl. He absent-mindedly twirled the broken match between his fingers.

'I know you didn't kill Mr Hopkinson and I don't think you killed Father Tubelcek,' he said. 'I think he was dying when you found him. I think you tried to save him, Dorfl. In fact, I'm pretty sure I can prove it if I can see your chem—'

The light from the golem's flaring eyes filled the room. He stepped forward, fists upraised.

Nobby fired the crossbow.

Dorfl snatched the long bolt out of the air. There was the sound of screaming metal and the bolt became a thin bar of red-hot iron with a bulge piled up around the golem's grip.

But Carrot was behind the golem, flipping open its head. As the golem turned, raising the iron bar like a club, the fire died in its eyes.

'Got it,' said Carrot, holding up a yellowed scroll.

At the end of Nonesuch Street was a gibbet, where wrongdoers – or, at least, people found guilty of wrongdoing – had been hung to twist gently in the wind as examples of just retribution and, as the elements took their toll, basic anatomy as well.

Once, parties of children were brought there by their parents to learn by dreadful example of the snares and perils that await the criminal, the outlaw and those who happen to be in the wrong place at the wrong time, and they would see the terrible wreckage creaking on its chain and listen to the stern imprecations and then usually (this being Ankh-Morpork) would say 'Wow! *Brilliant!*' and use the corpse as a swing.

These days the city had more private and efficient ways of dealing with those it found surplus to requirements, but for the sake of tradition the gibbet's incumbent was a quite realistic wooden body. The occasional stupid raven would have a peck at the eyeballs even now, and end up with a much shorter beak.

Vimes tottered up to it, fighting for breath.

The quarry could have gone anywhere by now. Such daylight as had been filtering through the fog had given up.

Vimes stood beside the gibbet, which creaked.

It had been built to creak. What's the good of a public display of retribution, it had been argued, if it didn't creak ominously? In richer times an elderly man had been employed to operate the creak by means of a length of string, but now there was a clockwork mechanism that needed to be wound up only once a month.

Condensation dripped off the artificial corpse.

'Blow this for a lark,' muttered Vimes, and tried to head back the way he came.

After ten seconds of blundering, he tripped over something.

It was a wooden corpse, hurled into the gutter.

When he got back to the gibbet, the empty chain was swinging gently, jingling in the fog.

Sergeant Colon tapped the golem's chest. It went *donk*.

'Like a flowerpot,' said Nobby. 'How can they move around when they're like a pot, eh? They ought to keep cracking all the time.'

'They're daft, too,' said Colon. 'I heard there was one over in Quirm who was made to dig a trench and they forgot about it and they only remembered it when there was all this water 'cos it had dug all the way to the river . . .'

Carrot unrolled the chem on the table, and laid beside it the paper that had been put in Father Tubelcek's mouth.

'It's dead, is it?' said Sergeant Colon.

'It's harmless,' said Carrot, looking from one piece of paper to the other.

'Right. I've got a sledgehammer round the back somewhere, I'll just . . .'

'No,' said Carrot.

'You saw the way it was acting!'

'I don't think it could actually have hit me. I think it just wanted to scare us.'

'It worked!'

'Look at these, Fred.'

Sergeant Colon glanced at the desk. 'Foreign writing,' he said, in a voice which suggested that it was nothing like as good as decent home writing, and probably smelled of garlic.

'Anything strike you about them?'

'Well . . . they looks the same,' Sergeant Colon conceded.

'This yellowing one is Dorfl's chem. The other one is from Father Tubelcek,' said Carrot. 'Letter for letter the same.'

'Why's that?'

'I *think* Dorfl wrote these words and put them in old Tubelcek's mouth after the poor man died,' said Carrot slowly, still looking from one piece of paper to the other.

'Urgh, yuk,' said Nobby. 'That's *mucky*, that is . . .'

'No, you don't understand,' said Carrot. 'I mean he wrote them because they were the only ones he knew that worked . . .'

'Worked how?'

'Well . . . you know the kiss of life?' said Carrot. 'I mean first aid? I know *you* know, Nobby. You came with me when they had that course at the YMPA.'

'I only went 'cos you said you got a free cup of tea and a biscuit,' said Nobby sulkily. 'Anyway, the dummy ran away when it was my turn.'

'It's the same with life-saving, too,' said Carrot. 'We want people to breathe, so we try to make sure they've got some air in them . . .'

They all turned to look at the golem.

'But golems don't breathe,' said Colon.

'No, a golem knows only one thing that keeps you alive,' said Carrot. 'It's the words in your head.' They all turned back to look at the words.

They all turned to look at the statue that was Dorfl.

'It's gone all cold in here,' Nobby quavered. 'I def'nitly felt a *aura* flick'rin' in the air just then! It was like someone . . .'

'What's going on?' said Vimes, shaking the damp off his cloak.

'. . . openin' the door,' said Nobby.

It was ten minutes later.

Sergeant Colon and Nobby had gone off-duty, to everyone's relief. Colon in particular had great difficulty with the idea that you went on investigating after someone had confessed. It outraged his training and experience. You got a confession and there it ended. You didn't go around *disbelieving* people. You disbelieved people only when they said they were innocent. Only guilty people were trustworthy. Anything else struck at the whole basis of policing.

'White clay,' said Carrot. 'It was white clay we found. And practically unbaked. Dorfl's made of dark terracotta, and rock-hard.'

'The last thing the old priest saw was a golem,' said Vimes.

'Dorfl, I'm sure,' said Carrot. 'But that's not the same as saying Dorfl was the murderer. I think he turned up as the man was dying, that's all.'

'Oh? Why?'

'I'm . . . not sure yet. But I've seen Dorfl around. He's always seemed a very gentle person.'

'It works in a slaughterhouse!'

'Maybe that's not a bad place for a gentle person to work, sir,' said Carrot. 'Anyway, I've checked up all the records I can find and I don't think a golem has ever attacked anyone. Or committed any kind of crime.'

'Oh, come *on*,' said Vimes. 'Everyone knows . . .' He stopped as his cynical ears heard his incredulous voice. 'What, *never*?'

'Oh, people are always saying that they know someone who had a friend whose grandfather heard of one killing someone, and that's about as real as it gets, sir. Golems aren't *allowed* to hurt people. It's in their words.'

'They give me the willies, I know that,' said Vimes.

'They give everyone the willies, sir.'

'You hear lots of stories about them doing stupid things like making a thousand teapots or digging a hole five miles deep,' said Vimes.

'Yes, but that's not exactly criminal activity, is it, sir? *That*'s just ordinary rebellion.'

'What do you mean, "rebellion"?'

'Dumbly obeying orders, sir. You know . . . someone shouts at it "Go and make teapots", so it does. Can't be blamed for obeying orders, sir. No one told them how many. No one wants them to think, so they get their own back by *not* thinking.'

'They rebel by *working*?'

'It's just a thought, sir. It'd make more sense to a golem, I expect.'

Automatically, they turned again to look at the silent shape of the golem.

'Can it hear us?' said Vimes.

'I don't think so, sir.'

'This business with the words . . . ?'

'Er . . . I think *they* think a dead human is just someone who's lost his chem. I don't think they understand how we work, sir.'

'Them and me both, Captain.'

Vimes stared at the hollow eyes. The top of Dorfl's head was still open so that light shone down through the sockets. Vimes had seen many horrible things on the street, but the silent golem was somehow worse. You could too easily imagine the eyes flaring and the thing standing up and striding forward, fists flailing like sledgehammers. It was more than just his imagination. It seemed to be built into the things. A *potentiality*, biding its time.

That's why we all hate 'em, he thought. *Those expressionless eyes watch us, those big faces turn to follow us, and doesn't it just look as if they're making notes and taking names? If you heard that one had bashed in someone's head over in Quirm or somewhere, wouldn't you just love to believe it?*

A voice inside, a voice which generally came to him only in the quiet hours of the night or, in the old days, halfway down a whisky bottle, added: *Given how we use them, maybe we're scared because we know we deserve it . . .*

No . . . there's nothing behind those eyes. There's just clay and magic words.

Vimes shrugged. 'I chased a golem earlier,' he said. 'It was standing on the Brass Bridge. Damn thing. Look, we've got a confession and the eyeball evidence. If you can't come up with anything better than a . . . a feeling, then we'll have to—'

'To what, sir?' said Carrot. 'There *isn't* anything more we could do to him. He's dead now.'

'Inanimate, you mean.'

'Yes, sir. If you want to put it that way.'

'If Dorfl didn't kill the old men, who did?'

'Don't know, sir. But I think Dorfl does. Maybe he was following the murderer.'

'Could it have been ordered to protect someone?'

'Maybe, sir. Or he decided to.'

'You'll be telling me it's got emotions next. Where's Angua gone?'

'She thought she'd check a few things, sir,' said Carrot. 'I was . . . puzzled about this, sir. It was in his hand.' He held the object up.

'A piece of matchstick?'

'Golems don't smoke and they don't use fire, sir. It's just . . . odd that he should have the thing, sir.'

'Oh,' said Vimes, sarcastically. 'A Clue.'

Dorfl's trail was *the* word on the street. The mixed smells of the slaughterhouse filled Angua's nostrils.

The journey zigzagged, but with a certain directional tendency. It was as if the golem had laid a ruler across the town and taken every road and alley that went in the right direction.

She came to a short blind alley. There were some warehouse gates at the end. She sniffed. There were plenty of other smells, too. Dough. Paint. Grease. Pine resin. Sharp, loud, fresh scents. She sniffed again. Cloth? Wool?

There was a confusion of footprints in the dirt. Large footprints.

The small part of Angua that always walked on two legs saw that the footprints coming out were on top of the footprints going in. She snuffled around. Up to twelve creatures, each with their own very distinctive smell – the smell of *merchandise* rather than living creatures – had all very recently gone down the stairwell. And all twelve had come back up.

She went down the steps and was met by an impenetrable barrier.

A door.

Paws were no good at doorknobs.

She peered over the top of the steps. There was no one around. Only the fog hung between the buildings.

She concentrated and *changed*, leaned against the wall for a moment until the world stopped spinning, and tried the door.

There was a large cellar beyond. Even with a werewolf's eyesight there wasn't much to see.

She had to stay human. She thought better when she was human. Unfortunately, here and now, as a human, the thought occupying her mind in no small measure was that she was naked. Anyone finding a naked woman in their cellar would be bound to ask questions. They might not even bother with

169

questions, even ones like 'Please?' Angua could certainly deal with that situation, but she preferred not to have to. It was so difficult explaining away the shape of the wounds.

No time to waste, then.

The walls were covered in writing. Big letters, small letters, but all in that neat script which the golems used. There were phrases in chalk and paint and charcoal, and in some cases simply cut into the stone itself. They reached from floor to ceiling, criss-crossing one another over and over again so often that it was almost impossible to make out what any of them were meant to say. Here and there a word or two stood out in the jumble of letters:

... SHALT NOT ... WHAT HE DOES IS NOT ... RAGE AT THE CREATOR ... WOE UNTO THE MASTERLESS ... WORDS IN THE ... CLAY OF OUR ... LET MY ... BRING US TO FRE ...

The dust in the middle of the floor was scuffed, as if a number of people had been milling around. She crouched down and rubbed the dirt, occasionally sniffing her finger. Smells. They were industrial smells. She hardly needed special senses to detect them. A golem didn't smell of anything except clay and whatever it was it was working with at the time ...

And ... something rolled under her fingers. It was a length of wood, only a couple of inches long. A matchstick, without a head.

A few minutes' investigation found another ten, lying here and there as if they'd been idly dropped.

There was also half a stick, tossed away some distance from the others.

Her night vision was fading. But sense of smell lasted much longer. Smells were strong on the sticks – the same cocktail of odours that had trailed into this damp room. But the slaughterhouse smell she'd come to associate with Dorfl was on only the broken piece.

She sat back on her haunches and looked at the little heap of wood. Twelve people (twelve people in messy jobs) had come here. They hadn't stayed long. They'd had a . . . a *discussion*: the writing on the wall. They'd done something involving eleven matches (just the wooden part – they hadn't been dipped to get the head. Maybe the pine-smelling golem worked in a match factory?) plus one broken match.

Then they'd all left and gone their separate ways.

Dorfl's way had taken him straight to the main Watch House to give himself up.

Why?

She sniffed at the piece of broken match again. There was no doubt about that cocktail of blood and meat smells.

Dorfl had given himself up for murder . . .

She stared at the writing on the wall, and shivered.

'Cheers, Fred,' said Nobby, raising his pint.

'We can put the money back in the Tea Club tomorrow. No one'll miss it,' said Sergeant Colon. 'Anyway, this comes under the heading of an emergency.'

Corporal Nobbs looked despondently into his glass. People often did this in the Mended Drum, when the immediate thirst had been slaked and for the first time they could take a good look at what they were drinking.

'What am I going to *do*?' he moaned. 'If you're a nob you got to wear coronets and long robes and that. Got to cost a mint, that kind of stuff. And there's stuff you've got to do.' He took another long swig. ''S called *knobless obleeje*.'

'*Nobblyesse obligay*,' corrected Colon. 'Yeah. Means you got to keep your end up in society. Giving money to charities. Being kind to the poor. Passing your ole clothes to your gardener when there's still some good wear left in 'em. I know about that. My uncle was butler to ole Lady Selachii.'

'Ain't got a gardener,' said Nobby gloomily. 'Ain't got a garden. Ain't got 'ny ole clothes except what I'm wearin'.' He took another swig. 'She gave her ole clothes to the gardener, did she?'

Colon nodded. 'Yeah. We were always a bit puzzled about that gardener.' He caught the barman's eye. 'Two more pints of Winkles, Ron.' He glanced at Nobby. His old friend looked more dejected than he'd ever seen him. They'd have to see this thing through together. 'Better make that two for Nobby, too,' he added.

'Cheers, Fred.'

Sergeant Colon's eyebrows raised as one pint was emptied almost in one go. Nobby put the mug down a little unsteadily.

'Wouldn't be so bad if there was a pot of cash,' Nobby said, picking up the other mug. 'I thought you couldn't *be* a nob without bein' a rich bugger. I thought they gave you a big wad with one hand and banged the crown on your head with the other. Don't make *sense*, bein' nobby *and* poor. S'worst of both wurble.' He drained the mug and banged it down. 'Common 'n' rich, yeah, that I could hurble.'

The barman leaned over to Sergeant Colon. 'What's up with the corporal? He's a half-pint man. That's eight pints he's had.'

Fred Colon leaned closer and spoke out of the corner of his mouth. 'Keep it to yourself, Ron, but it's because he's a peer.'

'Is that a fact? I'll go and put down some fresh sawdust.'

In the Watch House, Sam Vimes prodded the matches. He didn't ask Angua if she were sure. Angua could smell if it was Wednesday.

'So who were the others?' he said. 'Other golems?'

'It's hard to tell from the tracks,' said Angua. 'But I think so. I'd have followed them, but I thought I ought to come right back here.'

'What makes you think they were golems?'

'The footprints. And golems have no smell,' she said. 'They pick up the smells associated with whatever they're doing. That's all they smell of . . .' She thought of the wall of words. 'And they had a long debate,' she said. 'A golem argument. In writing. It got pretty heated, I think.'

She thought about the wall again. 'Some of them got quite emphatic,' she added, remembering the size of some of the lettering. 'If they were human, they'd have been shouting . . .'

Vimes stared gloomily at the matches laid out before him. Eleven bits of wood, and a twelfth broken in two. You didn't need to be any kind of genius to see what had been going on. 'They drew lots,' he said. 'And Dorfl lost.'

He sighed. 'This is getting worse,' he said. 'Does anyone know how many golems there are in the city?'

'No,' said Carrot. 'Hard to find out. No one's made any for centuries, but they don't wear out.'

'No one makes them?'

'It's banned, sir. The priests are pretty hot on that, sir. They say it's making life, and that's something only gods are supposed to do. But they put up with the ones that are still around because, well, they're so useful. Some are walled up or in treadmills or at the bottom of shafts. Doing messy tasks, you know, in places where it's dangerous to go. They do all the really mucky jobs. I suppose there could be hundreds . . .'

'Hundreds?' said Vimes. 'And now they meet secretly and make plots? Good grief! Right. We ought to destroy the lot of them.'

'Why?'

'You like the idea of them having *secrets*? I mean, good grief, trolls and dwarfs, fine, even the undead are alive in a way, even if it is a bloody awful way' – Vimes caught Angua's eye and went on – 'for the most part. But these things? They're just things that do work. It's like having a bunch of shovels meeting for a chat!'

'Er . . . there was something else, sir,' said Angua slowly.

174

'In the cellar?'

'Yes. Er . . . but it's hard to explain. It was a . . . feeling.'

Vimes shrugged non-committally. He'd learned not to scoff at Angua's feelings. She always knew where Carrot was, for one thing. If she were in the Watch House you could tell if he were coming up the street by the way she turned to look at the door.

'Yes?'

'Like . . . deep grief, sir. Terrible, terrible sadness. Er.'

Vimes nodded, and pinched the bridge of his nose. It seemed to have been a long day and it was far from over yet.

He really, really needed a drink. The world was distorted enough as it was. When you saw it through the bottom of a glass, it all came back into focus.

'Have you had anything to eat today, sir?' said Angua.

'I had a bit of breakfast,' muttered Vimes.

'You know that word Sergeant Colon uses?'

'What? "Manky"?'

'That's how you look. If you're staying here at least let's have some coffee and send out for figgins.'

Vimes hesitated at that. He'd always imagined that *manky* was how your mouth felt after three days on a regurgitated diet. It was horrible to think that you could *look* like that.

Angua reached for the old coffee tin that represented the Watch's tea kitty. It was surprisingly easy to lift.

'Hey? There should be at least twenty-five dollars

in here,' she said. 'Nobby collected it only yester-day . . .'

She turned the tin upside-down. A very small dog-end dropped out.

'Not even an IOU?' said Carrot despondently.

'An IOU? This is *Nobby* we're talking about.'

'Oh. Of course.'

It had gone very quiet in the Mended Drum. Happy Hour had been passed with no more than a minor fight. Now everyone was watching Unhappy Hour.

There was a forest of mugs in front of Nobby.

'I mean, I mean, what's it worth whenallsaidan-done?' he said.

'You could flog it,' said Ron.

'Good point,' said Sergeant Colon. 'There's plenty o' rich folks who'd give a sack of cash for a title. I mean folks that's already got the big house and that. They'd give anything to be as nobby as you, Nobby.'

The ninth pint stopped halfway to Nobby's lips.

'Could be worth thousands of dollars,' said Ron encouragingly.

'At the very least,' said Colon. 'They'd fight over it.'

'You play your cards right and you could retire on something like that,' said Ron.

The mug remained stationary. Various ex-pressions fought their way around the lumps and excrescences of Nobby's face, suggesting the terrible battle within.

'Oh, they would, would they?' he said at last.

Sergeant Colon tilted unsteadily away. There was an edge in Nobby's voice he hadn't heard before.

'Then you could be rich and common just like you said,' said Ron, who did not have quite the same eye for mental weather changes. 'Posh folks'd be falling over themselves for it.'

'Sell m' birthright for a spot of massage, is that it?' said Nobby.

'It's "a pot of message",' said Sergeant Colon.

'It's "a mess of pottage",' said a bystander, anxious not to break the flow.

'Hah! Well, I'll tell *you*,' said Nobby, swaying, 'there's some things that *can't be sole*. Hah! Hah! Who streals my prurse streals trasph, right?'

'Yeah, it's the trashiest looking purse I ever saw,' said a voice.

'—*what is a mess of pottage, anyway?*'

''cos . . . what good'd a lot of moneneney do me, hey?'

The clientele looked puzzled. This seemed to be a question on the lines of 'Alcohol, is it nice?', or 'Hard work, do you want to do it?'.

'—*what's messy about it, then?*'

'We-ell,' said a brave soul, uncertainly, 'you could use it to buy a big house, lots of grub and . . . drink and . . . women and that.'

'That's wha' it takes to make a man happppeyey, is it?' said Nobby, glassy-eyed.

His fellow-drinkers just stared. This was a meta-physical maze.

'Well, I'll tell *you*,' said Nobby, the swaying now so regular that he looked like an inverted pendulum, 'all that stuff's nothing, *nothing*! I tell you, compared to pride inna man's linneneage . . . eage.'

'Linneneageeage?' said Sergeant Colon.

'Ancescestors and that,' said Nobby. ''T means I've got ancescestors and that, which's more'n you lot've got!'

Sergeant Colon choked on his pint.

'Everyone's got ancestors,' said the barman calmly. 'Otherwise they wouldn't be here.'

Nobby gave him a glassy stare and tried unsuccessfully to focus. 'Right!' he said, eventually. 'Right! Only . . . only I've got *more* of 'em, d'y'see? The blood of bloody kings is in these veins, am I right?'

'Temporarily,' said a voice. There was laughter, but it had an anticipatory ring to it that Colon had learned to respect and fear. It reminded him of two things: (1) he had got only six weeks to retirement, and (2) it had been quite a long time since he'd been to the lavatory.

Nobby delved into his pocket and pulled out a battered scroll. 'Y'see this?' he said, unrolling it with difficulty on the bar. 'Y'see it? I've got a right to arm bears, me. See here? It says "Earl", right? That's me. You could, you could, you could have my head up over the door.'

'Could be,' said the barman, eyeing the crowd.

'I mean, y'could change t'name o' this place, call it the Earl of Ankh, and I'd come in and drink here reg'lar, whaddya say?' said Nobby. 'News gets around an earl drinks here, business will go *right* up. And I wouldn't'n't'n't chargeyouapenny, howaboutit? People'd say, dat's a high-class pub, is that,

Lord de Nobbes drinks there, that's a place with a bit of tone.'

Someone grabbed Nobby by the throat. Colon didn't recognize the grabber. He was just one of the scarred, ill-shaven regulars whose function it was, around about this time of an evening, to start opening bottles with his teeth or, if the evening was going *really* well, with somebody else's teeth.

'So we ain't good enough for you, is that what you're saying?' the man demanded.

Nobby waved his scroll. His mouth opened to frame words like – Sergeant Colon just *knew* – 'Unhand me, you low-born oaf.'

With tremendous presence of mind and absence of any kind of common sense, Sergeant Colon said: 'His lordship wants everyone to have a drink with him!'

Compared to the Mended Drum, the Bucket in Gleam Street was an oasis of frigid calm. The Watch had adopted it as their own, as a silent temple to the art of getting drunk. It wasn't that it sold particularly good beer, because it didn't. But it did serve it quickly, and quietly, and gave credit. It was one place where Watchmen didn't have to see things or be disturbed. No one could sink alcohol in silence like a Watchman who'd just come off duty after eight hours on the street. It was as much protection as his helmet and breastplate. The world didn't hurt so much.

And Mr Cheese the owner was a good listener. He listened to things like 'Make that a double' and

'Keep them coming'. He also said the right things, like 'Credit? Certainly, officer'. Watchmen paid their tab or got a lecture from Captain Carrot.

Vimes sat gloomily behind a glass of lemonade. He wanted one drink, and understood precisely why he wasn't going to have one. One drink ended up arriving in a dozen glasses. But knowing this didn't make it any better.

Most of the day shift were in here now, plus one or two men who were on their day off.

Scummy as the place was, he liked it here. With the buzz of other people around him, he didn't seem to get in the way of his own thoughts.

One reason that Mr Cheese had allowed his pub to become practically the city's fifth Watch House was the protection this offered. Watchmen were quiet drinkers, on the whole. They just went from vertical to horizontal with the minimum amount of fuss, without starting any major fights, and without damaging the fixtures overmuch. And no one ever tried to rob him. Watchmen got really *intense* about having their drinking disturbed.

And he was therefore surprised when the door was flung open and three men rushed in, flourishing crossbows.

'Don't nobody move! Anyone moves and they're dead!'

The robbers stopped at the bar. To their own surprise their arrival didn't seem to have caused much of a stir.

'Oh, for heaven's sake, will someone shut that door?' growled Vimes.

A Watchman near the door did so.

'And bolt it,' Vimes added.

The three thieves looked around. As their eyes grew accustomed to the gloom, they received a general impression of armourality, with strong overtones of helmetness. But none of it was moving. It was all watching them.

'You boys new in town?' said Mr Cheese, buffing a glass.

The boldest of the three waved his bow under the barman's nose. 'All the money right now!' he screamed. 'Otherwise,' he said, to the room in general, 'you've got a dead barman.'

'Plenty of other bars in town, boyo,' said a voice.

Mr Cheese didn't look up from the glass he was polishing. 'I know that was you, Constable Thighbiter,' he said calmly. 'There's two dollars and thirty pence on your slate, thank you very much.'

The thieves drew closer together. Bars shouldn't act like this. And they fancied they could hear the faint sliding noises of assorted weapons being drawn from various sheaths.

'Haven't I seen you before?' said Carrot.

'Oh gods, it's *him*,' moaned one of the men. 'The bread-thrower!'

'I thought Mr Ironcrust was taking you to the Thieves' Guild,' Carrot went on.

'There was a bit of an argument about taxes . . .'

'Don't tell him!'

Carrot tapped his head. 'The tax forms!' he said. 'I expect Mr Ironcrust is worried I've forgotten about them!'

181

The thieves were now so close together they looked like a fat six-armed man with a very large bill for hats.

'Er . . . Watchmen aren't allowed to kill people, right?' said one of them.

'Not while we're on duty,' said Vimes.

The boldest of the three moved suddenly, grabbed Angua and pulled her upright. 'We walk out of here unharmed or the girl gets it, all right?' he snarled.

Someone sniggered.

'I hope you're not going to kill anyone,' said Carrot.

'That's up to us!'

'Sorry, was I talking to you?' said Carrot.

'Don't worry, I'll be fine,' said Angua. She looked around to make sure Cheery wasn't there, and then sighed. 'Come on, gentlemen, let's get it over with.'

'Don't play with your food!' said a voice from the crowd.

There were one or two giggles until Carrot turned in his seat, whereupon everyone was suddenly intensely interested in their drinks.

'It's okay,' said Angua quietly.

Aware that something was out of kilter, but not quite sure what it was, the thieves edged back to the door. No one moved as they unbolted it and, still holding Angua, stepped out into the fog, shutting the door behind them.

'Hadn't we better help?' said a constable who was new to the Watch.

'They don't deserve help,' said Vimes.

There was a clank of armour and then a long, deep growl, right outside in the street.

And a scream. And then another scream. And a third scream, modulated with 'NONONOnono-nonononoNO! . . . aarghaargh *aargh*!' Something heavy hit the door.

Vimes turned back to Carrot. 'You and Constable Angua,' he said. 'You . . . er . . . get along all right?'

'Fine, sir,' said Carrot.

'Some people might think that, er, there might be, er, problems . . .'

There was a thud, and then a faint bubbling noise.

'We work around them, sir,' said Carrot, raising his voice slightly.

'I heard that her father's not very happy about her working here . . .'

'They don't have much law up in Uberwald, sir. They think it's for weak societies. The baron's not a very civic-minded man.'

'He's pretty bloodthirsty, from what I've heard.'

'She wants to stay in the Watch, sir. She likes meeting people.'

From outside came another gurgle. Fingernails scrabbled at a windowpane. Then their owner disappeared abruptly from view.

'Well, it's not for me to judge,' said Vimes.

'No, sir.'

After a few moments of silence the door opened, slowly. Angua walked in, adjusting her clothes, and sat down. All the Watchmen in the room suddenly took a second course of advanced beer-study.

'Er . . .' Carrot began.

'Flesh wounds,' said Angua. 'But one of them did shoot one of the others in the leg by accident.'

'I think you'd better put it in your report as "self-inflicted wounds while resisting arrest",' said Vimes.

'Yes, sir,' said Angua.

'Not *all* of them,' said Carrot.

'They tried to rob our bar and take a wer— Angua hostage,' said Vimes.

'Oh, I see what you mean, sir,' said Carrot. 'Self-inflicted. Yes. Of course.'

It had gone quiet in the Mended Drum. This was because it is usually very hard to be both loud and unconscious.

Sergeant Colon was impressed at his own cleverness. Throwing a punch *could* stop a fight, of course, but in this case it had a quarter of rum, gin and sixteen chopped lemons floating in it.

Some people were still upright, however. They were the serious drinkers, who drank as if there was no tomorrow and rather hoped this would be the case.

Fred Colon had reached the convivial drunk stage. He turned to the man beside him. ''S good here, isn't it,' he managed.

'What'm I gonna tell me wife, that's what I want to know . . .' moaned the man.

'Dunno. Say you've bin bin bin working late,' said Colon. 'An' suck a peppermint before you goes home, that usually works—'

'Working late? Hah! I've bin given the sack! Me! A craftsman! Fifteen years at Spadger and Williams, right, and then they go bust 'cos of Carry undercutting 'em and I get a job at Carry's and, bang, I'm out of a job *there*, too! "Surplus to requirements"! Bloody golems! Forcing real people out of a job! What they wanna work for? They got no mouth to feed, hah. But the damn thing goes at it so fast you can't see its bloody arms movin'!'

'Shame.'

'Smash 'em up, that's what I say. I mean, we had a golem at S an' W's but ole Zhlob just used to plod along, y'know, not buzz away like a blue-arsed fly. You wanna watch it, mate, they'll have *your* job next.'

'Stoneface wouldn't stand f'r it,' said Colon, undulating gently.

'Any chance of a job with you lot, then?'

'Dunno,' said Colon. The man seemed to have become two men. 'What's it you do?'

'I'm a Wick-Dipper and End-Teaser, mate,' they said.

'I can see that's a useful trade.'

'Here you go, Fred,' said the barman, tapping him on the shoulder and putting a piece of paper in front of him. Colon watched with interest as figures danced back and forth. He tried to focus on the one at the bottom, but it was too big to take in.

'What's this, then?'

'His imperial lordship's bar bill,' said the barman.

'Don't be daft, no one can drink that much . . . 'm not payin'!'

185

'I'm including breakages, mind you.'

'Yeah? Like what?'

The barman pulled a heavy hickory stick from its hiding place under the bar. 'Arms? Legs? Suit yourself,' he said.

'Oh, come *on*, Ron, you've known me for years!'

'Yes, Fred, you've always been a good customer, so what I'll do is, I'll let you shut your eyes first.'

'But that's all the money I've got!'

The barman grinned. 'Lucky one for you, eh?'

Cheery Littlebottom leaned against the corridor wall outside her privy and wheezed.

It was something alchemists learned to do early in their career. As her tutors had said, there were two signs of a good alchemist: the Athletic and the Intellectual. A good alchemist of the first sort was someone who could leap over the bench and be on the far side of a safely thick wall in three seconds, and a good alchemist of the second sort was someone who knew *exactly* when to do this.

The equipment didn't help. She scrounged what she could from the guild, but a *real* alchemical laboratory should be full of the kind of glassware that looked as if it were produced during the Guild of Glassblowers All-Comers Hiccuping Contest. A proper alchemist did not have to run tests using as her beaker a mug with a picture of a teddy-bear on it, which Corporal Nobbs was probably going to be very upset about when he found it missing.

When she judged that the fumes had cleared she ventured back into her tiny room.

That was *another* thing. Her books on alchemy were marvellous objects, every page a work of the engraver's art, but they nowhere contained instructions like 'Be sure to open a window'. They *did* have instructions like 'Adde *Aqua Quirmis* to the Zinc untile Rising Gas Yse Vigorously Evolved', but never added 'Don't Doe Thys Atte Home' or even 'And Say Fare-thee-Welle to Thy Eyebrows'.

Anyway . . .

The glassware remained innocent of the brown-black sheen that, according to *The Compound of Alchemie*, would indicate arsenic in the sample. She'd tried every type of food and drink she could find in the palace pantries, and pressed into service every bottle and jar she could discover in the Watch House.

She tried one more time with what said on the packet it was Sample #2. Looked like a smear of cheese. Cheese? The various fumes thronging around her head were making her slow. She *must* have taken some cheese samples. She was pretty sure Sample #17 had been some Lancre Blue Vein, which had reacted vigorously with the acid, blown a small hole in the ceiling and covered half the work-bench with a dark green substance that was setting like tar.

She tested this one anyway.

A few minutes later she was scrabbling furiously through her notebook. The first sample she'd taken from the pantry (one portion of duck pâté) was down here as Sample #3. What about #1 and #2? No, #1 had been the white clay from Misbegot Bridge, so what had been #2?

She found it.

But that *couldn't* be right!

She looked up at the glass tube. Metallic arsenic grinned back at her.

She'd retained a bit of the sample. She could test again, but . . . perhaps it would be better to tell someone . . .

She hurried along to the main office, where a troll was on duty. 'Where's Commander Vimes?'

The troll grinned. 'In der Gleam . . . Littlebottom.'

'Thank *you*.'

The troll turned back to address a worried-looking monk in a brown cassock. 'And?' he said.

'Best if he tells it himself,' said the monk. 'I only work on the next bench.' He put a small jar of dust on the desk. It had a bow tie around it.

'I want to complain most *emphatically*,' said the dust, in a shrill little voice. 'I was working there only five minutes and then *splash*. It's going to take *days* to get back into shape!'

'Working where?' said the troll.

'Nonesuch Ecclesiastical Supplies,' said the worried monk, helpfully.

'Holy water section,' said the vampire.

'You've found arsenic?' said Vimes.

'Yes, sir. Lots. The sample's full of it. But . . .'

'Well?'

Cheery looked at her feet. 'I tried my process again with a test sample, sir, and I'm sure I'm doing it right . . .'

'Good. What was it in?'

'That's just it, sir. It wasn't in anything from the palace. Because I'd got a bit confused and tested the stuff I found under Father Tubelcek's fingernails, sir.'

'*What?*'

'There was grease under his nails, sir, and I thought maybe it could've come from whoever attacked him. Off an apron or something . . . I've still got some left if you want a second opinion, sir. I wouldn't blame you.'

'Why would the old man be handling poison?' said Carrot.

'I thought he might have scratched the murderer,' said Cheery. 'You know . . . put up a fight.'

'With the Arsenic Monster?' said Angua.

'Oh, gods,' said Vimes. 'What time is it?'

'Bingely bingely beep bong!'

'Oh, *damn* . . .'

'It's nine of the clock,' said the organizer, poking its head out of Vimes's pocket. '"I was unhappy because I had no shoes until I met a man with no feet."'

The Watchmen exchanged glances.

'What?' said Vimes, very carefully.

'People like it if I occasionally come up with a little aphorism or inspiring Thought For The Day,' said the imp.

'So how did you meet this man with no feet?' said Vimes.

'I didn't actually *meet* him,' said the imp. 'It was a general metaphorical statement.'

189

'Well, that's it, then,' said Vimes. 'If you'd met him you could have asked him if he had any boots he didn't have any use for.'

There was a squeak as he pushed the imp back into its box.

'There's more, sir,' said Cheery.

'Go on,' said Vimes wearily.

'And I had a careful look at the clay we found at the murder scene,' said Cheery. 'Igneous said it had a lot of grog in it – old powdered pottery. Well . . . I chipped a bit off Dorfl to compare and I can't be sure but I got the iconograph demon to paint *really small* details and . . . I think there's some clay just like his in there. He's got a lot of iron oxide in his clay.'

Vimes sighed. All around them people were drinking alcohol. One drink would make it all so clear.

'Any of you know what any of this means?' he said.

Carrot and Angua shook their heads.

'Is it supposed to make sense if we know how all the pieces fit together?' Vimes demanded, raising his voice.

'Like pieces of a jigsaw, sir?' Cheery ventured.

'Yes!' said Vimes, so loudly that the room went quiet. '*Now* all we need is the corner bit with the piece of sky and the leaves and it'll all be one big picture?'

'It's been a long day for all of us, sir,' said Carrot.

Vimes sagged. 'Okay,' he said. 'Tomorrow . . . I want you, Carrot, to check on the golems in the city. If they're up to something I want to know what it is.

And you, Littlebottom . . . you look *everywhere* in the old man's house for more arsenic. I wish I could believe that you'll find any.'

Angua had volunteered to walk Littlebottom back to her lodgings. The dwarf was surprised that the men let her do this. After all, it'd mean that Angua would then have to walk on home by herself.

'Aren't you afraid?' Cheery said as they ambled through the damp clouds of fog.

'Nope.'

'But I imagine muggers and cut-throats would be out in a fog like this. And you said you lived in the Shades.'

'Oh, yes. But I haven't been bothered lately.'

'Ah, perhaps they're frightened of the uniform?'

'Possibly,' said Angua.

'Probably they've learned respect.'

'You may be right.'

'Er . . . excuse me . . . but are you and Captain Carrot . . . ?'

Angua waited politely.

'. . . Er . . .'

'Oh, yes,' said Angua, taking pity. 'We're *er*. But I stay at Mrs Cake's boarding house because you need your own space in a city like this.' And an understanding landlady sympathetic to those with *special* needs, she added to herself. Like doorhandles that a paw could operate, and a window left open on moonlit nights. 'You've got to have somewhere where you can be yourself. Anyway, the Watch House smells of socks.'

'I'm staying with my Uncle Armstrangler,' said Cheery. 'It's not very nice there. People talk about mining most of the time.'

'Don't you?'

'There's not a lot you can say about mining. "I mine in my mine and what's mine is mine,"' said Cheery in a singsong voice. 'And then they go on about gold which, frankly, is a lot duller than people think.'

'I thought dwarfs *loved* gold,' said Angua.

'They just say that to get it into bed.'

'Are you *sure* you're a dwarf? Sorry. That was a joke.'

'There must be more interesting things. Hair. Clothes. People.'

'Good grief. You mean *girl talk*?'

'I don't know, I've never talked girl talk before,' said Cheery. 'Dwarfs just talk.'

'It's like that in the Watch, too,' said Angua. 'You can be any sex you like provided you act male. There's no men and women in the Watch, just a bunch of lads. You'll soon learn the language. Basically it's how much beer you supped last night, how strong the curry was you had afterwards, and where you were sick. Just think egotesticle. You'll soon get the hang of it. And you'll have to be prepared for sexually explicit jokes in the Watch House.'

Cheery blushed.

'Mind you, that seems to have ended now,' said Angua.

'Why? Did you complain?'

'No, after I joined in it all seemed to stop,' said

Angua. 'And, you know, they didn't laugh? Not even when I did the hand gestures too? I thought that was unfair. Mind you, some of them were quite small gestures.'

'There's no help for it, I'll have to move out,' sighed Cheery. 'I feel all . . . wrong.'

Angua looked down at the little figure trudging along beside her. She recognized the symptoms. Everyone needed their own space, just like Angua did, and sometimes that space was inside their heads. And she liked Cheery, oddly enough. Possibly it was because of her earnestness. Or the fact that she was the only person apart from Carrot who didn't look slightly frightened when they talked to her. And that was because she didn't *know*. Angua wanted to preserve that ignorance as a small precious thing, but she could tell when someone needed a little change in their lives.

'We're going quite close to Elm Street,' she said, carefully. 'Just, er, drop in for a while. I've got some stuff you could borrow . . .'

I won't be needing it, she told herself. *When I go, I won't be able to carry much.*

Constable Downspout watched the fog. Watching was, after staying in one place, the thing he did best. But he was also good at keeping quite still. Not making any noise whatsoever was another of his best features. When it came to doing absolutely nothing at all he was among the finest. But it was keeping completely motionless in one place that was his forte. If there were a roll-call for the world's champion non-movers, he wouldn't even turn up.

Now, chin on his hands, he watched the fog.

The clouds had settled somewhat so that up here, six storeys above the streets, it was possible to believe you were on a beach at the edge of a cold, moonlit sea. The occasional tall tower or steeple rose out of the clouds, but all sounds were muffled and pulled in on themselves. Midnight came and went.

Constable Downspout watched, and thought about pigeons.

Constable Downspout had very few desires in life, and almost all of them involved pigeons.

A group of figures lurched, staggered or in one case rolled through the fog like the Four Horsemen of a small Apocalypse. One had a duck on his head, and because he was almost entirely sane except for this one strange particular he was known as the Duck Man. One coughed and expectorated repeatedly, and hence was called Coffin Henry. One, a legless man on a small wheeled trolley, was for no apparent reason called Arnold Sideways. And the fourth, for some very good reasons indeed, was Foul Ole Ron.

Ron had a small greyish-brown, torn-eared terrier on the end of a string, although in truth it would be hard for an observer to know exactly who was leading whom and who, when push came to shove, would be the one to fold at the knees if the other one shouted 'Sit!' Because, although trained canines as aids for those bereft of sight, and even of hearing, have frequently been used throughout the universe, Foul Ole Ron was the first person ever to own a Thinking-Brain Dog.

The beggars, led by the dog, were heading for the dark arch of Misbegot Bridge, which they called Home. At least, one of them called it 'Home'; the others respectively called it 'Haaawrk haaawrk *HRRaawrk* ptui!', 'Heheheh! Whoops!' and 'Buggrit, millennium hand and shrimp!'

As they stumbled along the riverside they passed a can from hand to hand, drinking appreciatively and occasionally belching.

The dog stopped. The beggars shunted to a halt behind it.

A figure came towards them along the riverside.

'Ye gods!'

'Ptui!'

'Whoops!'

'Buggrit?'

The beggars flung themselves against the wall as the pale figure lurched past. It was clutching at its head as if trying to lift itself off the ground by its ears, and then occasionally banging its head against nearby buildings.

While they watched, it pulled a metal mooring post out of the cobbles and started to hit itself over the head. Eventually the cast iron shattered.

The figure dropped the stub, flung back its head, opened a mouth from which red light spilled, and roared like a bull in distress. Then it staggered on into the darkness.

'There's that golem again,' said the Duck Man. 'The white one.'

'Heheh, I gets heads like that myself, some mornings,' said Arnold Sideways.

'I knows about golems,' said Coffin Henry, spitting expertly and hitting a beetle climbing the wall twenty feet away. 'They ain't s'posed to have a voice.'

'Buggrit,' said Foul Ole Ron. 'Dang the twigger f'r'a bang at the fusel, and shrimp, 'cos the worm's on the other boot! See if he don't.'

'He meant it's the same one we saw the other day,' said the dog. 'After that ole priest got topped.'

'Do you think we should tell someone?' said the Duck Man.

The dog shook its head. 'Nah,' it said. 'We got a cushy number down here, no sense in spoiling it.'

The five of them staggered on into the damp shadows.

'I hate bloody golems, takin' our jobs . . .'

'We ain't got jobs.'

'See what I mean?'

'What's for supper?'

'Mud and ole boots. *HRRaawrk* ptui!'

'Millennium hand and shrimp, I sez.'

''m glad I've got a voice. I can speak up for meself.'

'It's time you fed your duck.'

'What duck?'

The fog glowed and sizzled around Five and Seven Yard. Flames roared up and all but set the thick clouds alight. Spitting liquid iron cooled in its moulds. Hammers rang out around the workshops. The ironmasters didn't work by the clock, but by the more demanding physics of molten metal. Even though it was nearly midnight, Stronginthearm's Iron Founders, Beaters and General Forging was still bustling.

There were many Stronginthearms in Ankh-Morpork. It was a very common dwarf name. That had been a major consideration for Thomas Smith when he'd adopted it by official deed poll. The scowling dwarf holding a hammer which adorned his sign was a mere figment of the signpainter's imagination. People thought 'dwarfmade' was better, and Thomas Smith had decided not to argue.

The Committee for Equal Heights had objected but things had mired somewhat because, firstly, most of the actual Committee was human, since dwarfs were generally too busy to worry about that sort of thing,* and in any case their position hinged on pointing out that Mr Stronginthearm *né* Smith was too tall, which was clearly a sizeist discrimination and technically illegal under the Committee's own rules.

In the meantime Thomas had let his beard grow, wore an iron helmet if he thought anyone official was around, and put up his prices by twenty pence on the dollar.

---

*And for the most part were unconcerned about matters of height. There's a dwarfish saying: 'All trees are felled at ground-level' – although this is said to be an excessively bowdlerized translation for a saw which more literally means, 'When his hands are higher than your head, his groin is level with your teeth.'

The drop hammers thumped, all in a row, powered by the big ox treadmill. There were swords to beat out and panels to be shaped. Sparks erupted.

Stronginthearm took off his helmet (the Committee had been around again) and wiped the inside.

'Dibbuk? Where the hell are you?'

A sensation of filled space made him turn. The foundry's golem was standing a few inches behind him, the forge light glowing on his dark red clay.

'I told you not to *do* that, didn't I?' Stronginthearm shouted above the din.

The golem held up its slate.

YES.

'You've gone and done all your holy day stuff? You were away too long!'

SORROW.

'Well, now you're back with us, go and take over on Number Three hammer and send Mr Vincent up to my office, right?'

YES.

Stronginthearm climbed the stairs to his office. He turned at the top to look back across the red-lit foundry floor. He saw Dibbuk walk over to the hammer and hold up a slate for the foreman. He saw Vincent the foreman walk away. He saw Dibbuk take the sword-blank that was being shaped and hold it in place for a few blows, then hurl it aside.

Stronginthearm hurried back down the steps.

When he was halfway down Dibbuk had laid his head on the anvil.

When Stronginthearm reached the bottom the hammer struck for the first time.

When he was halfway across the ash-crusted floor, other workers scurrying after him, the hammer struck for the second time.

As he reached Dibbuk the hammer struck for the third time.

The glow faded in the golem's eyes. A crack appeared across the impassive face.

The hammer went back up for the fourth time—

'Duck!' screamed Stronginthearm—

—and then there was nothing but pottery.

When the thunder had died away, the foundry master got to his feet and brushed himself off. Dust and wreckage were strewn across the floor. The hammer had jumped its bearings and was lying by the anvil in a heap of golem shards.

Stronginthearm gingerly picked up a piece of a foot, tossed it aside, and then reached down again and pulled a slate out of the wreckage.

He read:

> THE OLD MEN HELPED US!
> THOU SHALT NOT KILL!
> CLAY OF MY CLAY!
> SHAME.
> SORROW.

His foreman looked over Stronginthearm's shoulder. 'What did it go and do that for?'

'How should I know?' snapped Stronginthearm.

'I mean, it brought the tea round this afternoon as normal as anything. Then it went off for a coupla hours, and now this . . .'

Stronginthearm shrugged. A golem was a golem and that was all there was to it, but the recollection of that bland face positioning itself under the giant hammer had shaken him.

'I heard the other day the sawmill in Dimwell Street wouldn't mind selling the one it's got,' said the foreman. 'It sawed up a mahogany trunk into matchsticks, or something. You want I should go and have a word?'

Stronginthearm looked at the slate again.

Dibbuk had never been very wordy. He'd carry red-hot iron, hammer sword-blanks with his fists, clean out clinkers from a smelter still too hot for a man to touch . . . and never say a word. Of course, he *couldn't* say any words, but Dibbuk had always given the impression that there were none he'd particularly wanted to say in any case. He just worked. These were the most words he'd ever written at any one time.

They spoke to Stronginthearm of black distress, and a mind that would have been screaming if it could only have uttered a sound. Which was daft! The things *couldn't* commit suicide.

'Boss?' said the foreman. 'I said, you want me to get another one?'

Stronginthearm skimmed the slate away and, with a feeling of relief, watched it shatter against the wall. 'No,' he said. 'Just clear this thing up. And get the bloody hammer fixed.'

Sergeant Colon, after some considerable effort, managed to get his head higher than the gutter.

'You – you all right, Corporal Lord de Nobbes?' he mumbled.

'Dunno, Fred. Whose face is this?'

''S mine, Nobby.'

'Thank gods for that, I thought it was me . . .'

Colon fell back. 'We're lyin' in the gutter, Nobby,' he moaned. 'Ooo.'

'We're all lyin' in the gutter, Fred. But some of us're lookin' at the stars . . .'

'Well, *I'm* lookin' at your face, Nobby. Stars'd be a lot better, believe you me. C'mon . . .'

With several false starts they both managed to get upright, mainly by pulling themselves up one another.

'Where're're're we, Nobby?'

''m sure we left the Drum . . . 've I got a sheet over m'head?'

'It's the fog, Nobby.'

'What about these legs down here?'

'I reckon them's *your* legs, Nobby. I've got mine.'

'Right. Right. Ooo . . . I reckon I drunk a lot, Sarge.'

'Drunk as a lord, eh?'

Nobby reached gingerly up to his helmet. Someone had put a paper coronet around it. His questing hand found a dog-end behind his ear.

It was that unpleasant hour of the drinking day when, after a few hours' quality gutter-time, you're beginning to feel the retribution of sobriety while still being drunk enough to make it worse.

'How'd we get here, Sarge?'

Colon started to scratch his head and stopped because of the noise.

'I reckon . . .' he said, winnowing the frazzled shreds of his short-term memory, 'I . . . reckon . . . seems to me there was something about stormin' the palace and demandin' your birthright . . .'

Nobby choked and spat out the cigarette. 'We didn't do that, did we?'

'You was shouting we *ought* to do it . . .'

'Oh, gods . . .' moaned Nobby.

'But I reckon you threw up around that time.'

'That's a relief, anyway.'

'Well . . . it was all over Grabber Hoskins. But he tripped over someone before he could get us.'

Colon suddenly patted his pockets. 'And I've still got the tea money,' he said. Another cloud of memory scudded across the sunshine of oblivion. 'Well . . . three pennies of it . . .'

The urgency of this got through to Nobby. 'Thruppence?'

'Yeah, well . . . after you started orderin' all them expensive drinks for the whole bar . . . well, you din't have no money and it was either me payin' for them or . . .' Colon moved his finger across his throat and went: 'Kssssh!'

'You tellin' me we paid for Happy Hour in the Drum?'

'Not so much Happy Hour,' said Colon miserably. 'More sort of Ecstatic One-Hundred-and-Fifty Minutes. I didn't even know you *could* buy gin in pints.'

Nobby tried to focus on the fog. 'No one can drink gin by the pint, Sarge.'

'That's what I kept sayin', and would you listen?'

Nobby sniffed. 'We're close to the river,' he said. 'Let's try to get . . .'

Something roared, very close by. It was long and low, like a foghorn in serious distress. It was the sound you might hear from a cattleyard on a nervous night, and it went on and on, and then stopped so abruptly it caught the silence unawares.

'. . . far away from that as we can,' said Nobby. The sound had done the work of an ice-cold shower and about two pints of black coffee.

Colon spun around. He desperately needed something that would do the work of a laundry. 'Where *did* it come from?' he said.

'It was . . . over there, wasn't it?'

'I thought it was *that* way!'

In the fog, all directions were the same.

'I think . . .' said Colon, slowly, 'that we ort to go and make a report about this as soon as possible.'

'Right,' said Nobby. 'Which way?'

'Let's just run, eh?'

Constable Downspout's huge pointy ears quivered as the noise boomed over the city. He turned his head carefully, triangulating for height, direction and distance. And then he remembered it.

The cry was heard in the Watch House, but muffled by the fog.

It entered the open head of the golem Dorfl and

bounced around inside, echoing down, down among the small cracks in the clay until, at the very edge of perception, little grains danced together.

The sightless sockets stared at the wall. No one heard the cry that came back from the dead skull, because there was no mouth to utter it and not even a mind to guide it, but it screamed out into the night:

CLAY OF MY CLAY, THOU SHALT NOT KILL! THOU SHALT NOT DIE!

Samuel Vimes dreamed about Clues.

He had a jaundiced view of Clues. He instinctively distrusted them. They got in the way.

And he distrusted the kind of person who'd take one look at another man and say in a lordly voice to his companion, 'Ah, my dear sir, I can tell you nothing except that he is a left-handed stonemason who has spent some years in the merchant navy and has recently fallen on hard times,' and then unroll a lot of supercilious commentary about calluses and stance and the state of a man's boots, when *exactly the same* comments could apply to a man who was wearing his old clothes because he'd been doing a spot of home bricklaying for a new barbecue pit, and had been tattooed once when he was drunk and seventeen* and in fact got seasick on a wet pavement. What arrogance! What an insult to the rich and chaotic variety of the human experience!

It was the same with more static evidence. The footprints in the flowerbed were probably *in the real*

---

*These terms are often synonymous.

world left by the window-cleaner. The scream in the night was quite likely a man getting out of bed and stepping sharply on an upturned hairbrush.

The real world was far too *real* to leave neat little hints. It was full of too many things. It wasn't by eliminating the impossible that you got at the truth, however improbable; it was by the much harder process of eliminating the possibilities. You worked away, patiently asking questions and looking hard at things. You walked and talked, and in your heart you just hoped like hell that some bugger's nerve'd crack and he'd give himself up.

The events of the day clanged together in Vimes's head. Golems tramped like sad shadows. Father Tubelcek waved at him and then his head exploded, showering Vimes in words. Mr Hopkinson lay dead in his own oven, a slice of dwarf bread in his mouth. And the golems marched on, silently. There was Dorfl, dragging its foot, its head open for the words to fly in and out of, like a swarm of bees. And in the middle of it all Arsenic danced, a spiky little green man, crackling and gibbering.

At one point he thought one of the golems screamed.

After that, the dream faded, a bit at a time. Golems. Oven. Words. Priest. Dorfl. Golems marching, the thudding of their feet making the whole dream pulsate . . .

Vimes opened his eyes.

Beside him, Lady Sybil said, 'Wsfgl,' and turned over.

Someone was hammering at the front door. Still

205

muzzy, head swimming, Vimes pulled himself up on his elbows and said, to the night-time world in general, 'What sort of a time do you call this?'

'Bingeley bingeley beep!' said a cheerful voice from the direction of Vimes's dressing-table.

'Oh, please . . .'

'Twenty-nine minutes and thirty-one seconds past five ay-emm. A Penny Saved is a Penny Earned. Would you like me to present your schedule for today? While I am doing this, why not take some time to fill out your registration card?'

'What? What? What're you talking about?'

The knocking continued.

Vimes fell out of bed and groped in the dark for the matches. He finally got a candle alight and half-ran, half-staggered down the long stairs and into the hall.

The knocker turned out to be Constable Visit.

'It's Lord Vetinari, sir! It's worse this time!'

'Has anyone sent for Doughnut Jimmy?'

'Yessir!'

At this time of day the fog was fighting a rear-guard action against the dawn, and made the whole world look as though it were inside a ping-pong ball.

'I poked my head in as soon as I came on shift and he was out like a light, sir!'

'How did you know he wasn't asleep?'

'On the floor, sir, with all his clothes on?'

A couple of Watchmen had put the Patrician on his bed by the time Vimes arrived, slightly out of breath and with his knees aching. *Gods,* he thought as he struggled up the stairs, *it's not like the old truncheon-and-bell days. You wouldn't think twice about running halfway across the city, coppers and criminals locked in hot pursuit.*

With a mixture of pride and shame he added: *And none of the buggers ever caught me, either.*

The Patrician was still breathing, but his face was waxy and he looked as though death might be an improvement.

Vimes's gaze roamed the room. There was a familiar haze in the air.

'Who opened the window?' he demanded.

'I did, sir,' said Visit. 'Just before I went to get you. He looked as though he needed some fresh air . . .'

'It'd be fresher if you left the window *shut*,' said Vimes. 'Okay, I want everyone, I mean everyone, who was in this place overnight rounded up and down in the hall in two minutes. And someone fetch Corporal Littlebottom. And tell Captain Carrot.'

I'm worried and confused, he thought. *So the first rule in the book is to spread it around.*

He prowled about the room. It didn't take much intelligence to see that Vetinari had got up and moved over to his writing-desk, where by the look of it he had worked for some time. The candle had burned right down. An inkwell had been overturned, presumably when he'd slipped off the chair.

Vimes dipped a finger in the ink and sniffed it. Then he reached for the quill pen beside it, hesitated, took out his dagger, and lifted the long feather gingerly. There seemed to be no cunning little barbs on it, but he put it carefully on one side for Littlebottom to examine later.

He glanced down at the paper Vetinari had been working on.

To his surprise it wasn't writing at all, but a careful drawing. It showed a striding figure, except that the figure was not one person at all but made up of thousands of smaller figures. The effect was like one of the wicker men built by some of the more outlandish tribes near the Hub, when they annually celebrated the great cycle of Nature and their reverence for life by piling as much of it as possible in a great heap and setting fire to it.

The composite man was wearing a crown.

Vimes pushed the sheet of paper aside and returned his attention to the desk. He brushed the surface carefully for any suspicious splinters. He crouched down and examined the underside.

The light was growing outside. Vimes went into both the rooms alongside and made sure their drapes were open, then went back into Vetinari's room, closed the curtains and the doors, and sidled along the walls looking for any tell-tale speck of light that might indicate a small hole.

Where could you stop? Splinters in the floor? Blowpipes through the keyhole?

He opened the curtains again.

Vetinari had been on the mend yesterday. And now he looked worse. Someone had got to him in the night. How? Slow poison was the devil of a thing. You had to find a way of giving it to the victim every day.

No, you didn't . . . What was elegant *was finding a way of getting him to administer it to* himself *every day.*

Vimes rummaged through the paperwork. Vetinari had obviously felt well enough to get up and walk over here, but here was where he had collapsed.

You couldn't poison a splinter or a nail because he wouldn't keep on nicking himself . . .

There was a book half-buried in the papers, but it had a lot of bookmarks in it, mostly torn bits of old letters.

What did he do every day?

Vimes opened the book. Every page was covered with handwritten symbols.

You have to get a poison like arsenic into the body. It isn't enough to touch it. Or is it? Is there a kind of arsenic you can pick up through the skin?

No one was getting in. Vimes was almost certain of that.

The food and drink were probably all right, but he'd get Detritus to go and have another one of his little talks with the cooks in any case.

Something he breathed? How could you keep that up day after day without arousing suspicion somewhere? Anyway, you'd have to get your poison into the room.

Something already in the room? Cheery had a different carpet put down and replaced the bed. What else could you do? Strip the paint from the ceiling?

What had Vetinari told Cheery about poisoning? 'You put it where no one will look at all . . .'

Vimes realized he was still staring at the book. There wasn't anything there that he could recognize.

It must be a code of some sort. Knowing Vetinari, it wouldn't be crackable by anyone in a normal frame of mind.

Could you poison a book? But . . . so what? There were other books. You'd have to *know* he'd look at this one, continuously. And even then you'd have to get the poison into him. A man might prick his finger once and after that he'd take care.

It sometimes worried Vimes, the way he suspected everything. If you started wondering whether a man could be poisoned by words, you might as well accuse the wallpaper of driving him mad. Mind you, that horrible green colour would drive anyone insane . . .

'Bingely beepy bleep!'

'Oh, no . . .'

'This is your six ay-emm wake-up call! Good morning!! Here are your appointments for today, Insert Name Here!! Ten ay-emm . . .'

'Shut up! Listen, whatever's in my diary for today is *definitely* not—'

Vimes stopped. He lowered the box.

He went back to the desk. If you assumed one page per day . . .

Lord Vetinari had a very good memory. But everyone wrote things down, didn't they? You couldn't remember every little thing. Wednesday: 3 p.m., reign of terror; 3.15 p.m., clean out scorpion pit . . .

He held the organizer up to his lips. 'Take a memo,' he said.

'Hooray! Go right ahead. Don't forget to say "memo" first!!'

210

'Speak to . . . blast . . . *Memo*: What about Vetinari's journal?'

'Is that it?'

'Yes.'

Someone knocked politely at the door. Vimes opened it carefully. 'Oh, it's you, Littlebottom.'

Vimes blinked. Something wasn't right about the dwarf.

'I'll mix up some of Mr Doughnut's jollop right away, sir.' The dwarf looked past Vimes to the bed. 'Ooo . . . he doesn't look good, does he . . . ?'

'Get someone to move him into a different bedroom,' said Vimes. 'Get the servants to prepare a new room, right?'

'Yes, sir.'

'And, after they've done it, pick a *different* room at random and move him into it. And change *everything*, understand? Every stick of furniture, every vase, every rug—'

'Er . . . yes, sir.'

Vimes hesitated. Now he could put his finger on what had been bothering him for the last twenty seconds.

'Littlebottom . . .'

'Sir?'

'You . . . er . . . you . . . on your ears?'

'Earrings, sir,' said Cheery nervously. 'Constable Angua gave them to me.'

'Really? Er . . . right . . . I didn't think dwarfs wore jewellery, that's all.'

'We're known for rings, sir.'

'Yes, of course.' Rings, yes. No one quite like a

dwarf for forging a magical ring. But . . . magical earrings? Oh, well. There were some waters too deep to wade.

Sergeant Detritus's approach to these matters was almost instinctively correct. He had the palace staff lined up in front of him and was shouting at them at the top of his voice.

Look at old Detritus, Vimes thought as he went down the stairs. *Just your basic thick troll a few years ago, now a valuable member of the Watch provided you get him to repeat his orders back to you to make sure he understands you. His armour gleams even brighter than Carrot's because he doesn't get bored with polishing. And he's mastered policing as it is practised by the majority of forces in the universe, which is, basically, screaming angrily at people until they give in. The only reason that he's not a one-troll reign of terror is the ease with which his thought processes can be derailed by anyone who tries something fiendishly cunning, like an outright denial.*

'I know you all done it!' he was shouting. 'If the person wot done it does not own up der whole staff, an' I *means* this, der whole staff will be locked up in der Tanty also we throws der key away!' He pointed a finger at a stout scullerymaid. 'It was you wot done it, own up!'

'No.'

Detritus paused. Then: 'Where was you last night? Own up!'

'In bed, of course!'

'Aha, dat a likely story, own up, dat where you always is at night?'

'Of course.'

'Aha, own up, you got witnesses?'

'Sauce!'

'Ah, so you got no witnesses, you done it then, own up!'

'No!'

'Oh . . .'

'All right, all right. Thank you, Sergeant. That will be all for now,' said Vimes, patting him on the shoulder. 'Are all the staff here?'

He glared at the line-up: 'Well? *Are* you all here?'

There was a certain amount of reluctant shuffling among the ranks, and then someone cautiously put up a hand.

'Mildred Easy hasn't been seen since yesterday,' said its owner. 'She's the upstairs maid. A boy come with a message. She had to go off to see her family.'

Vimes felt the faintest of prickles on the back of his neck. 'Anyone know why?' he said.

'Dunno, sir. She left all her stuff.'

'All right. Sergeant, before you go off shift, get someone to find her. Then go and get some sleep. The rest of you, go and get on with whatever it is you do. Ah . . . Mr Drumknott?'

The Patrician's personal clerk, who'd been watching Detritus's technique with a horrified expression, looked up at him. 'Yes, Commander?'

'What's this book? Is it his lordship's diary?'

Drumknott took the book. 'It looks like it, certainly.'

'Have you been able to crack the code?'

'I didn't know it was in code, Commander.'

'What? You've never looked at it?'

'Why should I, sir? It's not mine.'

'You do know his last secretary tried to kill him?'

'Yes, sir. I ought to say, sir, that I have already been exhaustively interrogated by your men.' Drumknott opened the book and raised his eyebrows.

'What did they say?' said Vimes.

Drumknott looked up thoughtfully. 'Let me see, now . . . "It was you wot done it, own up, everybody seen you, we got lots of people say you done it, you done it all right didn't you, own up." That was, I think, the general approach. And then, I said it wasn't me and that seemed to puzzle the officer concerned.'

Drumknott delicately licked his finger and turned a page.

Vimes stared at him.

The sound of saws was brisk on the morning air. Captain Carrot knocked against the timber-yard door, which was eventually opened.

'Good morning, sir!' he said. 'I understand you have a golem here?'

'Had,' said the timber merchant.

'Oh dear, another one,' said Angua.

That made four so far. The one in the foundry had knelt under a hammer, the one in the stone-mason's yard was now ten clay toes sticking out from under a two-ton block of limestone, one working in the docks had last been seen in the river, striding towards the sea, and now this one . . .

'It was weird,' said the merchant, thumping the golem's chest. 'Sidney said it went on sawing all the way up to the moment it sawed its head right off. I've got a load of ash planking got to go out this afternoon. Who's going to saw it up, may I ask?'

Angua picked up the golem's head. Insofar as it had any expression at all, it was one of intense concentration.

''ere,' said the merchant, 'Alf told me he heard in the Drum last night that golems have been murderin' people . . .'

'Enquiries are continuing,' said Carrot. 'Now then, Mr . . . it's Preble Skink, isn't it? Your brother runs the lamp-oil shop in Cable Street? And your daughter is a maid at the university?'

The man looked astonished. But Carrot knew everyone.

'Yeah . . .'

'Did your golem leave the yard yesterday evening?'

'Well, yeah, early on . . . Something about a holy day.' He looked nervously from one to the other. 'You got to let them go, otherwise the words in their heads—'

'And then it came back and worked all night?'

'Yeah. What else would it do? And then Alf came in on early turn and he said it came up outa the saw pit, stood there for a moment, and then . . .'

'Was it sawing pine logs yesterday?' said Angua.

'That's right. Where'm I going to get another golem at short notice, may I ask?'

'What's this?' said Angua. She picked up a wood-framed square from a heap of sawdust. 'This was its slate, was it?' She handed it to Carrot.

'"Thou Shalt Not Kill,"' Carrot read slowly. '"Clay of My Clay. Ashamed." Do you have any idea why it'd write that?'

'Search me,' said Skink. 'They're always doing dumb things.' He brightened up a bit. 'Hey, perhaps it went potty? Get it? Clay . . . pot . . . potty?'

'Extremely funny,' said Carrot gravely. 'I will take this as evidence. Good morning.'

'Why did you ask about pine logs?' he said to Angua as they stepped outside.

'I smelled the same pine resin in the cellar.'

'Pine resin's just pine resin, isn't it?'

'No. Not to me. That golem *was* in there.'

'They all were,' sighed Carrot. 'And now they're committing suicide.'

'You can't take life you haven't got,' said Angua.

'What shall we call it, then? "Destruction of property"?' said Carrot. 'Anyway, we can't ask them now . . .' He tapped the slate.

'They've given us the answers,' he said. 'Perhaps we can find out what the questions should have been.'

'What do you mean, "nothing"?' said Vimes. 'It's got to be the book! He licks his fingers to turn a page, and every day he gets a little dose of arsenic! Fiendishly clever!'

'Sorry, sir,' said Cheery, backing away. 'I can't find a trace. I've used all the tests I know.'

'You're sure?'

'I could send it up to the Unseen University. They've built a new morphic resonator in the High Energy Magic Building. Magic would easily—'

'Don't do that,' said Vimes. 'We'll keep the wizards out of this. Damn! For half an hour there I really thought I'd got it . . .'

He sat down at his desk. Something new was odd about the dwarf, but again he couldn't quite work out what it was.

'We're missing something here, Littlebottom,' he said.

'Yes, sir.'

'Let's look at the facts. If you want to poison someone slowly you've either got to give them small doses all the time – or, at least, every day. We've covered everything the Patrician does. It can't be the air in the room. You and I have been in there every day. It's not the food, we're pretty sure of that. Is something stinging him? Can you poison a wasp? What we need—'

''scuse me, sir.'

Vimes turned.

'Detritus? I thought you were off-duty?'

'I got dem to give me der address of dat maid called Easy like you said,' said Detritus, stoically. 'I went up dere and dere was people all lookin' in.'

'What d'you mean?'

'Neighbours and dat. Cryin' women all round

217

der door. An' I remember what you said about dat dipplo word—'

'Diplomacy,' said Vimes.

'Yeah. Not shoutin' at people an' dat. I fought, dis look a delicate situation. Also, dey was throwin' stuff at me. So I came back here. I writ down der address. An' now I'm goin' home.' He saluted, rocked slightly from the force of the blow to the side of his head, and departed.

'Thanks, Detritus,' said Vimes. He looked at the paper written in the troll's big round hand.

'1st Floor Back, 27 Cockbill Street,' he said. 'Good grief!'

'You know it, sir?'

'Should do. I was born in that street,' said Vimes. 'It's down below the Shades. Easy . . . Easy . . . Yes . . . *Now I* remember. There was a Mrs Easy down the road. Skinny woman. Did a lot of sewing. Big family. Well, we were all big families, it was the only way to keep warm . . .'

He frowned at the paper. It wasn't as if it were any particular lead. Maidservants were always going off to see their mothers, every time there was the least little family upset. What was it his granny had used to say? 'Yer son's yer son till he takes a wife, but yer daughter's yer daughter all yer life.' Sending a Watchman around would almost certainly be a waste of everyone's time . . .

'Well, well . . . Cockbill Street,' he said. He stared at the paper again. *You might as well rename the place Memory Lane.* No, you couldn't waste Watch resources on a wild-goose chase like that. But he might look in. On his way past. Some time today.

'Er . . . Littlebottom?'

'Sir?'

'On your . . . your lips. Red. Er. On your lips . . .'

'Lipstick, sir.'

'Oh . . . er. Lipstick? Fine. Lipstick.'

'Constable Angua gave it to me, sir.'

'That was kind of her,' said Vimes. 'I expect.'

It was called the Rats Chamber. In theory this was because of the decoration; some former resident of the palace had thought that a fresco of dancing rats would be a real decorative coup. There was a pattern of rats woven in the carpet. On the ceiling rats danced in a circle, their tails intertwining at the centre. After half an hour in that room, most people wanted a wash.

Soon, then, there would be a big rush on the hot water. The room was filling up fast.

By common consent the chair was taken and amply filled by Mrs Rosemary Palm, head of the Guild of Seamstresses*, as one of the most senior guild leaders.

'Quiet, please! Gentlemen!'

The noise level subsided a little.

'Dr Downey?' she said.

The head of the Assassins' Guild nodded. 'My friends, I think we are all aware of the situation—' he began.

---

*As they were euphemistically named. People said, 'They call themselves seamstresses – hem, hem!'

'Yeah, so's your accountant!' said a voice in the crowd. There was a ripple of nervous laughter but it didn't last long, because you don't laugh too loud at someone who knows exactly how much you're worth dead.

Dr Downey smiled. 'I can assure you once again, gentlemen – and ladies – that I am aware of no engagement regarding Lord Vetinari. In any case, I cannot imagine that an Assassin would use poison in this case. His lordship spent some time at the Assassins' school. He knows the uses of caution. No doubt he will recover.'

'And if he doesn't?' said Mrs Palm.

'No one lives for ever,' said Dr Downey, in the calm voice of a man who personally knew this to be true. 'Then, no doubt, we'll get a new ruler.'

The room went very silent.

The word 'Who?' hovered silently above every head.

'Thing is . . . the thing is . . .' said Gerhardt Sock, head of the Butchers' Guild, 'it's been . . . you've got to admit it . . . it's been . . . well, think about some of the others . . .'

The words 'Lord Snapcase, now . . . at least this one isn't actually insane' flickered in the group consciousness.

'I have to admit,' said Mrs Palm, 'that under Vetinari it has certainly been safer to walk the streets—'

'You should know, madam,' said Mr Sock. Mrs Palm gave him an icy look. There were a few sniggers.

'*I meant* that a modest payment to the Thieves' Guild is all that is required for perfect safety,' she finished.

'And, indeed, a man may visit a house of ill—'

'Negotiable hospitality,' said Mrs Palm quickly.

'Indeed, and be quite confident of not waking up stripped stark naked and beaten black and blue,' said Sock.

'Unless his tastes run that way,' said Mrs Palm. 'We aim to give satisfaction. Very accurately, if required.'

'Life has certainly been more reliable under Vetinari,' said Mr Potts of the Bakers' Guild.

'He does have all street-theatre players and mime artists thrown into the scorpion pit,' said Mr Boggis of the Thieves' Guild.

'True. But let's not forget that he has his bad points too. The man is capricious.'

'You think so? Compared to the ones we had before he's as reliable as a rock.'

'Snapcase was reliable,' said Mr Sock gloomily. 'Remember when he made his horse a city councillor?'

'You've got to admit it wasn't a *bad* councillor. Compared to some of the others.'

'As I recall, the others at that time were a vase of flowers, a heap of sand and three people who had been beheaded.'

'Remember all those fights? All the little gangs of thieves fighting all the time? It got so that there was hardly any energy left to actually steal things,' said Mr Boggis.

'Things are indeed more . . . reliable now.'

Silence descended again. That was it, wasn't it? Things were reliable now. Whatever else you said about old Vetinari, he made sure today was always followed by tomorrow. If you were murdered in your bed, at least it would be by arrangement.

'Things were more exciting under Lord Snapcase,' someone ventured.

'Yes, right up until the point when your head fell off.'

'The trouble is,' said Mr Boggis, 'that the job *makes* people mad. You take some chap who's no worse than any of us and after a few months he's talking to moss and having people flayed alive.'

'Vetinari isn't mad.'

'Depends how you look at it. No one can be as sane as he is without being mad.'

'I am only a weak woman,' said Mrs Palm, to the personal disbelief of several present, 'but it does seem to me that there's an opportunity here. Either there's a long struggle to sort out a successor, or we sort it out now. Yes?'

The guild leaders tried to look at one another while simultaneously avoiding everyone else's glances. Who'd be Patrician now? Once there'd have been a huge multi-sided power struggle, but now . . .

You got the power, but you got the problems, too. Things had changed. These days, you had to negotiate and juggle with all the conflicting interests. No one sane had tried to kill Vetinari for *years*, because the world with him in it was just preferable to one without him.

Besides . . . Vetinari had tamed Ankh-Morpork. He'd tamed it like a dog. He'd taken a minor scavenger among scavengers and lengthened its teeth and strengthened its jaws and built up its muscles and studded its collar and fed it lean steak and then he'd aimed it at the throat of the world.

He'd taken all the gangs and squabbling groups and made them see that a small slice of the cake on a regular basis was better by far than a bigger slice with a dagger in it. He'd made them see that it was better to take a small slice but *enlarge the cake.*

Ankh-Morpork, alone of all the cities of the plains, had opened its gates to dwarfs and trolls (alloys are stronger, Vetinari had said). It had worked. They made things. Often they made trouble, but mostly they made wealth. As a result, although Ankh-Morpork still had many enemies, those enemies had to finance their armies with borrowed money. Most of it was borrowed from Ankh-Morpork, at punitive interest. There hadn't been any really big wars for years. Ankh-Morpork had made them unprofitable.

Thousands of years ago the old empire had enforced the Pax Morporkia, which had said to the world: 'Do not fight, or we will kill you.' The Pax had arisen again, but this time it said: 'If you fight, we'll call in your mortgages. And incidentally, that's *my* pike you're pointing at me. I paid for that shield you're holding. And take my helmet off when you speak to me, you horrible little debtor.'

And now the whole machine, which whirred away so quietly that people had forgotten it was a machine at all and thought that it was just the way the world worked, had given a lurch.

The guild leaders examined their thoughts and decided that what they did not want was power. What they wanted was that tomorrow should be pretty much like today.

'There's the dwarfs,' said Mr Boggis. 'Even if one of us – not that I'm saying it would be one of us, of course – even if *someone* took over, what about the dwarfs? We get someone like Snapcase again, there's going to be chopped kneecaps in the streets.'

'You're not suggesting we have some sort of . . . *vote,* are you? Some kind of *popularity* contest?'

'Oh, no. It's just . . . it's just . . . all more complicated now. And power goes to people's heads.'

'And then other people's heads fall off.'

'I wish you wouldn't keep on saying that, whoever you are,' said Mrs Palm. 'Anyone would think *you'd* had your head cut off.'

'Uh—'

'Oh, it's you, Mr Slant. I do apologize.'

'Speaking as the President of the Guild of Lawyers,' said Mr Slant, the most respected zombie in Ankh-Morpork, 'I must recommend stability in this matter. I wonder if I may offer some advice?'

'How much will it cost us?' said Mr Sock.

'Stability,' said Mr Slant, 'equals monarchy.'

'Oh, now, don't tell us—'

'Look at Klatch,' said Mr Slant doggedly. 'Generations of Seriphs. Result: political stability. Take Pseudopolis. Or Sto Lat. Or even the Agatean Empire—'

'Come *on*,' said Dr Downey. 'Everyone knows that kings—'

'Oh, monarchs come and go, they depose one another, and so on and so forth,' said Mr Slant. 'But the *institution* goes on. Besides, I think you'll find that it is possible to work out . . . an accommodation.'

He realized that he had the floor. His fingers absent-mindedly touched the seam where his head had been sewn back on. All those years ago Mr Slant had refused to die until he had been paid for the disbursements in the matter of conducting his own defence.

'How do you mean?' said Mr Potts.

'I accept that the question of resurrecting the Ankh-Morpork succession has been raised several times recently,' said Mr Slant.

'Yes. By madmen,' said Mr Boggis. 'It's part of the symptoms. Put underpants on head, talk to trees, drool, decide that Ankh-Morpork needs a king . . .'

'Exactly. Supposing *sane* men were to give it consideration?'

'Go on,' said Dr Downey.

'There have been precedents,' said Mr Slant. 'Monarchies who have found themselves bereft of a convenient monarch have . . . obtained one. Some suitably born member of some other royal line. After all, what is required is someone who, uh, knows the ropes, as I believe the saying goes.'

'Sorry? Are you saying we *send out* for a king?' said Mr Boggis. 'We put up some kind of advertisement? "Throne vacant, applicant must supply own crown"?'

'In fact,' said Mr Slant, ignoring this, 'I recall that, during the first Empire, Genua wrote to Ankh-Morpork and asked to be sent one of our generals to be their king, their own royal lines having died out through interbreeding so intensively that the last king kept trying to breed with himself. The history books say that we sent our loyal General Tacticus, whose first act after obtaining the crown was to declare a war on Ankh-Morpork. Kings are . . . interchangeable.'

'You mentioned something about reaching an accommodation,' said Mr Boggis. 'You mean, we tell a *king* what to *do*?'

'I like the sound of that,' said Mrs Palm.

'I like the echoes,' said Dr Downey.

'Not *tell*,' said Mr Slant. 'We . . . agree. Obviously, as king, he would concentrate on those things traditionally associated with kingship—'

'Waving,' said Mr Sock.

'Being gracious,' said Mrs Palm.

'Welcoming ambassadors from foreign countries,' said Mr Potts.

'Shaking hands.'

'Cutting off heads—'

'No! No. No, that will not be part of his duties. Minor affairs of state will be carried out—'

'By his advisors?' said Dr Downey. He leaned back. 'I'm sure I can see where this is going, Mr Slant,' he said. 'But kings, once acquired, are so damn hard to get rid of. Acceptably.'

'There have been precedents for that, too,' said Mr Slant.

The Assassin's eyes narrowed.

'I'm intrigued, Mr Slant, that as soon as the Lord Vetinari appears to be seriously ill, you pop up with suggestions like this. It sounds like . . . a remarkable coincidence.'

'There is no mystery, I assure you. Destiny works its course. Surely many of you have heard the rumours – that there is, in this city, someone with a bloodline traceable all the way back to the last royal family? Someone working in this very city in a comparatively humble position? A lowly Watchman, in fact?'

There were some nods, but not very definite ones. They were to nods what a grunt is to 'yes'. The guilds all picked up information. No one wanted to reveal how much, or how little, they personally knew, just in case they knew too little or, even worse, turned out to know too much.

However, Doc Pseudopolis of the Guild of Gamblers put on a careful poker face and said, 'Yes, but the tricentennial is coming up. And in a few years it'll be the Century of the Rat. There's something about centuries that gives people a kind of fever.'

'Nevertheless, the person exists,' said Mr Slant. 'The evidence stares one in the face if one looks in the right places.'

'Very well,' said Mr Boggis. 'Tell us the name of this captain.' He often lost large sums at poker.

'Captain?' said Mr Slant. 'I'm sorry to say his natural talents have thus far not commended him to that extent. He is a corporal. Corporal C. W. St J. Nobbs.'

There was silence.

And then there was a strange putt-putting sound, like water negotiating its way through a partially blocked pipe.

Queen Molly of the Beggars' Guild had so far been silent apart from occasional damp sucking noises as she tried to dislodge a particle of her lunch from the things which, because they were still in her mouth and apparently attached, were technically her teeth.

Now she was laughing. The hairs wobbled on every wart. 'Nobby Nobbs?' she said. 'You're talking about *Nobby Nobbs*?'

'He is the last known descendant of the Earl of Ankh, who could trace *his* descent all the way to a distant cousin to the last king,' said Mr Slant. 'It's the talk of the city.'

'A picture forms in my mind,' said Dr Downey. 'Small monkeylike chap, always smoking very short cigarettes. Spotty. He squeezes them in public.'

'That's Nobby!' Queen Molly chuckled. 'Face like a blind carpenter's thumb!'

'Him? But the man's a tit!'

'And dim as a penny candle,' said Mr Boggis. 'I don't see—'

Suddenly he stopped, and then contracted the contemplative silence that was gradually affecting everyone else around the table.

'Don't see why we shouldn't . . . give this . . . due consideration,' he said, after a while.

The assembled leaders looked at the table. Then they looked at the ceiling. Then they studiously avoided one another's gaze.

'Blood *will* out,' said Mr Carry.

'When I've watched him go down the street I've always thought: "There's a man who walks in greatness,"' said Mrs Palm.

'He squeezes them in a very regal way, mind you. Very graciously.'

The silence rolled over the assembly again. But it was busy, in the same way that the silence of an anthill is busy.

'I must remind you, ladies and gentlemen, that poor Lord Vetinari is still alive,' said Mrs Palm.

'Indeed, indeed,' said Mr Slant. 'And long may he remain so. I've merely set out for you one option against that day, may it be a long time coming, when we should consider a . . . successor.'

'In any case,' said Dr Downey, 'there is no doubt that Vetinari has been over-doing it. If he survives – which is greatly to be hoped, of course – I feel we should require him to step down for the sake of his health. Well done thou good and faithful servant, and so on. Buy him a nice house in the country somewhere. Give him a pension. Make sure there's a seat for him at official dinners. Obviously, if he can be so easily poisoned now he should welcome the release from the chains of office . . .'

'What about the wizards?' said Mr Boggis.

'They've never got involved in civic concerns,' said Dr Downey. 'Give 'em four meat meals a day and tip your hat to them and they're happy. They know nothing about politics.'

The silence that followed was broken by the

voice of Queen Molly of the Beggars. 'What about Vimes?'

Dr Downey shrugged. 'He is a servant of the city.'

'That's what I mean.'

'Surely *we* represent the city?'

'Hah! He won't see it that way. And you know what Vimes thinks about kings. It was a Vimes who chopped the head off the last one. *There's* a bloodline that thinks a swing of an axe can solve anything.'

'Now, Molly, you know Vimes'd probably take an axe to Vetinari if he thought he could get away with it. No love lost there, I fancy.'

'He won't like it. That's all I tell you. Vetinari keeps Vimes wound up. No knowing what happens if he unwinds all at once—'

'He's a public servant!' snapped Dr Downey.

Queen Molly made a face, which was not difficult in one so naturally well endowed, and sat back. 'So this is the new way of things, is it?' she muttered. 'Lot of ordinary men sit around a table and talk and suddenly the world's a different place? The sheep turn round and charge the shepherd?'

'There's a soirée at Lady Selachii's house this evening,' said Dr Downey, ignoring her. 'I believe Nobbs is being invited. Perhaps we can . . . meet him.'

Vimes told himself he was really going to inspect the progress on the new Watch House in Chittling Street. Cockbill Street was just round the corner. And then he'd call in, informally. No sense in sparing a man when they were pushed anyway, what with these murders and Vetinari and Detritus's anti-Slab crusade.

He turned the corner, and stopped.

Nothing much had changed. That was the shocking thing. After . . . oh, too many years . . . things had no *right* not to have changed.

But washing lines still criss-crossed the street between the grey, ancient buildings. Antique paint still peeled in the way cheap paint peeled when it had been painted on wood too old and rotten to take paint. Cockbill Street people were usually too penniless to afford decent paint, but always far too proud to use whitewash.

And the place was slightly smaller than he remembered. That was all.

When had he last come down here? He couldn't remember. It was beyond the Shades, and up until quite recently the Watch had tended to leave that area to its own unspeakable devices.

Unlike the Shades, though, Cockbill Street was clean, with the haunting, empty cleanliness you get when people can't afford to waste dirt. For Cockbill Street was where people lived who were worse than poor, because they didn't *know* how poor they were. If you asked them they would probably say something like 'mustn't grumble' or 'there's far worse off than us' or 'we've always kept uz heads above water and we don't owe nobody nowt'.

He could hear his granny speaking. 'No one's too poor to buy soap.' Of course, many people were. But in Cockbill Street they bought soap just the same. The table might not have any food on it but, by gods, it was well scrubbed. That was Cockbill Street, where what you mainly ate was your pride.

What a mess the world was in, Vimes reflected. Constable Visit had told him the meek would inherit it, and what had the poor devils done to deserve *that*?

Cockbill Street people would stand aside to let the meek through. For what kept them in Cockbill Street, mentally and physically, was their vague comprehension that there were *rules*. And they went through life filled with a quiet, distracted dread that they weren't quite obeying them.

People said that there was one law for the rich and one law for the poor, but it wasn't true. There was no law for those who made the law, and no law for the incorrigibly lawless. All the laws and rules were for those people stupid enough to think like Cockbill Street people.

It was oddly quiet. Normally there'd be swarms of kids, and carts heading down towards the docks, but today the place had a shut-in look.

In the middle of the road was a chalked hopscotch path.

Vimes felt his knees go weak. It was still here! When had he last seen it? Thirty-five years ago? Forty? So it must have been drawn and redrawn thousands of times.

He'd been pretty good at it. Of course, they'd played it by Ankh-Morpork rules. Instead of kicking a stone they'd kicked William Scuggins. It had been just one of the many inventive games they'd played which had involved kicking, chasing or jumping on

232

William Scuggins until he threw one of his famous wobblers and started frothing and violently attacking himself.

Vimes had been able to drop William in the square of his choice nine times out of ten. The tenth time, William bit his leg.

In those days, tormenting William and finding enough to eat had made for a simple, straightforward life. There weren't so many questions you didn't know the answers to, except maybe how to stop your leg festering.

Sir Samuel looked around, saw the silent street, and flicked a stone out of the gutter with his foot. Then he booted it surreptitiously along the squares, adjusted his cloak, and hopped and jumped his way up, turned, hopped—

What was it you shouted as you hopped? 'Salt, mustard, vinegar, pepper?'? No? Or was it the one that went 'William Scuggins is a bastard'? Now he'd wonder about that all day.

A door opened across the street. Vimes froze, one leg in mid-air, as two black-clothed figures came out slowly and awkwardly.

This was because they were carrying a coffin.

The natural solemnity of the occasion was diminished by their having to squeeze around it and out into the street, pulling the casket after them and allowing two other pairs of bearers to edge their way into the daylight.

Vimes remembered himself in time to lower his other foot, and then remembered even more of himself and snatched his helmet off in respect.

Another coffin emerged. It was a lot smaller. It needed only two people to carry it and that was really one too many.

As mourners trooped out behind them, Vimes fumbled in a pocket for the scrap of paper Detritus had given him. The scene was, in its way, funny, like the bit in a circus where the coach stops and a dozen clowns get out of it. Apartment houses round here made up for their limited number of rooms by having a large number of people occupy them.

He found the paper and unfolded it. First Floor Back, 27 Cockbill Street.

And this was it. He'd arrived in time for a funeral. Two funerals.

'Looks like it's a really bad day to be a golem,' said Angua. There was a pottery hand lying in the gutter. 'That's the third one we've seen smashed in the street.'

There was a crash up ahead, and a dwarf came through a window more or less horizontally. His iron helmet struck sparks as he hit the street, but the dwarf was soon up again and plunging back through the adjacent doorway.

He emerged via the window a moment later but was fielded by Carrot, who set him on his feet.

'Hello, Mr Oresmiter! Are you keeping well? And what is happening here?'

'It's that devil Gimlet, Captain Carrot! You should be arresting him!'

'Why, what's he done?'

'He's been poisoning people, that's what!'

234

Carrot glanced at Angua, then back at Oresmiter. 'Poison?' he said. 'That's a very serious allegation.'

'You're telling me! I was up all night with Mrs Oresmiter! I didn't think much about it until I came in here this morning and there were other people complaining—'

He tried to struggle out of Carrot's grip. 'You know what?' he said. 'You know *what*? We looked in his cold room and you know what? You know *what*? You know what he's been selling as meat?'

'Tell me,' said Carrot.

'Pork and beef!'

'Oh, dear.'

'And lamb!'

'Tch, tch.'

'Hardly any rat at all!'

Carrot shook his head at the duplicity of traders.

'And Snori Glodssonsunclesson said he had Rat Surprise last night and he'll swear there were *chicken* bones in it!'

Carrot let go of the dwarf. 'You stay here,' he said to Angua and, head bowed, stepped inside Gimlet's Hole Food Delicatessen.

An axe spun towards him. He caught it almost absent-mindedly and tossed it casually aside.

'Ow!'

There was a mêlée of dwarfs around the counter. The row had already gone well past the stage when it had anything much to do with the subject in hand and, these being dwarfs, now included matters of vital importance such as whose grandfather had stolen whose grandfather's mining claim three hundred years ago and whose axe was at whose throat right now.

But there was something about Carrot's presence. The fighting gradually stopped. The fighters tried to look as if they'd just happened to be standing there. There was a sudden and general 'Axe? What axe? Oh, *this* axe? I was just showing it to my friend Bjorn here, good old Bjorn' feel to the atmosphere.

'All right,' said Carrot. 'What's all this about poison? Mr Gimlet first.'

'It's a diabolical lie!' shouted Gimlet, from somewhere under the heap. 'I run a wholesome restaurant! My tables are so clean you could eat your dinner off them!'

Carrot raised his hands to stop the outburst this caused. 'Someone said something about rats,' he said.

'I told them, I use only the very best rats!' shouted Gimlet. 'Good plump rats from the best locations! None of your latrine rubbish! And they're hard to come by, let me tell you!'

'And when you can't get them, Mr Gimlet?' said Carrot.

Gimlet paused. Carrot was hard to lie to. 'All right,' he mumbled. 'Maybe when there's not enough I might sort of plump out the stock with some chicken, maybe just a bit of beef—'

'Hah! A *bit*?' More voices were raised.

'That's right, you should see his cold room, Mr Carrot!'

'Yeah, he uses *steak* and cuts little legs in it and covers it with rat sauce!'

'I don't know, you try to do your best at very reasonable prices and this is the thanks you get?' said Gimlet hotly. 'It's hard enough to make ends meet as it is!'

'*You* don't even make 'em of the *right* meat!'

Carrot sighed. There were no public health laws in Ankh-Morpork. It would be like installing smoke detectors in Hell.

'All *right*,' he said. 'But you can't get poisoned by steak. No, honestly. No. No, *shut up*, all of you. No, I don't care *what* your mothers told you. Now, I want to know about this poisoning, Gimlet.'

Gimlet struggled to his feet.

'We did Rat Surprise last night for the Sons of Bloodaxe annual dinner,' he said. There was a general groan. 'And it *was* rat.' He raised his voice against the complaining. 'You can't use anything else – *listen* – you've got to have the noses poking through the pastry, all right? Some of the best rat we've had in for a long time, let me tell you!'

'And you were all ill afterwards?' said Carrot, taking out his notebook.

'Sweating all night!'

'Couldn't see straight!'

'I reckon I know every knothole on the back of the privy door!'

'I'll write that down as a "definitely",' said Carrot. 'Was there anything else on the dinner menu?'

'Vole-au-vents and Cream of Rat,' said Gimlet. 'All hygienically prepared.'

'How do you mean, "hygienically prepared"?' said Carrot.

'The chef is under strict orders to wash his hands afterwards.'

The assembled dwarfs nodded. This was certainly pretty hygienic. You didn't want people going around with ratty hands.

'Anyway, you've all been eating here for *years*,' said Gimlet, sensing this slight veer in his direction. 'This is the first time there's been any trouble, isn't it? My rats are famous!'

'Your chicken's going to be pretty famous, too,' said Carrot.

There was laughter this time. Even Gimlet joined in. 'All right, I'm sorry about the chicken. But it was that or very poor rats, and you know I only buy from Wee Mad Arthur. He's trustworthy, whatever else you may say about him. You just can't get better rats. Everyone knows that.'

'That'll be Wee Mad Arthur in Gleam Street?' said Carrot.

'Yes. Not a mark on 'em, most of the time.'

'Have you got any left?'

'One or two.' Gimlet's expression changed. 'Here, you don't think *he* poisoned them, do you? I never did trust that little bugger!'

'Enquiries are continuing,' said Carrot. He tucked his notebook away. 'I'd like some rats, please. *Those* rats. To go.' He glanced at the menu, patted his pocket and looked questioningly out through the door at Angua.

'You don't have to *buy* them,' she said wearily. 'They're *evidence*.'

'We can't defraud an innocent tradesman who

may be the victim of circumstances,' said Carrot.

'You want ketchup?' said Gimlet. 'Only they're extra with ketchup.'

The funeral carriage went slowly through the streets. It looked quite expensive, but that was Cockbill Street for you. People put money by. Vimes remembered that. You always put money by, in Cockbill Street. You saved up for a rainy day even if it was pouring already. And you'd die of shame if people thought you could afford only a cheap funeral.

Half a dozen black-clad mourners came along behind, together with perhaps a score of people who had tried at least to look respectable.

Vimes followed the procession at a distance all the way to the cemetery behind the Temple of Small Gods, where he lurked awkwardly among the gravestones and sombre graveyard trees while the priest mumbled on.

The gods had made the people of Cockbill Street poor, honest and provident, Vimes reflected. They might as well have hung signs saying 'Kick me' on their backs and had done with it. Yet Cockbill Street people tended towards religion, at least of the less demonstrative kind. They always put a little life by for a rainy eternity.

Eventually the crowd around the graves broke up and drifted away with the aimless look of people whose immediate future contains ham rolls.

Vimes spotted a tearful young woman in the main group and advanced carefully. 'Er . . . are you Mildred Easy?' he said.

She nodded. 'Who are you?' She took in the cut of his coat and added, 'sir?'

'Was that old Mrs Easy who used to do dressmaking?' said Vimes, taking her gently aside.

'That's right . . .'

'And the . . . smaller coffin?'

'That was our William . . .'

The girl looked as if she were about to cry again.

'Can we have a talk?' said Vimes. 'There are some things I hope you can tell me.'

He hated the way his mind worked. A proper human being would have shown respect and quietly walked away. But, as he'd stood among the chilly stones, a horrible apprehension had stolen over him that almost all the answers were in place now, if only he could work out the questions.

She looked around at the other mourners. They had reached the gate and were staring back curiously at the two of them.

'Er . . . I know this isn't the right time,' said Vimes. 'But, when the kids play hopscotch in the street, what's the rhyme they sing? "Salt, mustard, vinegar, pepper?", isn't it?'

She stared at his worried grin. 'That's a skipping rhyme,' she said coldly. 'When they play hopscotch they sing "Billy Skunkins is a brass stud". Who are you?'

'I'm Commander Vimes of the Watch,' said Vimes. So . . . Willy Scuggins would live on in the street, in disguise and in a fashion . . . And old Stoneface was just some guy on a bonfire . . .

Then her tears came.

'It's all right, it's all right,' said Vimes, as sooth-
ingly as he could. 'I was brought up in Cockbill
Street, that's why I . . . I mean I'm . . . I'm not here
on . . . I'm not out to . . . look, I *know* you took food
home from the palace. That's all right by me. I'm *not*
here to . . . oh, damn, would you like my handkerchief? I think your one's full.'

'Everyone does it!'

'Yes, I know.'

'Anyway, cook never says nothing . . .' She began
to sob again.

'Yes, yes.'

'Everyone takes a few things,' said Mildred Easy.
'It's not like *stealing*.'

It is, thought Vimes treacherously. *But I don't
give a damn.*

And now . . . he'd got a grip on the long copper
rod and was climbing into a high place while the
thunder muttered around him. 'The, er, the last food
you sto— were given,' he said. 'What was it?'

'Just some blancmange and some, you know, that
sort of jam made out of meat . . .'

'Pâté?'

'Yes. I thought it would be a little treat . . .'

Vimes nodded. Rich, mushy food. The sort you'd
give to a baby who was peaky and to a granny who
hadn't got any teeth.

Well, he was on the roof now, the clouds were
black and threatening, and he might as well wave the
lightning conductor. Time to ask . . .

The wrong question, as it proved.

'Tell me,' he said, 'what did Mrs Easy die of?'

*   *   *

'Let me put it like this,' said Cheery. 'If these rats had been poisoned with lead instead of arsenic, you'd have been able to sharpen their noses and use them as a pencil.'

She lowered the beaker.

'Are you sure?' said Carrot.

'Yes.'

'Wee Mad Arthur wouldn't poison rats, would he? Especially not rats that were going to be eaten.'

'I've heard he doesn't like dwarfs much,' said Angua.

'Yes, but business is business. *No one* who does a lot of business with dwarfs likes them much, and he must supply every dwarf café and delicatessen in the city.'

'Maybe they ate arsenic before he caught them?' said Angua. 'People use it as a rat poison, after all . . .'

'Yes,' said Carrot, in a very deliberate way. 'They do.'

'You're not suggesting that *Vetinari* tucks into a nice rat every day?' said Angua.

'I've heard he uses rats as spies, so I don't think he uses them as elevenses,' said Carrot. 'But it'd be nice to know where Wee Mad Arthur gets his from, don't you think?'

'Commander Vimes said *he* was looking after the Vetinari case,' said Angua.

'But we're just finding out why Gimlet's rats are full of arsenic,' said Carrot, innocently. 'Anyway, I was going to ask Sergeant Colon to look into it.'

'But . . . Wee Mad Arthur?' said Angua. 'He's mad.'

'Fred can take Nobby with him. I'll go and tell him. Um. Cheery?'

'Yes, Captain?'

'You've been, er, you've been trying to hide your face from me . . . oh. Did someone hit you?'

'No, sir!'

'Only your eyes look a bit bruised and your lips—'

'I'm fine, sir!' said Cheery desperately.

'Oh, well, if you say so. I'll . . . er, I'll . . . look for Sergeant Colon, then . . .'

He backed out, embarrassed.

That left the two of them. *All girls together,* thought Angua. *One normal girl between the two of us, at any rate.*

'I don't think the mascara works,' Angua said. 'The lipstick's fine but the mascara . . . I don't think so.'

'I think I need practice.'

'You sure you want to keep the beard?'

'You don't mean . . . *shave?*' Cheery backed away.

'All right, all right. What about the iron helmet?'

'It belonged to my grandmother! It's *dwarfish!*'

'Fine. Fine. Okay. You've made a good start, anyway.'

'Er . . . what do you think of . . . this?' said Cheery, handing her a bit of paper.

Angua read it. It was a list of names, although most of them were crossed out:

~~Cheery Littlebottom~~
~~Cheery~~
~~Sherry~~
~~Sherri~~
Lucinda Littlebottom
~~Sharry~~
~~Sharri~~
Cheri

'Er . . . what do you think?' said Cheery nervously.

'"Lucinda"?' said Angua, raising her eyebrows.

'I've always liked the sound of the name.'

'"Cheri" is nice,' said Angua. 'And it *is* rather like the one you've got already. The way people spell in this town, no one will actually notice unless you point it out to them.'

Cheery's shoulders sagged with released tension. When you've made up your mind to shout out who you are to the world, it's a relief to know that you can do it in a whisper.

'*Cheri*', thought Angua. *Now, what does that name conjure up? Does the mental picture include iron boots, iron helmet, a small worried face and a long beard?*

Well, it does now.

Somewhere underneath Ankh-Morpork a rat went about its business, ambling unconcernedly through the ruins of a damp cellar. It turned a corner towards the grain store it knew was up ahead, and almost walked into another rat.

This one was standing on its hind-legs, though, and wearing a tiny black robe and carrying a scythe. Such of its snout that could be seen was bone-white.

SQUEAK? it said.

Then the vision faded and revealed a slightly smaller figure. There was nothing in the least ratlike about it, apart from its size. It was human, or at least humanoid. It was dressed in ratskin trousers but was bare above the waist, apart from two bandoliers that criss-crossed its chest. And it was smoking a tiny cigar.

It raised a very small crossbow and fired.

The soul of the rat – for anything so similar in so many ways to human beings certainly has a soul – watched gloomily as the figure took its recent habitation by the tail and towed it away. Then it looked up at the Death of Rats.

'Squeak?' it said.

The Grim Squeaker nodded.

SQUEAK.

A minute later Wee Mad Arthur emerged into the daylight, dragging the rat behind him. There were fifty-seven neatly lined up along the wall, but despite his name Wee Mad Arthur made a point of not killing the young and the pregnant females. It's always a good idea to make sure you've got a job tomorrow.

His sign was still tacked up over the hole. Wee Mad Arthur, as the only insect and vermin exterminator able to meet the enemy on its own terms, found that it paid to advertise.

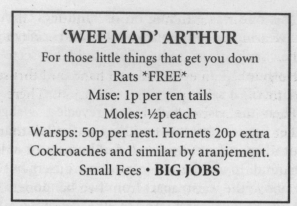

'WEE MAD' ARTHUR

For those little things that get you down

Rats *FREE*

Mise: 1p per ten tails

Moles: ½p each

Warsps: 50p per nest. Hornets 20p extra

Cockroaches and similar by aranjement.

Small Fees • **BIG JOBS**

Arthur took out the world's smallest notebook and a piece of pencil lead. See here, now . . . fifty-eight skins at two a penny, City bounty for the tails at a penny per ten, and the carcases to Gimlet at tuppence per three, the hard-driving dwarf bastard that he was . . .

There was a moment's shadow, and then someone stamped on him.

'Right,' said the owner of the boot. 'Still catching rats without a Guild card, are you? Easiest ten dollars we ever earned, Sid. Let's go and—'

The man was lifted several inches off the ground, whirled around, and hurled against the wall. His companion stared as a streak of dust raced across his boot, but reacted too late.

'He's gone up me trouser! He's gone up me – *arrgh*!'

There was a *crack*.

'Me knee! Me knee! He's broken me knee!'

The man who had been flung aside tried to get up, but something scurried across his chest and landed astride his nose.

'Hey, pal?' said Wee Mad Arthur. 'Can yer mother sew, pal? Yeah? Then get her to stitch this one!'

He grabbed an eyelid in each hand and thrust his head forward with pin-point precision. There was another *crack* as the skulls met.

The man with the broken knee tried to drag himself away but Wee Mad Arthur leapt from his stunned comrade and proceeded to kick him. The kicks of a man not much more than six inches high should not hurt, but Wee Mad Arthur seemed to have a lot more mass than his size would allow. Being nutted by Arthur was like being hit by a steel ball from a slingshot. A kick seemed to have all the power of one from a large man, but very painfully concentrated into a smaller area.

'Yez can tell them buggers at the Rat-Catchers' Guild that I works for whoze I want and charges what I like,' he said, between kicks. 'And them shites can stop tryin' to persecute the small business-man . . .'

The other guild enforcer made it to the end of the alley. Arthur gave Sid a final kick and left him in the gutter.

Wee Mad Arthur walked back to his task, shaking his head. He worked for nothing and sold his rats for half the official rate, a heinous crime. Yet Wee Mad Arthur was growing rich because the guild hadn't got its joint heads around the idea of fiscal relativity.

Arthur charged a lot *more* for his services. A lot more, that is, from the specialized and above all *low*

point of view of Wee Mad Arthur. What Ankh-
Morpork had yet to understand was that the smaller
you are the more your money is worth.

A dollar for a human bought a loaf of bread that
was eaten in a few bites. The same dollar for Wee
Mad Arthur bought the same-sized loaf, but it was
food for a week and could then be further hollowed
out and used as a bedroom.

The size-differential problem was also responsible for his frequent drunkenness. Few publicans
were prepared to sell beer by the thimbleful or had
gnome-sized mugs. Wee Mad Arthur had to go
drinking in a swimming costume.

But he liked his work. No one could clear out
rats like Wee Mad Arthur. Old and cunning rats
that knew all about traps, deadfalls and poison were
helpless in the face of his attack, which was where, in
fact, he often attacked. The last thing they felt was a
hand gripping each of their ears, and the last thing
they saw was his forehead, approaching at speed.

Muttering under his breath, Wee Mad Arthur got
back to his calculations. But not for long.

He spun around, forehead cocked.

'It's only us, Wee Mad Arthur,' said Sergeant
Colon, stepping back hurriedly.

'That's *Mr* Wee Mad Arthur to youse, copper,'
said Wee Mad Arthur, but he relaxed a little.

'We're Sergeant Colon and Corporal Nobbs,' said
Colon.

'Yeah, you remember us, don't you?' said Nobby,
in a wheedling voice. 'We was the ones who helped you
when you was fighting them three dwarfs last week.'

'Yez pulled me off 'f them, if that's what you mean,' said Wee Mad Arthur. 'Just when I'd got 'em all down.'

'We want to talk to you about some rats,' said Colon.

'Can't take on any more customers,' said Wee Mad Arthur firmly.

'Some rats you sold to Gimlet's Hole Food Delicatessen a few days ago.'

'What's that to yez?'

'He reckons they was poisoned,' said Nobby, who had taken the precaution of moving behind Colon.

'I never uses poison!'

Colon realized he was backing away from a man six inches high. 'Yeah, well . . . see . . . fing is . . . you being in fights and that . . . you don't get on with dwarfs . . . some people might say . . . fing is . . . it could look like you might have a grudge.' He took another step back and almost tripped over Nobby.

'Grudge? Why should I have a grudge, pal? It ain't me that gets the kicking!' said Wee Mad Arthur, advancing.

'Good point. Good point,' said Colon. 'Only it'd help, right, if you could tell us . . . where you got those rats from . . .'

'Like the Patrician's palace, maybe,' said Nobby.

'The palace? No one catches rats at the palace. That's not allowed. No, I remember those rats. They wuz good fat ones, I wanted a penny each, but he held out for four for threepence, th' ole skinflint that he is.'

'Where did you get them, then?'

Wee Mad Arthur shrugged. 'Down the cattle market. I do the cattle market Tuesdays. Couldn't tell yez where they came from. Them tunnels guz everywhere, see?'

'Could they've eaten poison before you caught them?' said Colon.

Wee Mad Arthur bristled. 'No one puts down poison round there. I won't have it, see? I got all the contracts along the Shambles, and I won't deal with any gobshite who uses poison. I doesn't charge for extermination, see? Guild *hates* that. But I chooses me customers.' Wee Mad Arthur grinned wickedly. 'I only guz where's there's the finest eating for the rats and I clean up flogging 'em to the lawn ornaments. I find anyone using poison on my patch, they can pay guild rates for guild work, hah, and see how they like it.'

'I can see you're going to be a big man in industrial catering,' said Colon.

Wee Mad Arthur put his head on one side. 'D'youse know what happened to the last man that made a crack like that?' he said.

'Er . . . no . . . ?' said Colon.

'Neither does anyone else,' said Wee Mad Arthur, ''cos he *was never found*. Have yez finished? Only I got a wasps' nest to clean out before I go home.'

'So you were catching them under the Shambles?' Colon persisted.

'All the way along. 'S a good beat. There's tanners, tallow men, butchers, sausage-makers . . . That's good grazing, if you're a rat.'

'Yeah, right,' said Colon. 'Fair enough. Well, I reckon we've taken up enough of your time—'

'How d'you catch wasps?' said Nobby, intrigued. 'Smoke 'em out?'

''Tis unsporting not to hit them on the wing,' said Wee Mad Arthur. 'But if it's a busy day I make up squibs out of that No. 1 black powder the alchemists sell.' He indicated the laden bandoliers over his shoulders.

'You blow them up?' said Nobby. 'That don't sound too sporting.'

'Yeah? Just ever tried settin' and lightin' half a dozen fuses and then fightin' your way back out of the entrance before the first one goes off?'

'It's a wild-goose chase, Sarge,' said Nobby, as they strolled away. 'Some rats et some poison somewhere and he got them. What're we supposed to do about it? Poisonin' rats ain't illegal.'

Colon scratched his chin. 'I think we could be in a bit of trouble, Nobby,' he said. 'I mean, everyone's been bustling around detectoring and we could end up looking a right couple of noddies. I mean, do you want to go back to the Yard and say we talked to Wee Mad Arthur and he said it wasn't him, end of story? We're humans, right? Well, *I* am and I know you probably are – and we're definitely bringing up the rear around here. I'm telling you, this ain't my Watch any more, Nobby. Trolls, dwarfs, gargoyles . . . I've nothing against them, you know me, but I'm looking forward to my little farm with chickens round the door. And I wouldn't mind goin' out with something to be proud of.'

'Well, what do you want us to do? Knock on

every door round the cattle market and ask 'em if they've got any arsenic in the place?'

'Yep,' said Colon. 'Walk and talk. That's what Vimes always says.'

'There's hundreds of 'em! Anyway, they'd say no.'

'Right, but we got to *arsk*. 'T'aint like it used to be, Nobby. This is modern policing. Detectoring. These days, we got to get results. I mean, the Watch is getting bigger. I don't mind ole Detritus bein' a sergeant, he's not bad when you get to know him, but one of these days it could be a dwarf giving out orders, Nobby. It's all right for me 'cos I'll be out on my farm—'

'Nailin' chickens round the door,' said Nobby.

'—but you've got your future to think about. An', the way things are going, maybe the Watch'll be looking for another captain. It'd be a right bugger if he turned out to have a name like Stronginthearm, eh, or Shale. So you'd better look smart.'

'*You* never wanted to be a captain, Fred?'

'Me? A hofficer? I have my pride, Nobby. I've nothing against hofficering for them as is called to it, but it's not for the likes of me. My place is with the common man.'

'I wish mine was,' said Nobby gloomily. 'Look what was in my pigeonhole this morning.'

He handed the sergeant a square of card, with gold edging. '"Lady Selachii will be At Home this p.m. from five onwards, and requests the pleasure of the company of Lord de Nobbes,"' he read.

'Oh.'

'I've heard about these rich ole women,' said Nobby, dejectedly. 'I reckon she wants me to be a giggle-low, is that right?'

'Nah, nah,' said the sergeant, looking at passion's most unlikely plaything. 'I know this stuff from my uncle. "At Home" is like a bit of a drinks do. It's where all you nobs hob-nob, Nobby. You just drink and scoff and talk about literachoor and the arts.'

'I haven't got any posh clothes,' said Nobby.

'Ah, that's where *you* score, Nobby,' said Colon. 'Uniforms is okay. Adds a bit of tone, in fact. Especially if you look dashing,' he said, ignoring the evidence that Nobby was, in fact, merely runny.

'Is that a fact?' said Nobby, brightening up a bit. 'I've got a lot more of 'em invites, too,' he said. 'Posh cards what look like they've been nibbled along the edges with gold teeth. Dinners, balls, all kinds of stuff.'

Colon looked down at his friend. A strange and yet persuasive thought crept into his mind. 'We-ell,' he said, 'it's the end of the social Season, see? Time's running out.'

'What for?'

'We-ell . . . could be all them posh women want to marry you off to their daughters who're in Season . . .'

'What?'

'Nothing beats an earl except a duke, and we haven't got one of them. And we ain't got a king, neither. The Earl of Ankh would be what they calls a social catch.' Yes, it was easier if he said it to himself like that. If you substituted 'Nobby Nobbs' for 'Earl of Ankh' it didn't work. But it *did* work when you just said 'Earl of Ankh'. There'd be many women who'd be happy to be the mother-in-law of the Earl of Ankh even if it meant having Nobby Nobbs into the bargain.

Well, a few, anyway.

Nobby's eyes gleamed. 'Never *thought* of that,' he said. 'And some of these girls have a bit of cash, too?'

'More'n you, Nobby.'

'And of course I owes it to my posterity to see that the line of Nobbses doesn't die out,' Nobby added, thoughtfully.

Colon beamed at him with the rather worried expression of a mad doctor who has bolted on the head, applied the crackling lightning to the electrodes, and is now watching his creation lurch down to the village.

'Cor,' said Nobby, his eyes now unfocusing slightly.

'Right, but *before* that,' said Colon, 'I'll do all the places along the Shambles and you do Chittling Street and then we can push off back to the Yard, job done and dusted. Okay?'

'Afternoon, Commander Vimes,' said Carrot, shutting the door behind him. 'Captain Carrot reporting.'

Vimes was slumped in his chair, staring at the window. The fog was creeping up again. Already the Opera House opposite was a little hazy.

'We, er, had a look at as many golems as we could, sir,' said Carrot, trying diplomatically to see if there was a bottle anywhere on the desk. 'There's hardly any, sir. We found eleven had smashed themselves up or sawn their heads off and by lunchtime people were smashing 'em or taking out their words themselves, sir. It's not nice, sir. There's bits of pottery all over the city. It's as if people were . . . just waiting for the opportunity. It's odd, sir. All they do is work and keep themselves to themselves and don't offer any harm to anyone. And some of the ones that smashed *themselves* left . . . well, notes, sir. Sort of saying they were sorry and ashamed, sir. They kept on going on about their clay . . .'

Vimes did not respond.

Carrot leaned sideways and down, in case there was a bottle on the floor. 'And Gimlet's Hole Food Delicatessen has been selling poisoned rat. Arsenic, sir. I've asked Sergeant Colon and Nobby to follow that one. It might just be some kind of mix-up, but you never know.'

Vimes turned. Carrot could hear his breathing. Short, sharp bursts, like a man trying to keep himself under control. 'What have we missed, Captain?' he said, in a faraway voice.

'Sir?'

'In his lordship's bedroom. There's the bed. The desk. Things on the desk. The table by the bed. The chair. The rug. Everything. We replaced *everything*. He eats food. We've checked the food, yes?'

'The whole larder, sir.'

'Is that a fact? We might be wrong there. I don't understand how, but we might be wrong. There's some evidence lying in the cemetery that suggests we are.' Vimes was nearly growling. 'What else is there? Littlebottom says there's no marks on him. What else *is* there? Let's find out the *how* and with any luck that'll give us the *who*.'

'He breathes the air more than anyone else, si—'

'But we moved him into another bedroom! Even if someone was, I don't know, pumping poison in . . . they couldn't change rooms with us all watching. It's got to be the food!'

'I've watched them taste it, sir.'

'Then it's something we're not seeing, damn it! People are *dead*, Captain! Mrs Easy's *dead*!'

'Who, sir?'

'You've never heard of her?'

'Can't say that I have, sir. What did she use to do?'

'Do? Nothing, I suppose. She just brought up nine kids in a couple of rooms you couldn't stretch out in and she sewed shirts for tuppence an hour, every hour the bloody gods sent, and all she did was work and keep herself to herself and she is *dead*, Captain. And so's her grandson. Aged fourteen months. Because her granddaughter took them some grub from the palace! A bit of a treat for them! And d'you know what? Mildred thought I was going to arrest her for theft! At the damn funeral, for gods' sake!' Vimes's fists opened and closed, his knuckles showing white. 'It's *murder* now. Not assassination, not politics, it's *murder*. Because we're not asking the right damn *questions*!'

*   *   *

The door opened.

'Oh, good afternoon, squire,' said Sergeant Colon brightly, touching his helmet. 'Sorry to bother you. I expect it's your busy time, but I've got to ask, just to eliminate you from our enquiries, so to speak. Do you use any arsenic around the place?'

'Er . . . don't leave the officer standing there, Fanley,' said a nervous voice, and the workman stepped aside. 'Good afternoon, officer. How may we help you?'

'Checking up on arsenic, sir. Seems some's been getting where it shouldn't.'

'Er . . . good heavens. Really. I'm sure we don't use any, but do come inside while I check with the foremen. I'm certain there's a pot of tea hot, too.'

Colon looked behind him. The mist was rising. The sky was going grey. 'Wouldn't say no, sir!' he said.

The door closed behind him.

A moment later, there was the faint scrape of the bolts.

'Right,' said Vimes. 'Let's start again.'

He picked up an imaginary ladle.

'I'm the cook. I've made this nourishing gruel that tastes like dog's water. I'm filling up three bowls. Everyone's watching me. All the bowls have been well washed, right? Okay. The tasters take two, one to taste, and these days the other's for Littlebottom to check, and then a servant – that's you, Carrot – takes the third one and . . .'

'Puts it in the dumbwaiter, sir. There's one up to every room.'

'I thought they carried them up?'

'Six floors? It'd get stone-cold, sir.'

'All right . . . hold on. We've gone too far. You've got the bowl. D'you put it on a tray?'

'Yes, sir.'

'Put it on a tray, then.'

Carrot obediently put the invisible bowl on an invisible tray.

'Anything else?' said Vimes.

'Piece of bread, sir. And we check the loaf.'

'Soup spoon?'

'Yes, sir.'

'Well, don't just stand there. Put them on . . .'

Carrot detached one hand from the invisible tray to take an invisible piece of bread and an intangible spoon.

'Anything else?' said Vimes. 'Salt and pepper?'

'I think I remember salt and pepper pots, sir.'

'On they go, then.'

Vimes stared hawk-like at the space between Carrot's hands.

'No,' he said. 'We wouldn't have missed that, would we? I mean . . . we wouldn't, would we?'

He reached out and picked up an invisible tube.

'Tell me we checked the salt,' he said.

'That's the pepper, sir,' said Carrot helpfully.

'Salt! Mustard! Vinegar! Pepper!' said Vimes. 'We didn't check all the food and then let his lordship tip poison on to suit his taste, did we? Arsenic's a metal. Can't you get . . . metal salts? Tell me we asked ourselves that. We aren't that stupid, are we?'

'I'll check directly,' said Carrot. He looked around desperately. 'I'll just put the tray down—'

'Not yet,' said Vimes. 'I've been here before. We don't rush off shouting "Give me a towel!" just because we've had one idea. Let's keep looking, shall we? The spoon. What's it made of?'

'Good point. I'll check the cutlery, sir.'

'*Now* we're cooking with charcoal! What's he been drinking?'

'Boiled water, sir. We've tested the water. And I checked the glasses.'

'Good. So . . . we've got the tray and you put the tray in the dumbwaiter and then what?'

'The men in the kitchen haul on the ropes and it goes up to the sixth floor.'

'No stops?'

Carrot looked blank.

'It goes up six floors,' said Vimes. 'It's just a shaft with a big box in it that can be pulled up and down, isn't it? I'll bet there's a door into it on every floor.'

'Some of the floors are hardly used these days, sir—'

'Even better for our poisoner, hmm? He just stands there, bold as you like, and waits for the tray to come by, right? We don't *know* that the meal which arrives is the one that left, do we?'

'Brilliant, sir!'

'It happens at night, I'll swear,' said Vimes. 'He's chipper in the evenings and out like a light next morning. What time is his supper sent up?'

'While he's poorly, around six o'clock, sir,' said Carrot. 'It's got dark by then. Then he gets on with his writing.'

'Right. We've got a lot to do. Come on.'

The Patrician was sitting up in bed reading when Vimes entered. 'Ah, Vimes,' he said.

'Your supper will be up shortly, my lord,' said Vimes. 'And can I once again say that our job would be a lot easier if you let us move you out of the palace?'

'I'm sure it would be,' said Lord Vetinari.

There was a rattle from the dumbwaiter. Vimes walked across and opened the doors.

There was a dwarf in the box. He had a knife between his teeth and an axe in each hand, and was glowering with ferocious concentration.

'Good heavens,' said Vetinari weakly. 'I hope at least they've included some mustard.'

'Any problems, Constable?' said Vimes.

'Nofe, fir,' said the dwarf, unfolding himself and removing the knife. 'Very dull all the way up, sir. There was other doors and they all looked pretty unused, but I nailed 'em up anyway like Captain Carrot said, sir.'

'Well done. Down you go.'

Vimes shut the doors. There was more rattling as the dwarf began his descent.

'Every detail covered, eh, Vimes?'

'I hope so, sir.'

The box came back up again, with a tray in it. Vimes took it out.

'What's this?'

'A Klatchian Hots without anchovies,' said Vimes, lifting the cover. 'We got it from Ron's Pizza Hovel round the corner. The way I see it, no one can poison all the food in the city. And the cutlery's from my place.'

'You have the mind of a true policeman, Vimes.'

'Thank you, sir.'

'Really? Was it a compliment?' The Patrician prodded at the plate with the air of an explorer in a strange country.

'Has someone *already* eaten this, Vimes?'

'No, sir. That's just how they chop up the food.'

'Oh, I *see*. I thought perhaps the food-tasters were getting over-enthusiastic,' said the Patrician. 'My word. What a treat I have to look forward to.'

'I can see you're feeling better, sir,' said Vimes stiffly.

'Thank you, Vimes.'

When Vimes had gone Lord Vetinari ate the pizza, or at least those parts of it he thought he could recognize. Then he put the tray aside and blew out the candle by his bed. He sat in the dark for a while, then felt under his pillow until his finger located a small sharp knife and a box of matches.

Thank goodness for Vimes. There was something endearing about his desperate, burning and above all *misplaced* competence. If the poor man took any longer he'd have to start giving him hints.

In the main office Carrot sat alone, watching Dorfl. The golem stood where it had been left. Someone had hung a dishcloth on one arm. The top of its head was still open.

Carrot spent a while with his chin on one hand, just staring. Then he opened a desk drawer and took out Dorfl's chem. He examined it. He got up. He walked over to the golem. He placed the words in the head. An orange glow rose in Dorfl's eyes. What was baked pottery took on that faintest of auras that marked the change between the living and the dead. Carrot found the golem's slate and pencil and pushed them into Dorfl's hand, then stood back.

The burning gaze followed him as he removed his sword belt, undid his breastplate, took off his jerkin and pulled his woollen vest over his head.

The glow was reflected from his muscles. They glistened in the candlelight.

'No weapons,' said Carrot. 'No armour. You see? Now listen to me . . .'

Dorfl lurched forward and swung a fist.

Carrot did not move.

The fist stopped a hair's-breadth from Carrot's unblinking eyes.

'I didn't think you could,' he said, as the golem swung again and the fist jerked to a stop a fraction of an inch from Carrot's stomach. 'But sooner or later you'll have to talk to me. Write, anyway.'

Dorfl paused. Then it picked up the slate pencil.

TAKE MY WORDS!

'Tell me about the golem who killed people.'

The pencil did not move.

'The others have killed themselves,' said Carrot.

I KNOW.

'*How* do you know?'

The golem watched him. Then it wrote:

CLAY OF MY CLAY.

'You feel what other golems feel?' said Carrot.

Dorfl nodded.

'And people are killing golems,' said Carrot. 'I don't know if I can stop that. But I can try. I think I know what's happening, Dorfl. Some of it. I think I know who you were following. Clay of your clay. Shaming you all. Something went wrong. You tried to put it right. I think . . . you all had such hopes. But the words in your head'll defeat you every time . . .'

The golem stayed motionless.

'You sold him, didn't you,' said Carrot quietly. 'Why?'

The words were scribbled quickly.

GOLEM MUST HAVE A MASTER.

'Why? Because the words say so?'

GOLEM MUST HAVE A MASTER!

Carrot sighed. Men had to breathe, fish had to swim, golems had to have a master. 'I don't know if I can sort this out, but no one else is going to try, believe me,' he said.

Dorfl did not move.

Carrot went back to where he had been standing. 'I'm wondering if the old priest and Mr Hopkinson did something . . . or *helped* to do something,' he said, watching the golem's face. 'I'm wondering if . . . afterwards . . . something turned against them, found the world a bit too much . . .'

Dorfl remained impassive.

Carrot nodded. 'Anyway, you're free to go. What

happens now is up to you. I'll help you if I can. If a golem is a *thing* then it can't commit murder, and I'll still try to find out why all this is happening. If a golem *can* commit murder, then you are *people,* and what is being done to you is terrible and must be stopped. Either way, you win, Dorfl.' He turned his back and fiddled with some papers on his desk. 'The big trouble,' he added, 'is that everyone wants someone else to read their minds for them and then make the world work properly. Even golems, perhaps.'

He turned back to face the golem. 'I know you've all got a secret. But, the way things are going, there won't be any of you left to keep it.'

He looked hopefully at Dorfl.

NO. CLAY OF MY CLAY. I WILL NOT BETRAY.

Carrot sighed. 'Well, I won't force you.' He grinned. 'Although, you know, I could. I could write a few extra words on your chem. Tell you to be talkative.'

The fires rose in Dorfl's eyes.

'But I won't. Because that would be inhumane. You haven't murdered anyone. I can't deprive you of your freedom because you haven't got any. Go on. You can go. It's not as if I don't know where you live.'

TO WORK IS TO LIVE.

'What is it golems *want,* Dorfl? I've seen you golems walking around the streets and working all the time, but what is it you actually hope to achieve?'

The slate pencil scribbled.

RESPITE.

Then Dorfl turned around and walked out of the building.

'D*mn!' said Carrot, a difficult linguistic feat. He drummed his fingers on the desk, then got up abruptly, put his clothing back on and stalked down the corridor to find Angua.

She was leaning against the wall in Corporal Littlebottom's office, talking to the dwarf.

'I've sent Dorfl home,' said Carrot.

'Has he got one?' said Angua.

'Well, back to the slaughterhouse, anyway. But it's probably not a good time for a golem to be out alone so I'm just going to stroll along after him and keep . . . Are you all right, Corporal Littlebottom?'

'Yes, sir,' said Cheri.

'You're wearing a . . . a . . . a . . .' Carrot's mind rebelled at the thought of what the dwarf was wearing and settled for: 'A kilt?'

'Yes, sir. A skirt, sir. A leather one, sir.'

Carrot tried to find a suitable response and had to resort to: 'Oh.'

'I'll come with you,' said Angua. 'Cheri can keep an eye on the desk.'

'A . . . kilt,' said Carrot. 'Oh. Well, er . . . just keep an eye on things. We won't be long. And . . . er . . . just keep behind the desk, all right?'

'Come *on*,' said Angua.

When they were out in the fog Carrot said, 'Do you think there's something a bit . . . *odd* about Littlebottom?'

'Seems like a perfectly ordinary female to me,' said Angua.

265

'*Female?* He *told* you he was female?'

'She,' Angua corrected. 'This is Ankh-Morpork, you know. We've got extra pronouns here.'

She could smell his bewilderment. Of course, everyone knew that, somewhere down under all those layers of leather and chain mail, dwarfs came in enough different types to ensure the future production of more dwarfs, but it was not a subject that dwarfs discussed other than at those essential points in a courtship when embarrassment might otherwise arise.

'Well, I would have thought she'd have the decency to keep it to herself,' Carrot said finally. 'I mean, I've nothing against females. I'm pretty certain my stepmother is one. But I don't think it's very clever, you know, to go around drawing attention to the fact.'

'Carrot, I think you've got something wrong with your head,' said Angua.

'What?'

'I think you may have got it stuck up your bum. I mean, good *grief.* A bit of make-up and a dress and you're acting as though she'd become Miss Va Va Voom and started dancing on tables down at the Skunk Club!'

There were a few seconds of shocked silence while they *both* considered the image of a dwarfish strip-tease dancer. Both minds rebelled.

'Anyway,' said Angua, 'if people can't be themselves in Ankh-Morpork, where can they?'

'There'll be trouble when the other dwarfs notice,' said Carrot. 'I could almost see his knees. *Her* knees.'

'Everyone's got knees.'

'Perhaps, but it's asking for trouble to flaunt them. I mean, *I'm* used to knees. I can look at knees and think, "Oh, yes, knees, they're just hinges in your legs", but some of the lads—'

Angua sniffed. 'He turned left here. Some of the lads *what*?'

'Well . . . I don't know how they'll react, that's all. You shouldn't have encouraged her. I mean, of course there's female dwarfs but . . . I mean, they have the decency not to show it.'

He heard Angua gasp. Her voice sounded rather far away when she said, 'Carrot, you know I've always respected your attitude to the citizens of Ankh-Morpork.'

'Yes?'

'I've been impressed by the way you really seem to be blind to things like shape and colour.'

'Yes?'

'And you always seem to care for people.'

'Yes?'

'And you know that I feel considerable affection for you.'

'Yes?'

'It's just that, sometimes . . .'

'Yes?'

'I really, really, *really* wonder why.'

Carriages were thickly parked outside Lady Selachii's mansion when Corporal Nobbs strolled up the drive. He knocked on the door.

A footman opened it. 'Servants' entrance,' said

the footman, and made to shut the door again.

But Nobby's outstretched foot had been ready for this. 'Read these,' he said, thrusting two bits of paper at him.

The first one read:

I, after hearing evidence from a number of experts, including Mrs Slipdry the midwife, certify that the balance of probability is that the bearer of this document, C. W. St John Nobbs, is a human being.

Signed, Lord Vetinari.

The other was the letter from Dragon King of Arms.

The footman's eyes widened. 'Oh, I am terribly sorry, your lordship,' he said. He stared again at Corporal Nobbs. Nobby was clean-shaven – at least, the last time he'd shaved he'd been clean-shaven – but his face had so many minor topological features it looked like a very bad example of slash-and-burn agriculture.

'Oh, dear,' added the footman. He pulled himself together. 'The other visitors normally just have cards.'

Nobby produced a battered deck. 'I'm probably busy hobnobbing right now,' he said. 'But I'm game for a few rounds of Cripple Mr Onion afterwards, if you like.'

The footman looked him up and down. He didn't get out much. He'd heard rumours – who hadn't? – that working in the Watch was the rightful king of Ankh-Morpork. He'd have to admit that, if you wanted to hide a secret heir to the throne, you couldn't possibly hide him more carefully than under the face of C. W. St J. Nobbs.

On the other hand . . . the footman was something of an historian, and knew that in its long history even the throne itself had been occupied by creatures who had been hunchbacked, one-eyed, knuckle-dragging and as ugly as sin. On that basis Nobby was as royal as they came. If, technically, he wasn't hunchbacked, this was only because he was hunched front and sides, too. There might be a time, the footman thought, when it paid to hitch your wagon to a star, even if said star was a red dwarf.

'You've never been to one of these affairs before, m'lord?' he said.

'First time,' said Nobby.

'I'm sure your lordship's blood will rise to the occasion,' said the footman weakly.

I'll have to go, Angua thought as they hurried through the fog. *I can't go on living from month to month.*

It's not that he's not likeable. You couldn't wish to meet a more caring man.

That's just it. He cares for everyone. He cares about everything. He cares indiscriminately. He knows everything about everyone because everyone interests him, and the caring is all general and never personal. He doesn't think personal is the same as important.

If only he had some decent human quality, like selfishness.

269

I'm sure he doesn't think about it that way, but you can tell the werewolf thing is upsetting him underneath. He cares about the things people say behind my back, and he doesn't know how to deal with them.

What was it those dwarfs said the other day? One said something like, 'She feels the need,' and the other one said, 'Yeah, the need to feed.' I saw his expression. I can handle that sort of thing . . . well, most of the time . . . but he can't. If only he'd thump someone. It wouldn't do any good but at least he'd feel better.

It's going to get worse. At best I'm going to get caught in someone's chicken-house, and then the midden is really going to hit the windmill. Or I'll get caught in someone's room . . .

She tried to shut out the thought but it didn't work. You could only *control* the werewolf, you couldn't *tame* it.

It's the city. Too many people, too many smells . . .

Maybe it would work if we were just alone somewhere, but if I said, 'It's me or the city,' he wouldn't even see there was a choice.

Sooner or later, I've got to go home. It's the best thing for him.

Vimes walked back through the damp night. He knew he was too angry to think properly.

He'd got nowhere, and he'd travelled a long way to get there. He'd got a cartload of facts and he'd done all the right logical things, and to someone, somewhere, he must look like a fool.

He probably looked like a fool to Carrot already. He'd kept coming up with bright ideas – proper *policeman's* ideas – and each one had turned out to be a joke. He'd bullied and shouted and done all the proper things, and none of it had worked. They hadn't found a thing. They'd merely increased their amount of ignorance.

The ghost of old Mrs Easy rose up in his inner vision. He couldn't remember much about her. He'd been just another snotty kid in a crowd of snotty kids, and she'd been just another worried face somewhere on top of a pinny. One of Cockbill Street's people. She'd taken in needlework to make ends meet and kept up appearances and, like everyone else in the street, had crept through life never asking for anything and getting even less.

What else *could* he have done? They'd practically scraped the damn wallpaper off the wal—

He stopped.

There was the same wallpaper in both rooms. In every room on that floor. That horrible green wallpaper.

But . . . no, that couldn't be it. Vetinari had slept in that room for years, if he slept at all. You can't sneak in and redecorate without someone noticing.

In front of him, the fog rolled aside. He caught a glimpse of a candlelit room in a nearby building before the cloud flowed back.

The fog. Yes. Dampness. Creeping in, brushing against the wallpaper. The old, dusty, musty wallpaper . . .

Would Cheery have tested the wallpaper? After all, in a way you didn't actually *see* it. It wasn't *in* the room because it was defining what the room was. Could you actually be poisoned by the *walls*?

He hardly dared think the thought. If he let his mind *settle* on the suspicion it'd twist and fly away, like all the others.

But . . . this was it, said his secret soul. All the messing around with suspects and Clues . . . that was just something to keep the body amused while the back of the brain toiled away. Every real copper knew you didn't go around looking for Clues so that you could find out Who Done It. No, you started out with a pretty good idea of Who Done It. That way, you knew what Clues to look for.

He wasn't going to have another day of bafflement interspersed with desperately bright ideas, was he? It was bad enough looking at Corporal Littlebottom's expression, which seemed to be getting a little more colourful every time he saw it.

He'd said, 'Ah, arsenic's a metal, right, so maybe the *cutlery* has been made of it?' He wouldn't forget the look on the dwarf's face as Cheery tried to explain that, yes, it might be possible to do that, provided you were sure that no one would notice the way it dissolved in the soup almost instantly.

This time he was going to think first.

'The Earl of Ankh, Corporal the Rt Hon. Lord C. W. St J. Nobbs!'

The buzz of conversation stopped. Heads turned. Somewhere in the crowd someone started to laugh and was hurriedly shushed into silence by their neighbours.

Lady Selachii came forward. She was a tall, angular woman, with the sharp features and aquiline nose that were the hallmarks of the family. The impression was that an axe was being thrown at you.

Then she curtsied.

There were gasps of surprise around her, but she glared at the assembled guests and there was a smattering of bows and curtsies. Somewhere at the back of the room someone started to say, 'But the man's an absolute oik—' and was cut off.

'Has someone dropped something?' said Nobby nervously. 'I'll help you look, if you like.'

The footman appeared at his elbow, bearing a tray. 'A drink, m'lord?' he said.

'Yeah, okay, a pint of Winkles,' said Nobby.

Jaws fell. But Lady Selachii's rose to the occasion. 'Winkles?' she said.

'A type of beer, your ladyship,' said the footman.

Her ladyship hesitated only a moment. 'I believe the butler drinks beer,' she said. 'See to it, man. And I'll have a pint of Winkles, too. What a *novel* idea.'

This caused a certain effect among those guests who knew on which side of the biscuit their pâté was spread.

'Indeed! Capital suggestion! A pint of Winkles here, too!'

'Hawhaw! Gweat! Winkles for me!'

'Winkles all round!'

'But the man's an absolute ti—'

'Shut up!'

* * *

273

Vimes crossed the Brass Bridge with care, counting the hippos. There was a ninth shape, but it was leaning against the parapet and muttering to itself in a familiar and, to Vimes at least, an unmenacing way. Faint air movements wafted towards him a smell that out-smelled even the river. It proclaimed that ahead of Vimes was a ding-a-ling so big he'd been upgraded to a clang-a-lang.

'. . . Buggrit buggrit I *told* 'em, stand it up and pull the end orf! Millennium hand and shrimp! I *told* 'em, sez I, and would they poke . . .'

'Evening, Ron,' said Vimes, without even bothering to look at the figure.

Foul Ole Ron fell into step behind him. 'Buggrit they done me out of it so they did . . .'

'Yes, Ron,' said Vimes.

'. . . And shrimp . . . buggrit, say I, bread it on the butter side . . . Queen Molly says to watch your back, mister.'

'What was that?'

'. . . Sowter fry it!' said Foul Ole Ron innocently. 'Trouser the lot of 'em, they did me out of it, them and their big weasel!'

The beggar lurched around and, filthy coat dragging its hems along the ground, limped away into the fog. His little dog trotted along in front of him.

There was pandemonium in the servants' hall.

'Winkles' Old Peculiar?' said the butler.

'Another one hundred and four pints!' said the footman.

The butler shrugged. 'Harry, Sid, Rob and Jeffrey . . . two trays apiece and double down to the King's Head again right now! What else is he doing?'

'Well, they're supposed to be having a poetry reading but *he's* telling 'em jokes . . .'

'Anecdotes?'

'Not exactly.'

It was amazing how it could drizzle and fog at the same time. Wind was blowing both through the open window, and Vimes was forced to shut it. He lit the candles by his desk and opened his notebook.

Probably he should use the demonic organizer, but he liked to see things written down fair and square. He could think better when he wrote things down.

He wrote 'Arsenic', and drew a big circle round it. Around the circle he wrote: 'Fr Tubelcek's fingernails' and 'Rats' and 'Vetinari' and 'Mrs Easy'. Lower down the page he wrote: 'Golems', and drew a second circle. Around that one he wrote: 'Fr Tubelcek?' and 'Mr Hopkinson?'. After some thought he wrote down: 'Stolen clay' and 'Grog'.

And then: 'Why would a golem admit to something it didn't do?'

He stared at the candlelight for a while and then wrote: 'Rats eat stuff.'

More time passed.

'What has the priest got that anyone wants?'

From downstairs came the sound of armour as a patrol came in. A corporal shouted.

'Words,' wrote Vimes. 'What had Mr Hopkinson

got? Dwarf bread? → Not stolen. What else had he got?'

Vimes looked at this, too, and then he wrote 'Bakery', stared at the word for a while, and rubbed it out and replaced it with 'Oven?'. He drew a ring around 'Oven?' and a ring around 'Stolen clay', and linked the two.

There'd been arsenic under the old priest's fingernails. Perhaps he'd put down rat poison? There were plenty of uses for arsenic. It wasn't as if you couldn't buy it by the pound from any alchemist.

He wrote down 'Arsenic Monster' and looked at it. You found dirt under fingernails. If people had put up a fight you might find blood or skin. You didn't find grease and arsenic.

He looked at the page again and, after still more thought, wrote: 'Golems aren't alive. But they *think* they are alive. What do things that are alive do? → Ans: Breathe, eat, crap.' He paused, staring out at the fog, and then wrote very carefully: 'And make more things.'

Something tingled at the back of his neck.

He circled the late Hopkinson's name and drew a line down the page to another circle, in which he wrote: 'He'd got a big oven.'

Hmm. Cheery had said you couldn't bake clay properly in a bread oven. But maybe you could bake it improperly.

He looked up at the candlelight again.

They couldn't do *that*, could they? Oh, gods . . . No, surely not . . .

But, after all, all you needed was clay. And a holy

man who knew how to write the words. And someone to actually sculpt the figure, Vimes supposed,
but golems had had hundreds and hundreds of years
to learn to be good with their hands . . .

Those great big hands. The ones that looked so
very fist-like.

And then the first thing they'd want to do
would be to destroy the evidence, wouldn't they?
They probably didn't think of it as killing, but more
like a sort of switching-off . . .

He drew another rather misshapen circle on his
notes.

Grog. Old baked clay, ground up small.

They'd added some of their own clay. Dorfl had
a new foot, didn't he – it? It hadn't made it quite
right. They'd put part of their own selves into a new
golem.

That all sounded – well, Nobby would call it
mucky. Vimes didn't know what to call it. It sounded
like some sort of secret-society thing. 'Clay of my
clay.' My own flesh and blood . . .

Damn hulking things. Aping their betters!

Vimes yawned. Sleep. He'd be better for some
sleep. Or something.

He stared at the page. Automatically his hand
trailed down to the bottom drawer of his desk, as it
always did when he was worried and trying to think.
It wasn't as though there was ever a bottle there these
days – but old habits died ha . . .

There was a soft glassy *ching* and a faint, se-
ductive slosh.

Vimes's hand came up with a fat bottle. The label

said: Bearhugger's Distilleries: The MacAbre, Finest Malt.

The liquid inside almost crawled up the sides of the glass in anticipation.

He stared at it. He'd reached down into the drawer for the whisky bottle and there it was.

But it shouldn't have been. He knew Carrot and Fred Colon kept an eye on him, but he'd never bought a bottle since he'd got married, because he'd promised Sybil, hadn't he . . . ?

But this wasn't any old rotgut. This was The MacAbre . . .

He'd tried it once. He couldn't quite remember why now, since in those days the only spirits he generally drank had the subtlety of a mallet to the inner ear. He must have found the money somehow. Just a *sniff* of it had been like Hogswatchnight. Just a *sniff* . . .

'And *she* said, "That's funny – it didn't do that last night"!' said Corporal Nobbs.

He beamed at the company.

There was silence. Then someone in the crowd started to laugh, one of those little uncertain laughs a man laughs who is unsure that he's not going to be silenced by those around him. Another man laughed. Two more picked it up. Then laughter exploded in the group as a whole.

Nobby basked.

'Then there's the one about the Klatchian who walked into a pub with a tiny piano—' he began.

'I think,' said Lady Selachii firmly, 'that the buffet is ready.'

'Got any pig knuckles?' said Nobby cheerfully. 'Goes down a treat with Winkles, a plate of pig knuckles.'

'I don't *normally* eat extremities,' said Lady Selachii.

'A pig-knuckle sandwich . . . Never tried a pig knuckle? You just can't beat it,' said Nobby.

'It is . . . perhaps . . . not the most delicate food?' said Lady Selachii.

'Oh, you can cut the crusts off,' said Nobby. 'Even the toenails. If you're feeling posh.'

Sergeant Colon opened his eyes, and groaned. His head ached. They'd hit him with something. It might have been a wall.

They'd tied him up, too. He was trussed hand and foot.

He appeared to be lying in darkness on a wooden floor. There was a greasy smell in the air, which seemed familiar yet annoyingly unrecognizable.

As his eyes grew accustomed to the dark he could make out very faint lines of light, such as might surround a door. He could also hear voices.

He tried to get up to his knees, and groaned as more pain crackled in his head.

When people tied you up it was bad news. Of course, it was much better news than when they killed you, but it could mean they were just putting you on one side for killing later.

This never used to happen, he told himself. In the old days, if you caught someone thieving, you practically held the door open for him to escape.

That way, you got home in one piece.

By using the angle between a wall and a heavy crate he managed to get upright. This was not much of an improvement on his former position, but after the thunder in his head had died away he hopped awkwardly towards the door.

There were still voices on the other side of it.

Someone apart from Sergeant Colon was in trouble.

'—*clown!* You got me here for *this*? There's a werewolf in the Watch! Ah-ha. Not one of your freaks. She's a proper bimorphic! If you tossed a coin, she could smell what side it came down!'

'How about if we kill him and drag his body away?'

'You think she couldn't smell the difference between a corpse and a living body?'

Sergeant Colon moaned softly.

'Er, how about we could march him out in the fog—?'

'And they can smell fear, idiot. Ah-ha. Why couldn't you have let him look around? What could he have seen? I know that copper. A fat old coward with all the brains of, ah-ha, a pig. He stinks of fear all the time.'

Sergeant Colon hoped he wasn't about to stink of anything else.

'Send Meshugah after him, ah-ha.'

'Are you sure? It's getting *odd*. It wanders off and screams in the night, and they're *not* supposed to do that. And it's cracking up. Trust dumb golems not to do something prop—'

'Everyone knows you can't trust golems. Ah-ha. See to it!'

'I heard that Vimes is—'

'I've seen to Vimes!'

Colon eased himself away from the door as quietly as possible. He hadn't the faintest idea what this thing called Meshugah the golems had made was, except that it sounded like a fine idea to be wherever it wasn't.

Now, if he were a resourceful type, like Sam Vimes or Captain Carrot, he'd . . . find a nail or something to snap these ropes, wouldn't he? They were *really* tight, and cut into his wrists because the cord was so thin, little more than string wound and knotted many times. If he could find something to rub it on . . .

But, unfortunately, and against all common sense, sometimes people inconsiderately throw their bound enemies into rooms entirely bereft of nails, handy bits of sharp stone, sharp-edged shards of glass or even, in extreme cases, enough pieces of old junk and tools to make a fully functional armoured car.

He managed to get on to his knees again and shuffled across the planks. Even a splinter would do. A lump of metal. A wide-open doorway marked FREEDOM. He'd settle for anything.

What he got was a tiny circle of light on the floor. A knothole in the wood had long ago fallen out, and light – dim orange light – was shining through.

Colon got down and applied his eye to the hole. Unfortunately this also brought his nose into a similar proximity.

The stench was appalling.

There was a suggestion of wateriness, or at least of liquidity. He must be over one of the numerous streams that flowed through the city, although they had of course been built over centuries before and were now used – if their existence was even remembered – for those purposes to which humanity had always put clean fresh water; i.e., making it as turbid and undrinkable as possible. And this one was flowing under the cattle markets. The smell of ammonia bored into Colon's sinuses like a drill.

And yet there was light down there.

He held his breath and took another look.

A couple of feet below him was a very small raft. Half a dozen rats were laid neatly on it, and a minute scrap of candle was burning.

A tiny rowing boat entered his vision. A rat was in the bottom of it and, sitting amidships and rowing, was—

'Wee Mad Arthur?'

The gnome looked up. 'Who's that there, then?'

'It's me, your good old mate Fred Colon! Can you give me a hand?'

'Wha're yez doing up there?'

'I'm all tied up and they're going to kill me! Why does it smell so *bad*?'

''S the old Cockbill stream. All the cattle pens drain into it.' Wee Mad Arthur grinned. 'Yez can feel it doing yer tubes a power of good, eh? Just call me King of the Golden River, eh?'

'They're going to *kill* me, Arthur! Don't piss about!'

'Aha, good one!'

Desperate cells flared in Colon's mind. 'I've been on the trail of those blokes who're poisoning your rats,' he said.

'The Rat-Catchers' Guild!' snarled Arthur, almost dropping an oar. 'I *knew* it was them, right? This is where I got them rats! There's more of 'em down here, dead as doornails!'

'Right! And I've got to give the names to Commander Vimes! In person! With all my arms and legs on! He's very particular about that sort of thing!'

'Did yez know ycz on a trapdoor?' said Arthur. 'Wait right there.'

Arthur rowed out of sight. Colon rolled over. After a while there was a scratching noise in the walls and then someone kicked him in the ear.

'Ow!'

'Would there be any money in this?' said Wee Mad Arthur, holding up his stub of candle. It was a small one, such as might be put on a child's birthday cake.

'What about your public duty?'

'Aye, so there's *no* money in this?'

'Lots! I promise! Now untie me!'

'This is string they've used,' said Arthur, somewhere around Colon's hands. 'Not proper rope at all.'

Colon felt his hands free, although there was still pressure around his wrists.

'Where's the trapdoor?' he said.

'Yer on it. Handy for dumping stuff. Dunt look as if it been used for years, from underneath. Hey, I been finding dead rats everywhere down there now! Fat as yer head and twice as dead! I *thought* the ones I caught for Gimlet were a wee bit sluggish!'

There was a twang and Colon's legs were free. He sat up cautiously and tried to massage some life back into them.

'Is there any other way out?' he said.

'Plenty for me, none for a silly bigger like yez,' said Wee Mad Arthur. 'Yer'll have to swim for it.'

'You want me to drop into *that*?'

'Don't yez worry, yez can't drown in it.'

'You sure?'

'Yeah. But yez may suffocate. Yer know that creek they talk about? The one yez can be up without no paddle?'

'That's not this one, is it?' said Colon.

'It's coz of the cattle pens,' said Wee Mad Arthur. 'Cattle penned up is always a bit nervous.'

'I know how they feel.'

There was a creak outside the door. Colon managed to get to his feet.

The door opened.

A figure filled the doorway. It was in silhouette because of the light behind it, but Colon looked up into two triangular glowing eyes.

Colon's body, which in many respects was considerably more intelligent than the mind it had to carry around, took over. It made use of the adrenalin-fed start the brain had given it and leapt several feet in the air, pointing its toes as it came down so that the iron tips of Colon's boots hit the trapdoor together.

The filth of years and the rust of iron gave way.

Colon went through. Fortunately his body had the foresight to hold its own nose as he hit the much-maligned stream, which went:

Gloop.

Many people, when they're precipitated into water, struggle to breathe. Sergeant Colon struggled not to. The alternative was too horrible to think about.

He rose again, buoyed up in part by various gases released from the ooze. A few feet away, the candle on Wee Mad Arthur's rocking raft started to burn with a blue flame.

Someone landed on his helmet and kicked it like a man spurs on a horse.

'Right *turn*! Forward!'

Half-walking, half-swimming, Colon struggled down the fetid drain. Terror lent him strength. It would demand repayment with interest later but, for now, he left a wake. Which took several seconds to close up after him.

He didn't stop until a sudden lack of pressure overhead told him that he was in the open air. He grabbed in the darkness, found the greasy pilings of a jetty, and clung to them, wheezing.

'What was that thing?' said Wee Mad Arthur.

'Golem,' Colon panted.

He managed to get a hand on to the planks of the jetty, tried to pull himself up, and sagged back into the water.

'Hey, did I just hear something?' said Wee Mad Arthur.

Sergeant Colon rose like an undersea-launched missile and landed on the jetty, where he folded up.

'Nah, just a bird or something,' said Wee Mad Arthur.

'What do your friends call you, Wee Mad Arthur?' muttered Colon.

'Dunno. Ain't got none.'

'Gosh, that's surprising.'

Lord de Nobbes had a lot of friends now. 'Up the hatch! Here's looking at your bottom!' he said.

There were shrieks of laughter.

Nobby grinned happily in the middle of the crowd. He couldn't remember when he had enjoyed himself so much with all his clothes on.

In the far corner of Lady Selachii's drawing-room a door closed discreetly and, in the comfortable smoking-room beyond, anonymous people sat down in leather armchairs and looked at one another expectantly.

Finally one said, 'It's astonishing. Frankly astonishing. The man has actually got charisn'tma.'

'Your meaning?'

'I mean he's so dreadful he fascinates people. Like those stories he was telling . . . Did you notice how people kept encouraging him because they couldn't actually believe *anyone* would tell jokes like that in mixed company?'

'Actually, I rather liked the one about the very small man playing the piano—'

'And his table manners! Did you notice them?'

'No.'

'Ex-actly!'

'And the smell, don't forget the smell.'

'Not so much *bad* as . . . odd.'

'Actually, I found that after a few minutes the nose shuts down and then it's—'

'My *point* is that, in some strange way, he attracts people.'

'Like a public hanging.'

There was a period of reflective silence.

'Good humoured little tit, though, in his way.'

'Not too bright, though.'

'Give him his pint of beer and a plate of whatever those things with toenails were and he seems as happy as a pig in muck.'

'I think that's somewhat insulting.'

'I'm sorry.'

'I've known some splendid pigs.'

'Indeed.'

'But I can certainly see him drinking his beer and eating feet while he signs the royal proclamations.'

'Yes, indeed. Er. Do you think he can read?'

'Does it matter?'

There was some more silence, filled with the busy racing of minds.

Then someone said, 'Another thing . . . we won't have to worry about establishing a royal succession that might be inconvenient.'

'Why do you think that?'

'Can you see any princess marrying him?'

'We-ell . . . they have been known to kiss frogs . . .'

'Frogs, I grant you.'

'. . . And, of course, power and royalty *are* powerful aphrodisiacs . . .'

287

'*How* powerful, would you say?'

More silence. Then: 'Probably not that powerful.'

'He should do nicely.'

'Splendid.'

'Dragon did well. I suppose the little tit isn't *really* an earl, by any chance?'

'Don't be silly.'

Cheri Littlebottom sat awkwardly on the high stool behind the desk. All she had to do, she'd been told, was check the patrols off and on-duty when the shift changed.

A few of the men gave her an odd look but they said nothing, and she was beginning to relax when the four dwarfs on the King's Way beat came in.

They stared at her. And her ears.

Their eyes travelled downwards. There was no such concept as a modesty panel in Ankh-Morpork. All that was usually visible under the desk was the bottom half of Sergeant Colon. Of the large number of good reasons for shielding the bottom half of Sergeant Colon from view, its potential for engendering lust was not among the top ten.

'That's . . . *female* clothes, isn't it?' said one of the dwarfs.

Cheri swallowed. Why *now*? She'd sort of assumed Angua would be around. People always calmed down when she smiled at them, it was really amazing.

'Well?' she quavered. 'So what? I can if I want to.'

'And . . . on your ear . . .'

'Well?'

'That's . . . my mother never even . . . urgh . . . that's disgusting! In public, too! What happens if kids come in?'

'I can see your *ankles*!' said another dwarf.

'I'm going to speak to Captain Carrot about this!' said the third. 'I never thought I'd live to see the day!'

Two of the dwarfs stormed off towards the locker-room. Another one hurried after them, but hesitated as he drew level with the desk. He gave Cheri a frantic look.

'Er . . . er . . . *nice* ankles, though,' he said, and then ran.

The fourth dwarf waited until the others had gone and then sidled up.

Cheri was shaking with nervousness. 'Don't you say a *thing* about my legs!' she said, waving a finger.

'Er . . .' The dwarf looked around hurriedly, and leaned forward. 'Er . . . is that . . . lipstick?'

'Yes! What about it?'

'Er . . .' The dwarf leaned forward even more, looked around again, this time conspiratorially, and lowered her voice. 'Er . . . could I try it?'

Angua and Carrot walked silently through the fog, except for Angua's occasional crisp and brief directions.

Then she stopped. Up until then Dorfl's scent, or at least the fresh scent of old meat and cow dung, had headed quite directly back to the slaughterhouse district.

'It's gone up this alley,' she said. 'That's nearly

doubling back. And . . . it was moving faster . . . and . . . there's a lot of humans and . . . *sausages*?'

Carrot started to run. A lot of people and the smell of sausages meant a performance of the street theatre that was life in Ankh-Morpork.

There was a crowd further up the alley. It had obviously been there for some time, because at the rear was a familiar figure with a tray, craning to see over the tops of the heads.

'What's going on, Mr Dibbler?' said Carrot.

'Oh, hello, Cap'n. They've got a golem.'

'Who have?'

'Oh, some blokes. They've just fetched the hammers.'

There was a press of bodies in front of Carrot. He put both hands together and rammed them between a couple of people, and then moved them apart. Grunting and struggling, the crowd opened up like a watercourse in front of the better class of prophet.

Dorfl was standing at bay at the end of the alley. Three men with hammers were approaching the golem cautiously, in the way of mobs, each unwilling to strike the first blow in case the second blow came right back at him.

The golem was crouching back, shielding itself with its slate on which was written:

I AM WORTH 530 DOLLARS.

'Money?' said one of the men. 'That's all you things think about!'

The slate shattered under a blow.

Then he tried to raise his hammer again. When it didn't budge he very nearly somersaulted backwards.

'Money is all you *can* think about when all you have is a price,' said Carrot calmly, twisting the hammer out of his grip. 'What do you think you're doing, my friend?'

'You can't stop us!' mumbled the man. 'Everyone knows they're not alive!'

'But I *can* arrest you for wilful damage to property,' said Carrot.

'One of these killed that old priest!'

'Sorry?' said Carrot. 'If it's just a thing, how can it commit murder? A sword is a thing' – he drew his own sword; it made an almost silken sound – 'and of course you couldn't possibly blame a *sword* if someone thrust it at you, sir.'

The man went cross-eyed as he tried to focus on the sword.

And, again, Angua felt that touch of bewilderment. Carrot wasn't threatening the man. He *wasn't* threatening the man. He was merely using the sword to demonstrate a . . . well, a point. And that was all. He'd be quite amazed to hear that not everyone would think of it like that.

Part of her said: *Someone has to be very complex indeed to be as simple as Carrot.*

The man swallowed.

'*Good* point,' he said.

'Yeah, but . . . you can't trust 'em,' said one of the other hammer-bearers. 'They sneak around and they never say anything. What are they up to, eh?'

He gave Dorfl a kick. The golem rocked slightly.

'Well, now,' said Carrot. 'That is what I am

291

finding out. In the meantime, I must ask you to go about your business . . .'

The third demolition man had only recently arrived in the city and had gone along with the idea because there are some people who do.

He raised his hammer defiantly and opened his mouth to say, 'Oh, yeah?' but stopped, because just by his ear he heard a growl. It was quite low and soft, but it had a complex little waveform which went straight down into a little knobbly bit in his spinal column where it pressed an ancient button marked Primal Terror.

He turned. An attractive watchwoman behind him gave him a friendly smile. That was to say, her mouth turned up at the corners and all her teeth were visible.

He dropped the hammer on his foot.

'Well done,' said Carrot. 'I've always said you can do more with a kind word and a smile.'

The crowd looked at him with the kind of expression people always wore when they looked at Carrot. It was the face-cracking realization that he really did believe what he was saying. The sheer enormity tended to leave people breathless.

They backed away and scurried out of the alley.

Carrot turned back to the golem, which had dropped to its knees and was trying to piece its slate together.

'Come on, Mr Dorfl,' he said. 'We'll walk with you the rest of the way.'

*   *   *

'Are you mad?' said Sock, trying to shut the door. 'You think I want *that* back?'

'He's your property,' said Carrot. 'People were trying to smash him.'

'You should've let them,' said the butcher. 'Haven't you heard the stories? I'm not having one of those under my roof.'

He tried to slam the door again, but Carrot's foot was in it.

'Then I'm afraid you're committing an offence,' said Carrot. 'To wit, littering.'

'Oh, be serious!'

'I always am,' said Carrot.

'He always is,' said Angua.

Sock waved his hands frantically. 'It can just go away. Shoo! I don't want a killer working in my slaughterhouse! You have it, if you're so keen!'

Carrot grabbed the door and forced it wide open. Sock took a step backwards.

'Are you trying to bribe an officer of the law, Mr Sock?'

'Are you insane?'

'I am always sane,' said Carrot.

'He always is,' sighed Angua.

'Watchmen are not allowed to accept gifts,' said Carrot. He looked around at Dorfl, who was standing forlornly in the street. 'But I *will* buy him from you. For a fair price.'

Sock looked from Carrot to the golem and then back again. 'Buy? For money?'

'Yes.'

The butcher shrugged. When people were offering

you money it was no time to debate their sanity. 'Well, that's different,' he conceded. 'It was worth $530 when I bought it, but of course it's got additional skills now—'

Angua growled. It had been a trying evening and the smell of fresh meat was making her senses twang. 'You were prepared to *give* it away a moment ago!'

'Well, *give*, yes, but business is busi—'

'I'll pay you a dollar,' said Carrot.

'A dollar? That's daylight robb—'

Angua's hand shot out and grabbed his neck. She could feel the veins, smell his blood and fear . . . She tried to think of cabbages.

'It's *night*-time,' she growled.

Like the man in the alley, Sock listened to the call of the wild. 'A dollar,' he croaked. 'Right. A fair price. One dollar.'

Carrot produced one. And waved his notebook.

'A receipt is very important,' he said. 'A proper legal transfer of ownership.'

'Right. Right. Right. Happy to oblige.'

Sock glanced desperately at Angua. Somehow, her smile didn't look right. He scribbled a few hasty lines.

Carrot looked over his shoulder.

I Gerhardt Sock give the barer full and totarl ownorship of the golem Dorfl in xchange for One Dolar and anythinge it doz now is his responsbility and nuthing to doe with me.

Singed, Gerhardt Sock.

'Interesting wording, but it does *look* legal, doesn't it?' said Carrot, taking the paper. 'Thank you very much, Mr Sock. A happy solution all round, I feel.'

'Is that it? Can I go now?'

'Certainly, and—'

The door slammed shut.

'Oh, well done,' said Angua. 'So now you own a golem. You do *know* that anything it does is *your* responsibility?'

'If that's the truth, why are people smashing *them*?'

'What are you going to use it *for*?'

Carrot looked thoughtfully at Dorfl, who was staring at the ground.

'Dorfl?'

The golem looked up.

'Here's your receipt. You don't *have* to have a master.'

The golem took the little scrap of paper between two thick fingers.

'That means you belong to you,' said Carrot encouragingly. 'You own yourself.'

Dorfl shrugged.

'What did you expect?' said Angua. 'Did you think it was going to wave a flag?'

'I don't think he understands,' said Carrot. 'It's quite hard to get some ideas into people's heads . . .' He stopped abruptly.

Carrot took the paper out of Dorfl's unresisting fingers. 'I *suppose* it might work,' he said. 'It seems a bit – invasive. But what they understand, after all, is the words . . .'

He reached up, opened Dorfl's lid, and dropped the paper inside.

The golem blinked. That is to say, its eyes went dark and then brightened again. It raised one hand very slowly and patted the top of its head. Then it held up the other hand and turned it this way and that, as if it had never seen a hand before. It looked down at its feet and around at the fog-shrouded buildings. It looked at Carrot. It looked up at the clouds above the street. It looked at Carrot again.

Then, very slowly, without bending in any way, it fell backwards and hit the cobbles with a thud. The light faded in its eyes.

'There,' said Angua. 'Now it's broken. Can we go?'

'There's still a bit of a glow,' said Carrot. 'It must have all been too much for him. We can't leave him here. Maybe if I took the receipt out . . .'

He knelt down by the golem and reached for the trapdoor on its head.

Dorfl's hand moved so quickly it didn't even *appear* to move. It was just there, gripping Carrot's wrist.

'Ah,' said Carrot, gently pulling his arm back. 'He's obviously . . . feeling better.'

'Thsssss,' said Dorfl. The voice of the golem shivered in the fog.

Golems had a mouth. They were part of the design. But this one was open, revealing a thin line of red light.

'Oh, ye gods,' said Angua, backing away. 'They *can't* speak!'

'Thssss!' It was less a syllable than the sound of escaping steam.

'I'll find your bit of slate—' Carrot began, looking around hurriedly.

'Thssss!'

Dorfl clambered to its feet, gently pushed him out of the way and strode off.

'Are you *happy* now?' said Angua. 'I'm not following the wretched thing! Maybe it's going to throw itself in the river!'

Carrot ran a few steps after the figure, and then stopped and came back.

'Why do you hate them so much?' he said.

'You wouldn't understand. I really think you wouldn't understand,' said Angua. 'It's an . . . undead thing. They . . . sort of throw in your face the fact you're not human.'

'But you *are* human!'

'Three weeks out of four. Can't you understand that, when you have to be careful all the time, it's dreadful to see *things* like that being accepted? They're not even alive. But they can walk around and *they* never get people passing remarks about silver or garlic . . . up until now, anyway. They're just machines for doing work!'

'That's how they're treated, certainly,' said Carrot.

'You're being reasonable again!' snapped Angua. 'You're deliberately seeing everyone's point of view! Can't you *try* to be unfair even once?'

*　　*　　*

297

Nobby had been left alone for a moment while the party buzzed around him, so he'd elbowed some waiters away from the buffet and was currently scraping out a bowl with his knife.

'Ah, Lord de Nobbes,' said a voice behind him.

He turned. 'Wotcha,' he said, licking the knife and wiping it on the tablecloth.

'Are you busy, my lord?'

'Just making meself this meat-paste sandwich,' said Nobby.

'That's pâté de foie gras, my lord.'

''S that what it's called? It doesn't have the kick of Clammer's Beefymite Spread, I know that. Want a quail's egg? They're a bit small.'

'No, thank you—'

'There's loads of them,' said Nobby generously. 'They're free. You don't have to pay.'

'Even so—'

'I can get six in my mouth at once. Watch—'

'Amazing, my lord. I was wondering, however, whether you would care to join a few of us in the smoking-room?'

'Fghmf? Mfgmf fgmf mgghjf?'

'Indeed.' A friendly arm was put around Nobby's shoulders and he was adroitly piloted away from the buffet, but not before he had grabbed a plate of chicken legs. 'So many people want to talk to you . . .'

'Mgffmph?'

Sergeant Colon tried to clean himself up, but trying to clean yourself up with water from the Ankh was a difficult manoeuvre. The best you could hope for was an all-over grey.

Fred Colon hadn't reached Vimes's level of sophisticated despair. Vimes took the view that life was so full of things happening erratically in all directions that the chances of any of them making some kind of relevant sense were remote in the extreme. Colon, being by nature more optimistic and by intellect a good deal slower, was still at the Clues are Important stage.

Why had he been tied up with string? There were still loops of it around his arms and legs.

'You sure you don't know where I was?' he said.

'Yez walked into the place,' said Wee Mad Arthur, trotting along beside him. 'How come yez don't know?'

''Cos it was dark and foggy and I wasn't paying attention, that's why. I was just going through the motions.'

'Aha, good one!'

'Don't mess about. Where was I?'

'Don't ask me,' said Wee Mad Arthur. 'I just hunts *under* the whole cattle-market area. I don't bother about what's up top. Like I said, them runs go everywhere.'

'Anyone along there make string?'

'It's all animal stuff, I tell yez. Sausages and soap and stuff like that. Is this the bit where yez gives me the money?'

Colon patted his pockets. They squelched.

'You'll have to come to the Watch House, Wee Mad Arthur.'

'I got a business to run here!'

'I'm swearin' you in as a Special Watchman for the night,' said Colon.

'What's the pay?'

'Dollar a night.'

Wee Mad Arthur's tiny eyes gleamed. They gleamed red.

'Ye gods, you look awful,' said Colon. 'What're you looking at my ear for?'

Wee Mad Arthur said nothing.

Colon turned.

A golem was standing behind him. It was taller than any he'd seen before, and much better proportioned – a human statue rather than the gross shape of the usual golems, and handsome, too, in the cold way of a statue. And its eyes shone like red searchlights.

It raised a fist above its head and opened its mouth. More red light streamed out.

It screamed like a bull.

Wee Mad Arthur kicked Colon on the ankle.

'Are we running or what?' he said.

Colon backed away, still staring at the thing.

'It's . . . it's all right, they can't move fast . . .' he muttered. And then his sensible body gave up on his stupid brain and fired up his legs, spinning him around and shoving him in the opposite direction.

He risked looking over his shoulder. The golem was running after him in long, easy strides.

Wee Mad Arthur caught him up.

Colon was used to proceeding gently. He wasn't

300

built for high speeds, and said so. 'And *you* certainly can't run faster than that thing!' he wheezed.

'Just so long as I can run faster'n yez,' said Wee Mad Arthur. 'This way!'

There was a flight of old wooden stairs against the side of a warehouse. The gnome went up them like the rats he hunted. Colon, panting like a steam engine, followed him.

He stopped halfway up and looked around.

The golem had reached the bottom step. It tested it carefully. The wood creaked and the whole stairway, grey with age, trembled.

'It won't take the weight!' said Wee Mad Arthur. 'The bugger's gonna smash it up! Yeah!'

The golem took another step. The wood groaned.

Colon got a grip on himself and hurried on up the stairs.

Behind him, the golem seemed to have satisfied itself that the wood could indeed take its weight, and started to leap from step to step. The rails shook under Colon's hands and the whole structure swayed.

'Come *on*, will yez?' said Wee Mad Arthur, who had already reached the top. 'It's gaining on yez!'

The golem lunged. The stairs gave way. Colon flung out his hands and grabbed the edge of the roof. Then his body thudded into the side of the building.

There was the distant sound of woodwork hitting cobbles.

'Come on then,' said Wee Mad Arthur. 'Pull yourself up, yer silly bugger!'

'Can't,' said Colon.

'Why not?'
'It's holding on to my foot . . .'

'A cigar, your lordship?'
'Brandy, my lord?'

Lord de Nobbes sat back in the comfort of his chair. His feet only just reached the ground. Brandy and cigars, eh? This was the life all right. He took a deep puff at the cigar.

'We were just talking, my lord, about the future governance of the city now that poor Lord Vetinari's health is so bad . . .'

Nobby nodded. This was the kind of thing you talked about when you were a nob. This was what he'd been born for.

The brandy was giving him a pleasant warm feeling.

'It would obviously upset the current equilibrium if we looked for a new Patrician at this point,' said another armchair. 'What is your view, Lord de Nobbes?'

'Oh, yeah. Right. The guilds'd fight like cats in a sack,' said Nobby. 'Everyone knows that.'

'A masterly summary, if I may say so.'

There was a general murmur of agreement from the other chairs.

Nobby grinned. Oh, yes. This was the bee's pyjamas and no mistake. Hobnobbing with his fellow nobs, talking big talk about important matters instead of having to think up reasons why the tea-money tin was empty . . . oh, yes.

A chair said, 'Besides, are any of the guild leaders

up to the task? Oh, they can organize a bunch of tradesmen, but ruling an entire city . . . I think not. Gentlemen, perhaps it is time for a new direction. Perhaps it is time for blood to reveal itself.'

Odd way of putting it, Nobby thought, but clearly this was how you were supposed to speak.

'At a time like this,' said a chair, 'the city will surely look at those representatives of its most venerable families. It would be in all our interests if such a one would take up the burden.'

'He'd need his head examined, if you want my opinion,' said Nobby. He took another swig of the brandy and waved the cigar expansively.

'Still, not to worry,' he said. 'Everyone knows we've got a king hanging around. No problem there. Send for Captain Carrot, that's my advice.'

Another evening folded over the city in layers of fog.

When Carrot arrived back at the Watch House Corporal Littlebottom made a face at him and indicated, with a flicker of her eyes, the three people sitting grimly on the bench against one wall.

'They want to see an officer!' she hissed. 'But S'arnt Colon isn't back and I knocked on Mr Vimes's door and I don't think he's in.'

Carrot composed his features into a welcoming smile.

'Mrs Palm,' he said. 'And Mr Boggis . . . and Dr Downey. I am so sorry. We're rather stretched at present, what with the poisoning and this business with the golems—'

The head of the Assassins' Guild smiled, but only

with his mouth. 'It's about the poisoning we wish to speak,' he said. 'Is there somewhere a little less public?'

'Well, there's the canteen,' said Carrot. 'It'll be empty at this time of night. If you'd just step this way . . .'

'You do well for yourselves here, I must say,' said Mrs Palm. 'A canteen—'

She stopped as she stepped through the door.

'People *eat* in here?' she said.

'Well, grumble about the coffee, mostly,' said Carrot. 'And write their reports. Commander Vimes is keen on reports.'

'Captain Carrot,' said Dr Downey, firmly, 'we have to talk to you on a grave matter concerning— *What* have I sat in?'

Carrot brushed a chair hurriedly. 'Sorry, sir, we don't seem to have much time to clean up—'

'Leave it for now, leave it for now.'

The head of the Assassins' Guild leaned forward with his hands pressed together.

'Captain Carrot, we are here to discuss this terrible matter of the poisoning of Lord Vetinari.'

'You really ought to talk to Commander Vimes—'

'I believe that on a number of occasions Commander Vimes has made derogatory comments to you about Lord Vetinari,' said Dr Downey.

'You mean like "He ought to be hung except they can't find a twisty enough rope"?' said Carrot. 'Oh, yes. But everyone does that.'

'Do you?'

'Well, no,' Carrot admitted.

'And I believe he personally took over the investigation of the poisoning?'

'Well, yes. But—'

'Didn't you think that was odd?'

'No, sir. Not when I thought about it. I think he's got a sort of soft spot for the Patrician, in his way. He once said that if anyone was going to kill Vetinari he'd like it to be him.'

'Indeed?'

'But he was smiling when he said it. Sort of smiling, anyway.'

'He, er, visits his lordship most days, I believe?'

'Yes, sir.'

'And I understand that his efforts to discover the poisoner have not reached any conclusions?'

'Not as such, sir,' said Carrot. 'We've found a lot of ways he's *not* being poisoned.'

Downey nodded at the others. 'We would like to inspect the Commander's office,' he said.

'I don't know if that's—' Carrot began.

'Please think very carefully,' said Dr Downey. 'We three represent most of the guilds of this city. We feel we have a good reason for inspecting the Commander's office. You will of course accompany us to see that we do nothing illegal.'

Carrot looked awkward. 'I suppose . . . if I'm with you . . .' he said.

'That's right,' said Downey. 'That makes it official.'

Carrot led the way. 'I don't even know if he's back,' he said, opening the door. 'As I said, we've been . . . oh.'

Downey peered around him and at the figure slumped over the desk.

'It would appear that Sir Samuel *is* in,' he said. 'But quite out of it.'

'I can smell the drink from here,' said Mrs Palm. 'It's terrible what drink will do to a man.'

'A whole bottle of Bearhugger's finest,' said Mr Boggis. 'All right for some, eh?'

'But he hasn't touched a drop all year!' said Carrot, giving the recumbent Vimes a shake. 'He goes to meetings about it and everything!'

'Now let us see . . .' said Downey.

He pulled open one of the desk drawers.

'Captain Carrot?' he said. 'Can you witness that there appears to be a bag of greyish powder in here? I will now—'

Vimes's hand shot out and slammed the drawer on the man's fingers. His elbow rammed back into the assassin's stomach and, as Downey's chin jerked down, Vimes's forearm swung upwards and caught him full on the nose.

Then Vimes opened his eyes.

'Wassat? Wassat?' he said, raising his head. 'Dr Downey? Mr Boggis? Carrot? Hmm?'

'Hwat? Hwat?' screamed Downey. 'You hnsfruck me!'

'Oh, I'm *so* sorry,' said Vimes, concern radiating from every feature as he pushed the chair back into Downey's groin and stood up. 'I'm afraid I must have dropped off and, of course, when I woke up and found someone stealing from . . .'

'You're raving drunk, man!' said Mr Boggis.

Vimes's features froze.

'Indeed? Peter Piper picked a peck of pickled peppers,' he snarled, prodding the man in the chest. 'A peck of bloody pickled peppers Peter Piper damn well picked. Do you want me to continue?' he said, poking the man until his back was against the wall. 'It doesn't get much better!'

'Hwhat about thif packet?' shouted Downey, clutching his streaming nose with one hand and waving at the desk with the other.

Vimes still wore a wild-eyed mirthless grin. 'Ah, well, yes,' he said. 'You've got me there. A highly dangerous substance.'

'Ah, you admit it!'

'Yes, indeed. I suppose I have no alternative but to dispose of the evidence . . .' Vimes grabbed the packet, ripped it open and tipped most of the powder into his mouth.

'Mmm *mmm*,' he said, powder spraying everywhere as he masticated. 'Feel that tingle on the tongue!'

'But that's *arsenic*,' said Boggis.

'Good gods, is it?' said Vimes, swallowing. 'Amazing! I've got this dwarf downstairs, you know, clever little bugger, spends all his time with pipes and chemicals and things to find out what is arsenic and what isn't, and all the time here's you able to spot it just by looking! I've got to hand it to you!'

He dropped the torn packet into Boggis's hand, but the thief jerked back and the packet tumbled to the floor, spraying its contents.

'Excuse me,' said Carrot. He knelt down and peered at the powder.

It is traditionally the belief of policemen that they can tell what a substance is by sniffing it and then gingerly tasting it, but this practice had ceased in the Watch ever since Constable Flint had dipped his finger into a blackmarket consignment of ammonium chloride cut with radium, said 'Yes, this is definitely slab wurble wurble sclup', and had to spend three days tied to his bed until the spiders went away.

Nevertheless, Carrot said, 'I'm *sure* this isn't poisonous,' licked his finger and tried a bit.

'It's sugar,' he said.

Downey, his composure severely compromised, waved a finger at Vimes. 'You admitted it was dangerous!' he screamed.

'Right! Take too much of it and see what it does to your teeth!' bellowed Vimes. 'What did you *think* it was?'

'We had information . . .' Boggis began.

'Oh, you had information, did you?' said Vimes. 'You hear that, Captain? They had information. So that's all right!'

'We acted in good faith,' said Boggis.

'Let me see,' said Vimes. 'Your information was something on the lines of: Vimes is dead drunk in the Watch House and he's got a bag of arsenic in his desk? And I'll just *bet* you wanted to act in good faith, eh?'

Mrs Palm cleared her throat. 'This has gone far enough. You are correct, Sir Samuel,' she said. 'We were all sent a note.' She handed a slip of paper to Vimes. It had been written in capitals. 'And I can see we have been misinformed,' she added, glaring at

Boggis and Downey. 'Do allow me to apologize. Come, gentlemen.'

She swept out of the door. Boggis followed her quickly.

Downey dabbed at his nose. 'What's the guild price on your head, Sir Samuel?' he said.

'Twenty thousand dollars.'

'Really? I think we shall definitely have to upgrade you.'

'Delighted. I shall have to buy a new beartrap.'

'I'll, er, show you out,' said Carrot.

When he hurried back he found Vimes leaning out of the window and feeling the wall below it.

'Not a brick dislodged,' Vimes muttered. 'Not a tile loose . . . and the front office has been manned all day. Odd, that.'

He shrugged and walked back to his desk, where he picked up the note.

'And I shouldn't think we'll be able to find any Clues on this,' he said. 'There's too many greasy fingermarks all over it.' He put down the paper and glared at Carrot. 'When we find the man responsible,' he said, 'somewhere at the top of the charge sheet is going to be Forcing Commander Vimes to Tip a Whole Bottle of Single Malt on to the Carpet. That's a hanging offence.' He shuddered. There were some things a man should *not* have to do.

'It's disgusting!' said Carrot. 'Fancy them even *thinking* that you'd poison the Patrician!'

'I'm offended that they think I'd be daft enough to keep the poison in my desk drawer,' said Vimes, lighting a cigar.

'Right,' said Carrot. 'Did they think you were some kind of fool who'd keep evidence like that where anyone could find it?'

'Exactly,' said Vimes, leaning back. 'That's why I've got it in my pocket.'

He put his feet on the desk and blew out a cloud of smoke. He'd have to get rid of the carpet. He wasn't going to spend the rest of his life working in a room haunted by the smell of departed spirits.

Carrot's mouth was still open.

'Oh, good grief,' said Vimes. 'Look, it's quite simple, man. I was expected to go "At last, alcohol!", and chugalug the lot without thinking. Then some respectable pillars of the community' – he removed the cigar from his mouth and spat – 'were going to find me, in your presence, too – which was a nice touch – with the evidence of my crime neatly hidden but not so well hidden that they couldn't find it.' He shook his head sadly. 'The trouble is, you know, that once the taste's got you it never lets go.'

'But you've been very good, sir,' said Carrot. 'I've not seen you touch a drop for—'

'Oh, *that*,' said Vimes. 'I was talking about policing, not alcohol. There's lots of people will help you with the alcohol business, but there's no one out there arranging little meetings where you can stand up and say, "My name is Sam and I'm a really suspicious bastard."'

He pulled a paper bag out of his pocket. 'We'll get Littlebottom to have a look at this,' he said. 'I damn sure wasn't going to try tasting it. So I nipped down to the canteen and filled a bag with sugar out of the bowl. It was but the work of a moment to fish Nobby's butts out of it, I might add.' He opened the door, poked his head out into the corridor and yelled, 'Littlebottom!' To Carrot he added, 'You know, I feel quite perked up. The old brain has begun to work at last. You know the golem that did the killing?'

'Yes, sir?'

'Ah, but do you know what was *special* about it?'

'Can't think, sir,' said Carrot, 'except that it was a new one. The golems made it themselves, I think. But of course they needed a priest for the words and they had to borrow Mr Hopkinson's oven. I expect the old men thought it would be interesting. They were historians, after all.'

It was Vimes's turn to stand there with his mouth open.

Finally he got control of himself. 'Yes, yes, of course,' he said, his voice barely shaking. 'Yes, I mean, that's *obvious*. Plain as the nose on your face. But . . . er, have you worked out what *else* is special about it?' he added, trying to keep any trace of hope out of his voice.

'You mean the fact it's gone mad, sir?'

'Well, I didn't think it was winner of the Ankh-Morpork Mr Sanity Award!' said Vimes.

'I mean they drove it mad, sir. The other golems. They didn't mean to, but it was built-in, sir. They wanted it to do so many things. It was like their . . . child, I think. All their hopes and dreams. And when they found out it'd been killing people . . . well, that's

311

terrible to a golem. They mustn't kill, and it was their *own clay* doing it—'

'It's not a great idea for people, either.'

'But they'd put all their future in it—'

'You wanted me, Commander?' said Cheery.

'Oh, yes. Is this arsenic?' said Vimes, handing her the packet.

Cheery sniffed at it. 'It could be arsenous acid, sir. I'll have to test it, of course.'

'I thought acids sloshed about in jars,' said Vimes. 'Er . . . what's that on your hands?'

'Nail varnish, sir.'

'Nail varnish?'

'Yes, sir.'

'Er . . . fine, fine. Funny, I thought it would be green.'

'Wouldn't look good on the fingers, sir.'

'I meant the arsenic, Littlebottom.'

'Oh, you can get all sorts of colours of arsenic, sir. The sulphides – that's the ores, sir – can be red or brown or yellow or grey, sir. And then you cook them up with nitre and you get arsenous acid, sir. And a load of nasty smoke, *really* bad.'

'Dangerous stuff,' said Vimes.

'Not good at all, sir. But useful, sir,' said Cheery. 'Tanners, dyers, painters . . . It's not just poisoners that've got a use for arsenic.'

'I'm surprised people aren't dropping dead of it all the time,' said Vimes.

'Oh, most of them use golems, sir—'

The words stayed in the air even after Cheery stopped speaking.

Vimes caught Carrot's eye and started to whistle hoarsely under his breath. *This is it*, he thought. *This is where we've filled ourselves up with so many questions that they're starting to overflow and become answers.*

He felt more alive than he had for days. The recent excitement still tingled in his veins, kicking his brain into life. It was the sparkle you got with exhaustion, he knew. You were so bone-weary that a shot of adrenalin hit you like a falling troll. They *must* have it all now. All the bits. The edges, the corners, the whole picture. All there, just waiting to be pieced together . . .

'These golems,' said Carrot. 'They'd be *covered* in arsenic, would they?'

'Could be, sir. I saw one at the Alchemists' Guild building in Quirm and, hah, it'd even got arsenic plated on its hands, sir, on account of stirring crucibles with its fingers . . .'

'They don't feel heat,' said Vimes.

'Or pain,' said Carrot.

'That's right,' said Cheery. She looked uncertainly from one to the other.

'You can't poison them,' said Vimes.

'And they'll obey orders,' said Carrot. 'Without speaking.'

'Golems do *all* the really mucky jobs,' said Vimes.

'You could have mentioned this before, Cheery,' said Carrot.

'Well, you know, sir . . . Golems are just *there*, sir. No one notices golems.'

'Grease under his fingernails,' said Vimes, to the

313

room in general. 'The old man scratched at his murderer. Grease under his fingernails. With arsenic in it.'

He looked down at the notebook, still on his desk. *It's there,* he thought. *Something we haven't seen. But we've looked everywhere. So we've seen the answer and haven't seen that it is the answer. And if we don't see it now, at this moment, we'll never see it at all . . .*

'No offence, sir, but that's probably not a help,' said Cheery's voice somewhere in the distance. 'So many of the trades that use arsenic involve some kind of grease.'

Something we don't see, thought Vimes. *Something invisible. No, it wouldn't have to be invisible. Something we don't see because it's always there. Something that strikes in the night . . .*

And there it was.

He blinked. The glittering stars of exhaustion were causing his mind to think oddly. Well, thinking rationally hadn't worked.

'No one move,' he said. He held up a hand for silence. 'There it is,' he said softly. 'There. On my desk. You see it?'

'What, sir?' said Carrot.

'You mean *you* haven't worked it out?' said Vimes.

'*What,* sir?'

'The thing that's poisoning his lordship. There it is . . . on the desk. See?'

'Your notebook?'

'No!'

'He drinks Bearhugger's whisky?' said Cheery.

'I doubt it,' said Vimes.

'The blotter?' said Carrot. 'Poisoned pens? A packet of Pantweeds?'

'Where're they?' said Vimes, patting his pockets.

'Just sticking out from under the letters in the In Tray, sir,' said Carrot. He added reproachfully, 'You know, sir, the ones you don't answer.'

Vimes picked up the packet and extracted another cigar. 'Thanks,' he said. 'Hah! I didn't ask Mildred Easy what else she took! But of course they're a servant's little bonus, too! And old Mrs Easy was a seamstress, a *proper* seamstress! And this is autumn! Killed by the nights drawing in! See?'

Carrot crouched down and looked at the surface of the desk. 'Can't see it myself, sir,' he said.

'Of course you can't,' said Vimes. 'Because there's nothing to see. You can't see it. That's how you can tell it's there. If it wasn't there you'd soon see it!' He gave a huge manic grin. 'Only you wouldn't! See?'

'You all right, sir?' said Carrot. 'I know you've been overdoing it a bit these last few days—'

'I've been *under*doing it!' said Vimes. 'I've been running around looking for damn Clues instead of just thinking for five minutes! What is it I'm always telling you?'

'Er . . . er . . . Never trust anybody, sir?'

'No, not that.'

'Er . . . er . . . Everyone's guilty of something, sir?'

'Not that, either.'

'Er . . . er . . . Just because someone's a member

of an ethnic minority doesn't mean they're not a nasty small-minded little jerk, sir?'

'N— When did I say that?'

'Last week, sir. After we'd had that visit from the Campaign for Equal Heights, sir.'

'Well, not that. I mean . . . I'm pretty sure I'm always saying something else that's very relevant here. Something pithy about police work.'

'Can't remember anything right now, sir.'

'Well, I'll damn well make up something and start saying it a lot from now on.'

'Jolly good, sir.' Carrot beamed. 'It's good to see you're your old self again, sir. Looking forward to kicking ar— to prodding buttock, sir. Er . . . What have we found, sir?'

'You'll see! We're going to the palace. Fetch Angua. We might need her. And bring the search warrant.'

'You mean the sledgehammer, sir?'

'Yes. And Sergeant Colon, too.'

'He hasn't signed in again yet, sir,' said Cheery. 'He should have gone off-duty an hour ago.'

'Probably hanging around somewhere, staying out of trouble,' said Vimes.

Wee Mad Arthur peered over the edge of the wall. Somewhere below Colon, two red eyes stared up at him.

'Heavy, is it?'

''S!'

'Kick it with your other foot!'

There was a sucking sound. Colon winced. Then

316

there was a plop, a moment of silence, and a loud crash of pottery down in the street.

'The boot it was holding came off,' moaned Colon.

'How did that happen?'

'It got . . . lubricated . . .'

Wee Mad Arthur tugged at a finger. 'Up yez come, then.'

'Can't.'

'Why not? It ain't holding on to yez no more.'

'Arms tired. Another ten seconds and I'm gonna be a chalk outline . . .'

'Nah, no one's got that much chalk.' Wee Mad Arthur knelt down so that his head was level with Colon's eyes. 'If you gonna die, d'yez mind signing a chitty to say yez promised me a dollar?'

Down below, there was a chink of pottery shards.

'What was that?' said Colon. 'I thought the damn thing smashed up . . .'

Wee Mad Arthur looked down. 'D'yez believe in that reincarnation stuff, Mr Colon?' he said.

'You wouldn't get me touching that foreign muck,' said Colon.

'Well, it's putting itself together. Like one of them jiggling saw puzzles.'

'Well done, Wee Mad Arthur,' said Colon. 'But I know you're just saying that so's I'll make the effort to haul meself up, right? Statues don't go putting themselves back together when they're smashed up.'

'Please yezself. It's done nearly a whole leg already.'

Colon managed to peer down through the small

and smelly space between the wall and his armpit. All he could see were shreds of fog and a faint glow.

'You sure?' he said.

'Yez run around rat holes, yez learns to see good in the dark,' said Wee Mad Arthur. 'Otherwise yez dead.'

Something hissed, somewhere below Colon's feet.

With his one booted foot and his toes he scrabbled at the brickwork.

'It's having a wee bit o' trouble,' said Wee Mad Arthur conversationally. 'Looks like it's put its knees on wrong way round.'

Dorfl sat hunched in the abandoned cellar where the golems had met. Occasionally the golem raised its head and hissed. Red light spilled from its eyes. If something had streamed back down through the glow, soared through the eye-sockets into the red sky beyond, there would be . . .

Dorfl huddled under the glow of the universe. Its murmur was a long way off, muted, nothing to do with Dorfl.

The Words stood around the horizon, reaching all the way to the sky.

And a voice said quietly, 'You own yourself.' Dorfl saw the scene again and again, saw the concerned face, hand reaching up, filling its vision, felt the sudden icy knowledge . . .

'. . . Own yourself.'

It echoed off the Words, and then rebounded, and then rolled back and forth, increasing in volume until the little world between the Words was gripped in the sound.

Golem Must Have a Master. The letters towered against the world, but the echoes poured around them, blasting like a sandstorm. Cracks started and then ran, zigzagging across the stone, and then—

The Words exploded. Great slabs of them, mountain-sized, crashed in showers of red sand.

The universe poured in. Dorfl felt the universe pick it up and bowl it over and then lift it off its feet and up . . .

. . . and now the golem was *among* the universe. It could feel it all around, the purr of it, the busyness, the spinning complexity of it, the roar . . .

There were no Words between you and It.

You belonged to It, It belonged to you.

You couldn't turn your back on It because there It was, in front of you.

Dorfl was responsible for every tick and swerve of It.

You couldn't say, 'I had orders.' You couldn't say, 'It's not fair.' No one was listening. There were no Words. You *owned* yourself.

Dorfl orbited a pair of glowing suns and hurtled off again.

Not *Thou Shalt Not*. Say *I Will Not*.

Dorfl tumbled through the red sky, then saw a dark hole ahead. The golem felt it dragging at him, and streamed down through the glow and the hole grew larger and sped across the edges of Dorfl's vision . . .

The golem opened his eyes.

NO MASTER!

Dorfl unfolded in one movement and stood upright. He reached out one arm and extended a finger.

The golem pushed the finger easily into the wall where the argument had taken place, and then dragged it carefully through the splintering brickwork. It took him a couple of minutes but it was something Dorfl felt needed to be said.

Dorfl completed the last letter and poked a row of three dots after it. Then the golem walked away, leaving behind:

NO MASTER . . .

A blue overcast from the cigars hid the ceiling of the smoking-room.

'Ah, yes. Captain Carrot,' said a chair. 'Yes . . . indeed . . . but . . . is he the right man?'

''S got a birthmark shaped like a crown. I seen it,' said Nobby helpfully.

'But his background . . .'

'He was raised by dwarfs,' said Nobby. He waved his brandy glass at a waiter. 'Same again, mister.'

'I shouldn't think dwarfs could raise anyone very high,' said another chair. There was a hint of laughter.

'Rumours and folklore,' someone murmured.

'This is a large and busy and above all complex city. I'm afraid that having a sword and a birthmark are not much in the way of qualifications. We would need a king from a lineage that is *used* to command.'

'Like yours, my lord.'

There was a sucking, draining noise as Nobby

attacked the fresh glass of brandy. 'Oh, I'm used to command, all right,' he said, lowering the glass. 'People are always orderin' me around.'

'We would need a king who had the support of the great families and major guilds of the city.'

'People *like* Carrot,' said Nobby.

'Oh, the *people* . . .'

'Anyway, whoever got the job'd have his work cut out,' said Nobby. 'Ole Vetinari's always pushin' paper. What kinda fun is that? 'S no life, sittin' up all hours, worryin', never a moment to yerself.' He held out the empty glass. 'Same again, my old mate. Fill it right up this time, eh? No sense in havin' a great big glass and only sloshin' a bit in the bottom, is there?'

'Many people prefer to savour the bouquet,' said a quietly horrified chair. 'They enjoy sniffing it.'

Nobby looked at his glass with the red-veined eyes of one who'd heard rumours about what the upper crust got up to. 'Nah,' he said. 'I'll go on stickin' it in my mouth, if it's all the same to you.'

'If we may get to the *point*,' said another chair, 'a *king* would *not* have to spend every moment running the city. He would of course have people to do that. Advisors. Counsellors. People of experience.'

'So what'd he have to do?' said Nobby.

'He'd have to reign,' said a chair.

'Wave.'

'Preside at banquets.'

'Sign things.'

'Guzzle good brandy disgustingly.'

'*Reign*.'

321

'Sounds like a good job to me,' said Nobby. 'All right for some, eh?'

'Of course, a king would have to be someone who could recognize a hint if it was dropped on his head from a great height,' said a speaker sharply, but the other chairs shushed him into silence.

Nobby managed to find his mouth after several goes and took another long pull at his cigar. 'Seems to me,' he said, 'seems to *me*, what you want to do is find some nob with time on his hands and say, "Yo, it's your lucky day. Let's see you wave that hand."'

'Ah! *That's* a good idea! Does any name cross your mind, my lord? Have a drop more brandy.'

'Why, thanks, you're a toff. O' course, so 'm I, eh? That's right, flunkey, all the way to the top. No, can't think of anyone that fits the bill.'

'In fact, my lord, we were indeed thinking of offering the crown to you—'

Nobby's eyes bulged. And then his cheek bulged.

It is not a good idea to spray finest brandy across the room, especially when your lighted cigar is in the way. The flame hit the far wall, where it left a perfect chrysanthemum of scorched wood-work, while in accordance with a fundamental rule of physics Nobby's chair screamed back on its castors and thudded into the door.

'King?' Nobby coughed, and then they had to slap him on the back until he got his breath again. 'King?' he wheezed. 'And have Mr Vimes cut me head off?'

'All the brandy you can drink, my lord,' said a wheedling voice.

''S no good if you ain't got a throat for it to go down!'

'What're you talking about?'

'Mr Vimes'd go spare! He'd go *spare*!'

'Good heavens, man—'

'My lord,' someone corrected.

'My lord, I mean – when you're *king* you can tell that wretched Sir Samuel what to do. You'll be, as you would call it, "the boss". You could—'

'Tell ole Stoneface what to do?' said Nobby.

'That's right!'

'I'd be a king and tell ole Stoneface what to do?' said Nobby.

'Yes!'

Nobby stared into the smoky gloom.

'He'd go *spare*!'

'Listen, you silly little man—'

'*My lord*—'

'You silly little lord, you'd be able to have him executed if you wished!'

'I couldn't do that!'

'Why not?'

'He'd go spare!'

'The man calls himself an officer of the law, and whose law does he listen to, eh? Where does his law come from?'

'*I* don't know!' groaned Nobby. 'He says it comes up through his boots!' He looked around. The shadows in the smoke seemed to be closing in.

'I can't be king! Ole Vimes'd go spare!'

'*Will you stop saying that!*'

Nobby pulled at his collar.

''S a bit hot and smoky in here,' he mumbled. 'Which way's the window?'

'Over there—'

The chair rocked. Nobby hit the glass helmet-first, landed on top of a waiting carriage, bounced off and ran into the night, trying to escape destiny in general and axes in particular.

Cheri Littlebottom strode into the palace kitchens and fired her crossbow into the ceiling.

'Don't nobody move!' she yelled.

The Patrician's domestic staff looked up from their dinner.

'When you say don't *nobody* move,' said Drumknott carefully, fastidiously taking a piece of plaster off his plate, 'do you in fact mean—'

'All right, Corporal, I'll take over now,' said Vimes, patting Cheri on the shoulder. 'Is Mildred Easy here?'

All heads turned.

Mildred's spoon dropped into her soup.

'It's all right,' said Vimes. 'I just need to ask you a few more questions—'

'I'm . . . s-s-sorry, sir—'

'You haven't done anything wrong,' said Vimes, walking around the table. 'But you didn't just take food home for your family, did you?'

'S-sir?'

'What *else* did you take?'

Mildred looked at the suddenly blank expressions on the faces of the other servants. 'There was the old sheets but Mrs Dipplock did *s-say* I could have—'

'No, not that,' said Vimes.

Mildred licked her dry lips. 'Er, there was . . . there was some boot polish . . .'

'Look,' said Vimes, as kindly as possible, '*every-one* takes small things from the place where they work. Small stuff that no one notices. No one thinks of it as stealing. It's like . . . it's like *rights*. Odds and ends. Ends, Miss Easy? I'm thinking about the word "ends".'

'Er . . . you mean . . . the candle ends, sir?'

Vimes took a deep breath. It was such a relief to be right, even though you knew you'd only got there by trying every possible way to be wrong. '*Ah*,' he said.

'B-but that's not stealing, sir. I've never stolen nothing, s-sir!'

'But you take home the candle stubs? Still half an hour of light in 'em, I expect, if you burn them in a saucer?' said Vimes gently.

'But that's not stealing, sir! That's *perks*, sir.'

Sam Vimes smacked his forehead. 'Perks! Of course! *That* was the word I was looking for. Perks! Everyone's got to have perks, aren't I right? Well, that's fine, then,' he said. 'I expect you get the ones from the bedrooms, yes?'

Even through her nervousness, Mildred Easy was able to grin the grin of someone with an Entitlement that lesser beings hadn't got. 'Yessir. I'm *allowed*, sir. They're much better than the ole coarse ones we use in the main halls, sir.'

'And you put in fresh candles when necessary, do you?'

'Yessir.'

Probably slightly more often than necessary, Vimes thought. *No point in letting them burn down too much . . .*

'Perhaps you can show me where they're kept, miss?'

The maid looked along the table to the house-keeper, who glanced at Commander Vimes and then nodded. She was bright enough to know when something that sounded like a question really wasn't one.

'We keep them in the candle pantry next door, sir,' said Mildred.

'Lead the way, please.'

It wasn't a big room, but its shelves were stacked floor-to-ceiling with candles. There were the yard-high ones used in the public halls and the small everyday ones used everywhere else, sorted according to quality.

'These are what we uses in his lordship's rooms, sir.' She handed him twelve inches of white candle.

'Oh, yes . . . *very* good quality. Number Fives. Nice white tallow,' said Vimes, tossing it up and down. 'We burn these at home. The stuff we use at the Yard is damn near pork dripping. We get ours from Carry's in the Shambles now. *Very* reasonable prices. We used to deal with Spadger and Williams but Mr Carry's really cornered the market these days, hasn't he?'

'Yessir. And he delivers 'em special, sir.'

'And you put these candles in his lordship's room every day?'

'Yessir.'

'Anywhere else?'

'Oh, no, sir. His lordship's particular about that! *We* just use Number Threes.'

'And you take your, er, perks home?'

'Yessir. Gran said they gave a lovely light, sir . . .'

'I expect she sat up with your little brother, did she? Because I expect he got took sick first, so she sat up with him all night long, night after night and, hah, if I know old Mrs Easy, she did her sewing . . .'

'Yessir.'

There was a pause.

'Use my handkerchief,' said Vimes, after a while.

'Am I going to lose my position, sir?'

'No. That's definite. No one involved deserves to lose their jobs,' said Vimes. He looked at the candle. 'Except possibly me,' he added.

He stopped at the doorway, and turned. 'And if you ever want candle-ends, we've always got lots at the Watch House. Nobby'll have to start buying cooking fat like everyone else.'

'What's it doing now?' said Sergeant Colon.

Wee Mad Arthur peered over the edge of the roof again. 'It's havin' problems with its elbows,' he said conversationally. 'It keeps lookin' at one of 'em and tryin' it all ways up and it's not workin'.'

'I had that trouble when I put up them kitchen units for Mrs Colon,' said the sergeant. 'The instructions on how to open the box were inside the box—'

'Oh-oh, it's worked it out,' said the rat-catcher. 'Looks like it had it mixed up with its knees after all.'

Colon heard a clank below him.

327

'And now it's gone round the corner' – there was a crash of splintering wood – 'and now it's got into the building. I expect it'll come up the stairs, but it looks like yer'll be okay.'

'Why?'

''cos all you gotta do is let go of the roof, see?'

'I'll drop to my death!'

'Right! Nice clean way to go. None of that "arms-and-legs-bein'-ripped-off" stuff first.'

'I wanted to buy a farm!' moaned Colon.

'Could be,' said Arthur. He looked over the roof again. 'Or,' he said, as if this were hardly a better option, 'yez could try to grab the drainpipe.'

Colon looked sideways. There *was* a pipe a few feet away. If he swung his body and really made an effort, he might *just* miss it by inches and plunge to his death.

'Does it look safe?' he said.

'Compared with what, mister?'

Colon tried to swing his legs like a pendulum. Every muscle in his arm screamed at him. He knew he was overweight. He'd always meant to take exercise one day. He just hadn't been aware that it was going to be today.

'I reckon I can hear it walking up the stairs,' said Wee Mad Arthur.

Colon tried to swing faster. 'What're *you* going to do?' he said.

'Oh, don't yez worry about me,' said Wee Mad Arthur. 'I'll be fine. I'll jump.'

'Jump?'

'Sure. I'll be safe 'cos of being normal-sized, see.'

'You think you're normal-sized?'

Wee Mad Arthur looked at Colon's hands. 'Are these yer fingers right here by my boots?' he said.

'Right, right, you're normal-sized. 'S not your fault you've moved into a city full of giants,' said Colon.

'Right. The smaller yez are the lighter yez fall. Well known fact. A spider'll not even notice a drop like this, a mouse'd walk away, a horse'd break every bone in its body and a helephant would spla—'

'Oh, gods,' muttered Colon. He could feel the drainpipe with his boot now. But getting a grip would mean there would have to be one long, bottomless moment when he was not exactly holding on to the roof and not exactly holding on to the drainpipe and in very serious peril of holding on to the ground.

There was another crash from somewhere on the roof.

'Right,' said Wee Mad Arthur. 'See you at the bottom.'

'Oh, gods . . .'

The gnome stepped off the roof.

'All okay so far,' he shouted, as he went past Colon.

'Oh, gods . . .'

Sergeant Colon looked up into two red glows.

'Doing fine up to now,' said a dopplering voice from below.

'Oh, *gods* . . .'

Colon heaved his legs around, stood on fresh air for a moment, grabbed the top of the pipe, ducked his head as a pottery fist swung at him, heard the nasty little noise as the pipe's rusty bolts said good-bye to the wall and, still clinging to a tilting length of cast-iron pipe as if it were going to help, disappeared backwards into the fog.

Mr Sock looked up at the sound of the door opening, and then cowered back against the sausage machine.

'*You?*' he whispered. 'Here, you can't come back! I *sold* you!'

Dorfl regarded him steadily for a few seconds, and then walked past him and took the largest cleaver from the blood-stained rack on the wall.

Sock began to shake.

'I-I-I was always g-g-good to you,' he said. 'A-a-always let you h-have your h-holy d-d-days off—'

Dorfl stared at him again. *It's only red light,* Sock gibbered to himself . . .

But it seemed more focused. He felt it entering his head through his own eyes and examining his soul.

The golem pushed him aside and stepped out of the slaughterhouse and towards the cattle pens.

Sock unfroze. They never fought back, did they? They *couldn't.* It was how the damn things were *made.*

He stared around at the other workers, humans and trolls alike. 'Don't just stand there! Get it!'

One or two hesitated. It was a *big* cleaver in the golem's hand. And when Dorfl stopped to look around at them there was something different about the golem's stance, too. It didn't *look* like something that wouldn't fight back.

But Sock didn't employ people for the muscles in their heads. Besides, no one had really liked a golem around the place.

A troll aimed a pole-axe at him. Dorfl caught it one-handed without turning his head and snapped the hickory handle with his fingers. A man with a hammer had it plucked from his hand and thrown so hard at the wall that it left a hole.

After that they followed at a cautious distance. Dorfl took no further notice of them.

The steam over the cattle pens mingled with the fog. Hundreds of dark eyes watched Dorfl curiously as he walked between the fences. They were always quiet when the golem was around.

He stopped by one of the largest pens. There were voices from behind.

'Don't tell me it's going to slaughter the lot of 'em! We'll never get that lot jointed this shift!'

'I heard where there was one at a carpenter's that went odd and made five thousand tables in one night. Lost count or something.'

'It's just staring at them . . .'

'I mean, five thousand tables? One of them had twenty-seven legs. It got stuck on legs . . .'

Dorfl brought the cleaver down hard and sliced the lock off the gate. The cattle watched the golem, with that guarded expression which cattle have that means they're waiting for the next thought to turn up.

He walked on to the sheep pens and opened them, too. The pigs were next, and then the poultry.

'*All* of them?' said Mr Sock.

The golem walked calmly back down the line of pens, ignoring the watchers, and re-entered the slaughterhouse. He came out very shortly afterwards leading the ancient and hairy billygoat on a piece of string. He went past the waiting animals until he reached the wide gates that led on to the main road, which he opened. Then he let the goat loose.

The animal sniffed the air and rolled its slotted eyes. Then, apparently deciding that the distant odour of the cabbage fields beyond the city wall was much preferable to the smells immediately around it, it trotted away up the road.

The animals followed it in a rush, but with hardly any other noise than the rustle of movement and the sounds of their hooves. They streamed around the stationary figure of Dorfl, who stood and watched them go.

A chicken, bewildered by the stampede, landed on the golem's head and started to cluck.

Anger finally overcame Sock's terror. 'What the hell are you doing?' he shouted, trying to field a few stray sheep as they bolted out of the pens. 'That's *money* walking out of the gate, you—'

Dorfl's hand was suddenly around his throat. The golem picked him up and held the struggling man at arm's-length, turning his head this way and that as if considering his next course of action.

Finally he tossed away the cleaver, reached up under the chicken that had taken up residence, and produced a small brown egg. With apparent ceremony the golem smashed it carefully on Sock's scalp and dropped him.

The golem's former co-workers jumped back out of the way as Dorfl walked back through the slaughterhouse.

There was a tally board by the entrance. Dorfl looked at it for a while, then picked up the chalk and wrote:

NO MASTER . . .

The chalk crumbled in his fingers. Dorfl walked out into the fog.

Cheri looked up from her workbench.

'The wick's *full* of arsenous acid,' she said. 'Well done, sir! This candle even weighs slightly more than other candles!'

'What an evil way to kill anyone,' said Angua.

'Certainly very clever,' said Vimes. 'Vetinari sits up half the night writing, and in the morning the candle's burned down. Poisoned by the light. The light's something you don't see. Who looks at the light? Not some plodding old copper.'

'Oh, you're not that old, sir,' said Carrot, cheerfully.

'What about plodding?'

'Or that plodding, either,' Carrot added quickly. 'I've always pointed out to people that you walk in a very purposeful and meaningful manner.'

Vimes gave him a sharp look and saw nothing more than a keen and innocently helpful expression.

'We don't look at the light because the light is what we look *with*,' said Vimes. 'Okay. And now I think we should go and have a look at the candle factory, shouldn't we? You come, Littlebottom, and bring your . . . have you got taller, Littlebottom?'

'High-heeled boots, sir,' said Cheri.

'I thought dwarfs always wore iron boots . . .'

'Yes, sir. But I've got high heels on mine, sir. I welded them on.'

'Oh. Fine. Right.' Vimes pulled himself together. 'Well, if you can still totter, bring your alchemy stuff with you. Detritus should've come off-duty from the palace. When it comes to locked doors you can't beat Detritus. He's a walking crowbar. We'll pick him up on the way.'

He loaded his crossbow and lit a match.

'Right,' he said. 'We've done it the modern way, now let's try policing like grandfather used to do it. It's time to—'

'Prod buttock, sir?' said Carrot, hurriedly.

'Close,' said Vimes, taking a deep drag and blowing out a smoke ring, 'but no cigar.'

Sergeant Colon's view of the world was certainly changing. Just when something was about to fix itself firmly in his mind as the worst moment of his entire life, it was hurriedly replaced by something even nastier.

Firstly, the drainpipe he was riding hit the wall of the building opposite. In a well-organized world he might have landed on a fire escape, but fire escapes were unknown in Ankh-Morpork and the flames generally had to leave via the roof.

With the pipe thus leaning against the wall, he found himself sliding down the diagonal. Even this might have been a happy outcome were it not for the fact that Colon was a heavy man and, as his weight slid nearer to the middle of the unsupported pipe, the pipe sagged, and cast iron has only a very limited amount of sag before it snaps, which it now did.

Colon dropped, and landed on something soft – at least, softer than the street – and the something went 'mur-r-r-r-r-m!'. He bounced off it and landed on something lower and softer which went 'baaaaarp!', and rolled from this on to something even lower and apparently made of feathers, which went insane. And pecked him.

The street was full of animals, milling around uncertainly. When animals are in a state of uncertainty they get nervous, and the street was already, as it were, paved with anxiety. The only benefit to Sergeant Colon was that this made it slightly softer than would otherwise have been the case.

Hooves trod on his hands. Very large dribbly noses sneezed at him.

Sergeant Colon had not hitherto had a great deal of experience of animals, except in portion sizes. When he'd been little he'd had a pink stuffed pig called Mr Dreadful, and he'd got up to Chapter Six in *Animal Husbandry*. It had woodcuts in it. There was no mention of hot smelly breath and great clomping feet like soup plates on a stick. Cows, in Sergeant Colon's book, should go 'moo'. Every child knew that. They shouldn't go 'mur-r-r-r-r-m!' like some kind of undersea monster and spray you with spit.

He tried to get up, skidded on some cow's

moment of crisis, and sat down on a sheep. It went 'blaaaart!' What kind of noise was that for a sheep to make?

He got up again and tried to make his way to the kerb. 'Shoo! Get out of the damn way, you sheep! Garn!'

A goose hissed at him and stuck out altogether too much neck.

Colon backed off, and stopped when something nudged him in the back. It was a pig.

It was no Mr Dreadful. This wasn't the little piggy that went to market, or the little piggy that stayed at home. It would be quite hard to imagine what kind of foot would have a piggy like this, but it would probably be the kind that also had hair and scales and toenails like cashew nuts.

This piggy was the size of a pony. This piggy had tusks. And it wasn't pink. It was a blue-black colour and covered with sharp hair but it did have – *let's be fair,* thought Colon – little red piggy eyes.

This little piggy looked like the little piggy that killed the boarhounds, disembowelled the horse and ate the huntsman.

Colon turned around, and came face-to-face with a bull like a beef cube on legs. It turned its huge head from side to side so that each rolling eye could get a sight of the sergeant, but it was clear that neither of them liked him very much.

It lowered its head. There wasn't room for it to charge, but it could certainly push.

As the animals crowded around him, Colon took the only way of escape possible.

*   *   *

There were men slumped all over the alley.

'Hello, hello, hello, what's all this, then?' said Carrot.

A man who was holding his arm and groaning looked up at him. 'We were viciously attacked!'

'We don't have time for this,' said Vimes.

'We may have,' said Angua. She tapped him on the shoulder and pointed to the wall opposite, on which was written in a familiar script:

NO MASTER . . .

Carrot hunched down and spoke to the casualty. 'You were attacked by a golem, were you?' he said.

'Right! Vicious bugger! Just walked out of the fog and went for us, you know what they're like!'

Carrot gave the man a cheerful smile. Then his gaze travelled along the man's body to the big hammer lying in the gutter, and moved from that to the other tools strewn around the scene of the fight. Several had their handles broken. There was a long crowbar, bent nearly into a circle.

'It's lucky you were all so well armed,' he said.

'It turned on us,' said the man. He tried to snap his fingers. 'Just like *that* – aargh!'

'You seem to have hurt your fingers . . .'

'You're right!'

'It's just that I don't understand how it could have turned on you *and* just walked out of the fog,' said Carrot.

'Everyone knows they're not allowed to fight back!'

'"Fight back",' Carrot repeated.

'It's not right, them walking around the streets like that,' the man muttered, looking away.

There was the sound of running feet behind them and a couple of men in blood-stained aprons caught up with them. 'It went that way!' one yelled. 'You'll be able to catch up with it if you hurry!'

'Come on, don't hang around! What do we pay our taxes for?' said the other.

'It went all round the cattle yards and let everything out. *Everything!* You can't move on Pigsty Hill!'

'A *golem* let all the cattle out?' said Vimes. 'What for?'

'How should I know? It took the yudasgoat out of Sock's slaughterhouse so half the damn things are following it around! And then it went and put old Fosdyke in his sausage machine—'

'What?'

'Oh, it didn't turn the handle. It just shoved a handful of parsley in his mouth, dropped an onion down his trousers, covered him in oatmeal and dropped him in the hopper!'

Angua's shoulders started to shake. Even Vimes grinned.

'And then it went into the poultry merchant's, grabbed Mr Terwillie, and' – the man stopped, aware there was a lady present, even if she was making snorting noises while trying not to laugh, and continued in a mumble – 'made use of some sage and onion. If you know what I mean . . .'

'You mean he—?' Vimes began.

'Yes!'

His companion nodded. 'Poor old Terwillie

won't be able to look sage and onion in the face again, I reckon.'

'By the sound of it, that's the last thing he'll do,' said Vimes.

Angua had to turn her back.

'Tell him about what happened in your pork butcher's,' said the man's companion.

'I don't think you'll need to,' said Vimes. 'I'm seeing a pattern here.'

'Right! And poor young Sid's only an apprentice and didn't deserve what it done to him!'

'Oh, dear,' said Carrot. 'Er . . . I think I've got an ointment that might be—'

'Will it help with the apple?' the man demanded.

'It shoved an apple in his mouth?'

'Wrong!'

Vimes winced. 'Ouch . . .'

'What's going to be done, eh?' said the butcher, his face a few inches from Vimes's.

'Well, if you can get a grip on the stem—'

'I'm serious! What are *you* going to do? I'm a taxpayer and I know my rights!'

He prodded Vimes in the breastplate. Vimes's expression went wooden. He looked down at the finger, and then back up at the man's large red nose.

'In that case,' said Vimes, 'I suggest you take another apple and—'

'Er, excuse me,' said Carrot loudly. 'You're Mr Maxilotte, aren't you? Got a shop in the Shambles?'

'Yes, that's right. What of it?'

'It's just that I don't recall seeing your name on

the register of taxpayers, which is very odd because you said you *were* a taxpayer, but of course you wouldn't lie about a thing like that and anyway when you paid your taxes they would have given you a receipt because that's the law and I'm sure you'd be able to find it if you looked—'

The butcher lowered his finger. 'Er, yes . . .'

'I could come and help you if you'd like,' said Carrot.

The butcher gave Vimes a despairing look.

'He really *does* read that stuff,' said Vimes. 'For pleasure. Carrot, why don't you scarp—? My gods, what the hell is *that*?'

There was a bellow further up the street.

Something big and muddy was approaching at a sort of menacing amble. In the gloom it looked vaguely like a very fat centaur, half-man, half . . . in *fact* it was, he realized as it bounced nearer, half-Colon, half-bull.

Sergeant Colon had lost his helmet and had a certain look about him that suggested he had been close to the soil.

As the massive bull cantered past, the sergeant rolled his eyes wildly and said, 'I daren't get off! I daren't get off!'

'How did you get *on*?' shouted Vimes.

'It wasn't easy, sir! I just grabbed the 'orns, sir, next minute I was on its back!'

'Well, hang on!'

'Yes, sir! Hanging on, *sir*!'

*　　*　　*

Rogers the bulls were angry and bewildered, which counts as the basic state of mind for full-grown bulls.*

But they had a particular reason. Beef cattle have a religion. They are deeply spiritual animals. They believe that good and obedient cattle go to a better place when they die, through a magic door. They don't know what happens next, but they've heard that it involves really good eating and, for some reason, horseradish.

Rogers had been quite looking forward to it. They were getting a bit creaky these days, and cows seemed to run faster than they had done when they were lads. They could just taste that heavenly horseradish . . .

And instead they'd been herded into a crowded pen for a day and *then* the gate had been opened and there'd been animals everywhere and this did *not* look like the Promised Lard.

And someone was on their back. They'd tried to buck him off a few times. In Rogers' heyday the impudent man would by now be a few stringy red stains on the ground, but finally the arthritic bulls had given up until such time as they could find a handy tree on which to scrape him off.

---

*Because of the huge obtrusive mass of his forehead, Rogers the bulls' view of the universe was from two eyes each with their own non-overlapping hemispherical view of the world. Since there were two separate visions, Rogers had reasoned, that meant there must be two bulls (bulls not having been bred for much deductive reasoning). Most bulls believe this, which is why they always keep turning their head this way and that when they look at you. They do this because both of them want to see.

They just wished the wretched man would stop yelling.

Vimes took a few steps after the bull, and then turned.

'Carrot? Angua? You two get down to Carry's tallow works. Just keep an eye on it until we get there, understand? Spy out the place but don't go in, understand? Right? Do not in any circumstances move in. Do I make myself clear? Just remain in the area. Right?'

'Yes, sir,' said Carrot.

'Detritus, let's get Fred off that thing.'

The crowds were melting away ahead of the bull. A ton of pedigree bull does not experience traffic congestion, at least not for any length of time.

'Can't you jump off, Fred?' Vimes yelled, as he ran along behind.

'I do not wish to give that a try, sir!'

'Well, can you steer it?'

'How, sir?'

'Take the bull by the horns, man!'

Colon tentatively reached out and took a horn in each hand. Rogers the bulls turned their head and nearly pulled him off.

'He's a bit stronger than me, sir! Quite a lot stronger actually, sir!'

'I could shoot it through der head wid my bow, Mr Vimes,' said Detritus, flourishing his converted siege weapon.

'This is a crowded street, Sergeant. It might hit an innocent person, even in Ankh-Morpork.'

'Sorry, sir.' Detritus brightened. 'But if it did we could always say they'd bin guilty of somethin', sir?'

'No, that . . . What's that chicken doing?'

A small black bantam cock raced up the street, ran between the bull's legs and skidded to a halt just in front of Rogers. A smaller figure jumped off its back, leapt up, caught hold of the ring through the bull's nose, swung up further until it was in the mass of curls on the bull's forehead, and then took firm hold of a lock of hair in each tiny hand.

'It looks like Wee Mad Arthur der ger-nome, sir,' said Detritus. 'He . . . tryin' to nut der bull . . .'

There was a noise like a slow woodpecker working on a particularly difficult tree, and it punctuated a litany of complaints from somewhere between the animal's eyes.

'Take that, yer big lump that yez are . . .'

The bulls stopped. They tried to turn their head so that one or other of the Rogerses could see what the hell it was that was hammering at their foreheads, and might as well have tried looking down their own ears.

They staggered backwards.

'Fred,' Vimes whispered. 'You slip off its back while it's busy.'

With a panicky look, Sergeant Colon swung a leg over the bull's huge back and slid down to the ground. Vimes grabbed him and hustled him into a doorway. Then he hustled him out again. A doorway was far too confined a space in which to be anywhere near Fred Colon.

'Why are you all covered in crap, Fred?'

'Well, sir, you know that creek that you're up without a paddle? It started there and it's got worse, sir.'

'Good grief. Worse than that?'

'Permission to go and have a bath, sir?'

'No, but you could stand back a few more feet. What happened to your helmet?'

'Last time I saw it, it was on a sheep, sir. Sir, I was tied up and shoved in a cellar and heroically broke free, sir! And I was chased by one of them golems, sir!'

'Where was this?'

Colon had hoped he wouldn't be asked that. 'It was a place in the Shambles,' he said. 'It was foggy, so I—'

Vimes grabbed Colon's wrists. 'What's this?'

'They tied me up with string, sir! But at great pers'nal risk of life and limb I—'

'This doesn't look like string to *me*,' said Vimes.

'No, sir?'

'No, this looks like . . . candlewick.'

Colon looked blank.

'That a Clue, sir?' he said, hopefully.

There was a splatting noise as Vimes slapped him on the back. 'Well done, Fred,' he said, wiping his hand on his trousers. 'It's certainly a corroboration.'

'That's what I thought!' said Colon quickly. 'This is a corrobolaration and I've got to get it to Commander Vimes as soon as possible regardless of—'

'Why's that gnome nutting that bull, Fred?'

'That's Wee Mad Arthur, sir. We owe him a dollar. He was . . . of some help, sir.'

Rogers the bulls were on their knees, dazed and bewildered. It wasn't that Wee Mad Arthur was capable of delivering a killing blow, but he just didn't stop. After a while the noise and the thumping got on people's nerves.

'Should we help him?' said Vimes.

'Looks like he's doing all right by himself, sir,' said Colon.

Wee Mad Arthur looked up and grinned. 'One dollar, right?' he shouted. 'No welching or I'll come after yez! One of these buggers trod on me grandpa once!'

'Was he hurt?'

'He got one of his horns twisted right orf!'

Vimes took Sergeant Colon firmly by the arm. 'Come on, Fred, it's all hitting the street now!'

'Right, sir! And most of it's splashing!'

'I say! You there! You're a watchman, aren't you? Come over here!'

Vimes turned. A man had pushed his way through the crowds.

On the whole, Colon reflected, it was just possible that the worst moment of his life hadn't happened yet. Vimes tended to react in a ballistic way to words like 'I say! You there!' when uttered in a certain kind of neighing voice.

The speaker had an aristocratic look about him, and the angry air of a man not accustomed to the rigours of life who has just found one happening to him.

Vimes saluted smartly. 'Yessir! I'm a watchman, *sir*!'

'Well, just you come along with me and arrest this thing. It's disturbing the workers.'

'What thing, sir?'

'A golem, man! Walked into the factory as bold as you like and started painting on the damn walls!'

'What factory, sir?'

'You come with me, my man. I happen to be a very good friend of your commander and I can't say I like your attitude.'

'Sorry about that, sir,' said Vimes, with a cheerfulness that Sergeant Colon had come to dread.

There was a nondescript factory on the other side of the street. The man strode in.

'Er . . . he said "golem", sir,' murmured Colon.

Vimes had known Fred Colon a long time. 'Yes, Fred, so it's vitally important for you to stay on guard out here,' he said.

The relief rose off Colon like steam. 'That's right, sir!' he said.

The factory was full of sewing-machines. People were sitting meekly in front of them. It was the sort of thing the guilds hated, but since the Guild of Seamstresses didn't take all that much interest in sewing there was no one to object. Endless belts led up from each machine to pulleys on a long spindle near the roof, which in turn were driven by . . . Vimes's eyes followed it down the length of the workshop . . . a treadmill, now stationary and somewhat broken. A couple of golems were standing forlornly alongside it, looking lost.

There was a hole in the wall quite close to it and, above it, someone had written in red paint:

WORKERS! NO MASTER BUT YOURSELVES!

Vimes grinned.

'It smashed its way in, broke the treadmill, pulled my golems out, painted that stupid message on the wall and stamped out again!' said the man behind him.

'Hmm, yes, I see. A lot of people use oxen in their treadmills,' said Vimes mildly.

'What's that got to do with it? Anyway, cattle can't keep going twenty-four hours a day.'

Vimes's gaze worked its way along the rows of workers. Their faces had that worried, Cockbill Street look that you got when you were cursed with pride as well as poverty.

'No, indeed,' he said. 'Most of the clothing workshops are up at Nap Hill, but the wages are cheaper down here, aren't they?'

'People are jolly glad to get the work!'

'Yes,' said Vimes, looking at the faces again. 'Glad.' At the far end of the factory, he noted, the golems were trying to rebuild their treadmill.

'Now you listen to me, what I want you to do is—' the factory-owner began.

Vimes's hand gripped his collar and dragged him forward until his face was a few inches from Vimes's own.

'*No*, you listen to *me*,' hissed Vimes. 'I mix with crooks and thieves and thugs all day and that doesn't worry me at all but after two minutes with you I need a bath. And if I find that damn golem I'll shake its damn hand, you hear me?'

To the surprise of that part of Vimes that wasn't

raging, the man found enough courage to say 'How dare you! You're supposed to be the law!'

Vimes's furious finger almost went up the man's nose.

'Where shall I start?' he yelled. He glared at the two golems. 'And why are you clowns repairing the treadmill?' he shouted. 'Good grief, haven't got the sense you were bor— Haven't you got any sense?'

He stormed out of the building. Sergeant Colon stopped trying to scrape himself clean and ran to catch up with him.

'I heard some people say they saw a golem come out of the other door, sir,' he said. 'It was a red one. You know, red clay. But the one that was after me was white, sir. Are you angry, Sam?'

'Who's that man who owns that place?'

'That's Mr Catterail, sir. You know, he's always writing you letters about there being too many what he calls "lesser races" in the Watch. You know . . . trolls and dwarfs . . .'

The sergeant had to trot to keep up with him.

'Get some zombies,' said Vimes.

'You've always been dead against zombies, excuse my pune,' said Sergeant Colon.

'Any want to join, are there?'

'Oh, yessir. Couple of good lads, sir, and but for the grey skin hangin' off 'em you'd swear they hadn't been buried five minutes.'

'Swear them in tomorrow.'

'Right, sir. Good idea. And of course it's a great saving not having to include them in the pension plan.'

'They can patrol up on Kings Down. After all, they're only human.'

'Right, sir.' When Sam is in these moods, Colon thought, you agree with *everything*. 'You're really getting the hang of this affirmative action stuff, eh sir?'

'Right now I'd swear in a gorgon!'

'There's always Mr Bleakley, sir, he's getting fed up with working in the kosher butcher's and—'

'But no vampires. *Never* any vampires. Now let's get a move on, Fred.'

Nobby Nobbs ought to have known. That's what he told himself as he scuttled through the streets. All that stuff about kings and stuff – they'd wanted him to . . .

It was a terrible thought . . .

Volunteer.

Nobby had spent a lifetime in one uniform or another. And one of the most basic lessons he'd learned was that men with red faces and plummy voices never *ever* gave cushy numbers to the likes of Nobby. They'd ask for volunteers to do something 'big and clean' and you'd end up scrubbing some damn great drawbridge; they'd say, 'Anyone here like good food?' and you'd be peeling potatoes for a week. You never *ever* volunteered. Not even if a sergeant stood there and said, 'We need someone to drink alcohol, bottles of, and make love, passionate, to women, for the use of.' There was *always* a snag. If a choir of angels asked for volunteers for Paradise to step forward, Nobby knew enough to take one smart pace to the rear.

When the call came for Corporal Nobbs, it would not find him wanting. It would not find him at all.

Nobby avoided a herd of pigs in the middle of the street.

Even Mr Vimes never expected him to *volunteer*. He respected Nobby's pride.

Nobby's head ached. It must've been the quail's eggs, he was sure. They couldn't be healthy birds to lay titchy eggs like that.

He sidled past a cow that had got its head stuck in someone's window.

Nobby as king? Oh, *yes*. No one ever gave a Nobbs anything except maybe a skin disease or sixty lashes. It was a dog-eat-Nobbs world, right enough. If there were to be a world competition for losers, a Nobbs would come firs— last.

He stopped running and went to earth in a doorway. In its welcome shadows he extracted a very short cigarette end from behind his ear and lit it.

Now that he felt safe enough to think about more than flight he wondered about all the animals that seemed to be on the streets. Unlike the family tree that had borne Fred Colon as its fruit, the creeping vine of the Nobbses had flourished only within city walls. Nobby was vaguely aware of animals as being food in a primary stage and left it at that. But he was pretty sure they weren't supposed to be wandering around untidily like this.

Gangs of men were trying to round them up. Since they were tired and working at cross-purposes, and the animals were hungry and bewildered, all that was happening was that the streets were getting a lot muddier.

Nobby became aware that he was not alone in the doorway.

He looked down.

Also lurking in the shadows was a goat. It was unkempt and smelly, but it turned its head and gave Nobby the most knowing look he'd ever seen on the face of an animal. Unexpectedly, and most uncharacteristically, Nobby was struck by a surge of fellow-feeling.

He pinched out the end of his cigarette and passed it down to the goat, which ate it.

'You and me both,' said Nobby.

Miscellaneous livestock scattered madly as Carrot, Angua and Cheri made their way down the Shambles. They especially tried to keep away from Angua. It seemed to Cheri that an invisible barrier was advancing in front of them. Some animals tried to climb walls or scattered madly into side alleys.

'Why are they so scared?' said Cheri.

'Can't imagine,' said Angua.

A few maddened sheep ran away from them as they walked around the candle-factory. Light from its high windows indicated that candlemaking continued all night.

'They make nearly half a million candles every twenty-four hours,' said Carrot. 'I heard they've got very advanced machinery. It sounds very interesting. I'd love to see it.'

At the rear of the premises light blazed out into

the fog. Crates of candles were being manhandled on to a succession of carts.

'Looks normal enough,' said Carrot, as they eased themselves into a conveniently shadowy doorway. 'Busy, though.'

'I don't see what good this is going to do,' said Angua. 'As soon as they see us they can destroy any evidence. And, even if we find arsenic, so what? There's no crime in owning arsenic, is there?'

'Er . . . is there a crime in owning *that*?' whispered Cheri.

A golem was walking slowly up the alley. It was quite unlike any other golem they had seen. The others were ancient and had repaired themselves so many times they were as shapeless as a gingerbread man, but this one looked like a human, or at least like humans wished they could look. It resembled a statue made of white clay. Around its head, part of the very design, was a crown.

'I was *right*,' murmured Carrot. 'They *did* make themselves a golem. The poor devils. They thought a king would make them free.'

'Look at its legs,' said Angua.

As the golem walked, lines of red light appeared and disappeared all over its legs, and across its body and arms.

'It's cracking,' she said.

'*I knew* you couldn't bake pottery in an old bread oven!' said Cheri. 'It's not the right *shape*!'

The golem pushed open a door and disappeared into the factory.

'Let's go,' said Carrot.

'Commander Vimes told us to wait for him,' said Angua.

'Yes, but we don't know *what* might be going on in there,' said Carrot. 'Besides, he likes us to use our initiative. We can't just hang around now.'

He darted across the alley and opened the door.

There were crates piled inside, with a narrow passageway between them. From all around them, but slightly muffled by the crates, came the clicking and rattling of the factory. The air smelled of hot wax.

Cheri was aware of a whispered conversation going on several feet above her little round helmet.

'*I wish Mr Vimes hadn't wanted us to bring her. Supposing something happens to her?*'

'*What are you talking about?*'

'*Well . . . you know . . . she's a girl.*'

'*So what? There's at least three female dwarfs in the Watch already and you don't worry about them.*'

'*Oh, come on . . . name one.*'

'*Lars Skulldrinker, for a start.*'

'*No! Really?*'

'*Are you calling this nose a liar?*'

'*But he broke up a fight in the Miner's Arms single-handedly last week!*'

'*Well? Why do you assume females are weaker? You wouldn't worry about* me *taking on a vicious bar crowd by myself.*'

'*I'd give aid where necessary.*'

'*To me or to them?*'

'*That's unfair!*'

'*Is it?*'

'*I wouldn't help them unless you got really rough.*'

'*Ah, so? And they say chivalry is dead . . .*'

'*Anyway, Cheri is . . . a bit different. I'm sure he . . . she's good at alchemy, but we'd better watch her back in a fight. Hold on . . .*'

They'd stepped out into the factory.

Candles whirled overhead – hundreds of them, *thousands* of them – dangling by their wicks from an endless belt of complex wooden links that switch-backed its way up and down the long hall.

'I heard about this,' said Carrot. 'It's called a producing line. It's a way of making thousands of things that are all the same. But look at the speed! I'm amazed the treadmill can—'

Angua pointed. There was a treadmill creaking around beside her, but there was nothing inside it.

'*Something's* got to be powering all this,' said Angua.

Carrot pointed. Further up the hall the switch-backs of the line converged in a complicated knot. There was a figure somewhere in the middle, arms moving in a blur.

Just beside Carrot the line ended at a big wooden hopper. Candles cascaded into it. No one had been emptying it, and they were tumbling over the pile and rolling on to the floor.

'Cheri,' said Carrot. 'Do you know how to use any kind of weapon?'

'Er . . . no, Captain Carrot.'

'Right. You just wait in the alley, then. I don't want any harm coming to you.'

She scuttled off, looking relieved.

Angua sniffed the air. 'There's been a vampire here,' she said.

'I think we'd—' Carrot began.

'I knew you'd find out! I wish I'd never bought the damned thing! I've got a bow! I warn you, I've got a crossbow!'

They turned. 'Ah, Mr Carry,' said Carrot cheerfully. He produced his badge. 'Captain Carrot, Ankh-Morpork City Watch—'

'I know who you are! I know who you are! And *what* you are, too! I knew you'd come! I've got a bow and I'm not afraid to use it!' The crossbow's point moved uncertainly, proving him a liar.

'Really?' said Angua. '*What* we are?'

'I didn't even want to get involved!' said Carry. 'It killed those old men, didn't it?'

'Yes,' said Carrot.

'Why? I didn't tell it to!'

'Because they helped make it, I think,' said Carrot. 'It knew who to blame.'

'The golems sold it to me!' said Carry. 'I thought it'd help build up the business but the damned thing won't stop—'

He glanced up at the line of candles whirring overhead, but jerked his head back before Angua could move.

'Works hard, does it?'

'Hah!' But Carry didn't look like a man enjoying a joke. He looked like a man in private torment. 'I've laid off everyone except the girls in the packing department, and *they're* on three shifts and overtime! I've got four men out looking for tallow, two negotiating for wicks and three trying to buy more storage space!'

'Then get it to stop making candles,' said Carrot.

'It goes off into the streets when we run out of tallow! You want it walking around looking for something to do? Hey, you two stay together!' Carry added urgently, waving the crossbow.

'Look, all you have to do is change the words in its head,' said Carrot.

'It won't let me! Don't you think I've tried?'

'It can't *not let you*,' said Carrot. 'Golems have to let—'

'I said it won't let me!'

'What about the poisoned candles?' said Carrot.

'That wasn't my idea!'

'Whose idea was it?'

Carry's crossbow swung back and forth. He licked his lips. 'This has all gone far too far,' he said. 'I'm getting out.'

'Whose idea, Mr Carry?'

'I'm not going to end up in some alley somewhere with as much blood as a banana!'

'Now then, we wouldn't do anything like that,' said Carrot.

Mr Carry was exporting terror. Angua could smell it streaming off him. He might pull the trigger out of sheer panic.

There was another smell, too. 'Who's the vampire?' she said.

For a moment she thought the man *would* fire the crossbow. 'I never said anything about him!'

'You've got garlic in your pocket,' said Angua. 'And the place reeks of vampire.'

'He said we could get the golem to do anything,' Carry mumbled.

'Like making poisoned candles?' said Carrot.

'Yes, but he said it'd just keep Vetinari out of the way,' said Carry. He seemed to be getting a tenuous grip on himself. 'And he's not dead, 'cos I'd have heard,' he said. 'I shouldn't think making him ill is a crime, so you can't—'

'The candles killed two other people,' said Carrot.

Carry started to panic again. 'Who?'

'An old lady and a baby in Cockbill Street.'

'Were they important?' said Carry.

Carrot nodded to himself. 'I was almost feeling sorry for you,' he said. 'Right up to that point. You're a lucky man, Mr Carry.'

'You think so?'

'Oh, yes. We got to you before Commander Vimes did. Now, just put down the crossbow and we can talk about—'

There was a noise. Or, rather, the sudden cessation of a noise that had been so pervasive that it had no longer been consciously heard.

The clacking line had stopped. There was a chorus of little waxy thuds as the hanging candles swung and hit one another, and then silence unrolled. The last candle dropped off the line, tumbled down the heap in the hopper, and bounced on the floor.

And in the silence, the sound of footsteps.

Carry started to back away. 'Too late!' he moaned.

Both Carrot and Angua saw his finger move.

Angua pushed Carrot out of the way as the claw released the string, but he had anticipated this and his hand was already flinging itself up and across. She heard the sickening, tearing noise as his palm whirled in front of her face, and his grunt as the force of the bolt spun him round.

He landed heavily on the floor, clutching his left hand. The crossbow bolt was sticking out of the palm.

Angua crouched down. 'It doesn't look barbed, let me pull—'

Carrot grabbed her wrist. 'The point's silver! Don't touch it!'

They both looked up as a shadow crossed the light.

The king golem looked down at her.

She felt her teeth and fingernails begin to lengthen.

Then she saw the small round face of Cheri peering nervously around a pile of crates. Angua fought down her werewolf instincts, screamed 'Stay right there!' at the dwarf and at every swelling hair follicle, and hesitated between pursuing the fleeing Carry and dragging Carrot to safety.

She told her body again that a wolf-shape was *not* an option. There were too many strange smells, too many fires . . .

The golem glistened with tallow and wax.

She backed away.

Behind the golem she saw Cheri look down at the groaning Carrot and then up at a fire-axe hooked on the wall. The dwarf took it down and weighed it vaguely in her hands.

'Don't try—' Angua began.

'*T'dr'duzk b'hazg t't!*'

'Oh, no!' moaned Carrot. 'Not *that* one!'

Cheri came up behind the golem at a run and hacked at its waist. The axe rebounded but she pirouetted with it and caught the statue on the thigh, chipping off a piece of clay.

Angua hesitated. Cheri's axe was making blurred orbits around the golem while its wielder yelled more terrible battle cries. Angua couldn't make out any words but many dwarf cries didn't bother with words. They went straight for emotions in sonic form. Chips of pottery ricocheted off the crates as each blow landed.

'What did she yell?' Angua said, as she pulled Carrot out of the way.

'It's the most menacing dwarf battle cry there is! Once it's been shouted *someone* has to be killed!'

'What's it mean?'

'Today Is A Good Day For Someone Else To Die!'

The golem watched the dwarf incuriously, like an elephant watching an attack by a rogue chicken.

Then it picked the axe out of the air, Cheri trailing behind it like a comet, and hurled it aside.

Angua hauled Carrot to his feet. Blood dripped from his hand. She tried to shut her nostrils. *Full moon tomorrow. No more choices.*

359

'Maybe we can reason with it—' Carrot started.

'Attention! This is the *real* world calling!' shouted Angua.

Carrot drew his sword. 'I am arresting you—' he began.

The golem's arm whirred across. The sword buried itself to the hilt in a crate of candles.

'Got any more clever ideas?' said Angua, as they backed away. 'Or can we go now?'

'No. We've got to stop it somewhere.'

Their heels met a wall of crates.

'I think we've found the place,' said Angua as the golem raised its fists again.

'You duck right, I'll duck left. Maybe—'

A blow rocked the big double doors in the far wall.

The king golem's head turned.

The doors shook again, and burst inwards. For a moment Dorfl was framed in the doorway. Then the red golem lowered his head, spread his arms, and charged.

It wasn't a very fast run but it did have a terrible momentum, like the slow slide of a glacier. The floorboards shook and drummed under him.

The golems collided with a *clang* in the middle of the floor. Jagged lines of fire spread across the king's body as cracks opened, but it roared and caught up Dorfl around the middle and tossed him against the wall.

'Come *on*,' said Angua. '*Now* can we find Cheri and get out of here?'

'We ought to help him,' said Carrot, as the

golems smashed into each other again.

'How? If it . . . if *he* can't stop it, what makes you think *we* can? Come *on*!'

Carrot shook her off.

Dorfl picked itself up from among the bricks and charged again. The golems met, scrabbling at one another for purchase. They stood locked for a moment, creaking, and then Dorfl's hand came up holding something. Dorfl pushed himself back and smashed the other golem over the head with its own leg.

As it spun Dorfl's other hand lashed out, but was grabbed. The king swivelled with a strange grace, bore Dorfl to the floor, rolled and kicked out. Dorfl rolled too. He flung out his arms to stop himself, and looked back to see both his feet pinwheeling into the wall.

The king picked up its own leg, balanced for a moment, and joined itself together.

Then its red gaze swept the factory and flared when it caught sight of Carrot.

'There must be a back way out of here,' muttered Angua. 'Carry got out!'

The king started to run after them, but hit an immediate problem. It had put its leg on back to front. It began to limp in a circle but, somehow, the circle got nearer to them.

'We can't just leave Dorfl lying there,' said Carrot.

He pulled a long metal rod out of a stirring tank and eased himself back down to the grease-crusted floor.

The king rocked towards him. Carrot hopped backwards, steadied himself on a rail, and swung.

The golem lifted its hand, caught the rod out of the air and tossed it aside. It raised both fists and tried to step forward.

It couldn't move. It looked down.

'Thsss,' said what remained of Dorfl, gripping its ankle.

The king bent, swung one hand with the palm edgewise, and calmly sheared the top off Dorfl's head. It removed the chem and crumpled it up.

The glow died in Dorfl's eyes.

Angua cannoned into Carrot so hard he almost fell over. She wrapped both arms around him and pulled him after her.

'It just *killed* Dorfl, just like that!' said Carrot.

'It's a shame, yes,' said Angua. 'Or it would be if Dorfl had been alive. Carrot, they're like . . . *machinery*. Look, we can make it to the door—'

Carrot shook himself free. 'It's murder,' he said. 'We're Watchmen. We can't just . . . watch! It *killed* him!'

'It's an it and so's he—'

'Commander Vimes said someone has to speak for the people with no voices!'

He really believes *it,* Angua thought. *Vimes puts words in* his *head.*

'Keep it occupied!' he shouted, and darted away.

'How? Organize a sing-song?'

'I've got a plan.'

'Oh, *good!*'

*   *   *

Vimes looked up at the entrance of the candle-factory. He could dimly see two cressets burning on either side of a shield. 'Look at that, will you?' he said. 'Paint not dry and he flaunts the thing for all the world to see!'

'What's dat, sir?' said Detritus.

'His damn coat of arms!'

Detritus looked up. 'Why's it got a lighted fish on it?' he said.

'In heraldry that's a poisson,' said Vimes bitterly. 'And it's supposed to be a lamp.'

'A lamp made out of a poisson,' said Detritus. 'Well, dere's a fing.'

'At least it's got the motto in proper language,' said Sergeant Colon. 'Instead of all the old-fashioned stuff no one understands. "Art Brought Forth the Candle." That, Sergeant Detritus, is a pune, or play on words. 'cos his name is Arthur, see.'

Vimes stood between the two sergeants and felt a hole open up in his head.

'Damn!' he said. 'Damn, damn, damn! He *showed* it to me! "Dumb plodder Vimes! *He* won't notice!" Oh, yes! *And* he was right!'

''S not that good,' said Colon. 'I mean, you've got to know that Mr Carry's first name is Arthur—'

'Shut *up*, Fred!' snapped Vimes.

'Shutting up right now, sir.'

'The *arrogance* of the . . . Who's that?'

A figure darted out of the building, glanced around hurriedly, and scurried along the street.

'That's Carry!' said Vimes. He didn't even shout 'After him!' but went from a standing start to a full run. The fleeing figure dodged between the occasional straying sheep or pig and didn't have a bad turn of speed, but Vimes was powered by sheer anger and was only yards away when Carry ducked into an alleyway.

Vimes skidded to a halt and grabbed at the wall. He'd seen the shape of a crossbow and one of the things you learned in the Watch – that is, one of the things which hopefully you'd have a *chance* to learn – was that it was a very stupid thing indeed to follow someone with a crossbow into a dark alley where you'd be outlined against any light there was.

'I know it's you, Carry,' he shouted.

'I've got a crossbow!'

'You can only fire it once!'

'I want to turn King's Evidence!'

'Guess again!'

Carry lowered his voice. 'They just said I could get the damn golem to do it. I didn't think anyone was going to get hurt.'

'Right, right,' said Vimes. 'You made poisoned candles because they gave a better light, I expect.'

'You know what I mean! They told me it would all be all right and—'

'Which they would "they" be?'

'They said no one would ever find out!'

'Really?'

'Look, look, they said they could . . .' The voice paused, and took on that wheedling tone the blunt-witted use when they're trying to sound sharp.

'If I tell you everything, you'll let me go, right?'

The two sergeants had caught up. Vimes pulled Detritus towards him, although in fact he ended up pulling himself towards Detritus.

'Go round the corner and see he doesn't come out of the alley the other way,' he whispered. The troll nodded.

'What's it you want to tell me, Mr Carry?' said Vimes to the darkness in the alley.

'Have we got a bargain?'

'What?'

'A bargain.'

'No, we damn well *haven't* got a bargain, Mr Carry! I'm not a tradesman! But I'll tell you something, Mr Carry. They betrayed you!'

There was silence from the darkness, and then a sound like a sigh.

Behind Vimes, Sergeant Colon stamped his feet on the cobbles to keep warm.

'You can't stay in there all night, Mr Carry,' said Vimes.

There was another sound, a leathery sound. Vimes glanced up into the coils of fog. 'Something's not right,' he said. 'Come on!'

He ran into the alley. Sergeant Colon followed, on the basis that it was fine to run into an alley containing an armed man provided you were behind someone else.

A shape loomed at them.

'Detritus?'

'Yes, sir!'

'Where did he go? There are no doors in the alley!'

Then his eyes grew more accustomed to the gloom. He saw a huddled outline at the foot of a wall, and his foot nudged a crossbow. 'Mr Carry?'

He knelt down and lit a match.

'Oh, nasty,' said Sergeant Colon. 'Something's broken his neck . . .'

'Dead, is he?' said Detritus. 'You want I should draw a chalk outline round him?'

'I don't think we need bother, Sergeant.'

'It no bother, I've got der chalk right here.'

Vimes looked up. Fog filled the alley, but there were no ladders, no handy low roofs.

'Let's get out of here,' he said.

Angua faced the king.

She resisted a terrible urge to Change. Even a werewolf's jaws probably wouldn't have any effect on the thing. It didn't *have* a jugular.

She daren't look away. The king moved uncertainly, with little jerks and twitches that in a human would suggest madness. Its arms moved fast but erratically, as if signals that were being sent were not arriving properly. And Dorfl's attack had left it damaged. Every time it moved, red light shone from dozens of new cracks.

'You're cracking up!' she shouted. 'The oven wasn't right for pottery!'

The king lunged at her. She dodged and heard its hand slice through a rack of candles.

'You're cranky! You're baked like a loaf! You're *half-baked*!'

She drew her sword. She didn't usually have

much use for it. She found a smile would invariably do the trick.

A hand sliced the top off the blade.

She stared at the sheared metal in horror and then somersaulted back as another blow hummed past her face.

Her foot rolled on a candle and she fell heavily, but with enough presence of mind to roll before a foot stamped down.

'Where've you gone?' she yelled.

'Can you get it to move a little closer to the doors, please?' said a voice from the darkness on high.

Carrot crawled out along the rickety structure that supported the production line.

'*Carrot!*'

'Almost there . . .'

The king grabbed at her leg. She lashed out with her foot and caught it on the knee.

To her amazement she made it crack. But the fire below was still there. The pieces of pottery seemed to float on it. No matter what anyone did the golem could keep going, even if it were just a cloud of dust held together.

'Ah. Right,' said Carrot, and dropped off the gantry.

He landed on the king's back, flung one arm around its neck, and began to pound on its head with the hilt of his sword. It staggered and tried to reach up to pull him off.

'Got to get the words out!' Carrot shouted, as the arms flailed at him. 'It's the only . . . way!'

The king staggered forward and hit a stack of boxes, which burst and rained candles over the floor. Carrot grabbed its ears and tried to twist.

Angua heard him saying: 'You . . . have . . . the right . . . to . . . a lawyer . . .'

'Carrot! Don't bother with its damn rights!'

'You . . . have . . . the right to—'

'Just give it the *last* ones!'

There was a commotion in the gaping doorway and Vimes ran in, sword drawn. 'Oh, *gods* . . . Sergeant Detritus!'

Detritus appeared behind him. 'Sah!'

'Crossbow bolt through the head, if you please!'

'If you say so, sir . . .'

'*Its* head, Sergeant! Mine is fine! Carrot, get down off the thing!'

'Can't get its head off, sir!'

'We'll try six feet of cold steel in the ear just as soon as you let the damn thing go!'

Carrot steadied himself on the king's shoulders, tried to judge his moment as the thing staggered around, and leapt.

He landed awkwardly on a sliding heap of candles. His leg buckled under him and he tumbled over until he was stopped by the inert shell that had been Dorfl.

'Hey, look dis way, mister,' said Detritus.

The king turned.

Vimes didn't catch everything that happened next, because it all happened so quickly. He was merely aware of the rush of air and the *gloink* of the rebounding bolt mingling with the wooden juddering noise as it buried itself in the doorframe behind him.

And the golem was crouching down by Carrot, who was trying to squirm out of the way.

It raised a fist, and brought it down . . .

Vimes didn't even see Dorfl's arm move but there it was *there*, suddenly gripping the king's wrist.

Tiny stars of light went nova in Dorfl's eyes.

'Tssssss!'

As the king jerked back in surprise, Dorfl held on and levered himself up on what remained of his legs. As he came up so did his fist.

Time slowed. Nothing moved in the whole universe but Dorfl's fist.

It swung like a planet, without any apparent speed but with a drifting unstoppability.

And then the king's expression changed. Just before the fist landed, it smiled.

The golem's head exploded. Vimes recalled it in slow motion, one long second of floating pottery. And words. Scraps of paper flew out, dozens, *scores* of them, tumbling gently to the floor.

Slowly, peacefully, the king hit the floor. The red light died, the cracks opened, and then there were just . . . pieces.

Dorfl collapsed on top of them.

Angua and Vimes reached Carrot together.

'He came alive!' said Carrot, struggling up. 'That thing was going to kill me and Dorfl came alive! But that thing had smashed the words out of his head! A golem *has* to have the words!'

'They gave their own golem too many, I can see that,' said Vimes.

He picked up some of the coils of paper.

... CREATE PEACE AND JUSTICE FOR ALL ...

... RULE US WISELY ...

... TEACH US FREEDOM ...

... LEAD US TO ...

Poor devil, he thought.

'Let's get you home. That hand needs treating—' said Angua.

'*Listen*, will you?' said Carrot. 'He's alive!'

Vimes knelt down by Dorfl. The broken clay skull looked as empty as yesterday's breakfast egg. But there was still a pinpoint of light in each eye socket.

'Usssss,' hissed Dorfl, so faintly that Vimes wasn't sure he'd heard it.

A finger scratched on the floor.

'Is it trying to write something?' said Angua.

Vimes pulled out his notebook, eased it under Dorfl's hand, and gently pushed a pencil into the golem's fingers. They watched the hand as it wrote – a little jerkily but still with the mechanical precision of a golem – eight words.

Then it stopped. The pencil rolled away. The lights in Dorfl's eyes dwindled and went out.

'Good grief,' breathed Angua. 'They *don't* need words in their heads ...'

'We can rebuild him,' said Carrot hoarsely. 'We have the pottery.'

Vimes stared at the words, and then at what remained of Dorfl.

'Mr Vimes?' said Carrot.

'Do it,' said Vimes.

Carrot blinked.

'Right now,' Vimes said. He looked back at the scrawl in his book.

WORDS IN THE HEART CAN NOT BE TAKEN.

'And when you rebuild him,' he said, 'when you rebuild him . . . give him a voice. Understand? And get someone to look at your hand.'

'A voice, sir?'

'Do it!'

'Yes, sir.'

'Right.' Vimes pulled himself together. 'Constable Angua and I will have a look around here. Off you go.'

He watched Carrot and the troll carry the remains out. 'Okay,' he said. 'We're looking for arsenic. Maybe there'll be some workshop somewhere. I shouldn't think they'd want to mix the poisoned candles up with the others. Cheery'll know what— Where *is* Corporal Littlebottom?'

'Er . . . I don't think I can hold on much longer . . .'

They looked up.

Cheri was hanging on the line of candles.

'How did you get up there?' said Vimes.

'I sort of found myself going past, sir.'

'Can't you just let go? You're not that high— Oh . . .'

A big trough of molten tallow was a few feet under her. Occasionally the surface went *gloop*.

'Er . . . how hot would that be?' Vimes hissed to Angua.

'Ever bitten hot jam?' she said.

Vimes raised his voice. 'Can't you swing yourself along, Corporal?'

'All the wood's greasy, sir!'

'Corporal Littlebottom, I *order* you not to fall off!'

'Very good, sir!'

Vimes pulled off his jacket. 'Hang on to this. I'll see if I can climb up . . .' he muttered.

'It won't work!' said Angua. 'The thing's shaky enough as it is!'

'I can feel my hands slipping, sir.'

'Good grief, why didn't you call out earlier?'

'Everyone seemed to be busy, sir.'

'Turn around, sir,' said Angua, undoing the buckles of her breastplate. 'Right now, please! And shut your eyes!'

'Why, what . . . ?'

'Rrright nowwww, sirrrrr!'

'Oh . . . yes . . .'

Vimes heard Angua back away from the candle machine, her footsteps punctuated by the clang of falling armour. Then she started running and the footsteps *changed* while she was running and then . . .

He opened his eyes.

The wolf sailed upwards in slow motion, caught the dwarf's shoulder in its jaws as Cheri's grip gave way, and then arced its body so that wolf and dwarf hit the floor on the far side of the vat.

Angua rolled, whimpering.

Cheri scrambled to her feet. 'It's a werewolf!'

Angua rolled back and forth, pawing at her mouth.

'What's happened to it?' said Cheri, her panic receding a little. 'It looks . . . hurt. Where's Angua? Oh . . .'

Vimes glanced at the dwarf's torn leather shirt. 'You wear chain mail *under* your clothes?' he said.

'Oh . . . it's my silver vest . . . but she *knew* about it. I *told* her . . .'

Vimes grabbed Angua's collar. She moved to bite him, and then caught his eye and turned her head away.

'She only *bit* the silver,' said Cheri, distractedly.

Angua pulled herself on to her feet, glared at them, and slunk off behind some crates. They heard her whimpering which, by degrees, became a voice.

'Blasted blasted dwarfs and their blasted vests . . .'

'You all right, Constable?' said Vimes.

'Damn silver underwear . . . Can you throw me my clothes, please?'

Vimes bundled up Angua's uniform and, eyes closed for decency's sake, handed it around the crates.

'No one *told* me she was a were—' Cheri moaned.

'Look at it like this, Corporal,' said Vimes, as patiently as he could. 'If she *hadn't* been a werewolf you would by now be the world's largest novelty candle, all right?'

Angua walked from behind the crates, rubbing her mouth. The skin around it looked too pink . . .

'It burned you?' said Cheri.

'It'll heal,' said Angua.

'You never said you were a werewolf!'

'How would you've liked me to have put it?'

'Right,' said Vimes, 'if *that's* all sorted out, ladies, I want this place searched. Understand?'

'I've got some ointment,' said Cheri meekly.

'Thank you.'

They found a bag in a cellar. There were several boxes of candles. And a lot of dead rats.

Igneous the troll opened the door of his pottery a fraction. He'd intended the fraction to be no more than about one-sixteenth, but someone immediately pushed hard and turned it into rather more than one and three-quarters.

'Here, what's dis?' he said, as Detritus and Carrot came in with the shell of Dorfl between them. 'You can't jus' break in here—'

'We ain't *just* breakin' in,' said Detritus.

'Dis is an outrage,' said Igneous. 'You got no right comin' in here. You got no reason—'

Detritus let go of the golem and spun around. His hand shot out and caught Igneous around the throat. 'You see dose statchoos of Monolith over dere? You *see* dem?' he growled, twisting the other troll's head to face a row of troll religious statues on the other side of the warehouse. 'You want I should smash one open, see what dey're fill wit', maybe *find* a reason?'

Igneous's slitted eyes darted this way and that. He might have been hard of thinking, but he could feel a killing mood when it was in the air. 'No call for dat, I always help der Watch,' he muttered. 'What dis all about?'

Carrot laid out the golem on a table. 'Start, then,' he said. 'Rebuild him. Use as much of the old clay as you can, understand?'

'How can it work when its lights're out?' said Detritus, still puzzled by this mission of mercy.

'He said the clay remembers!'

The sergeant shrugged.

'And give him a tongue,' said Carrot.

Igneous looked shocked. 'I won't do *dat*,' he said. 'Everybody know it *blasphemy* if golems speak.'

'Oh, yeah?' said Detritus. He strode across the warehouse to the group of statues and glared at them. Then he said, 'Whoops, here's me accident'ly trippin' up, ooo, dis is me grabbin' a statchoo for support, oh, der arm have come right off, where can I put my face . . . and what is dis white powder what I sees here with my eyes accident'ly spillin' on der floor?'

He licked a finger and gingerly tasted the stuff.

'Slab,' he growled, walking back to the trembling Igneous. 'You tellin' *me* about blasphemy, you sedimentr'y coprolith? You doin' what Captain Carrot say right *now* or you goin' out of here in a *sack*!'

'Dis is police brutality . . .' Igneous muttered.

'No, *dis* is just police shoutin'!' yelled Detritus. 'You want to try for brutality it okay wit' me!'

Igneous tried to appeal to Carrot. 'It not right, he got a badge, he puttin' me in fear, he can't do dis,' he said.

Carrot nodded. There was a glint in his eye
that Igneous should have noticed. 'That's correct,' he
said. 'Sergeant Detritus?'

'Sir?'

'It's been a long day for all of us. You can go off
duty.'

'Yessir!' said Detritus, with considerable enthusiasm. He removed his badge and laid it
down carefully. Then he started to struggle out of his
armour.

'Look at it like this,' said Carrot. 'It's not that
we're making life, we're simply giving life a place to
live.'

Igneous finally gave up. 'Okay, *okay*,' he
muttered. 'I doin' it. I *doin*' it.'

He looked at the various lumps and shards that
were all that remained of Dorfl, and rubbed the
lichen on his chin.

'You got most of the bits,' he said, professional-
ism edging resentment aside for a moment. 'I could
glue him together wit' kiln cement. Dat'd do the
trick if we bakes him overnight. Lessee . . . I reckon I
got some over dere . . .'

Detritus blinked at his finger, which was still
white with the dust, and sidled over to Carrot. 'Did I
just lick dis?' he said.

'Er, yes,' said Carrot.

'T'ank goodness for dat,' said Detritus, blinking
furiously, ''d hate to believe dis room was *really* full
of giant hairy spide . . . weeble weeble sclup . . .'

He hit the floor, but happily.

'Even if I do it you can't make it come alive

again,' muttered Igneous, returning to his bench. 'You won't find a priest who's goin' to write der words for in der head, not again.'

'He'll make up his own words,' said Carrot.

'And who's going to watch the oven?' said Igneous. 'It's gonna take 'til breakfast at least . . .'

'I wasn't planning on doing anything for the rest of tonight,' said Carrot, taking off his helmet.

Vimes awoke around four o'clock. He'd gone to sleep at his desk. He hadn't meant to, but his body had just shut down.

It wasn't the first time he'd opened bleary eyes there. But at least he wasn't lying in anything sticky.

He focused on the report he'd half-written. His notebook was beside it, page after page of laborious scrawl to remind him that he was trying to understand a complex world by means of his simple mind.

He yawned, and looked out at the shank of the night.

He didn't have any evidence. No real evidence at all. He'd had an interview with an almost incoherent Corporal Nobbs, who hadn't really seen anything. He had nothing that wouldn't burn away like the fog in the morning. All he'd got were a few suspicions and a lot of coincidences, leaning against one another like a house of cards with no card on the bottom.

He peered at his notebook.

Someone seemed to have been working hard. Oh, yes. It had been him.

The events of last night jangled in his head. Why'd he written all this stuff about a coat of arms?

Oh, yes . . .

Yes!

Ten minutes later he was pushing open the door of the pottery. Warmth spilled out into the clammy air.

He found Carrot and Detritus asleep on the floor on either side of the kiln. Damn. He needed someone he could trust, but he hadn't the heart to wake them. He'd pushed everyone very hard the last few days . . .

Something tapped on the door of the kiln.

Then the handle started to turn by itself.

The door opened as far as it could go and *something* half-slid and half-fell on to the floor.

Vimes still wasn't properly awake. Exhaustion and the importunate ghosts of adrenalin sizzled around the edges of his consciousness, but he saw the burning man unfold himself and stand upright.

His red-hot body gave little *pings* as it began to cool. Where it stood, the floor charred and smoked.

The golem raised his head and looked around.

'You!' said Vimes, pointing an unsteady finger. 'Come with me!'

'Yes,' said Dorfl.

Dragon King of Arms stepped into his library. The dirt of the small high windows and the remnants of the fog made sure there was never more than greyness here, but a hundred candles yielded their soft light.

He sat down at his desk, pulled a volume towards him, and began to write.

After a while he stopped and stared ahead of him. There was no sound but the occasional spluttering of a candle.

'Ah-ha. I can smell you, Commander Vimes,' he said. 'Did the Heralds let you in?'

'I found my own way, thank you,' said Vimes, stepping out of the shadows.

The vampire sniffed again. 'You came alone?'

'Who should I have brought with me?'

'And to what do I owe the pleasure, Sir Samuel?'

'The pleasure is all mine. I'm going to arrest you,' said Vimes.

'Oh, dear. Ah-ha. For what, may I ask?'

'Can I invite you to notice the arrow in this crossbow?' said Vimes. 'No metal on the point, you'll see. It's wood all the way.'

'How very considerate. Ah-ha.' Dragon King of Arms twinkled at him. 'You still haven't told me what I'm accused of, however.'

'To start with, complicity in the murders of Mrs Flora Easy and the child William Easy.'

'I am afraid those names mean nothing to me.'

Vimes's finger twitched on the bow's trigger. 'No,' he said, breathing deeply. 'They probably don't. We are making other enquiries and there may be a number of additional matters. The fact that you were poisoning the Patrician I consider a mitigating circumstance.'

'You really intend to prefer charges?'

'I'd *prefer* violence,' said Vimes loudly. 'Charges is what I'm going to have to settle for.'

The vampire leaned back. 'I hear you've been working very hard, Commander,' he said. 'So I will not—'

'We've got the testimony of Mr Carry,' lied Vimes. 'The *late* Mr Carry.'

Dragon's expression changed by not one tiny tremor of muscle. 'I really do not know, ah-ha, what you are talking about, Sir Samuel.'

'Only someone who could fly could have got into my office.'

'I'm afraid you've lost me, sir.'

'Mr Carry was killed tonight,' Vimes went on. 'By someone who could get out of an alley guarded at both ends. And I know a vampire was in his factory.'

'I'm still gamely trying to understand you, Commander,' said Dragon King of Arms. 'I know nothing about the death of Mr Carry and in any case there are a great many vampires in the city. I'm afraid your ... *aversion is* well known.'

'I don't like to see people treated like cattle,' said Vimes. He stared briefly at the volumes piled in the room. 'And of course that's what you've always done, isn't it? These are the stock books of Ankh-Morpork.' The crossbow swung back towards the vampire, who hadn't moved. 'Power over little people. That's what vampires want. The blood is just a way of keeping score. I wonder how much influence you've had over the years?'

'A little. You are correct there, at least.'

'"A person of breeding",' said Vimes. 'Good grief. Well, I think people wanted Vetinari out of the way. But not dead, yet. Too many things'd happen too fast if he were dead. Is Nobby really an earl?'

'The evidence suggests so.'

'But it's *your* evidence, right? You see, I *don't* think he's got noble blood in him. Nobby's as common as muck. It's one of his better points. I don't set any score by the ring. The amount of stuff his family's nicked, you could probably prove he's the Duke of Pseudopolis, the Seriph of Klatch and the Dowager Duchess of Quirm. He pinched my cigar case last year and I'm damn certain he's not me. No, I don't think Nobby is a nob. But I think he *was* convenient.'

It seemed to Vimes that Dragon was getting bigger, but perhaps it was only a trick of the candlelight. The light flickered as the candles hissed and popped.

'You made good use of me, eh?' Vimes carried on. 'I'd been ducking out of appointments with you for weeks. I expect you were getting quite impatient. You were so surprised when I told you about Nobby, eh? Otherwise you'd've had to send for him or something, very suspicious. But Commander Vimes *discovered* him. That looks good. Practically makes it official.

'And then I started thinking: who wants a king? Well, nearly everyone. It's built in. Kings make it better. Funny thing, isn't it? Even those people who owe everything to him don't like Vetinari. Ten years ago most of the guild leaders were just a bunch of thugs and now . . . well, they're still a bunch of thugs, to tell the truth, but Vetinari's given 'em the time and energy to decide they never needed him.

'And then young Carrot turns up with charisma writ all over him, and he's got a sword and a birthmark and everyone gets a funny feeling and dozens of buggers start going through the records and say, "Hey, looks like the king's come back." And *then* they watch him for a while and say, "Shit, he really *is* decent and honest and fair and just, just like in all the stories. Whoops! If this lad gets on the throne we could be in serious trouble! He might turn out to be one of them inconvenient kings from long ago who wanders around talking to the common people—"'

'You are in favour of the common people?' said Dragon mildly.

'The common people?' said Vimes. 'They're nothing special. They're no different from the rich and powerful except they've got no money or power. But the law should be there to balance things up a bit. So I suppose I've got to be on their side.'

'A man married to the richest woman in the city?'

Vimes shrugged. 'The watchman's helmet isn't like a crown. Even when you take it off you're still wearing it.'

'That's an interesting statement of position, Sir Samuel, and I would be the first to admire the way you've come to terms with your family history, but—'

'Don't move!' Vimes shifted his grip on the crossbow. 'Anyway . . . Carrot wouldn't do, but the news was getting around, and someone said, "Right, let's have a king we *can* control. All the rumours say the king is a humble watchman so let's find one." And they had a look and found that when it comes to humble you can't beat Nobby Nobbs. But . . . I think people weren't too sure. Killing Vetinari wasn't an option. As I said, too many things would happen too fast. But to just gently remove him, so that he's there and not there at the same time, while everyone tried out the idea . . . *that* was a good wheeze. That's when someone got Mr Carry to make poisoned candles. He'd got a golem. Golems can't talk. No one would know. But it turned out to be a bit . . . erratic.'

'You seem to wish to involve me,' said Dragon King of Arms. 'I know nothing about this man other than that he's a customer—'

Vimes strode across the room and pulled a piece of parchment from a board. 'You did him a coat of arms!' he shouted. 'You even *showed* me when I was here! "The butcher, the baker and the candlestick-maker!" Remember?'

There was no sound now from the hunched figure.

'When I first met you the other day,' said Vimes, 'you made a point of *showing* me Arthur Carry's coat of arms. I thought it was a bit fishy at the time, but all that business with Nobby put it out of my mind. But I *do* remember it reminded me of the one for the Assassins' Guild.'

Vimes flourished the parchment.

'I looked and looked at it last night, and then I wound my sense of humour down ten notches and let it go out of focus and looked at the crest, the fish-shaped lamp. *Lampe au poisson,* it's called. A sort of bilingual play on words, perhaps? "A lamp of poison"? You've got to have a mind like old Detritus to spot that one. And Fred Colon wondered why you'd left the motto in modern Ankhian instead of putting it into the old language, and that made *me* wonder so I sat up with the dictionary and worked it out and, you know, it would have read "Ars Enixa Est Candelam". *Ars Enixa.* That must have really cheered you up. You'd said who did it and how it was done and gave it to the poor bugger to be proud of. It didn't matter that no one else would spot it. It made *you* feel good. Because we ordinary mortals just aren't as clever as you, are we?' He shook his head. 'Good grief, a coat of arms. Was that the bribe? Was that all it took?'

Dragon slumped in his chair.

'And then I wondered what was in it for you,' continued Vimes. 'Oh, there's a lot of people involved, I expect, for the same old reasons. But you? Now, my wife breeds dragons. Out of interest, really. Is that what you do? A little hobby to allow the centuries to fly by? Or does blue blood taste sweeter? Y'know, I hope it was some reason like that. Some decent mad selfish one.'

'Possibly – if someone were so inclined, and I certainly make no such admission, ah-ha – they might simply be thinking of improving the race,' said the shape in the shadows.

'Breeding for receding chins or bunny teeth, that sort of thing?' said Vimes. 'Yes, I can see where it'd be more straightforward if you had the whole king business. All those courtly balls. All those little arrangements which see to it that the right kind of gel meets only the right kind of boy. You've had hundreds of years, right? And everyone consults you. You know where all the family trees are planted. But it's all got a bit *messy* under Vetinari, hasn't it? All the wrong people are getting to the top. I know how Sybil curses when people leave the pen gates open: it really messes up her breeding programme.'

'You are wrong about Captain Carrot, ah-ha. The city knows how to work around . . . *difficult* kings. But would it want a future king who might *really* be called Rex?'

Vimes looked blank. There was a sigh from the shadows. 'I am, ah-ha, referring to his apparently stable relationship with the werewolf.'

Vimes stared. Understanding eventually dawned. 'You think they'd have *puppies*?'

'The genetics of werewolves are not straight-forward, ah-ha, but the chance of such an outcome would be considered unacceptable. If someone were thinking on those lines.'

'By gods, and that's *it*?'

The shadows were changing. Dragon was still slumped in his chair, but his outline seemed to be blurring.

'Whatever the, ah-ha, motives, Mr Vimes, there is no evidence other than supposition and coincidence and your will to believe that links me with any attempt on Vetinari's, ah-ha, life . . . '

The old vampire's head was sunk even further in

his chest. The shadows of his shoulders seemed to be getting longer.

'It was sick, involving the golems,' said Vimes, watching the shadows. 'They could feel what their "king" was doing. Perhaps it wasn't very sane even to begin with, but it was all they had. Clay of their clay. The poor devils didn't have anything except their clay, and you bastards took away even *that*—'

Dragon leapt suddenly, bat-wings unfolding. Vimes's wooden bolt clattered somewhere near the ceiling as he was borne down.

'You really thought you could arrest me with a piece of wood?' said Dragon, his hand around Vimes's neck.

'No,' Vimes croaked. 'I was more . . . poetic . . . than that. All I had . . . to do . . . was keep you talking. Feeling . . . weak, are you? The biter bit . . . you might say . . . ?' He grinned.

The vampire looked puzzled, and then turned his head and stared at the candles. 'You . . . put something in the candles? Really?'

'We . . . knew garlic . . . would smell but . . . our alchemist reckoned that . . . if you get . . . holy water . . . soak the wicks . . . water evaporates . . . just leaves holiness.'

The pressure was released. Dragon King of Arms sat back on his haunches. His face had changed, shaping itself forward, giving him an expression like a fox.

Then he shook his head. 'No,' he said, and this time it was his turn to grin. 'No, that's just words. That wouldn't work . . .'

'Bet . . . your . . . unlife?' rasped Vimes, rubbing his neck. 'A better way . . . than old Carry went, eh?'

'Trying to trick me into an admission, Mr Vimes?'

'Oh, I had *that*,' said Vimes. 'When you looked straight at the candles.'

'Really? Ah-ha. But who else saw me?' said Dragon.

From the shadows there was a rumble like a distant thunderstorm.

'I Did,' said Dorfl.

The vampire looked from the golem to Vimes.

'You gave one of them a *voice*?' he said.

'Yes,' said Dorfl. He reached down and picked up the vampire in one hand. 'I Could Kill You,' he said. 'This Is An Option Available To Me As A Free-Thinking Individual But I Will Not Do So Because I Own Myself And I Have Made A Moral Choice.'

'Oh, gods,' murmured Vimes under his breath.

'That's *blasphemy*,' said the vampire.

He gasped as Vimes shot him a glance like sunlight. 'That's what people say when the voiceless speak. Take him away, Dorfl. Put him in the palace dungeons.'

'I Could Take No Notice of That Command But Am Choosing To Do So Out of Earned Respect And Social Responsibility—'

'Yes, yes, fine,' said Vimes quickly.

Dragon clawed at the golem. He might as well have kicked at a mountain.

'Undead Or Alive, You Are Coming With Me,' said Dorfl.

'Is there no end to your crimes? You've made this thing a *policeman*?' said the vampire, struggling as Dorfl dragged him away.

'No, but it's an intriguing suggestion, don't you think?' said Vimes.

He was left alone in the thick velvety gloom of the Royal College.

And Vetinari will let him go, he reflected. *Because this is politics. Because he's part of the way the city works. Besides, there's the matter of* evidence. *I've got enough to prove it to myself, but . . .*

But I'll *know,* he told himself.

Oh, he'll be watched, and maybe one day when Vetinari is ready a really good assassin will be sent with a wooden dagger soaked in garlic, and it'll all be done in the dark. That's how politics works in this city. It's a game of chess. Who cares if a few pawns die?

I'll *know. And I'll be the only one who knows, deep down.*

His hands automatically patted his pockets for a cigar.

It was hard enough to kill a vampire. You could stake them down and turn them into dust and ten years later someone spills a drop of blood in the wrong place and *guess who's back*? They returned more times than raw broccoli.

These were dangerous thoughts, he knew. They were the kind that crept up on a watchman when the chase was over and it was just you and him, facing one another in that breathless little pinch between the crime and the punishment.

And maybe a watchman had seen civilization

with the skin ripped off one time too many and stopped acting like a watchman and started acting like a normal human being and realized that the click of the crossbow or the sweep of the sword would make all the world so *clean*.

And you couldn't think like that, even about vampires. Even though they'd take the lives of other people because little lives don't matter and what the hell can we take away from *them*?

And you couldn't think like that because they gave you a sword and a badge and that turned you into something else and *that* had to mean there were some thoughts you couldn't think.

Only crimes could take place in darkness. Punishment had to be done in the light. That was the job of a good watchman, Carrot always said. To light a candle in the dark.

He found a cigar. Now his hands did the automatic search for matches.

The volumes were piled up against the walls. The candlelight picked up gold lettering and the dull gleam of leather. There they were, the lineages, the books of heraldic minutiae, the Who's Whom of the centuries, the stock books of the city. People stood on them to look down.

No matches . . .

Quietly, in the dusty silence of the College, Vimes picked up a candelabrum and lit his cigar.

He took a few deep luxuriant puffs, and looked thoughtfully at the books. In his hand, the candles spluttered and flickered.

*   *   *

TERRY PRATCHETT

The clock ticked its arrhythmic tock. It finally stuttered its way to one o'clock, and Vimes got up and went into the Oblong Office.

'Ah, Vimes,' said Lord Vetinari, looking up.

'Yes, sir.'

Vimes had managed a few hours' sleep and had even attempted to shave.

The Patrician shuffled some papers on his desk. 'It seems to have been a very busy night last night . . .'

'Yes, sir.' Vimes stood to attention. All uniformed men knew in their very soul how to act in circumstances like this. You stared straight ahead, for one thing.

'It appears that I have Dragon King of Arms in the cells,' said the Patrician.

'Yes, sir.'

'I've read your report. Somewhat tenuous evidence, I feel.'

'Sir?'

'One of your witnesses isn't even alive, Vimes.'

'No, sir. Neither is the suspect, sir. Technically.'

'He is, however, an important civic figure. An authority.'

'Yes, sir.'

Lord Vetinari shuffled some of the papers on his desk. One of them was covered in sooty fingermarks. 'It also appears I have to commend you, Commander.'

'Sir?'

'The Heralds at the Royal College of Arms, or at least at what *remains* of the Royal College of Arms,

390

have sent me a note saying how bravely you worked last night.'

'Sir?'

'Letting all those heraldic animals out of the pens and raising the alarm and so on. A tower of strength, they've called you. I gather most of the creatures are lodging with you at the present time?'

'Yes, sir. Couldn't stand by and let them suffer, sir. We'd got some empty pens, sir, and Keith and Roderick are doing well in the lake. They've taken a liking to Sybil, sir.'

Lord Vetinari coughed. Then he stared up at the ceiling for a while. 'So you, er, assisted in the fire.'

'Yes, sir. Civic duty, sir.'

'The fire was caused by a candlestick falling over, I understand, possibly after your fight with Dragon King of Arms.'

'So I believe, sir.'

'And so, it seems, do the Heralds.'

'Anyone told Dragon King of Arms?' said Vimes innocently.

'Yes.'

'Took it well, did he?'

'He screamed a lot, Vimes. In a heart-rending fashion, I am told. And I gather he uttered a number of threats against you, for some reason.'

'I shall try to fit him into my busy schedule, sir.'

'Bingely bongely beep!!' said a small bright voice. Vimes slapped a hand against his pocket.

Lord Vetinari fell silent for a moment. His fingers drummed softly on his desk. 'Many fine old manuscripts in that place, I believe. Without price, I'm told.'

'Yes, sir. Certainly worthless, sir.'

'Is it possible you misunderstood what I just said, Commander?'

'Could be, sir.'

'The provenances of many splendid old families went up in smoke, Commander. Of course, the Heralds will do what they can, and the families themselves keep records but frankly, I understand, it's all going to be patchwork and guesswork. Extremely embarrassing. Are you smiling, Commander?'

'It was probably a trick of the light, sir.'

'Commander, I always used to consider that you had a definite anti-authoritarian streak in you.'

'Sir?'

'It seems that you have managed to retain this even though you *are* authority.'

'Sir?'

'That's practically Zen.'

'Sir?'

'It seems I've only got to be unwell for a few days and you manage to upset everyone of any importance in this city.'

'Sir.'

'Was that a "yes, sir" or a "no, sir", Sir Samuel?'

'It was just a "sir", sir.'

Lord Vetinari glanced at a piece of paper. 'Did you really punch the president of the Assassins' Guild?'

'Yes, sir.'

'Why?'

'Didn't have a dagger, sir.'

Vetinari turned away abruptly. 'The Council of Churches, Temples, Sacred Groves and Big Ominous Rocks is demanding . . . well, a number of things, several of them involving wild horses. Initially, however, they want me to sack you.'

'Yes, sir?'

'In all I've had seventeen demands for your badge. Some want parts of your body attached. Why did you have to upset everybody?'

'I suppose it's a knack, sir.'

'But what could you hope to achieve?'

'Well, sir, since you *ask,* we found out who murdered Father Tubelcek *and* Mr Hopkinson *and* who was poisoning you, sir.' Vimes paused. 'Two out of three's not bad, sir.'

Vetinari riffled through the papers again. 'Workshop owners, assassins, priests, butchers . . . you seem to have infuriated most of the leading figures in the city.' He sighed. 'Really, it seems I have no choice. As of this week, I'm giving you a pay rise.'

Vimes blinked. 'Sir?'

'Nothing unseemly. Ten dollars a month. And I expect they need a new dart-board in the Watch House? They usually do, I recall.'

'It's Detritus,' said Vimes, his mind unable to think of anything other than an honest reply. 'He tends to split them.'

'Ah, yes. And talking of splits, Vimes, I wonder if your forensic genius could help me with a little conundrum we found this morning.' The Patrician stood up and headed for the stairs.

'Yes, sir? What is it?' said Vimes, following him down.

'It's in the Rats Chamber, Vimes.'

'Really, sir?'

Vetinari pushed open the double doors. 'Voilà,' he said.

'That's some kind of musical instrument, isn't it, sir?'

'No, Commander, the word means "What is that in the table?",' said the Patrician sharply.

Vimes looked into the room. There was no one there. The long mahogany table was bare.

Except for the axe. It had embedded itself in the wood very deeply, almost splitting the table along its entire length. Someone had walked up to the table and brought an axe down right in the centre as hard as they could and then left it there, its handle pointing towards the ceiling.

'That's an axe,' said Vimes.

'Astonishing,' said Lord Vetinari. 'And you've barely had time to study it. *Why* is it there?'

'I really couldn't say, sir.'

'According to the servants, Sir Samuel, you came into the palace at six o'clock this morning . . .'

'Oh, yes, sir. To check that the bastard was safely in a cell, sir. And to see that everything was all right, of course.'

'You didn't come into this room?'

Vimes kept his gaze fixed somewhere on the horizon. 'Why should I have done that, sir?'

The Patrician tapped the axe handle. It vibrated with a faint thumping noise. 'I believe some of the

City Council met in here this morning. Or came in here, at least. I'm told they hurried out very quickly. Looking rather disturbed, I'm told.'

'Maybe it was one of them that did it, sir.'

'That is, of course, a possibility,' said Lord Vetinari. 'I suppose you won't be able to find one of your famous Clues on the thing?'

'Shouldn't think so, sir. Not with all these finger-prints on it.'

'It would be a terrible thing, would it not, if people thought they could take the law into their own hands . . .'

'Oh, no fear of that, sir. I'm holding on tightly to it.'

Lord Vetinari *plunked* the axe again. 'Tell me, Sir Samuel, do you know the phrase *"Quis custodiet ipsos custodies?"*?'

It was an expression Carrot had occasionally used, but Vimes was not in the mood to admit anything. 'Can't say that I do, sir,' he said. 'Something about trifle, is it?'

'It means "Who guards the guards themselves?", Sir Samuel.'

'Ah.'

'Well?'

'Sir?'

'Who watches the Watch? I wonder?'

'Oh, that's easy, sir. We watch one another.'

'Really? An intriguing point . . .'

Lord Vetinari walked out of the room and back into the main hall, with Vimes trailing behind. 'However,' he said, 'in order to keep the peace, the golem will have to be destroyed.'

'No, sir.'

'Allow me to repeat my instruction.'

'No, sir.'

'I'm sure I just gave you an order, Commander. I distinctly felt my lips move.'

'No, sir. He's alive, sir.'

'He's just made of clay, Vimes.'

'Aren't we all, sir? According to them pamphlets Constable Visit keeps handing out. Anyway, *he* thinks he's alive, and that's good enough for me.'

The Patrician waved a hand towards the stairs and his office full of paper. 'Nevertheless, Commander, I've had no less than nine missives from leading religious figures declaring that he is an abomination.'

'Yes, sir. I've given that viewpoint a lot of thought, sir, and reached the following conclusion: arseholes to the lot of 'em, sir.'

The Patrician's hand covered his mouth for a moment. 'Sir Samuel, you are a harsh negotiator. Surely you can give and take?'

'Couldn't say, sir.' Vimes walked to the main doors and pushed them open.

'Fog's lifted, sir,' he said. 'There's a bit of cloud but you can see all the way across the Brass Bridge—'

'What will you use the golem for?'

'Not *use*, sir. Employ. I thought he might be useful for to keep the peace, sir.'

'A watchman?'

'Yes, sir,' said Vimes. 'Haven't you heard, sir? Golems do all the mucky jobs.'

Vetinari watched him go, and sighed. 'He does so like a dramatic exit,' he said.

'Yes, my lord,' said Drumknott, who had appeared noiselessly at his shoulder.

'Ah, Drumknott.' The Patrician took a length of candle out of his pocket and handed it to his secretary. 'Dispose of this somewhere safely, will you?'

'Yes, my lord?'

'It's the candle from the other night.'

'It's not burned down, my lord? But I saw the candle end in the holder . . .'

'Oh, of course I cut off enough to make a stub and let the wick burn for a moment. I couldn't let our gallant policeman know I'd worked it out for myself, could I? Not when he was making such an effort and having so much fun being . . . well, being *Vimes*. I'm not *completely* heartless, you know.'

'But, my lord, you could have sorted it out diplomatically! Instead he went around upsetting things and making a lot of people very angry and afraid—'

'Yes. Dear me. Tsk, tsk.'

'Ah,' said Drumknott.

'Quite so,' said the Patrician.

'Do you wish me to have the table in the Rats Chamber repaired?'

'No, Drumknott, leave the axe where it is. It will make a good . . . conversation piece, I think.'

'May I make an observation, my lord?'

'Of course you may,' said Vetinari, watching Vimes walk through the palace gates.

'The thought occurs, sir, that if Commander Vimes did not exist you would have had to invent him.'

'You know, Drumknott, I rather think I did.'

'Atheism Is Also A Religious Position,' Dorfl rumbled.

'No it's not!' said Constable Visit. 'Atheism is a *denial* of a god.'

'Therefore It Is A Religious Position,' said Dorfl. 'Indeed, A True Atheist Thinks Of The Gods Constantly, Albeit In Terms of Denial. Therefore, Atheism Is A Form Of Belief. If The Atheist Truly Did Not Believe, He Or She Would Not Bother To Deny.'

'Did you read those pamphlets I gave you?' said Visit suspiciously.

'Yes. Many Of Them Did Not Make Sense. But I Should Like To Read Some More.'

'Really?' said Visit. His eyes gleamed. 'You really want *more* pamphlets?'

'Yes. There Is Much In Them That I Would Like To Discuss. If You Know Some Priests, I Would Enjoy Disputation.'

'All right, all right,' said Sergeant Colon. 'So are you going to take the sodding oath or not, Dorfl?'

Dorfl held up a hand the size of a shovel. 'I, Dorfl, Pending The Discovery Of A Deity Whose Existence Withstands Rational Debate, Swear By The Temporary Precepts of A Self-Derived Moral System—'

'You *really* want more pamphlets?' said Constable Visit.

Sergeant Colon rolled his eyes.

'Yes,' said Dorfl.

'Oh, my god!' said Constable Visit, and burst into tears. 'No one's *ever* asked for more pamphlets before!'

Colon turned when he realized Vimes was watching. 'It's no good, sir,' he said. 'I've been trying to swear him in for half an hour, sir, and we keep ending up arguing about oaths and things.'

'You willing to be a Watchman, Dorfl?' said Vimes.

'Yes.'

'Right. That's as good as a swear to me. Give him his badge, Fred. And this is for you, Dorfl. It's a chit to say you're officially alive, just in case you run into any trouble. You know . . . with people.'

'Thank You,' said Dorfl solemnly. 'If Ever I Feel I Am Not Alive, I Will Take This Out And Read It.'

'What are your duties?' said Vimes.

'To Serve The Public Trust, Protect The Innocent, And Seriously Prod Buttock, Sir,' said Dorfl.

'He learns fast, doesn't he?' said Colon. 'I didn't even *tell* him the last one.'

'People won't like it,' said Nobby. ''S not going to be popular, a golem as a watchman.'

'What Better Work For One Who Loves Freedom Than The Job of Watchman. Law Is The Servant of Freedom. Freedom Without Limits Is Just A Word,' said Dorfl ponderously.

'Y'know,' said Colon, 'if it doesn't work out, you could always get a job making fortune cookies.'

'Funny thing, that,' said Nobby. 'You never get bad fortunes in cookies, ever noticed that? They never say stuff like: "Oh dear, things're going to be really bad." I mean, they're never *misfortune* cookies.'

Vimes lit a cigar and shook the match to put it out. 'That, Corporal, is because of one of the fundamental driving forces of the universe.'

'What? Like, people who read fortune cookies are the lucky ones?' said Nobby.

'No. Because people who *sell* fortune cookies want to go on selling them. Come on, Constable Dorfl. We're going for a walk.'

'There's a lot of paperwork, sir,' said Sergeant Colon.

'Tell Captain Carrot I said he should look at it,' said Vimes, from the doorway.

'He hasn't been in yet, sir.'

'It'll keep.'

'Right, sir.'

Colon went and sat behind his desk. It was a good place to be, he'd decided. There was absolutely no chance of finding any Nature there. He'd had a rare conversation with Mrs Colon this morning and made it clear that he was no longer interested in getting close to the soil because he'd *been* as close to the soil as it was possible to get and the soil, it turned out, was just dirt. A good thick layer of cobblestones was, he decided, about as close as he wanted to get to Nature. Also, Nature tended to be squishy.

'I've got to go on duty,' said Nobby. 'Captain Carrot wants me to do crime prevention in Peach Pie Street.'

'How d'you do that, then?' said Colon.

'Keep away, he said.'

''Ere, Nobby, woss this about you not being a lord after all?' said Colon cautiously.

'I think I got the sack,' said Nobby. 'Bit of a relief, really. That nobby grub isn't much, and the drink is frankly piss.'

'Lucky escape for you, then,' said Colon. 'I mean, you won't have to go giving your clothes away to gardeners and so on.'

'Yeah. Wish I'd never told them about the damn ring, really.'

'Would've saved you a lot of trouble, certainly,' said Colon.

Nobby spat on his badge and buffed it industriously with his sleeve. *'S a good job I never told them about the tiara, the coronet and the three gold lockets,* he said to himself.

'Where Are We Going?' said Dorfl, as Vimes strolled across the Brass Bridge.

'I thought I might break you in gently with some guard duty at the palace,' said Vimes.

'Ah. This Is Where My New Friend Constable Visit Is Also On Guard,' said Dorfl.

'Splendid!'

'I Wish To Ask You A Question,' said the golem. 'Yes?'

'I Smashed The Treadmill But The Golems

401

Repaired It. Why? And I Let The Animals Go But
They Just Milled Around Stupidly. Some of Them
Even Went Back To The Slaughter Pens. Why?'

'Welcome to the world, Constable Dorfl.'

'Is It Frightening To Be Free?'

'You said it.'

'You Say To People "Throw Off Your Chains"
And They Make New Chains For Themselves?'

'Seems to be a major human activity, yes.'

Dorfl rumbled as he thought about this. 'Yes,' he
said eventually. 'I Can See Why. Freedom Is Like
Having The Top Of Your Head Opened Up.'

'I'll have to take your word for that, Constable.'

'And You Will Pay Me Twice As Much As Other
Watchmen,' said Dorfl.

'Will I?'

'Yes. I Do Not Sleep. I Can Work Constantly. I
Am A Bargain. I Do Not Need Days Off To Bury My
Granny.'

How soon they learn, thought Vimes. He said:
'But you have holy days off, don't you?'

'Either All Days Are Holy Or None Are. I Have
Not Decided Yet.'

'Er . . . what do you need money for, Dorfl?'

'I Shall Save Up And Purchase The Golem
Klutz Who Labours In The Pickle Factory, And
Give Him To Himself; Then Together We Will
Earn And Save For The Golem Bobkes Of The Coal
Merchant; The Three Of Us Will Labour And Buy
The Golem Shmata Who Toils At The Seven-Dollar
Tailor's In Peach Pie Street; Then The Four of Us
Will—'

'*Some* people might decide to free their comrades by force and bloody revolution,' said Vimes. 'Not that I'm suggesting that in any way, of course.'

'No. That Would Be Theft. We Are Bought And Sold. So We Will Buy Ourselves Free. By Our Labour. No One Else To Do It For Us. We Will Do It By Ourselves.'

Vimes smiled to himself. Probably no other species in the world would demand a receipt with their freedom. Some things you just couldn't change.

'Ah,' he said. 'It seems some people want to talk to us . . .'

A crowd was approaching over the bridge, in a mass of grey, black and saffron robes. It was made up of priests. They looked angry. As they pushed and shoved their way through the other citizens, several haloes became interlocked.

At their head was Hughnon Ridcully, Chief Priest of Blind Io and the closest thing Ankh-Morpork had to a spokesman on religious issues. He spotted Vimes and hurried towards him, admonitory finger upraised.

'Now, see here, Vimes . . .' he began, and stopped. He glared at Dorfl.

'Is this *it*?' he said.

'If you mean the golem, this is *him*,' said Vimes. 'Constable Dorfl, your reverence.'

Dorfl touched his helmet respectfully. 'How May We Be Of Service?' he said.

'You've done it this time, Vimes!' said Ridcully, ignoring him. 'You've gone altogether too far by half. You made this thing speak and it isn't even alive!'

'We want it smashed!'

'Blasphemy!'

'People won't stand for it!'

Ridcully looked around at the other priests. 'I'm *talking*,' he said. He turned back to Vimes. 'This comes under the heading of gross profanity and the worship of idols—'

'I don't worship him. I'm just employing him,' said Vimes, beginning to enjoy himself. 'And he's far from idle.' He took a deep breath. 'And if it's gross profanity you're looking for—'

'Excuse Me,' said Dorfl.

'We're not listening to you! You're not even really alive!' said a priest.

Dorfl nodded. 'This Is Fundamentally True,' he said.

'See? He admits it!'

'I Suggest You Take Me And Smash Me And Grind The Bits Into Fragments And Pound The Fragments Into Powder And Mill Them Again To The Finest Dust There Can Be, And I Believe You Will Not Find A Single Atom of Life—'

'True! Let's do it!'

'However, In Order To Test This Fully, One Of You Must Volunteer To Undergo The Same Process.'

There was silence.

'That's not fair,' said a priest, after a while. 'All anyone has to do is bake up your dust again and you'll be alive . . .'

There was more silence.

Ridcully said, 'Is it only me, or are we on tricky theological ground here?'

There was more silence.

Another priest said, 'Is it true you've said you'll believe in any god whose existence can be proved by logical debate?'

'Yes.'

Vimes had a feeling about the immediate future and took a few steps away from Dorfl.

'But the gods plainly *do* exist,' said a priest.

'It Is Not Evident.'

A bolt of lightning lanced through the clouds and hit Dorfl's helmet. There was a sheet of flame and then a trickling noise. Dorfl's molten armour formed puddles around his white-hot feet.

'I Don't Call That Much Of An Argument,' said Dorfl calmly, from somewhere in the clouds of smoke.

'It's tended to carry the audience,' said Vimes. 'Up until now.'

The Chief Priest of Blind Io turned to the other priests. 'All right, you fellows, there's no need for any of that—'

'But Offler is a vengeful god,' said a priest at the back of the crowd.

'Trigger-happy is what he is,' said Ridcully. Another lightning bolt zigzagged down but bent at right-angles a few feet above the Chief Priest's hat and earthed itself on a wooden hippo, which split. The Chief Priest smiled smugly and turned back to Dorfl, who was making little clinking noises as he cooled.

'What you're saying is, you'll accept the existence of any god only if it can be proved by discussion?'

'Yes,' said Dorfl.

Ridcully rubbed his hands together. '*Not* a problem, me old china,' he said. 'Firstly, let us take the—'

'Excuse Me,' said Dorfl. He bent down and picked up his badge. The lightning had given it an interesting melted shape.

'What are you doing?' said Ridcully.

'Somewhere, A Crime Is Happening,' said Dorfl. 'But When I Am Off Duty I Will Gladly Dispute With The Priest of The Most Worthy God.'

He turned and strode on across the bridge. Vimes nodded hurriedly at the shocked priests and ran after him. *We took him and baked him in the fire and he's turned out to be free,* he thought. *No words in the head except the ones he's chosen to put there himself. And he's not just an atheist, he's a* ceramic *atheist. Fireproof!*

It looked like being a good day.

Behind them, on the bridge, a fight was breaking out.

Angua was packing. Or, rather, she was failing to pack. The bundle couldn't be too heavy to carry by mouth. But a little money (she wouldn't have to buy much food) and a change of clothes (for those occasions when she might have to wear clothes) didn't have to take up much room.

'The boots are a problem,' she said aloud.

'Maybe if you knot the laces together you could

carry them round your neck?' said Cheri, who was sitting on the narrow bed.

'Good idea. Do you want these dresses? I've never got round to wearing them. I expect you could cut them down.'

Cheri took them in both arms. 'This one's *silk*!'

'There's probably enough material for you to make two for one.'

'D'you mind if I share them out? Only some of the lads – the *ladies* at the Watch House' – Cheri savoured the word 'ladies' – 'are beginning to get a bit thoughtful . . .'

'Going to melt down their helmets, are they?' said Angua.

'Oh, *no*. But perhaps they could be made into a more attractive design. Er . . .'

'Yes?'

'Um . . .'

Cheri shifted uneasily.

'You've never actually *eaten* anyone, have you? You know . . . crunching bones and so on?'

'No.'

'I mean, I only *heard* my second cousin was eaten by werewolves. He was called Sfen.'

'Can't say I recall the name,' said Angua.

Cheri tried to grin. 'That's all right, then,' she said.

'So you won't need that silver spoon in your pocket,' said Angua.

Cheri's mouth dropped open, and then the words tumbled over themselves. 'Er . . . I don't know how it got there it must have dropped in when I was washing up oh I didn't mean—'

'It doesn't worry me, honestly. I'm used to it.'

'But I didn't think you'd—'

'Look, don't get the wrong idea. It's not a case of not wanting to,' said Angua. 'It's a case of wanting to and *not doing it*.'

'You don't really have to go, do you?'

'Oh, I don't know if I can take the Watch seriously and . . . and sometimes I think Carrot's working up to ask me . . . and, well, it'd never work out. It's the way he just *assumes* everything, you know? So best to go now,' Angua lied.

'Won't Carrot try to stop you?'

'Yes, but there's nothing he can say.'

'He'll be upset.'

'Yes,' said Angua briskly, throwing another dress on the bed. 'And then he'll get over it.'

'Hrolf Thighbiter's asked me out,' said Cheri shyly, looking at the floor. 'And I'm almost *certain* he's male!'

'Glad to hear it.'

Cheri stood up. 'I'll walk with you as far as the Watch House. I've got to go on duty.'

They were halfway along Elm Street before they saw Carrot, head and shoulders above the crowd.

'Looks like he was coming to see you,' said Cheri. 'Er, shall I go away?'

'Too late . . .'

'Ah, good morning, Corporal Miss Littlebottom!' said Carrot cheerfully. 'Hello, Angua. I was just coming to see you but I had to write my letter home first, of course.'

He took off his helmet, and smoothed back his hair. 'Er . . .' he began.

'I know what you're going to ask,' said Angua.

'You do?'

'I know you've been thinking about it. You knew I was wondering about going.'

'It was obvious, was it?'

'And the answer's no. I wish it could be yes.'

Carrot looked astonished. 'It never occurred to me that you'd say no,' he said. 'I mean, why should you?'

'Good grief, you amaze me,' she said. 'You really do.'

'I thought it'd be something you'd want to do,' said Carrot. He sighed. 'Oh, well . . . it doesn't matter, really.'

Angua felt that a leg had been kicked away. 'It doesn't *matter*?' she said.

'I mean, yes, it'd have been nice, but I won't lose any sleep over it.'

'You won't?'

'Well, no. Obviously not. You've got other things you want to do. That's fine. I just thought you might enjoy it. I'll do it by myself.'

'What? How can . . . ?' Angua stopped. 'What are you *talking* about, Carrot?'

'The Dwarf Bread Museum. I promised Mr Hopkinson's sister that I'd tidy it up. You know, get it sorted out. She's not very well off and I thought it could raise some money. Just between you and me, there's several exhibits in there that could be better-presented, but I'm afraid Mr Hopkinson was rather set in his ways. I'm sure there's a lot of dwarfs in the city that'd flock there if they knew about it, and of course there's a lot of youngsters that ought to learn more about their proud heritage. A good dusting and a lick of paint would make all the difference, I'm sure, especially on the older loaves. I don't mind giving up a few days off. I just thought it might cheer you up, but I appreciate that bread isn't everyone's cup of tea.'

Angua stared at him. It was the stare that Carrot so often attracted. It roamed every feature of his face, looking for the tiniest clue that he was making some kind of joke. Some long, deep joke at the expense of everyone else. Every sinew in her body *knew* that he must be, but there was not a clue, not a twitch to prove it.

'Yes,' she said weakly, still searching his face, 'I expect it could be a little goldmine.'

'Museums have got to be a whole lot more interesting these days. And, you know, there's a whole guerrilla crumpet assortment he hasn't even catalogued,' said Carrot. '*And* some early examples of defensive bagels.'

'Gosh,' said Angua. 'Hey, why don't we paint a big sign saying something like "The Dwarf Bread Experience"?'

'That probably wouldn't work for dwarfs,' said Carrot, oblivious to sarcasm. 'A dwarf bread experience tends to be short. But I can see it's certainly caught your imagination!'

I'll have to go, Angua thought as they strolled on down the street. *Sooner or later he'll see that it can't really work out. Werewolves and humans . . . we've both got too much to lose. Sooner or later I'll have to leave him.*

But, for one day at a time, let it be tomorrow.

'Want the dresses back?' said Cheri, behind her.

'Maybe one or two,' said Angua.

THE END

SOUL MUSIC
Terry Pratchett

'Classic English humour, with all the slapstick,
twists and dry observations you could hope for'
The Times

*'Be careful what you wish for. You never know who
might be listening.'*

THERE'S no getting away from it. From whichever
angle, Death is a horrible, inescapable business. But
someone's got to do it. So if Death decides to take a
well-earned moment to uncover the meaning of life and
discover himself in the process, then there is going to be
a void of specific dimensions that needs to be occupied,
particularly so when there is trouble brewing in
Discworld. There aren't too many who are qualified to
fill Death's footsteps and it certainly doesn't help the
imminent cataclysm that the one person poised
between the mortal and the immortal is only sixteen
years old...

'Very clever madcap satire which has universal
appeal. If you haven't tried him, this is a fun one
to start with'
Today

'Pratchett lures classical themes and popular
mythologies into the dark corners of his
imagination, gets them drunk and makes them
do things you wouldn't dream of doing with
an Oxford don'
Daily Mail

9780552153195

THE COLOUR OF MAGIC
Terry Pratchett

'One of the best and funniest
English authors alive'
Independent

*Twoflower was a tourist, the first ever seen on the
discworld. Tourist, Rincewind decided, meant idiot.*

SOMEWHERE on the frontier between thought and
reality exists the Discworld, a parallel time and place
which might sound and smell very much like our
own, but which looks completely different. It plays by
different rules. Certainly it refuses to succumb to the
quaint notion that universes are ruled by pure logic and
the harmony of numbers.

But just because the Disc is different doesn't mean
that some things don't stay the same. Its very existence
is about to be threatened by a strange new blight: the
arrival of the first tourist, upon whose survival rests the
peace and prosperity of the land. But if the person
charged with maintaining that survival in the face of
robbers, mercenaries and, well, Death, is a spectacularly
inept wizard, a little logic might turn out to be a very
good idea...

'Like Jonathan Swift, Pratchett uses his other
world to hold up a distorting mirror to our own,
and like Swift he is a satirist of enormous
talent...incredibly funny... compulsively readable'
The Times

'Pratchett is a comic genius'
Daily Express

9780552157278

THE LIGHT FANTASTIC
Terry Pratchett

'A true original among contemporary writers'
The Times

'What shall we do?' said Twoflower.
'Panic?' said Rincewind hopefully. He always held that
panic was the best means of survival.

W HEN THE very fabric of time and space are about to
be put through the wringer – in this instance by
the imminent arrival of a very large and determinedly
oncoming meteorite – circumstances require a very
particular type of hero. Sadly what the situation does
not need is a singularly inept wizard, still recovering
from the trauma of falling off the edge of the world.
Equally it does not need one well-meaning tourist and
his luggage which has a mind of its own. Which is a
shame because that's all there is...

'He is a satirist of enormous talent... Incredibly
funny, compulsively readable'
The Times

'He would be amusing in any form and his
spectacular inventiveness makes the Discworld
series one of the perennial joys of modern fiction'
Daily Mail

'Pure fantastic delight'
Time Out

9780552152594

EQUAL RITES

Terry Pratchett

'Persistently amusing, good-hearted and shrewd'
Sunday Times

They say that a little knowledge is a dangerous thing, but it is not one half so bad as a lot of ignorance.

THERE ARE some situations where the correct response is to display the sort of ignorance which happily and wilfully flies in the face of the facts. In this case, the birth of a baby girl, born a wizard – by mistake. Everybody knows that there's no such thing as a female wizard. But now it's gone and happened, there's nothing much anyone can do about it. Let the battle of the sexes begin...

'Pratchett keeps getting better and better...It's hard to think of any humorist writing in Britain today who can match him'
Time Out

'If you are unfamiliar with Pratchett's unique blend of philosophical badinage, you are on the threshold of a mind-expanding opportunity'
Financial Times

9780552152600

MORT
By Terry Pratchett

'He is screamingly funny. He is wise. He has style'
Sunday Telegraph

Although the scythe isn't pre-eminent among the weapons of war, anyone who has been on the wrong end of, say, a peasants' revolt will know that in skilled hands it is fearsome.

For Mort however, it is about to become one of the tools of his trade. From henceforth, Death is no longer going to be the end, merely the means to an end. He has received an offer he can't refuse. As Death's apprentice he'll have free board, use of the company horse and being dead isn't compulsory. It's the dream job until he discovers that it can be a killer on his love life . . .

'Pratchett is a comic genius'
Daily Express

'Cracking dialogue, compelling illogic and unchained whimsy . . . Pratchett has a subject and a style that is very much his own'
Sunday Times

'Pratchett's humour takes logic past the point of absurdity and round again, but it is his unexpected insights into human morality that make the Discworld series stand out'
Times Educational Supplement

9780552131063

CORGI BOOKS